A novel inspired by the daring true story of the White Rose!

The TRAITOR

V.S. ALEXANDER

Author of *The Magdalen Girls*

MORE RIVETING HISTORICAL FICTION
BY V. S. ALEXANDER

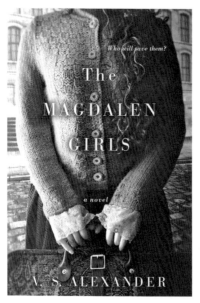

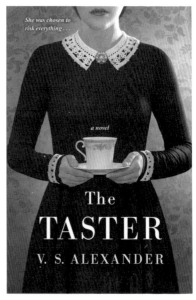

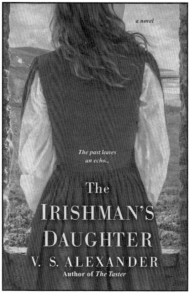

Books by V. S. Alexander

THE MAGDALEN GIRLS

THE TASTER

THE IRISHMAN'S DAUGHTER

THE TRAITOR

Published by Kensington Publishing Corporation

THE
TRAITOR

V. S. Alexander

KENSINGTON BOOKS
www.kensingtonbooks.com

KENSINGTON BOOKS are published by

Kensington Publishing Corp.
119 West 40th Street
New York, NY 10018

All Kensington titles, imprints, and distributed lines are available at special quantity discounts for bulk purchases for sales promotion, premiums, fund-raising, and educational or institutional use.

Special book excerpts or customized printings can also be created to fit specific needs. For details, write or phone the office of the Kensington Sales Manager: Kensington Publishing Corp., 119 West 40th Street, New York, NY 10018. Attn.: Sales Department. Phone: 1-800-221-2647.

Kensington and the K logo Reg. U.S. Pat. & TM Off.

ISBN-13: 978-1-4967-2041-2 (ebook)
ISBN-10: 1-4967-2041-5 (ebook)
Kensington Electronic Edition: March 2020

ISBN-13: 978-1-4967-2039-9
ISBN-10: 1-4967-2039-3
First Kensington Trade Paperback Edition: March 2020

10 9 8 7 6 5 4 3 2 1

Printed in the United States of America

To those who fought and died for freedom

PROLOGUE

Kristallnacht, November 9, 1938
The Night of Broken Glass

In the dark, the mind can play tricks.

That's what I thought when the sounds entered my ears, faint at first, like the play of droplets in a fountain, followed by distant crashes that cracked and splintered the air. I wiped the sleep from my eyes, reached for my glasses, and peered out the window above my desk. The silver clock on my desk read past one in the morning. It was November ninth, the fifteenth anniversary of the failed Beer Hall Putsch, a time of National Socialist memorials and celebrations across Germany for the martyred Nazis. Everyone should have been asleep, but other equally ominous noises filled the air as well.

Muffled laughs and jeers filtered through my window. I opened the latch, hearing the voices spreading across Munich, which seemed to come from every corner of the city, from the very earth itself. Indistinct voices, broken in the air, chanting, *"Juden, Juden, Juden,"* fell upon my ears. I shivered against the shouted barrage of anger and hate.

I switched on my desk lamp and a sickly yellow glow washed over the papers that lay upon my blotter—I'd spent long hours studying before bed. I rubbed my tired eyes, put on my glasses, cupped my hands around my face, and peered through the soot-smudged window of my fourth-story bedroom on Rumfordstrasse.

I looked beyond the needlelike spire of the Church of St. Peter, "Old Peter" as my mother and father called it, and past the stone buildings that lined the streets, smoke spiraling up in a corkscrew, pummeling the clouds that concealed the full moon. Flames flickered on the horizon as the dark smoke spread across the sky like ink dropped in a bucket of water.

Munich was constructed of stone and wood, and the fire brigade would be there soon enough to extinguish the blaze. A feeling I had known few times before settled in my stomach. The sensation reminded me of the time, as a child of seven, I had wandered away from my mother in a department store when we first came to Munich. A peculiar fear filled me. A kind old man dressed in a blue suit that smelled of tobacco and spicy cologne helped me find my mother. The man spoke German with a heavy accent and wore a round cap on his gray head. My mother swept me into her arms and forgot about her anger with me for wandering off. She told me later that if it hadn't been for the Jewish man, someone might have snatched me away. Her voice was flat and calm, nothing like the voices outside my window.

This November evening brought that earlier dread back to me, a crushing culmination, like brick piled upon brick, of the changes that had swept across the city as National Socialism spread at first in small steps then in insidious leaps and bounds. My Jewish friends, who had once been numerous since the time the old gentleman had been my deliverer years earlier, were now distant, many telling me that I was better off without them. Their words saddened me as they drifted away. I wanted to keep them as friends even as they preferred not to be seen or heard, sheltering in their homes like secretive, silent mice.

In 1938, the Reich pressed its incrimination and repression not only upon my family but upon every citizen who wasn't a fervent Nazi. Sometimes the tension that vibrated through Munich bordered on paranoia, with a terrible, blood-churning excitement that came with a terrible cost—one never knew when the Gestapo might come for your neighbor or you.

As these thoughts raced through my mind, the fire grew

larger, the overcast reflecting a hellish mixture of blazing yellow and orange, streaked by flowering blooms of black. Then, there were more crashes, the sounds of ripping metal and breaking glass, but no alarms sounded.

At sixteen, I was too young to leave my parents' house without permission, but old enough to be curious—and frightened— by what I saw and heard. I tiptoed down the hall and peered into my parents' bedroom. They slept undisturbed under their blankets, their sleepy breaths rising and falling in rhythm.

I crept back to my room, turned off my lamp, and tried to fall asleep while fearing for the city I called home.

"Talya," my mother shouted the next morning at my door.

I shot up in bed. "Yes?"

Mary, my mother, tapped her foot as she always did when I had overslept.

"You'll be late for school." She turned in the hall toward the kitchen, her black dress ruffling around her body, her shoes clicking on the wooden floor. My mother always kept her bourgeois attitude, despite the fact that living in Germany was harder than both my parents had anticipated after leaving our Russian home behind. She always looked, no matter the time of day, as if she was going shopping. Another habit that she refused to give up was calling me by the diminutive form of my name. That mannerism irritated me because I was no longer a child—I had turned sixteen on the sixteenth of May. All of my girlfriends, and certainly the boys I knew and liked at school, called me by my full name—Natalya.

"There's no school today—it's a national holiday." I yawned and stretched toward the window to see if the fire was still burning.

She returned, her eyes flashing in irritation at my sleepy attitude. "Herr Hitler has canceled the holiday. Herr Hess is speaking tonight. No matter if there's school. If not, you can find yarn for me so I can mend your father's socks."

I was at a loss. If the holiday was canceled, would stores be open or closed? And the task of finding dry goods was becoming almost impossible as the availability of fabrics dried up to support the needs of the expanding Wehrmacht. I washed, dressed, and joined my parents at the breakfast table.

"Did you see the fire?" I asked my mother after I sat down.

My mother busied herself with the pots on the stove and didn't answer. My father, Peter, lifted a spoonful of porridge to his mouth and gave me a stern look. His eyes narrowed and he said, "Hooligans. Such nonsense." He took a bite and pointed the spoon at me. "Stay away from them."

"How do you know they were hooligans?" I asked.

My father's black brows bunched over the bridge of his nose. "Many people are reluctant to talk these days, but some do, even early in the morning, when neighbors gather in the hall."

"I don't associate with troublemakers," I assured him as I dug into my oatmeal. My father's approach to life, unlike my mother's breezier style, was all business, suitable for a strict disciplinarian. As I grew into my teenage years, I resented the absolute commands that he spewed toward me like platitudes. "No" and "don't" were principle words in his vocabulary.

After eating, I returned to my room and studied the algebra problem I'd been working on the previous evening. Frustrated by my inability to solve it, I tossed the troublesome paper and pen next to my biology text. The book lay open to its title page with the spread-winged eagle perched on the encircled swastika; it gleamed up at me as if its black ink had been printed yesterday. We lived with those symbols every day—we had no choice.

I cleaned my glasses and wondered if I could sneak out with my friend Lisa Kolbe. She was more knowledgeable about life and worldly interests than I was. I believed she was prettier, more outgoing, with a less melancholy outlook than mine— inherited from her German parents—far different from living in my Russian father's household. Lisa had a way of making friends that I also admired. We'd known each other for years because we were only a few months apart in age and lived in the same building.

Two taps sounded on the floor from the ceiling below. They were soft, but I felt their vibrations through my shoes. Lisa was sending me our long-held signal to meet. I put on my coat and walked to the sitting room.

My father was finishing his tea and reading an illegal book— a German translation of the *Summa Theologica* of St. Thomas Aquinas. He kept it, and a few other illegals concealed behind the bookcase, as if their makeshift hiding place would never be discovered. My father would have refrained from reading a banned book in public, and because our family kept to ourselves, there was little likelihood his cache would be found.

I watched him for a moment as his eyes drank in the words. Soon he would put down his reading and go to the apothecary shop where he worked as an assistant to the pharmacist—a job similar to the one he held in Russia before we moved to Munich.

My mother gave me Reichsmark for black yarn if I should happen to find a store open. This came after a stern admonition from my father, "Make sure you stick to your business." I kissed my parents good-bye and stepped into the dusty hall, being careful to tread lightly down the steps. Lisa stood in the half-dark corridor, attired in her tights and jacket, her face partially lit by the single bulb at the top of the stairs. Her blonde hair, verging on silver, was cut in a stylish sweep around her face and ears. The upturned mouth I knew so well offered the usual appearance of a pert smile.

"So where are we headed?" she asked.

"Out for yarn."

"Exciting," she replied and feigned a yawn.

"I know."

"My parents have left for work." Her smile shifted to a mischievous grin. "We must see what happened last night!"

I was as excited as she was about discovering what had gone on, and more than willing to stretch the limits of my father's orders. We sprinted down the remaining steps and out the door. A listless breeze carried the lingering odor of burned wood.

"Did you see the fire?" I asked as we walked through the narrow streets of the city center. To the west, the twin towers of the Frauenkirche loomed near the central square of the Marienplatz.

"Only the red in the sky."

We were engrossed by the strange timbre of the day. The streets were quiet, but here and there people strode past, eyes cast downward, barely giving us a glance. Sometimes they disappeared up alleyways like phantoms in the shadows.

Several young men sat on benches smoking cigarettes, or leaned against buildings, looking as if they were fighting off the effects of a long, drunken night. They were members of the SA, "brownshirts," as we called them. One particularly surly fellow with a thick jaw and full head of sandy-colored hair ordered us to stop. "*Juden?*" he asked. We shook our heads and said "*Nein*," and after we presented our school papers, which we always carried with us, he let us go.

"Can't they tell we're not Jews?" Lisa asked, but I knew she was trying to make a joke. Her words dripped with sarcasm. One of our dear friends, a Jewish girl whom we hadn't seen in several months, was as blonde and blue-eyed as any Aryan could be. Yet, she was subject to the laws oppressing the Jews. Nothing about these restrictions was fair.

Soon we came upon the building that had burned—a synagogue. I had passed by it many times. It was a solid stone building with a large circular window encased in what appeared to be a turret, but the flames had charred everything, leaving the window a round, empty hole like the removed eye of a Cyclops. Most of the roof had collapsed upon itself. The stone masonry stood blackened, but some parts had been turned the color of ash by the intense flames. The structure with its burned-out arched windows and doors was as ugly now as the naked trees that stood apart from it.

We dared not move too close because members of the SA guarded the building, keeping those away who might want to loot it or perhaps save an artifact. Two women stood behind us, tears streaming down their cheeks as they dabbed their eyes with handkerchiefs. From their muffled sobs, I could tell they didn't want to call attention to themselves.

They shuffled away and a nicely dressed young man strode to my side and took off his hat. He was tall with hair a mixture of blond and brown, parted on the left and swept back to the right in the style most men wore. His wide-set eyes were framed by an attractive face, and even with a glance I surmised that he was intelligent and a bit on the cunning side. From his rigid stance to the set jaw, he exuded those qualities.

"The SA set it on fire with gasoline, and then tried to throw the Rabbi in the flames," he said in a low voice while staring at the synagogue. "He wanted to save the Torah scrolls."

Lisa and I looked at each other, not sure what to say.

"They're dogs, all of them," he continued. "They had the Rabbi arrested. He'll end up in Dachau for sure. Pigs." He turned our way. "Who are you?"

I started to answer, but Lisa stepped in front of me and said, "It's none of your business. Who are you to ask?"

Being the introvert, I fell silent, feeling somewhat sorry for the man who had expressed his sympathy for the Rabbi and the tragic arson. Out of kindness, I smiled at him and his eyes locked upon mine. A jolt of attraction sparked between us for a second, and the hair on my arms prickled with gooseflesh.

"I'm sorry to bother you, but I won't forget you," the man said and tipped his hat. After giving me a look, he disappeared around a street corner behind us.

"That was strange," I told my friend, while absentmindedly positioning my glasses on my nose. The electric thrill still lingered on my body. Lisa stood composed, sassy, and stylish a few steps away. I'd never considered myself to be pretty, always judging myself: tall and gangly with perhaps too much black hair. My glasses didn't help my confidence with boys either.

"Let's leave before we become more conspicuous," Lisa said, implying that by merely observing the synagogue we had already done so.

She was right. One always had to toe the line—to be the good German and not make waves or create a fuss, because any action outside the law could lead to misfortune.

As we left, I asked Lisa, "What has become of our Jewish friends? I fear for them now more than ever." And behind that question was a broader indisputable fact: Lisa and I didn't agree with the Reich's laws and doctrines. There was no exact day we formed that viewpoint, but the propaganda from the state-run newspapers and radio, the men who marched off to war and never came back, the rationing, the building tension in the air allowed us to reach that conclusion. We silently understood what the consequences were for such thinking. But what could we do about the Nazis?

As we walked about Munich, we saw the destruction that was perpetrated for the "protection" of Jewish property—the looting of goods by the SA and others. Many people emerged to look at the damage, walking like the dead as they passed broken windows, burned storefronts, and looted showrooms. Lisa and I knew that the world was changing for the worse.

At the Schwarz Restaurant windows were broken out; Adolf Salberg Fineries on Neuhauserstrasse had been firebombed— the large *Salberg* sign was a twisted mass of metal; Heinrich Rothschild's hat and finery store had been vandalized and words against Jews whitewashed on the windows; the Sigmund Koch music store looted; display windows smashed at Bernheimer home furnishings and art store; and perhaps most shocking of all, the large, popular department store, Uhlefelder on Rosental, had been looted and vandalized.

My father worked for one of the few remaining Jewish business owners in Munich. Lisa and I found him standing on the sidewalk in front of the broken windows of the apothecary, shards of glass like fractured diamonds littering the street.

"What are you doing here?" my father asked sternly when we approached. His broad jaw, so typical of the men in his Russian family, was clenched. "Your mother sent you out for yarn, not to roam the streets." He picked up a broom propped against the side of the shop and pointed the handle at us. "Go home! Now! You've seen enough."

Mr. Bronstein, my father's boss, poked his head out of the shattered window. His pinched face, red eyes, and trembling hands showed the pain incurred by the destruction at his shop. Two brownshirts strolled down the street. My father threw the broom down, grabbed Lisa and I by the shoulders, and whispered to us to stand still.

"Are you a Jew?" one of the men shouted from down the street.

My father shook his head but stared defiantly at them.

"Go on, then," the man ordered, strolling toward us and placing his hand over his holstered pistol. "Where is Bronstein?"

The owner, small and thin, appeared in the doorway. The man rushed at Mr. Bronstein, shoved him inside the store, and shouted, "Clean up your mess, dirty Jew. Is this how you run a business? Well, you won't for long. You have to pay for this damage." A slap and a cry echoed from the shop.

My father swiveled us on the sidewalk toward our home, his arms trembling as he guided us. We walked home in silence. As we neared our door, I realized that overnight Germany had embraced death over life.

The yarn was forgotten.

PART 1

---•◦•---

THE WHITE ROSE

CHAPTER 1

July 1942

If I had believed the world was flat, the steppes would have provided the proof as the earth spread in an unbroken line to a distant horizon. The vast land stretched before me, a patchwork of green grasses that undulated in wind-whipped waves along with the brown stubs of harvested winter wheat, other fields dissected only by the gray bark of infrequent trees or the cubed wooden frames of farmhouses not destroyed in the Wehrmacht's advance.

I was on a cramped train, separated from the army men, heading to the Russian Front as a volunteer nurse for the German Red Cross.

Some of the fields had been burned and only the blackened earth remained, but as surely as the sun rose, the ground had to be tilled and tended by the solitary figures of peasant farmers, who stood with pitchforks in hand or sat upon a horse-drawn wagon—if the poor people could force another crop from the ground.

Somehow a lucky few had survived. Perhaps the Wehrmacht needed the workers, toiling under slave labor to transport grain back to Germany, or perhaps they had been spared from death by a "beneficent" Nazi officer.

It was the first time I had been in Russia since our family had fled from Leningrad during the first phase of the Five-Year

Plan in 1929. I was seven years old then. My father had seen firsthand the disappearance of those who didn't meet the work quotas set up by Joseph Stalin—they vanished in the night never to be seen again, usually sent to their deaths in labor camps. My father had scraped enough money together for us to move to Germany, where he hoped we would have a better life. Because my mothers' parents were German, we were granted citizenship before the full rise of National Socialism.

But the war was in full bloom after the September 1, 1939, invasion of Poland and depending on the train's location, we looked out upon a land that retained its raw beauty or rolled past a landscape blasted by conflict. In Warsaw, I witnessed the desperation of Polish nationals, who had surrendered everything to the Nazis except their humanity, as I slipped a piece of candied sugar to a little girl who offered me a flower, while gazing upon the brick ghetto walls that confined so many Jews. Soldiers herded emaciated people in and out of the gates, marching them in lines toward some unknown destination. I had become numb to the horrors, learning over the years that I could do little to fight against the Reich.

In those lands yet untouched by war's deadly grip, the tall birches shimmered in East Prussia, the wide steppes of Russia opened to gently swelling hills; and, at those times, with the train windows open, the wheels clacking in rhythmic motion along the tracks, the July heat dissipating with the setting sun— in those times—one could almost forget the cares of war and pretend that all was right with the world.

But there were other distractions on the long trip to the Front. I traveled with a young woman named Greta, also a volunteer nurse, whom I knew little about other than she had her own plans, as I did, to eventually return to Munich.

Because my father worked in a field related to medicine, I was drawn to it and, furthermore, I had no better idea what to do with my life. I had come to volunteer nursing after my experiences in the League of German Girls. Administering medical care to the ill gave me satisfaction. Changing bandages, helping children who suffered from cuts and scrapes, and learning about the body became my "profession" in the years following 1939. Although nursing allowed me to get away from my strict father and not immediately give in to the pressure to marry and produce children, as the Reich demanded, one strong disadvantage remained. The German Red Cross became a potent arm of the Nazi regime. We were expected to embrace the Reich's teachings on Aryan supremacy and blindly follow Hitler—both of which I innocently ignored in thinking and action. My father's strictness had inadvertently instilled an anxious tension inside me, which fed my natural shyness. But something stronger bubbled in me as well: an urge to be free, to be my own woman, a nascent rebelliousness.

One night Greta offered me a smoke as I read a biology text in our cramped quarters. The book offered little excitement, but any gathered kernels of knowledge I hoped would help me secure a medical career as a woman under National Socialism.

Not being a smoker, I declined her offer. Cigarettes weren't cheap and were often sold on the black market. I wondered where she had gotten them. "Good" women weren't supposed to smoke, but one of the reasons many became volunteer nurses was for the occasional freedom it offered from such restrictions. Mostly, cigarettes went to soldiers. She also held up a bottle of clear liquid. The red label, printed in Polish, read *Wódka*, and when Greta pulled out the stopper, the odor of the sharp, medicinal spirit floated past me.

She looked older than her years. The emerging frown lines on her face and the chewed cuticles on her fingers led me to believe that her life had not been happy. Perhaps they were signs of anxiety about the war, or life in general, but she couldn't have been much more than my age of twenty. Still, she made herself pretty in a way that was aimed at the men traveling with us.

Greta sat in the chair opposite mine, sitting backward to the forward motion of the train as we sped over the vast plain. She lit her cigarette and a plume of smoke rushed to my face but dispersed quickly out the open window. I closed my book.

"Have you spoken to any of them?" She hitched her right

thumb over her shoulder and rested her left elbow on the lip of the window, keeping the lit end of the cigarette near the opening. The spark flared red in the rushing wind.

"A few," I replied. "I try not to get too familiar." I had no desire to foster romantic relationships with army or medical corpsmen. I was headed to the Front to do a job, not get a husband; and, after all, being somewhat fatalistic, I wondered how long a potential mate would be alive in these dire times. The war on the Eastern Front was dragging on despite the Reich's claims of victory after victory. To be held by a man, to taste his lips upon mine, would be nice had such a prospect occurred, but a relationship seemed a matter of secondary importance considering how men were dying for the Reich.

Greta took a drag on her cigarette, took a gulp of vodka, and then held the bottle out to me.

I pulled down the shade on our compartment door. "Where did you get this contraband?"

"A lady never tells." Greta smiled wryly and tapped her nails on the bottle. "Some of them are very good-looking, including the Russian. Whatever happened to all those lectures about racial purity we had to sit through? Natalya *Petrovich*? Alexander *Schmorell*?"

Her question irked me—I was a native Russian living in Germany—my parents never let me forget that fact. We knew the Reich rumblings about the *Untermensch*, the subhumans, but non-Jewish Russians living in Germany had mostly been able to live as citizens, particularly those already assimilated. One had little choice in the Reich but to obey; still, I was proud to be traveling to my homeland on what I considered a mission of mercy. I took the bottle and tipped it back, the strong drink burning my throat, the fire settling in a warm ball in my stomach.

"We're all German now. Have a look at my papers. The Reich needs men . . . and nurses." After what had happened to my Jewish friends since the Nazis came to power, I wanted nothing to do with creating a new racial order in the East—a thought repugnant to me. All I was concerned about was saving lives, and if that compassion extended to my fellow Russians, so be it. Of course, I didn't really know what the future held.

She shrugged off my rebuff and continued her daydreams about men. "It's hard to choose from among them," she said, her eyes on my mouth as it puckered from another swig of liquor.

"Not the best vodka I've ever had," I said, although my experience with drink was limited.

"One of them is Russian, he told me so. Alexander. Nicelooking . . ." Greta puffed on her cigarette, which had prematurely burned to her fingertips in the train's rushing wake, and then tossed it out the window. "But the one he's traveling with—a real doll." She fanned her fingers in front of her face.

I took another gulp of the vodka and a dull stupor overtook me. I yawned and stretched out in my seat, which served as an uncomfortable bed. "The sun has set. We need to pull down the blackout shades."

"Another dull night with only dreams to keep me company," Greta said, and settled back in her seat. "Things will pick up when we get to the Front."

I wondered if she was right, for I feared the Front would bring only tragedy and misery. My excitement about returning to Russia was tempered by the prospect of what might lay ahead. Secretly, I wondered if I was prepared to deal with what I might witness. I deflected the phantom images of dead and wounded soldiers, the bombed-out buildings that filled my mind—mental pictures reinforced by the destruction I had seen in Warsaw. They didn't fade easily.

After what seemed like an endless trip through Russia, we arrived in early August at Vyazma and the home of the 252nd Division, to which the men were assigned. Greta and I stepped out of our car to stretch our legs. Our eventual stop would be to the northwest in the town of Gzhatsk, about 180 kilometers west of Moscow.

I had barely stepped onto the ground to the sound of blaring military music when Greta cocked her head toward the men she had spoken about. "There they are." She discreetly pointed at them as they exited their car, located farther up the train from ours. "They hang together like thieves."

Greta identified them: Hans, tall with dark hair and the handsome profile of a movie actor, a pleasing face of wonderful proportion, a thin nose over sensuous lips, a slight cleft to the chin, and inquisitive eyes under dark brows; Willi, with slick-backed blond hair, which sometimes hung in wind-pushed wisps across his forehead. He was handsome as well, with an oval face and broad chin, a man who looked the most prone to silence and grave thoughts of the three. The last was the "Russian" as Greta called him, a man she had heard the others call "Alex." He was tall and lanky, with a full head of hair sweeping back from his face. He seemed to be the one who smiled the most, with fun in his soul, who perhaps didn't take life as seriously as the others.

I gave them a cursory glance, more interested in putting names to faces than in cultivating romantic notions.

I was unprepared for what I saw after my gaze shifted from the men. Vyazma was little more than the shattered remains of buildings surrounded by craters blasted into the earth. One wooden church, the only intact structure in the village, stood perched on a small hill. Nothing moved among the rubble except the German troops. I wondered where all the life had gone. Had its people been killed, all animal life destroyed by the advance?

The loudspeakers installed by the Wehrmacht blared into my ears. I walked away from the train, leaving Greta and the others behind, and stood next to a burned-out home, nothing more than blackened timbers and the shell of a window. The smell of death, like rotted meat, filled my nose. I spun away, unable to stand the stench, and discovered the source. Beyond the house lay the corpse of a decaying dog. Swarms of black flies buzzed around its body. The animal reminded me of a dog left to fend on its own after a Jewish family in Munich had disappeared. It was taken care of for a time by neighbors, but then it too vanished, like the village before me. Nothing but desiccated earth remained in a town that had once brimmed with life.

After boarding the train, on our way to Gzhatsk, my mood deepened as the shadows lengthened over the plains. I found it hard to believe that the war in Russia had been going on for more than a year with hundreds of thousands of men, maybe a million or more, traveling this route in the military surge to take Moscow, Leningrad to the north, and the Russian cities to the south. Greta must have recognized my reluctance to talk, because even though we were compartment mates, she left me to my thoughts and socialized with the two other nurses on board.

Something—at first inexplicable—was happening. When I gazed from the train at the vast landscape, the summer wind lashing the birches, the rain and the sun painting the trees in resplendent splashes of silver, I felt at one with the earth, at one with my native country, profound memories resurrecting from my distant childhood. A kind of "Russian fever" had overtaken me as if I had become part of the land of Dostoyevsky, Tolstoy, and Pushkin, leaving Goethe and Schiller behind. Something stirred in my soul, opening me to unfamiliar feelings that disturbed me but at the same time thrilled me. An ecstatic emptiness, a heaven filled with stars yet undefined by space, melancholy tempered by shining hope, overcame me. Deeply buried yearnings stirred within me as I recalled what it was like to be a child in Leningrad, unaware of my parents' worries about Stalin, and, later, Hitler.

Instead of life on the busy streets of Munich, I understood what it was to be free of constraints. Ribbons of rivers, lush meadows, and verdant woods spread out before me. I saw for the first time what Hitler desired in his perverted megalomania, his Lebensraum, the territory he desired for Germany and the ever-expanding Reich. The "subhumans" would be the tenders of the fields, the Aryan race the masters. But Hitler and his henchmen had not taken into account the fullness and determination of the Russian spirit, and a splinter of that essence pricked my skin. That fact was never clearer to me than when we reached Gzhatsk.

The city, like Vyazma, lay in ruins. Churches, shops, and homes had been obliterated in the drive to subjugate Moscow. The Front was a mere ten kilometers away, and shells burst within earshot. A few even landed near Gzhatsk, shaking the earth with their explosions. What people remained here, outside of troops, wandered about the destroyed city with soil smeared on their ragged clothes and shock in their eyes. Little emotion showed as they passed us—well-fed Germans on our way to a medical camp in the woods safely away from the danger of bullets and bombs. A strong and prevailing sadness filled my heart upon seeing these people.

For several days, we set up additional tents, made sure our uniforms, aprons, and supplies were unpacked, listened to medical lectures from stuffy Wehrmacht doctors, played cards, and offered aid to the small number of wounded in camp. Some of the medical corpsmen, including Willi and Alex, passed around vodka in the evening. I could tell by the sighing and excessive cigarette smoking that everyone was itching to do something besides sit in camp. At night, the shells would crash near the city and light up the woods with their explosive flares.

The first truckload of new casualties arrived about a week later. Everyone jumped into their roles, the medical corpsmen and the nurses attending the doctors. One physician ordered me to help Alex, who leaned over a man with a nearly severed leg. The soldier's head lolled on the gurney and he mouthed words I couldn't hear above the shouted orders, the clanging of metal medical tables and instruments, and moans of the wounded. Alex pulled on his gloves and apron and I did the same.

"What's he saying?" I asked.

"Something about killing Hitler," Alex said. "He says if he loses his leg, he'll shoot the Führer." He bent down and studied the tourniquet and the large gash in the man's limb. The bandages, soaked with blood, had turned from crimson to brownish red. "I have bad news for him. When he comes to, he'll find his left leg missing. The shrapnel cut most of the way through.

All we can do is make him comfortable until the doctor lops it off."

I sensed that Alex was horrified by the man's injuries, but that, as a medical corpsman, he fought against the nightmarish atmosphere of the tent. The joie de vivre that ran through him lifted his spirits.

"Natalya, isn't it?"

I nodded.

His eyes brightened despite the misery around us. "Get fresh bandages and we'll clean the injury and apply antiseptic." He studied his surroundings as the medical staff dashed about the large tent. "It's going to be a while before the doctor can operate." Hans and Greta hovered over a nearby bench where a man lay bleeding from a gaping shoulder wound.

I gathered the bandages and returned to the gurney. The now delirious soldier had clutched Alex's shoulders and pulled him so close he was screaming in his ear. My comrade shushed the man and pushed him down on his makeshift bed. Alex attempted to calm him as an orderly administered a shot of morphine. Alex and I worked as a team until the wound had been cleaned and dressed. Under the influence of the drug, the soldier slipped into sleep.

When the wounded in our care had been attended to, Alex and I stripped off our gear and stepped outside, clear of the tent and away from the commotion. He ran his fingers through his cliff of hair, lit his black pipe, and puffed on it. The smoke dispersed in hazy shafts in the few rays of sun that penetrated the thick canopy.

"You do good work," Alex said between puffs and stretches of his long legs. "You hope to remain a nurse?"

"Probably," I said, and sat on the damp earth beneath a pine tree. The cool air bathed me with its woody fragrance, a refreshing change from the stifling conditions and antiseptic smell of the stuffy tent. "That's why I'm here—to find out. I've passed my Abitur and I may decide to go on in biology or philosophy at the university." I picked up some decaying brown needles and threw them absentmindedly in the direction of the tent. "That soldier was out of his mind with pain, but then we've all been under strain the past few years—dealing with rations . . . conditions we have no control over. . . ."

Alex sat beside me. The smoke from his pipe encircled us with a pleasant, earthy scent that reminded me of a fall campfire—and it kept the mosquitoes away. "Yes, he was saying things he shouldn't have . . . words he could be executed for if anyone was to report him." He chomped down on the pipe stem. "That is, if someone felt it necessary to *betray* him."

". . . necessary to betray . . ." His words astonished me. "War changes everything, despite our rules and regulations," I replied after his comment had sunk in. "Drinking and smoking are forbidden, yet nearly everyone does it. Greta wears makeup when she can. Why should we worry about things like getting tipsy or having a cigarette when our next breath could be extinguished by a bullet?" I looked toward the medical tent, partially obscured by pine branches. "No court would convict a man who was crazed with pain."

"I wouldn't be so sure. . . . We *are* dealing with the Reich." He leaned back in the circular shade of the tree and thought for a moment. "How would you like to do something that's strictly forbidden?"

A thrill raced through me at his unexpected question. "I guess I'd have to know how forbidden this something is?"

"You can keep a secret—after all, you're Russian like me."

"Yes," I said, and added to protect myself, "but we're Germans too."

He paused and then said, "Fraternization with the enemy." He spoke matter-of-factly, as if the words meant nothing more than "let's have breakfast."

I assumed he didn't mean clandestine meetings with Russian soldiers or partisans, but I wasn't really sure of his objective. No matter his exact intent, such activity was risky. I must have displayed some hesitation, because he settled against the tree as if nothing had been said.

"I've met a woman who has welcomed me into her home—Sina," he said. "Willi and Hans have met other Russians, but

I'd like to take you to Sina's if you're game. We drink and sing songs, sometimes dance. It's something to look forward to in this terrible time."

"You'd never met her before coming here?"

Alex laughed. "Never. Hans, Willi, and I like meeting the people. We feel we can learn something from our *enemies*." His voice lifted on the last word in a sarcastic jibe and then lowered. "All Russians are family to me."

Half of me wanted to go, but the other half was worried about being found out. If we were caught, the least punishment for me might mean expulsion from my work and a trip back to Munich shrouded in disgrace, at worst conviction of a crime and imprisonment. I'd often thought of prison, and my neighbors and friends who had disappeared. Even talking about them was like committing a crime.

Alex's eyes retained their sparkle despite the deep shadows. I found it hard to resist his charm, bordering on good-natured innocence, so I nodded despite my natural inclination to stay at the camp. "It would be an adventure, Alex. I'd like to meet a fellow Russian."

He smiled broadly and tapped the embers of his pipe on a patch of soggy ground. "Tonight, then. Please call me 'Shurik'— all my best friends do."

That evening, as we walked to a farmhouse on the outskirts of the city, Alex told me about *his* Russian family. His mother had died when he was small, and his father, a doctor, decided to move the family to Munich when Alex was four years old. A nanny became his surrogate mother and spoke to him in Russian, as my parents had after we left Leningrad. Therefore, we were both fluent in Russian and German.

Alex was even more rhapsodic about Russia than I, although both of us were affected by our rediscovered love of the country. Weaving in and out of the woods, we talked about customs and holidays and pranks we remembered from our childhoods, filling us with laughter. We traveled several kilometers down a dirt road far away from the military camp. The evening breeze whispered underneath the pines like a soft brush stroked against velvet. But on the eastern horizon, gunfire traced in yellow streaks and volleys of shells exploded in vibrant bursts against the deepening twilight.

The farmhouse, on the southern edge of a forested patch of land, resembled a string of huts jumbled together. There was no electricity here; an oil lamp burned brightly in the window. A cow lowed from one of the huts to the south of the main house, and near there stood a chicken roost smothered in downy feathers.

A grasshopper flew on waxy wings from a weedy patch in the middle of the road and I jumped from the sudden scare. I landed against Alex and he laughed at my girlish behavior. A large white moth circled us and then flitted away toward the yellow lamplight.

Alex grabbed my hand and pulled me to a stop. "There's something I want you to know before we go inside," he said. "Sina loves me and I believe she will love you, but I've told her certain things that only a few people know."

"Your chums, Hans and Willi, I suppose," I said without thinking.

He turned toward the east, facing the indigo light layering the horizon. I followed his gaze and was still able to make out his eyes, which had transformed from their usual joyful look to one of solemnity. "Hans knows more about me than almost anyone." He dug his bootheel into the soft earth. "I never wanted to be here. In fact, I didn't want to swear allegiance to Hitler and the Wehrmacht. I asked to be discharged from service, but my request was denied." He turned and looked at me with large, questioning eyes. "You may understand. . . ." He pointed to the hut. "As Sina does. . . ."

I did understand, but the only courageous affirmation I could muster was a nod.

"Let's go inside," he said. "Sina will be waiting."

Alex stepped to the door, knocked, and called the woman's name. Sina, probably not much older than we, welcomed "Shurik" and me with a kiss on both cheeks and invited us in. Even though the war raged only a few kilometers from her home, she seemed to be in good spirits and looked nothing like the peasant woman I had pictured in my mind. She was thin, with long black hair braided artfully around her head. She wore no babushka or long apron covering a simple dress. Instead, she was attired in a feminine version of a navy man's suit, a blue pinstripe blouse with an overlapping collar held together by white buttons and a matching skirt, which flowed to her bare ankles.

The hut was comfortable and warm. An additional kind of warmth came from the glow of life inside. The meager furnishings consisted of a small table, a chair, and a pine bed large enough to fit the woman and her two small children, Dimitri and Anna. They sat on their knees at one side of the table and spooned soup from wooden bowls. A samovar and several books sat on the opposite end; a guitar and balalaika lay with their fingerboards crossed at the foot of the bed; red and gold weavings of poppies, and bold geometric designs in red and blue stitching adorned what would otherwise have been bare wooden walls. A painted icon of a weeping Christ hung above the bed in a sparkling silver frame.

"Sit, sit," Sina insisted. "I don't have enough chairs. Shurik, you sit on the floor on the old rug."

Alex obliged, crossing his long legs and exposing the black military boots under his gray uniform pants.

"I have no tea," Sina said, "so let us drink vodka." She dipped like a graceful swan and withdrew a brown bottle from under the bed. Taking three samovar cups, she poured the vodka, and handed us our two.

"*Za Zdarovje,*" Alex said, raising the cup to our health, followed by toasts to our meeting and friendship.

Sina sat on the bed with her legs folded underneath her thin body. Dimitri and Anna put their bowls in a washbasin and took their places on either side of their mother. "So, you are new to Russia," she said to me.

I put the samovar cup on the table, having drained its contents. "I was born in Russia, like Shurik, but I haven't been back since my parents left Leningrad when I was seven. I'm a volunteer nurse."

Sina lifted her hands in a wild flourish. "You've missed nothing. Stalin and Bolshevism have ruined our country and killed more of our people than we can count—"

I interrupted her. "That's why we left—because of the Five-Year Plan. My father had friends who disappeared in the night never to be seen again."

"Then came the purges of the Terror," Sina continued. "It's lucky we have an army at all. Many military officers were liquidated because the General Secretary thought they might be a threat to his power." Her eyes blazed from across the room. "And we believed the Germans had come to liberate us from Stalin. . . . We were wrong." She lowered her head and shook it slowly. "Instead, they're killing us where we stand, and we are burning our homes and crops so the Wehrmacht will get no use from them." Her hand crept toward the pillows to her right. "We've been instructed to kill Germans."

"Do you have a husband?" I asked, wanting to steer the subject away from killing.

"Oh, yes, a strong, handsome man whom the Nazis would shoot on sight if they could get their hands on him." She lifted her hands from the bed and fluttered her arms like wings. "But he's free as a bird now. I see him when he can sneak away, deep in the night, in the dark, when we both can take refuge from our troubles."

"He's a partisan," Alex said, turning his head toward me from his seat on the rug. "A man of conviction and principles fighting against . . ."

He stopped, but I suspected the next word to come from his mouth might have been "evil."

Alex reached for a book on the table and lifted it in front of him. "*Crime and Punishment*—one of my favorites. We can read from it if you'd like."

Sina's right hand inched toward the pillows until her fingers rested underneath one of the slipcases. I considered her movement a bit strange, but had no idea what she was doing until she withdrew a black pistol from its hiding place.

I gasped and felt the blood drain from my head.

Alex thumbed through the book, apparently unaware of Sina's action. "Dostoyevsky," he said, without looking up, "is the most Christian of all the Russian writers, in my opinion." He lifted his gaze from the pages for a moment and glanced at our host.

The black barrel was pointed directly at us. I was behind Alex and, from above, a rich thatch of brownish hair swirled around the part in back. I couldn't see his face, but I wondered if the color had drained from his as it had from mine.

Without raising his voice, he said, "Sina, please put that away—you might accidentally shoot one of us."

"It wouldn't be an accident," she replied. Her children sat calmly by her side looking intently at both of us—me in the chair and Alex sitting on the rug in front of me.

"We're supposed to kill all Germans," she said and paused. "But you aren't like all Germans. In fact, you'll never be rid of the Slav in your soul."

The trigger clicked and the hammer popped into its resting place. I yelped, but there was no explosion, no bullet smashing into my skin.

"See, you've done nothing but frighten Natalya," Alex calmly shook a finger at her. "Shame on you."

I clutched the side of the chair to keep from shaking out of the seat. "You scared me to death, Sina. That was a dirty trick."

"An old trick," Alex said. "I lived through it the first night we met, and I should have warned you, but I didn't know she repeated it for all the Germans she meets." He turned his head and gave me a wink.

"I'm not stupid enough to keep a loaded pistol around my children." Sina smiled, returned the weapon to its place under the pillow, and swept up Dimitri and Anna in a bear hug. "Soon they will be old enough to handle the pistol themselves. I look forward to seeing them kill their first enemy fighter."

The thought of Russian children taking shots at German soldiers appalled me. Dimitri and Anna would be slaughtered like
pigs. "May I have another drink?" I asked, lifting my cup.

"Please, help yourself," Sina said.

I poured another vodka. The liquor took over and my shock
faded to a shaky tension; we sang and laughed for several hours
until Sina played a melancholy folk song on the balalaika. The
melody seemed somewhat familiar from long ago in my childhood, but was now too distant in my memory for me to join in.
Alex knew it by heart and sang with Sina while I did a slow clap
in time with the beat. The children danced in front of the bed,
joining arms and moving their legs in unified step.

The hour grew late and rain pattered against the walls, keeping us there longer than we'd anticipated. The oil lamp flickered,
but rather than replacing the fuel, Sina allowed it to sputter out
and we talked in the dark as the children settled into bed. We
adults looked through the open window as shells exploded in
the east, illuminating the starry expanse, now free of clouds,
with brilliant bursts of yellow and white.

As the night lingered, Sina, slowed by vodka and perhaps
her own sadness, sang a melody that brought tears to my eyes.
It started low, never leaving the minor key, and then grew to a
high pitch, until I thought the wooden rafters would split from
the sound. Finally, the tune dissipated in a soft shift to a major
key and died on the breeze that wafted into the hut.

I nudged Alex's head, which rested against my legs. "It's time
to get back to camp, or we'll be reported missing." My words
tripped thick and heavy off my tongue.

"Yes," Alex said, and pushed himself up on all fours before
standing on wobbly legs.

We said our farewells, kissed Sina, and promised to visit another night. Alex vowed that on our next trip he would abstain
from vodka long enough to have an intelligent discussion about
Pushkin and Tolstoy. Sina agreed and, with a final wave of her
hand, shut the door.

"She's delightful," I said to Alex, and wondered if that was
the best way to describe her. Sina was exotic to me, different in

a way I had never experienced except in the far reaches of my memory when vague images of Leningrad came to mind. But even those people dredged up from the past were different from her. There was no way to compare the city folk I knew as a child to country folk ravaged by German troops.

We weaved up the road toward camp as I looked into a sky profuse with stars. "I can reach up and touch them," I said, shifting my glasses and craning my neck toward the heavens.

Unaware of where I was stepping, I missed a large puddle by the width of my foot and decided to take off my shoes to avoid coating them with muddy water. I wrapped my arms around Alex's waist and savored the still warm feeling of the vodka in my stomach and the cool, damp earth squishing between my toes. In the morning, I would pay dearly for my excess. However, rinsing off the mud would be easier than ridding myself of a hangover.

In spite of the evening's indulgences, I'd found a true friend in Alex. That alone made the night worthwhile.

The rain began in earnest a few days later and turned the camp into a morass of swampy earth and dripping branches. I imagined what the colder fall and winter weather would bring, when conditions would truly worsen.

Wounded soldiers poured into the camp daily, and the onslaught of injuries, many horrific, made me question my decision to be a nurse. Often I stumbled to bed bone weary and bleary eyed from long hours in the medical tent. One stiff-necked surgeon in particular was a stickler for rules and regulations, including limited rest breaks; no small talk among medics, aides, and nurses; and no smoking in the camp. He made everyone's life miserable, including my own, performing his surgeries while criticizing my dressing of wounds, my administration of medicines and hypodermics, thus further eroding my confidence. I was thrilled and relieved when he was transferred unexpectedly to a unit farther north.

Alex, Hans, Willi, and another medic, Hubert Furtwängler, often ate lunch together on nice days at a spot near camp, their table dappled in the sunlight coursing through the overhanging limbs of an oak. The men were a snapshot in time, their canteens and tin cups scattered between half-eaten loaves of bread and thick slices of cheese. When the workload was light or they could sneak away for a break, they sat on a fence post near a damaged building and smoked. The thought struck me that they had banded together in a fraternal bond.

The three of them, minus Hubert, often gathered in hushed conversations that ended abruptly when an outsider approached. On the few times I was asked to join them—mostly I passed by with a quick hello—the talk turned to the mundane: the weather, the thrill of duty or its opposite, the drudgery of the medical tent, our longing for home and friends.

I was certain these men, when alone, talked about other things as well—forbidden topics—that only this group dared discuss. I had no proof of this other than the way they interacted with one another: cautious, quiet, hunched, as if secrets were being shared. Any astute Gestapo agent would have questioned them for their actions. One time when they sat smoking, I spotted the remains of a swastika carved into the dirt. Alex had hurriedly tried to blot it out with his boot. The top half of the symbol had been crossed out with a large X.

By September, Willi and Hubert had been deployed to other battalions on the Front and Alex had taken ill. I received this news from Hans.

"Alex has diphtheria." We stood in a grove of birch trees whose tops had turned to a brilliant burnished gold.

"Diphtheria?" I was shocked because most of us had been immunized against the disease.

"He's burning up from a high fever, and confined to his bed," Hans said. "Apparently, he didn't get the vaccine." His handsome face looked drawn in the pale light, his cheeks sunken as if the medical corps and its uneven rhythm of work, from boredom to frenzy, and the effects of lackluster army rations had taken their toll. He took off his cap and swatted at a buzzing fly. "I'll be lucky if I don't come down with it myself. We've given too much blood for the troops, our resistance is low—and there are so many infections in Russia. Well, I don't need to tell you that. . . ." His lips parted in a half smile, the facial expression I had seen him display most often.

"Please give him my best wishes, if you see him before I do," I said.

"I will." Hans placed his cap back on his head. "Walk with me . . . please."

I stepped in sync beside him as we headed in the direction of Sina's home, away from the birch forest and into a clearing where the land stretched to the horizon on all sides and the gray clouds skimmed above us.

Hans took a deep breath, and he seemed to grow lighter from the air. "I'm tired of death . . . and the war."

"You need something to take your mind off it," I said.

"It's hard being alone now that Alex is sick and Willi and Hubert are gone." He uttered a faint laugh. "I can never take my mind off it—war will be on my mind as long as we are in it . . . and probably long after."

"You're very serious," I said.

His gaze narrowed, his brows tightened, as if I had maligned him.

"I didn't mean that as an insult," I said quickly. "I meant that you look at things in a different way from other men. The war has touched you."

We stopped near a rivulet that swirled in a shallow pool on the road and then bubbled into a nearby field. I bent down and stuck a finger in the cool water. I looked back to our camp, which lay hidden by the trees, to the east and west, where the land ended in rolling hills, and then to the south, where the fields spread out to the horizon. Down the road, Sina's hut stood outlined against the haze.

"I've been to Sina's with Alex," Hans said. "Did he tell you what we did the other day?"

Not having seen Alex for several days, I shook my head.

"We buried a Russian we found on the plain not far from

here." He squatted near the flowing water and dipped his hand into it. "His head had separated from his rump and his private parts had decayed. Worms crawled out of his half-rotten clothes. We had almost filled the grave with soil when we found another arm. We made a Russian cross, which we put in the earth at the head of the grave." He paused. "Now his soul can rest in peace." Hans bowed his head. "Maybe that's how Alex contracted diphtheria."

He looked up at me. "I feel such sympathy for the Russian people—knowing what they've been through at the hands of our army. I fear that there's much more going on that we don't know about as medics and nurses. I think the SS keeps their actions a secret even from the generals. You're Russian—I'm sure this killing bothers you as well."

The water reflected the tortured look on his face, but before I had a chance to answer, his mood shifted to one of joy. "Have you heard my choir? I put it together with a few Russian girls and POWs. . . . We do the best we can. I love music and I long to dance. The other night we danced until we collapsed."

I'd heard the songs, sometimes joyous, sometimes faint, often somber, drift through the medical tent, but work, darkness, and fatigue had kept me from investigating. The voices seemed to come from far away, at odd times of day and night, like the songs of distant angels. "I'd like to hear them. My friend in Munich, Lisa Kolbe, knows more about the arts than I do, and I've learned something about music from her."

"Did you know I have a brother serving here in the same sector?" Hans asked.

"No. Do you see him?"

He stood up from the rushing water and looked to the west. "A few miles from here. His name is Werner. I ride over on horseback when I can." Hans opened his arms in a grand gesture, which seemed to unleash a sweep of energy into the air. "I've developed a passion for riding, and it won't let go of me," he said, his voice filling with enthusiasm. "There's nothing to beat galloping across the plain astride a fast horse, forging your way like an arrow through the head-high steppe grass, and riding back into the forest at sunset, weary to the point of exhaustion, with your head still glowing from the heat of the day and blood throbbing in every fingertip." He paused, seeming on the brink of fatigue from his description. "It's the finest delusion I've succumbed to, because in a certain sense you have to delude yourself. The men call it 'Russian fever' but that's a clumsy, feeble expression."

"I've used the term myself," I said, somewhat embarrassed by the admission.

"It's something like this: When you see the world in all its enchanting beauty, you're sometimes reluctant to concede that the other side of the coin exists. The antithesis exists here, as it does everywhere, if only you open your eyes to it. But here the antithesis is accentuated by war to such an extent that a weak person sometimes can't endure it."

We stepped across the rivulet and walked into a field filled with tall grasses. We had traveled for about ten minutes, when we came to a Russian cross sticking out of the ground. "This is where we buried him," Hans said. "He was probably a good man, a Christian man, with a family and children. No one will ever know because he will lie here until the end of time." He looked up from the grave toward the broad steppe, the grass swaying in the wind, and a tear rolled down his cheek. "So, you intoxicate yourself. You see only one side in all its splendor and glory."

As I watched, he bowed his head and said a silent prayer. A wave, like an electric charge, prickled up my skin, a sense of joy akin to ecstasy washed over me, unlike any feeling I had experienced before. The sensation jolted me so much that I leaned against him.

Flushed from their feeding by an unseen visitor, a flock of gray-and-black jackdaws flew over our heads, cawing their shrill cry. A burst of sunlight lit the grave and then was consumed by the murky clouds as quickly as it had appeared.

Hans moved away from me, his hands clutched by his sides.

"I don't know you. . . . I shouldn't be talking of such things. . . . Alex likes you and trusts you."

I didn't know what to say. What was he offering me—friendship, something more? Was he testing me, in slow steps, to see if I could be trusted? His face flushed almost to the point of red-hot anger. Whatever he carried inside was eating him up, although I got the sense that such an intimate display of passion was a rarity.

"Our days and nights are ruled by those who would commit evil and immoral acts," I responded, attempting to placate him. "We can only do what's right and offer praise and support when it's deserved and condemnation when it's justified. We must be strong in the face of moral corruption."

"The Reich must be condemned."

I stepped back, stunned by his words, and took a deep breath as we stood near the grave. I agreed but was unwilling to say so to a man I barely knew. "That thought must remain between you and me. You should not repeat it to anyone else."

"This is why I fight—not for Germany, but for all men."

I squeezed his hand and he smiled. We left the grave and proceeded back to camp, saying little as we walked. The overcast sky, except for a few sparkling breaks of sun, held fast through the afternoon and portended a bleak and dreary fall. That evening, as I sat in the dark with Greta, I recalled Hans's words, and the bleak grave and the cawing jackdaws appeared in my head. Feeling a bit light-headed, I was overwhelmed by contrasting thoughts of a hopeful peace and a long war filled with death and destruction. I didn't sleep well for several nights.

Alex recovered but Hans exhibited symptoms similar to diphtheria that put him in bed for several days. Alex withdrew a bit after his illness—not that he was unfriendly—but he, like Hans, seemed to be carrying an increasing weight on his shoulders. Our work kept us busy when the trucks and wagons rolled in carrying their cargo of dying and wounded men.

One late September morning, I decided to take advantage of

some free time. I bundled up and walked along the dirt road leading to Sina's. About halfway there, I reached a path, turning into a field alongside the birch forest, which had been cut into the tall grasses by trucks. Large puddles were scattered along its route, but the trail fueled my curiosity and I welcomed a change of scenery from my usual walk southward.

I had never been down it; in fact, it had escaped my attention. The vegetation lay crushed and dead under the weight of the tires while the brown and green stalks swayed in the air on each side; the earth was tamped hard in spots like rock, but spongy in other places.

The wind had picked up overnight as the first breath of winter poured in from the north. The small patches of sunlight on my shoulders did little to warm me, and I tried as best I could to stay out of the shade. The muddy tracks kept me sidestepping in and out of the shadows.

The birch branches, holding leaves that had turned from gold to a reddish purple, shuddered and bent in the gusts as their branches knocked against each other, and if not for the gale, the forest would have been silent. The path turned into a section of woods that had been cleared of trees. My senses sharpened in the gloom as the sound of an engine took me by surprise.

The engine revved behind me and tires spun in the mud. There were no *Verboten* signs at the beginning of the trail, no posted reason for me not to be here, but instinct told me to keep out of sight. The ground squished underneath my shoes as I knelt behind several trees that had been chopped down and piled upon one another. Through a narrow opening between the logs, I spotted a large truck, open in the back, with the black-and-white iron cross on its doors. About twenty people, surrounded by four armed SS guards and their commander, huddled against the wood panels that held them in back. The people were easy to identify as Russian by their attire; and, to my deepening horror, I recognized the faces of Sina and her two children, Dimitri and Anna.

The truck sped past me at a fast clip, bouncing over the rough path, splashing muddy water in its wake and coating the surrounding trees with the sloppy mix. As soon as the vehicle disappeared around a curve, I dashed back to the path in pursuit until I found a suitable hiding place nestled in a thick grove of trees. I had to see what was happening to Sina and her children.

The truck, its human cargo shuddering like tenpins as the brakes screeched, came to a halt near a shallow ravine within the forest. After that, my mind became foggy, hazy, in a scene that played out before me like a film in slow motion.

SS guards open the wooden gate on the back, one of them so kind as to even help an older woman wrapped in her flannel coat and kerchief to the wet ground. Russian men, mostly older with gray beards and long hair, some in work clothes, some in what look like pajamas, join the line of captives. Children look at their mothers with wide eyes, while grasping at coat sleeves as they totter along in small, hurried steps. The SS herd them along like cattle, shoving their machine gun barrels into the prisoners' backs. The wood, silent, without song, without air, is claimed by the cold hand of Death.

The SS line them up between the two hillocks, the men with their hands clasped behind their necks, the women with heads bowed, the children, their eyes flashing between their guards and their mothers. Twenty or more here to die like animals led to slaughter.

"Scum. Subhuman." The SS taunt them from their superior position atop the hill.

A song floats on the air, the one that Sina played in her home for Alex and me, and one by one the others join in until it fills the air with its melancholy melody.

A man shouts, "Quiet, pigs," while the Commander counts down—four, three, two, one—then four SS armed with machine guns fire at once, a terrible volley of bullets, spent casings flashing copper in the air, smoke searing the air gray and black.

They fall like limp dolls to the ground, holes exploded in flesh, the exiting bullets striking in watery puffs against the damp earth, the prisoners' blood turning dark on their coats and shirts.

I want to scream but no sound comes from my mouth. Horror. Blood, much more blood than I'd ever seen on the operating table, or on the gurneys as men die. Sina is spread-eagled on the ground, Dimitri and Anna, also dead, clutching her coat.

My hands rushed to my mouth to stop a scream as I fell back against a tree. Any uttered word, the fact that I've seen the unbelievable, could mean my death. I ran from my hiding place, loping along the path, hoping that the truck wouldn't bear down upon me, fear punching me with adrenaline. I would be at peace if I were dead—after what my eyes had seen, I didn't know if I would rest again. Then, I questioned what I had seen. Was it just an illusion caused by a fevered mind?

Soon I came to the dirt road and collapsed in tears near the path. When I was able to walk again, I discovered another horror. On the southern horizon a fire burned, sending black smoke spiraling into the sky. Sina's house was engulfed in flames.

I wiped my eyes and staggered back to camp, like a woman overcome with sickness, unsure what to say or do. The truck caught up to me and slowed until one of the Wehrmacht drivers greeted me with a wave. The grim SS guards and the Commander in the back of the truck stared at me while they smoked their cigarettes, white stubs clenched between gritted teeth.

When I reached camp, I didn't want to talk to anyone and kept my distance from Alex, Hans, and Greta.

After a sleepless night, I assisted a doctor the next day with a soldier who died on the table from a horrible chest wound. His last words to me as the doctor deserted him were, "Tell my parents I love them."

My heart ached for the solider and for the slaughtered Russians who had died because a tyrant had deemed them unworthy of life. I was a Russian, too, but my family and I had been of service to Germany and in fact were accepted as Germans—but how long would that last?

Grief dragged me down for days before finally transforming

into a growing rage against the man who had spawned the horrible crime I had witnessed—Adolf Hitler.

Hans was only half-right in his assessment that the Reich needed to be condemned. The Reich needed to be destroyed. The thought thrilled and horrified me at the same time.

CHAPTER 2

I never told anyone about what I had seen in the birch forest. I tried to wipe the barbarous crime from my memory if only to keep from going mad. A slip of the tongue, even to men I trusted, like Alex and Hans, might end in disaster. The SS guards and their commanding officer in the back of the empty truck occupied my thoughts like an ever-present, insidious disease. Their blank, white faces hovered like death heads over me.

Hans's father, Robert, was arrested in August for making a derogatory remark about Hitler and was sentenced to four months in prison after being turned in by a woman in his office. Still, Hans went about his medical duties in September and October in his usual careful way, but I could tell he was seething inside about his father's arrest, as was Alex for a different reason. He went into a period of withdrawal and mourning after Sina's death. The two of them were like pots about to boil over on a hot stove.

Hans was so stubborn about his resistance to the Reich that he wouldn't sign a petition for his father's clemency hearing that his mother had sent along in a letter. His pride was too great to give in to Hitler. He was even so bold as to tell me that he wondered why people feared prison, and, by logical extension, its outcome—death. When he was younger, he had been imprisoned for participating in youth groups that weren't sanctioned by the Nazis. According to Hans, prison could be a time for reflection, self-assessment, even a religious awakening.

As we struggled through the short days and the long nights of October, we learned that we would be leaving Russia soon. This news depressed Alex because he had grown fond of our homeland, as I had. He promised to keep Russian mud on his boots and confessed that he had kept his vow never to shoot a Russian or a German soldier because he wanted no part of killing.

After we left Gzhatsk, Willi and Hubert met up with us at our assembly point in Vyazma on the thirtieth of October. Despite the reunion, Alex's sadness at leaving was palpable; his face was sallow, drawn, and careworn, and he moped about like a lost puppy. He told me one day that he suspected that Sina and her children had been imprisoned after the farm had burned. I wanted to tell him what happened, but I feared for both of our lives if the truth came out.

On the first of November, we left Russia for Germany. I was eager to be home, but also anxious because I faced an uncertain future in nursing. My traveling companion, Greta, sensed my reluctance to talk and spent her time flirting with men or gossiping with the other women.

"Did you hear about their adventures?" she asked me one day as we chugged toward Poland.

"Whose adventures?" Of course, she was baiting me with her question.

She flicked at her index finger with her thumb and smiled coyly at me. Her lips were painted flame red, lipstick and powder never far from reach in her leather purse. Men, smoking, and drinking were her weaknesses, but loyalty to her friends, especially those in the Reich, was her strength. The cigarettes and other contraband she obtained so easily led me to believe that she was well acquainted with those in high places in the black market.

"You know who," she said and pouted. "You spent a lot of time with them."

I knew perfectly well she was referring to Alex and Hans, but I was determined not to give her the pleasure of prying into my business. She pulled down the window, lit a cigarette with a flourish, and watched as flecks of ash and smoke fluttered away on the wind. The compartment air mixed with the telltale odor of burned tobacco and the cool freshness of the Russian steppe.

"In Gzhatsk, they got into a fight with a few men from the Party," Greta said. "It was an ugly scene and fists were thrown. They got out of that scrap without being arrested—they must know how to evade the law." She laughed.

She took another drag and absentmindedly pulled brown specs of tobacco from her pink tongue. Her lips left a bright red smudge around the end of the cigarette.

"How do you know they were in a fight?" I asked.

"People see things," she said, and leaned forward in her seat as if she was telling me a secret. "And people talk. I'd be careful of the company you keep. I've heard they read books they shouldn't."

My lips quivered, and I hoped I hadn't given away my irritation, let alone my annoyance at the implication that the "company" I kept was less than desirable, perhaps even traitorous.

"And they skipped the delousing line in Vyazma to go shopping." She inhaled and blew the smoke toward my face, but the wind whipped it away. "Now they have a samovar for hot tea anytime they want it. Quite a luxury to spend your hard-earned medic money on."

We had all gone through the delousing process before boarding the train, but I didn't recall seeing the men there. Had they gone on a spending spree instead? "It's none of my business what they do," I said.

"Ah, but it is your business." Her lips curled into a cagey smile. "It's the Reich's business . . . *everything* is the Reich's business—if we are to win this war."

I picked up my biology book and ignored her while she finished her cigarette. Greta soon wandered off to find a more personable companion. I read the rest of the evening, before going to bed.

A few days later, at the Polish border, we stopped at the gate.

I had a clear view from my opened compartment window on the left side of the train.

Three army guards herded shabbily dressed Russian prisoners into a nearby field. One by one, the guards kicked, spit on, and smashed their rifle butts into the prisoners' backs.

In a split second, Hans, Willi, and Alex leapt from the car behind me and assaulted the soldiers.

"You son of a bitch," Willi screamed over the commotion while pummeling one of the guards on the back with his fists. He ripped the rifle from the man's shoulder and threw it on the ground.

"Keep your hands off them, bastards," Alex yelled as he confronted another.

Hans, for his part, shoved one of the guards to the ground and kept him pinned there with his foot.

The train stopped only briefly, and by the time the dumbfounded guards knew what had hit them, the cars had started to roll again.

Hans, Alex, and Willi darted for their compartment door as the guards regrouped. I looked back as my three friends, in running turns, clasped the railing and hoisted themselves aboard. Willi was the last in, and, in a final act of defiance, turned round and saluted the guards with his finger.

I took a deep breath and leaned back in my seat. As I feared, Greta had witnessed the incident from another car. When she took her seat across from me, she shot me a look that reinforced her "be careful of the company you keep" attitude. She said nothing, but her furrowed brows and constricted facial muscles revealed all I needed to know about what she'd seen. I was sure she might report them to the SS when we arrived in Munich.

Berlin was only a blur from the train window, a dark and somber city as gray as the autumn weather, its buildings slick and spotted black with rain.

My mother and father welcomed me after I arrived in Munich. While I waited for classes to begin, I pondered what to do with my life. My parents had moved in January of 1940, a little more than a year after *Kristallnacht*, to a smaller apartment in Schwabing near Leopoldstrasse. This came about for two reasons: The house was closer to the university, where my father felt I belonged, and the rent was cheaper—he had taken a pay cut in his new position as a retail clerk for a German pharmacist.

Many students lived in the district, so the housing turnover was great, making it easier for my parents to find a new apartment, although the building wasn't as nice as the one we had moved out of. My parents lived on the third floor of a nineteenth-century wood-and-stone structure that had been covered later with white stucco.

Despite settling back into a strained familiarity with my mother and father, I never mentioned the atrocity near the camp. I knew *they* would be better off not knowing, if the SS knocked on their door. In the Reich, your grandmother was as likely to turn you in as your grandson. Everyone in Germany had that fear—even Nazis knew they had to watch their step.

Since *Kristallnacht*, my father had kept to himself, preferring to keep his personal and business life private and away from Nazi eyes. My mother suffered under his recalcitrance, and the days and nights of laughter and dance had disappeared. I couldn't wait to find another living arrangement, paying my own way, allowing me to be on my own and away from my father's strict silence.

When I did speak of Russia, I told my parents about the happy times with Sina and Alex, my feelings for the country, and my reluctance to continue nursing as a profession, an outgrowth of my experiences at the Front. After seeing the horrors of war firsthand, I told my father that I didn't have the stomach for it. He strongly suggested I continue in the profession, telling me he wanted a "better life for his grandchildren" than he had given his daughter. The job security would be better than other courses of study, he said. I was touched by his concern for my future, but still undecided. My tales of the Russian Front left my parents wistful, but, like me, caught in the middle of a war. There was no going back to a devastated Russia. Our only choice was to accept what was happening in Hitler's Germany.

On a Saturday of the break between classes, I met up with my friend Lisa Kolbe, who had been continuing her art and music studies at the university. We decided to visit the Haus der Deutschen Kunst, for it had been many years since I had visited a museum.

Since my parents had moved, Lisa and I hadn't seen as much of each other as we used to, although we did run into each other occasionally at the Café Luitpold. The trip to the museum was more suited to Lisa's tastes than mine, but I was happy to do anything to get out of the apartment rather than look through rain-spattered windows on a cold and windy day.

"I can't be a doctor in the Reich, and I've had my fill of nursing," I complained to Lisa as we climbed the steps to the museum and took shelter under its massive portico on Prinz-regentenstrasse near the Englischer Garten. We had met near the Odeonsplatz in the center of Munich, where the memorial to the fallen Nazis of Hitler's failed Putsch had been erected at the Feldherrnhalle. Walking quickly through the rain, we bypassed the east side of the Feldherrnhalle, with its massive Gothic arches and stone lions, where Germans were required to honor the "martyrs" by giving the Nazi salute, or face arrest.

We shook the rain from our umbrellas and coats and stepped past the museum's massive doors. The monumental size of the building, one of the first in Hitler's architectural plan for the Reich, always awed me with its huge galleries, long halls, and tall ceilings with recessed lighting. A solemn woman, wearing a gray suit with a Party pin tacked to it, hair tied back in a bun, took our trappings and handed us our coat check tickets.

"I think you should do what makes you happy," Lisa announced as we proceeded to the first gallery. "Biology is a good major. Sophie Scholl is studying biology and philosophy." She was referring to Hans's sister, whom Lisa had befriended at the university, but I'd not met.

The thought of changing my life's direction unsettled me, but perhaps Lisa was right. My head whirled as I listened to my internal arguments: obey my father or do what instinct told me was best for me. Since returning from Russia, I'd been haunted by nightmares of the vilest kind: large, festering wounds; severed limbs; decapitations; soldiers with the cruelest injuries; and, the vision I feared most, the slaughter of Sina, her children, and the other Russians. Those horrors played in my mind at night, conjured by my fevered brain. Often I got only a few hours of sleep.

"You look tired," Lisa said, and smoothed her silvery-blonde hair behind her ears. Her locks had grown longer in the months since I'd seen her, but she looked healthy and pretty in her impish way, her demeanor seemingly unaffected by the war. We walked into the first gallery, where the lighting accentuated her intense blue eyes, upturned mouth, and cheeky smile.

"Still tripe," she whispered to me as she viewed the artworks and spread her arms in a wide circle. "Goebbels can spout off all day about the 'triumph of German art,' but it's still boring as hell."

I surveyed the gallery and concluded that Lisa was right despite my limited knowledge about sculpture and painting. The monumental sculptures of naked men shaking hands in comradeship, the boring and classically carved busts that sat like severed heads on pedestals, left me cold and unmoved as if I were standing in a mausoleum rather than a museum. Nothing about the pedestrian Bavarian landscapes, the massive paintings of bucolic German farmers pitching hay, or the tastefully composed female nudes generated an emotion in me. We continued on to an equally boring room.

"We've been through a lot," Lisa said as she observed the paintings, including one of Hitler in battle armor. "Do you remember how excited we were when we first became members of the Young Girls League?"

"Yes, we thought the world would be different and good," I said.

We sat on one of the tufted benches in the center of the gallery and stared at the grotesque caricature of Hitler attired in gleaming silver, carrying a Nazi flag in his right hand while astride a black horse. It was propaganda at its best—not art—mythologizing, romanticizing a demon who appeared unshakable, invincible.

I shook my head and said, "We were wrong."

"And then those monotonous stints in the League of German Girls and the Reichsarbeitsdienst," Lisa said. "Imagine us working on farms and then me teaching children music and art—and you volunteering as a nurse's aide." She laughed and flexed her right arm. "At least we got some exercise on the farm."

"Monotonous is right." I thought back to the endless days and nights, it seemed, of work, National Socialist stories, home parties to discuss German culture and arts as long as the topics fit the Party's requirements; days and nights of rules and regulations: no smoking, no makeup, no sexual relations. *No, no, no.*

"Tell me about Russia," Lisa said as she looked toward the opposite end of the gallery, where a couple of uniformed soldiers passed through another chamber.

Lisa was my best friend in Munich, but I didn't want to burden her with my nightmares. I felt somewhat guilty about keeping her in the dark, but my horrible secret had to remain buried. "There's not much to tell," I pretended. "Russia was fascinating—wonderful, in fact—the work was depressing and exhausting." Someday, I knew I'd reveal what I had seen; otherwise, I wouldn't be able to live with myself.

As if reading my thoughts, Lisa responded, "When the time is right, you'll tell me . . . when you're ready." She sighed. "Remember how excited we were when our teacher took us to the Degenerate Art exhibit? The president of the Reichskammer called it an 'exorcism of evil.' More people attended that exhibit than you'd ever see here. You could drive a Panzer through these galleries and not hit anyone."

I recalled my feelings on that day in late July 1937 as we toured the narrow, arcaded rooms of the Residenz near the Hofgarten, where the Degenerate Art exhibit had been hastily housed. What a difference from the museum we sat in now! That day we were greeted by the stark wooden figure of the crucified Christ as we climbed the stairs to the first room. His tortured face, the crown of thorns thrusting out from his head, the ribs painfully showing through his emaciated skin, the wound in his side spurting a brown plug of blood, horrified us, but forced us to imagine the pain He had endured. A piece of wood, ugly, yet so supremely powerful in its carving, elicited emotions in us from compassion to revulsion for His suffering.

Our art teacher, Herr Lange, a zealous Nazi, had laughed so hard at the "perverted spectacle" that he'd taken off his horn-rimmed glasses to wipe away tears. A black-coated SS officer, who also happened to be in attendance, congratulated Herr Lange on his good taste and championed him to "teach these young minds a thing or two about good art." I'd looked at Lisa, and we silently communicated our displeasure at the officer's remarks. Of course, we couldn't say anything in opposition to the Reich, or even roll our eyes at the effrontery and stupidity of the SS man and our teacher. I found the art fascinating and many of the pictures touched my emotions with their raw power, particularly the expressive and colorful landscapes, and the arching composition and expressive painting of Franz Marc's *Two Cats, Blue and Yellow*.

The exhibit with its abstract forms and geometric landscapes, its misfit subjects, nearly all denigrated with Nazi slogans labeling the art as "effrontery," "filth for filth's sake," blaming the Jew and the Negro for the "racial idea of degenerate art," sent shock waves through the crowds. One slogan painted on the wall excoriated the artists with the words *They had four years' time*—four years to adjust their artistic styles to conform to Hitler's ideals—four years to cleanse their souls and change their way of thinking.

Many Germans snickered and laughed their way through the exhibit, and I wondered if this response was a true indication of their feelings or a nervous reaction masking their shame. But many held on to their hats or purses and, like sad dogs, skulked their way through the rooms, their blank faces reflecting a deeper despair. *They knew.* They knew and could do nothing about it.

Lisa nudged me from my reflection and I wondered what I, or we, had done to necessitate such a gesture. I looked at her and she responded by rolling her eyes and flicking her head backward. I glanced to my side and caught sight of a man who had taken a seat behind us on the double-rowed bench. His broad shoulders and muscular back pushed against his jacket and although I only got a glimpse of his face, I judged him to be handsome.

"Yes, this art is wonderful," I said to Lisa, and with a hurried look acknowledged her cue. "I'm so glad you brought me here."

"Let's move on to the next gallery," Lisa added, and rose from her seat.

A finger tapped my right shoulder. Taken aback, I flinched but turned to face the man. He looked vaguely familiar, bringing up the disconcerting feeling one has of trying to remember an acquaintance from the past. He *was* handsome with a strong, angular chin, dimpled cheeks, and wide-set blue eyes. Most German women would have considered him an ideal Aryan husband.

Lisa stopped, rooted to her spot on the marble floor.

"Pardon me," he asked in a charming baritone voice, "do you know where the Josef Thorak sculpture *Kameradschaft* might be?"

I was of no help because I had little interest in the boring art. Lisa's mouth narrowed and her blue eyes flashed under her almost white eyebrows. "I don't know how you could've missed it," she said. "It's in the gallery behind us, with the other large sculptural nudes." She pointed to the last room we had been in.

He laughed halfheartedly and smiled. "I'm sorry to have bothered you." He turned to go but halted, looked back, and said. "Have we met? I believe I've seen you both before."

Suddenly, it struck me who he was; the intelligent, cunning,

smile gave him away—I remembered his face from that disturbing day—he had talked to us in November 1938 during *Kristallnacht*, the day after the destruction.

"On the morning after the synagogues were burned, if I'm
not mistaken," I said. "You stood behind us . . . and then disappeared." I recalled the electric jolt of attraction that I felt at the
time—one I'd thought he'd sensed as well.

His already dazzling smile brightened and he skirted the
bench. "Of course," he said, and put a finger to his temple as if
attempting to recall the memory. "And other times as well . . .
long ago at the Degenerate Art exhibit . . . and at Café Luitpold." He walked closer and stopped within an arm's length of
me. "You both have coffee there sometimes? Am I right?"

An uncomfortable, nerves-taut tingle prickled over me.
Clearly, he knew much more about us than we knew about him.
Lisa stood rigidly by my side, exhibiting the same unease.

"I'm sorry," he said and bowed slightly. "I'm Garrick Adler.
I shouldn't have been so forward, but it's rare that I'm in a museum and I found myself wandering—a bit lost."

He held out his hand, and I shook it, his grip firm and warm.

Garrick approached Lisa and with some reluctance, she
shook his hand and said, "You seem to know a lot about us,
and we know nothing about you."

He sat next to me on the bench and encouraged Lisa to sit to
his right. "I can remedy that quickly," he said as Lisa took her
seat. "It's wonderful to sit between two such lovely ladies."

I cringed. My assessment that he had a wife or many girlfriends apparently had been wrong. "Flattery is unnecessary,
Herr Adler. We're in no need of it."

Lisa nodded and smiled through clenched teeth, showing her
impatience and ready willingness to withdraw from Garrick's
company.

"I'm sure you'd like the Arno Breker sculptures," Lisa said
after her smile settled. "We can guide you to them on our
way out."

"Isn't he the Führer's favorite?" Garrick asked in a voice
overflowing with sincerity.

"Yes," Lisa replied, "and he's fond of Adolf Ziegler's female nudes as well."

He swiped his fingers through the voluminous wave of hair flowing away from the part on his head. "Oh, I've seen them . . . very nice." His eyes glazed a bit in a thoughtful look. "Was your teacher Herr Lange? I must have been a year or two ahead of you, but I could swear I saw you at the Degenerate Art exhibit."

"So, what do you do?" I asked, trying to steer the conversation away from us. Lisa exhaled and sank against the bench.

"I work for the Reich insurance agency here in Munich. Pretty boring, really, but it makes me feel I'm doing some good for people—keeping those who are ill from falling into poverty and despair."

"Just like Clara Barton," Lisa said.

Blood rose to my face.

Garrick jerked his head toward her. "What?"

"Nothing," Lisa said.

When he turned back to me, rage smoldered in his eyes but subsided as he spoke. "I've taken enough of your time—I should be going if I want to see the Thorak sculpture." He got up from the bench.

Lisa tapped her wristwatch. "We should be going too."

"Before I leave . . . I don't believe I've gotten your names."

"Natalya Petrovich," I said, "and Lisa Kolbe."

"It was a pleasure to see you again," he said and started to raise his hand in the Nazi salute. Instead, his arm fell to his side as if shame, or some other emotion, had caused him to reconsider. "Perhaps I'll see you at the café." He walked around the bench and into the gallery behind us.

I scowled at Lisa after he left. "*Clara Barton?* It probably wasn't smart to needle him."

"It was intended as a jab," Lisa replied. "I doubt if he even knows who she was. I wish you hadn't given him our names."

"Why not? It would only make him suspicious if we didn't."

"Make something up. He'd never know."

I shook my head in amazement at her paranoia, but perhaps

she was right; we didn't know Garrick Adler. But why was Lisa so concerned about giving her name? If anything, I was the one who needed to watch what I said after what I'd seen in Russia. "Why don't you want your name known?"

She shook her head.

"Do you recall seeing Garrick when I was at the Front?" I asked.

"I've never seen him, other than after that terrible night in 1938. If he's seen us, he was spying. We need to be cautious—I don't trust anyone who can overhear a conversation."

We left the gallery and strolled through the building until we were back at the entrance. We put on our coats, gathered our umbrellas, and stepped out on the portico. The wind whipped around the stone columns in a cold blast. The rain had slowed to a drizzle, but the gusts rendered the umbrellas useless.

Apparently, Garrick had had his fill of the museum, for I spotted him a block ahead of us, his build and long stride unmistakable.

"It seems he's headed my way toward Schwabing," I said. "I'll see where he goes."

"What do you think he's up to?" Lisa asked.

Her question deflated me, my sadness festering from the cruel fact that we had to watch every word we said, censor every public conversation, look with distrust upon every human interaction and emotion, and spend sleepless nights wondering whether the Gestapo was surging up the stairs to arrest us. "I don't know, but he's certainly attractive."

Lisa clicked her tongue and pointed the tip of her closed umbrella at me. "Those are dangerous words. He's good-looking, but I'd be careful."

"I'm a pretty good judge of character," I said, wiping the mist from my glasses.

"That's not what I'm worried about."

"What then?" I asked irritably.

"A man like that can *make* you fall in love. Away from your father's clutches you're susceptible."

"Don't be absurd. No man is going to *make* me fall in love."

"And why isn't he in the army?"

"I don't know. Perhaps he has some medical condition—I've seen plenty of men who couldn't serve for one reason or another—or the work he does is critical."

"Not in insurance. He could be replaced by a hundred others."

We came to the large avenue that led toward the apartment building my parents used to live in. Lisa and I hugged each other and said good-bye, promising to meet again after I had decided upon my course of study.

I trundled on through the drizzle, clutching my umbrella with my right hand, clenching my coat tightly about my neck with my left, trying to keep up with Garrick as he disappeared around a corner, turning north onto Ludwigstrasse. Large stone buildings lined each side of the street leading to the university, each one as gray and dreary as the falling night, blackout curtains clinging to the windows.

Garrick passed under the triumphal arch of the Siegestor, with its sculpted chariot atop, and into Schwabing, where I lived with my parents. He turned onto one of the shadowy streets, the trees stripped of leaves by November winds, bark wet and dripping from the drizzle, the two of us nearly alone in the fading day. Smells permeated the chilly air, so different from the fresh, clean sweep of the wind on the Russian steppes. Here, the odors of cooked sausage, potatoes, and eggs mixed with car exhaust and spent heating fuel.

He opened the door to a two-story house, its arched doorway, stones, and gabled roof neat and tidy in their Bavarian cleanliness. I stood behind a tree on the other side of the street and watched as a dark figure pulled the curtain down on a front window on the upper story. A warm yellow light flared from a side window and Garrick appeared with a notebook in hand, pen resting on his lips. He removed the pen from his mouth and wrote in his book; and, as if pleased with his words, he held it like a hymnal before closing it. Then, the shade was drawn and the room went black.

I gripped my umbrella and headed toward my parents' apartment somewhat ashamed that I was stalking a man, as he had perhaps stalked us.

As I walked, I wondered what he had written. Whatever he had penned, it had taken only a moment. A strange sensation came over me, and, in my mind, I was standing next to him as he wrote the names in his book.

Natalya Petrovich and *Lisa Kolbe.*

CHAPTER 3

The early weeks of November were filled with excitement, and I rarely had time to think about anything except the university and moving.

I decided upon biology as a major, rearranged my class schedule, and removed myself from the rolls of volunteer nurses. My father, less than pleased with my choice, still hoped for a nursing career for me. He was somewhat mollified because my new major was at least related to my previous field and might allow me to work in a research capacity. Both he and my mother hinted (in their own ways, but the meaning was clear) that it was time for me to think about finding a husband, in addition to getting a job. That way, if I couldn't find work after my studies, or the Reich came calling on me to produce children, I'd have a husband to support me. They didn't take into account that men were scarce. These conversations with my father were one-sided and precipitated tension between us. I was treated like a child, I thought.

After several stressful weeks of living at home, I resolved to find an apartment of my own.

As luck would have it, my father had made friends with a widow by the name of Frau Hofstetter, who lived a few blocks from my parents in Schwabing. He would often slide her a few extra aspirin, or hard-to-get packets of bath salts, across the apothecary counter. The Frau always expressed her eternal gratitude, secretly, of course, because giving such "gifts" was a crime.

One day, she told my father of her hope to find a young woman to help care for her: to do dishes, tidy up, and to "make sure I'm not dead in the morning." These responsibilities came with a small payment each month and the free use of an extra bedroom with its own entrance on the front of the house.

The bedroom joined the other rooms by a main connecting hallway. The opportunity to hear "movement" in the dull rooms and to "know that someone is there" gave the widow great satisfaction. The new tenant would have kitchen and bathroom privileges, and, if required, access to the small sitting room where the Frau spent most of her time.

Spending my free time caring for a seventy-five-year-old woman was less than thrilling, but the opportunity was too good to pass up. My father's income was barely enough to support my mother and him, food shortages were rampant, and, most important, I needed my freedom. The time had come to make my own way in the world.

It didn't take long for me to pack the few things I owned and move to my new home. I accomplished it all in a couple of trips, and, by the time classes were in full swing, I was settled into the Frau's residence.

My room was pleasant and faced south, toward the street. A few streaks of November sun splashed through the window in the early morning. As the seasons changed, the room would be brilliantly lit in the spring and summer, perhaps dappled with light from quivering oak leaves. The furniture consisted of a bed, framed by an antique walnut headboard with carved foxes and hunting dogs cavorting across its top, a modest curved kneehole dresser with a bluish mirror from the 1920s, and a simple, but solid, mahogany chair, which sat next to a small table.

The inside door led to a hallway lit only from the sunlight coming in from the main entrance. The other rooms extended from this hall and led also to Frau Hofstetter's bedroom at the back of the house. I surmised my landlady was more comfortable away from the street noise and also enjoyed her access to the tiny garden behind her room.

We saw each other daily, as I completed my list of tasks. For the most part, the Frau ambled about her home clad in a house-dress with her gray stockings rolled down to her ankles. When the temperature would fall, the stockings would rise. Often she fell asleep in the small sitting room with a newspaper or book covering her lap. I was responsible for cleaning, but she insisted on cooking. If my studies prevented me from eating, she would knock on my door while balancing a plate of food, usually extra potatoes and fried eggs from her supper. She was generous, but also insistent that I be meticulous in my work.

Much of my time was spent studying at my dresser under the glare of my old desk lamp, or curled up in bed, attempting to read from the soft glow of an oil lamp. My only company at night was the hiss and rattle of the radiators.

In early December, Lisa and I received an invitation from Hans and his sister Sophie for dessert, wine, and conversation at their apartment on Josefstrasse, where they lived in two large separate rooms. Lisa came for me that frigid night, the air as clean and crisp as ice, and we trundled our way shivering and rattling down the streets.

Sophie, whom I recognized as someone I'd seen in an audi-torium class, answered the door. Her brown hair ran down her neck to her shoulders and rested in a rather severe wave across her forehead. A boyish quality infused her face, and depending on how she turned her head, she gave the appearance of having somewhat masculine features. She exuded a seriousness in her manner, a like characteristic of her brother, her eyes searching, her lips often pursed. She welcomed Lisa with an affectionate "hello," and introduced herself to me. I told her that I was a friend of her brother's, which elicited an immediate warm smile.

I took off my glasses and swiped at the lenses with a clean handkerchief, the transition from cold to heat momentarily blinding me with condensation. When I put them on again, the rooms came into view. They were sparse but retained a cozy feel:

pictures adorned the flowered wallpaper, chairs and pillows invited the visitors to take their places in comfort. The table held cakes, an assortment of chocolate and vanilla pastries, tea, and wine. A bottle of schnapps sat gleaming like a spirit overlord at the end of the table. It appeared that Hans and Sophie had their own connections when it came to obtaining food and drink.

I studied the crowd of guests. Willi Graf and Alex Schmorell were missing from the gathering—I thought they might be attending—but a few others were unexpected.

Professor Kurt Huber, for one. I recognized him as the instructor of the class that Sophie and I attended. He sat hunched in the corner as if he were sitting on pins and needles, crossing and uncrossing his legs, smoothing his pant legs with his hands. His long, oval face was topped by a half-bald pate adorned only by the graying hair that grew halfway back and down the sides of his head. He glanced at me and then turned away. Having no reason to introduce myself, I decided to wait until the evening's social strictures had relaxed under the influence of the Riesling wine.

But my indifference toward Professor Huber turned to surprise as another face came into view.

Garrick Adler was seated on a pillow embroidered with green vines and the purple trumpets of morning glories, his legs crossed in front of him. I had missed him when I first came in because his body was partially concealed behind a chair. Garrick smiled in his bright way and I felt a blush rise in my cheeks, a signal of his attractiveness. However, my ardor was dampened by the suspicious nature so masterfully orchestrated by the Reich and instilled in all of us.

Lisa wandered off to speak to Hans and an artist friend. Knowing few in the crowd, I found myself drawn to the food and drinks table—my shyness overcoming any urge to converse with anyone. I sat in a chair across the room and couldn't help peeking at Garrick now and then. He was speaking to a man I didn't know and as soon as their conversation ended, I felt his gaze upon me before I glanced his way. He got up from the floor, grabbed his pillow, and plopped it next to my feet.

"I didn't expect to see you here," he said.

I found myself admiring his bright smile and broad shoulders, and he looked up at me like an adoring puppy. Then, I pictured him writing *Natalya* and *Lisa* in his book the night I had followed him and the thought sent a shiver up my spine. Was it paranoia or reality? Despite that disturbing image, I found his attention flattering.

"A last-minute invitation . . ."

"How do you know Hans and Sophie?" he asked, filling in my broken thought.

I wondered how much I should reveal, but also considered that anyone who knew the Scholls well enough to be invited to a house party would know something about them.

"I served with Hans on the Eastern Front for three months before we were called home. I was a nurse and he was a medic. We're both at the university now." I threaded my fingers together and placed my hands in my lap, trying to quell my social discomfort. "I've seen Sophie in class, but we've just met."

"We've been friends for about a year," Garrick offered. Dimples formed at the end of his smile. "They're interesting people of the right sort."

I was perplexed by what he meant. "Right sort?"

He placed his arms behind him like pillars and leaned back in a comfortable pose. His long legs stretched in front of mine, blocking me from leaving the chair. "Politically . . . and they're nice people. Solid Germans with their feet on the ground. They understand politics and literature."

Hans had already communicated his feelings to me about the Nazis when we were in Russia. His words, "The Reich must be condemned," came rushing back. I couldn't carry on the conversation without lying or incriminating myself, so I nodded in an absentminded way. Thinking of a ploy to end our talk, I asked Garrick, "Would you mind getting me a glass of wine?" I offered a bemused smile. "I seem to be boxed in."

"Of course," he said, and rose from his resting place. "Don't go away . . . I have a question to ask you."

The hair on the back of my neck bristled. *A question?* I had no idea what he had in mind. I had questions for him but didn't know him well enough to ask. He glided off to the table and was about to lift a glass, when he was engaged in conversation by a woman, a slim brunette whom I didn't know.

"I think you have an admirer." Lisa stood beside me with a wineglass in one hand and a dish holding a chocolate pastry in the other.

"Shhh," I ordered. "I don't need a boyfriend or a husband. My studies come first."

She chuckled. "That's what you say now, but remember what I said about men who can *make* you fall in love."

"Yes. You needn't remind me."

Even as I objected to my friend, part of me basked in the attention Garrick offered. I was the quiet and shy one compared to Lisa, who always seemed prettier and more vivacious than I. It was the first time any man had really *looked* at me, and he was coming close to overriding any objections I might hold. Any woman would have found him a prize, as confirmed by the one at the table, who grasped his arm, touched his shoulder, and threw her head back in flirtatious laughter.

Garrick finally disengaged himself from her; she pouted as he walked away. "Good evening, Lisa," he said with little warmth upon his return. He handed me the glass and took his spot on the pillow.

"You remembered," Lisa said flatly.

"I never forget a name or a pretty face."

"Flatterer," Lisa said, and turned on her heels.

Garrick sighed and leaned back on his elbows.

"You don't drink?" I asked.

"Rarely. It doesn't agree with me." He tapped his jacket pocket and lifted the flap, exposing the top of a cigarette pack. "I smoke now and then—it calms me down."

I sipped my wine and let its warmth settle in my stomach. "You don't seem the type who would get upset easily."

"Oh, yes," he said. "Sometimes the war gets on my nerves. I see what's happening and there's nothing at the insurance service I can do about it." His mood darkened and he stared across the room at nothing in particular. "Our men come home in boxes, and I have to deal with the grieving widows and parents and my nerves can be overwrought." He tapped his right leg. "I can't serve."

"I'm sorry," I said, sympathy pricking me for the injury he suffered. "The Russian Front wasn't a day at the fair, either. Much of what I had to deal with was upsetting—so much so that I decided to suspend my volunteer nursing in favor of my studies."

"That's a shame." He pushed himself off his elbows and leaned toward me. "Let's not talk about the war, it's too depressing." His mood brightened in a flash. "Regarding that question I mentioned." He paused and gazed at the floor before looking up at me. "May I ask you out—that is, if you don't have other engagements?"

His question caught me off guard, and I'm sure my eyes widened in surprise at his sudden proposal.

Before I could answer, Hans clapped his hands and called for everyone's attention. I was relieved to be saved by our host as the group gathered around him and took their places in chairs or on pillows and cushions.

Hans, who looked much more relaxed than he had been in Russia, quieted the room in his role as the congenial master of the group. He offered a rare smile, leaned against the table, welcomed us to his home with Sophie, and joked about living with his sister. Their arrangement had fostered a "new amicability," he said. After sparring with the group, he read poetry from Schiller and Goethe, which went on for some time, and his words were applauded by the crowd except for one—Professor Huber.

The academician rose as the last poem ended, and, after pulling on his coat, walked past Hans and Sophie and out the door without so much as a good-bye. A blast of bitter wind cut through the room. Hans continued his congenial banter with the crowd, apparently unaffected by the professor's exit. He talked for some time about various subjects: philosophy, ethics, man as a social being. I shifted uncomfortably in my seat as the hour grew late; Garrick watched Hans with a studied intensity.

As the evening drew to a close, I still hadn't answered Garrick's question about going out. We were interrupted at times by Lisa and Sophie, who spent most of the evening talking with each other.

"How was Stuttgart?" I heard Sophie ask a young woman, and then address a similar question a few minutes later to another woman. "How was Hamburg?"

Both of these young women answered in the affirmative and talked with some animation about the beauty of both cities. The conversations seemed out of place and Garrick must have felt the same way, for he listened with one ear cocked toward them before turning his attention back to me. Mostly, these intrusive discussions were a welcome distraction to small talk with Garrick as I drank my second glass of wine.

Finally, I had to give him some kind of answer. I screwed up my courage, for it was the first time I had been asked out by a man rather than a collegial schoolboy. The image of my strict father intruded in my thoughts. I took a breath. "I'm busy with classes until the break, and I live with a seventy-five-year-old woman who doesn't like to be disturbed."

The smile that had graced his face most of the night faded. "That's not a 'no.'"

"I guess not." I put the empty wineglass on the small table next to my chair. "If I can spare the time, I'll let you know." He seemed somewhat placated by my noncommittal reply and grasped my hand warmly.

"I look forward to it," he said. "Let me give you my phone number and address."

Of course, I knew where he lived, having followed him home after the museum visit. I didn't reveal my own, only a few blocks from his, as he handed me a hurriedly scribbled note.

Lisa appeared next to my chair with our coats. "Time to make a discreet exit before we're regaled with more poetry."

Garrick laughed and stood up on his long legs. He was at

least a head taller than I was, and I was considered tall for a woman. Lisa gave me my coat and I put it on, placing the address in the pocket.

"It was nice to see you both again," he said. "I should be getting home myself."

We said our good-byes to Hans and Sophie and headed for the door. Lisa pushed me past it with a friendly shove as she hurried us to the street. "Quick, let's get out of here before your admirer follows you home."

The streets were pitch-dark, devoid of light from the extinguished streetlamps, the homes shrouded by blackout curtains as we walked. The only sources of light were a small sliver of moon and the steady stars that sent their cold beams cutting through breaks in the swiftly flowing clouds.

Garrick's interest quickened my thoughts and my step. My kisses had been limited to schoolboys, with little romantic attraction flowering from my lips. Those were minor crushes that came to nothing. My father had kept a close watch on me; my mother didn't object to his intention of keeping his daughter pure for her marriage day. He didn't have to worry—I was shy and uncertain with men and certainly wouldn't have given away my virginity. Any fascination I had with the body came merely from studying it, but with Garrick I had the strange feeling that the world of love might open for me. However, I wasn't rushing into anything because, in these times, keeping to yourself, not drawing attention, was the best way to stay out of trouble.

"How do you think my hair would look if I cut it shorter?" I asked Lisa, and wrapped a few strands of my shoulder-length locks around my fingers. I was thinking of Lisa's style, which was similar to the woman who had struck up the conversation with Garrick.

"My God, Natalya," Lisa replied with horror biting into her voice. "You can't be serious." We turned the corner toward my apartment, and I caught the look of concern on her face despite the dim light. "You're not going out with *him*?" Her words sounded like a command rather than a friendly question. "You don't even know him."

"How can I get to know him, if I don't go out?" I asked. "He doesn't seem like a bad man. He said things tonight that made me reconsider my impression of him. He has a leg injury that keeps him from serving."

We strolled up to my apartment. Frau Hofstetter's neat, tidy house was as bland and unremarkable, like a dark cube in the shadows, as every other dwelling on the block.

"Forget Garrick for a few minutes," Lisa said. "Can I come in—out of the cold? I have something to share with you."

I was somewhat leery of the hour and of disturbing the landlady. "I suppose—as long as we're quiet."

"Don't worry—what I have to tell you requires secrecy—in a way, silence."

I opened the door and we stepped into the dark, the blackout curtains drawn. By the time I switched on my lamp, Lisa had taken off her shoes, removed her coat, and settled under it on my bed with her back resting against the walnut headboard. As the radiator clanged, I lifted the chair from its normal resting place at the dresser and positioned it at the end of the bed.

"Come closer," Lisa said and then shivered. "It's cold in here."

What is so important! What does she have to tell me?

Intrigued by her somber expression, I moved the chair closer to the headboard and leaned toward her.

She fluffed my pillow and settled back again. "Have you heard of the White Rose?"

I shook my head.

"Are you sure your landlady's asleep?" Lisa asked.

I looked at my watch. "At this hour she's tucked away in bed."

"What I have to tell you can never be repeated." Her voice hummed low under the radiator's noise. "Hans, Sophie, and Alex have taken a stand against the Reich."

My heart beat faster at her words.

Lisa's arms trembled as she struggled to keep her emotions in check.

"This is a very dangerous business, but something has to be done," she continued. "Everyone in the White Rose was chosen for their intelligence, their convictions, and their politics, including me."

I wanted to wrap my arms around her as the words spilled from her mouth and tears, close to falling, glistened in her eyes.

"What have you done?" I asked, shaking, as if the coldness of the room had entered my bones. "Are you in danger?"

"Let me finish." She straightened her back against the headboard and looked at me. "Hans and Alex wrote four leaflets against the Reich that were mailed in June and July before you went to the Front. Some were distributed at the university. The words are treasonous—questioning the will of the German people to stand up against a corrupt government, a dictatorship of evil; calling National Socialism a 'cancerous ulcer'; pointing out that since Poland fell, three hundred thousand Jews have been murdered. . . ."

My breath caught and my stomach twisted from my memory of seeing Sina and her children slaughtered by the SS. On top of my agony came the sudden realization that others knew about the heinous crimes being committed. *Others know!* I felt as if chains had dropped from my body.

"Stop, please stop." Shame flooded me because I had been unable to tell anyone my terrible secret. Lisa put a finger to my lips as I struggled to keep from collapsing, humiliation washing over me, my hands shaking from knowing that I now could take a stand as well—but only if I placed my life and my parents' lives at risk in order to fight the evil that had overtaken our homeland. But what could I do?

Leaning forward, Lisa clasped my hands in hers. "They want you." Her words sounded like a sacrament, a holy whisper. "Hans and Alex have been watching you since you traveled to the Front. They want you to join the group."

"Me?"

"You'll help me mail and deliver leaflets. We can write them ourselves with their approval. Alex and Hans wrote the first four and they'll soon be working on a fifth. In the meantime, they want the movement to expand its targets. The Reich already believes the White Rose is a national organization. The Gestapo is running scared. We are making a difference." She paused. "Our mailing locations will be Vienna and Nuremberg."

I held my arms close to my body to quell the violent shivering that threatened to consume me. "Sophie talked to two women about Stuttgart and Hamburg. Was that about the leaflets?"

Lisa rose from the bed, retrieved my coat, and wrapped it around me. "Yes. I know this is a shock, but think about what I've said. We are the first, and, remember, *something* has to be done."

I breathed deeply and leaned back in the chair. After a few minutes of reflection, I told Lisa what I had seen at the Front—revealing for the first time what I witnessed—stopping several times to wipe away tears, drained from the emotions coursing through me.

Lisa lay sprawled under her coat as I ended my story. We stared at each other for a long time, both of us knowing that what I had told her could get us killed.

"I have to get home or my parents will send for the police," Lisa finally said. "We don't want that." She got off the bed, put on her coat, and walked behind my chair. She leaned over and embraced me in a powerful hug.

I was worried that she might be harassed by the authorities as she walked home. "It's after eleven. Stay here—it's late." I extricated myself from her arms and got up from the chair.

"No, I'll be fine. I know the less-traveled streets by heart. Class tomorrow."

I hugged her once more as she headed toward the door.

"One last thing," she said, clutching the knob. "Don't say a word of this to anyone, most of all Garrick. He's being watched as well, but so far he's not won over the group. He says all the right things, but Hans wants to find out more about him."

"Of course," I replied, knowing that Lisa held no fondness for Garrick from the beginning.

Lisa opened the door and dissolved into the wreath of shadows hanging upon the street. Soon she had disappeared in the night.

Exhausted, I collapsed on my bed. I woke up at three in the morning, my lamp still aglow on my desk. I switched it off and crawled back under the blankets, hoping my dreams would be free of thoughts of imprisonment and execution, the horrors of war, or the budding admission in my mind that I was more than curious about Garrick Adler.

The following Saturday morning while washing up in my parents' tiny bathroom, I heard my mother's strangled scream. They had invited me over for breakfast, as they often did on weekends. As always, I was glad for a respite from my work at Frau Hofstetter's and an invitation to enjoy my mother's cooking.

My mother stood at the front window, her fingers clenched into fists at her side. I rushed to her, as did my father, and spotted a black sedan parked in front of their apartment. The car idled, white puffs of exhaust billowing from its pipes before evaporating into the December air.

My heart rocketed into my throat when three men, one an SS officer in his black leather trench coat, the other two in brown coats, alighted swiftly from the car and with an aura of Reich formality strode up the walk.

"Whatever happens, neither of you say a word," my father cautioned, his face blanched with fear. "You know nothing."

I looked at him in horror; something was dreadfully wrong. The downstairs door was often open and I listened, my heart thudding in my chest, for footsteps on the stairs.

All was silent before the muffled creak of their shoes sounded in the hall. Two violent knocks echoed in the apartment before my father, silencing us with a finger to his lips, answered.

The SS officer stood behind the two men in the brown coats. One of them cracked a thin smile and announced he was from the Gestapo. "Herr Petrovich?" he asked in a voice that hinted of disdain behind its pleasant veneer. My mother leaned against me and the tremble in her bones settled in mine. Still, she was remarkably composed, in control of her shaky emotions as we watched what was unfolding before our eyes; but we had to be, we had no choice.

My father nodded and asked what business they had.

"We would like you to come with us," the man said and the other two slipped into the apartment, their eyes darting around the room as if my parents were suspected of the most terrible treason.

I started to speak, but my father's intense glare warned me not to open my mouth. I complied, all the while struggling to silence my fear. My parents had never supported the Nazi Party, but had never disparaged it as far as I knew. I couldn't imagine what the Gestapo was doing in their apartment—at first, I thought they might have come for me because of what I'd revealed to Lisa. I quickly dismissed that thought—Lisa would never have betrayed me.

The first man took my father by the arm and ushered him into the hall. The SS man and the other Gestapo agent headed for my father's bookcase. With one swipe of his gloved hand, the black-clad thug overturned the case, sending the books crashing to the floor. Several volumes of my father's illegal books tumbled from their hiding place along with the others.

The second Gestapo agent picked up two of the books, including the Aquinas my father was so fond of, and held them in his gloved hands. The brown leather surrounding his fingers glinted like polished amber in the bright morning light.

"Do you know anything about these books, Frau Petrovich?" the agent asked my mother. His thin mustache wriggled on his upper lip as he spoke.

My mother shook her head, but said nothing.

"I'd advise you to stay at home for the next several days," the SS officer said. He turned on his heels along with the other agent. Clutching several books, they rushed away, leaving the door open as they hurried down the staircase.

My mother and I ran to the window. The agent who had grabbed my father shoved him into the backseat of the waiting sedan and climbed in beside him. The other agent and the SS officer tossed the books in the trunk and then took their seats as driver and lookout. The car's motor revved and the vehicle accelerated down the street out of sight.

We were left staring out the window. Without a word, my mother went to the kitchen. She lifted the spatula to stir the eggs, but it dropped from her trembling fingers as she collapsed in front of the stove.

I held her in my arms and stroked her hair.

"Oh, my God, what will become of him," she sobbed.

I tried to quiet her. As her weeping faded, the silence grew ominous—the street even devoid of traffic—as if the Gestapo and SS had chased all life away. My fear transformed into a white anger behind my eyes. I knew what I must do.

I vowed, as I cradled my mother, to resist Hitler, his Reich, and his henchmen.

I would join the White Rose.

CHAPTER 4

By the following Monday, my father had been convicted of making a "slanderous statement" and of fostering "subversion" against the Reich and was sentenced to six months in prison. He had been reported by a woman who "overheard" him talking to another customer at the apothecary about the books he read and lamenting the fact that he could not read what he wanted because of Hitler.

My mother and I attended the trial at the Palace of Justice, but we weren't allowed to speak. In fact, my father's defense attorney made no case at all. He shook his head at the judge and muttered a plea for clemency, his sole statement, a tactic which froze my mother in her seat with terror and infuriated me. In fact, the mockery of a trial cemented my resolve to join the White Rose.

We were able to see my father only for a few minutes outside the courtroom. He clutched my mother's hands and said, "Don't mount an appeal; it will only make things worse. Live your lives as if nothing has happened." The guards led him away to Stadelheim Prison, a large stone facility southeast of the city that had a long history of violent and notable criminals, including the Führer himself.

After he was gone, we stood sobbing in the hall. My mother clutched my hand and noted, as anger rose within me, that what I'd experienced since Kristallnacht was part of the Reich's plan not only for Jews and Russians, but for all Germans. I'd known this every day since Hitler took power, but now the terror had come to our family. Killing, ripping families apart, had become commonplace and we had done *nothing*.

I was able to follow my father's wishes in the days following his imprisonment, for the most part, by immersing myself in my studies. I visited my mother when I could. She, also, seemed to be bearing up better than I'd expected (perhaps it was a stoic Russian characteristic), cooking, cleaning an already spotless apartment, and crossing off the days of the week on a calendar with my father's release date circled in red.

About a week after my father was convicted, Lisa asked me to meet her at an address in Schwabing I'd never been to. She was secretive about what we'd be doing, but having made up my mind that I would take my own stand against the Nazis, I followed her instructions after ending my day with the Frau.

As I approached the building, another large three-story home populated mostly by students, I was happy to be under cover of darkness. It is one thing to trust a friend, but entirely another to place your life in their hands.

Lisa was leaning against the bark of a large tree, her dark clothing blending in with the night, the north wind whipping at her coat. The red-tipped flare of her cigarette caught my eye, and it struck me that she would only be smoking if she was certain that the police wouldn't be walking by.

She said nothing to me, and offered only a melancholy smile. Crushing the cigarette underneath her heel, she turned in a fierce sweep toward a narrow path on the side of the building, brushing past the naked branches of lilacs, and opening a door spotted with a rainbow of paint colors.

"Welcome to the studio of Dieter Frank," Lisa said, closing and locking the door with a brass key. We were plunged into a cavern of darkness. The room smelled damp, musty, and of linseed, and oil paints. She switched on a battered brass floor lamp and a dismal basement room appeared before me.

The artist's studio was in disarray: Canvases lay askew in the corners; two easels sat near the room's center on either side of a large oak table piled with paper and drawings; an unmade bed occupied space under a small window on the rear wall. A blackout curtain covered the window.

I studied the art on the easels. Dieter's paintings were pleasing if you liked grand figures in stiff poses, much like the Reich-approved art housed in the museum.

"Are you sure we're in the right place?" I asked Lisa, questioning the role the artist might have in the White Rose.

Lisa took off her coat, lit another cigarette, and walked to an easel. "This is what Dieter Frank really paints." She flipped over the top canvas, revealing a startling jumble of lines and geometric forms.

"Much like Kandinsky," Lisa said, "but Dieter, in his vision, has managed to make them somehow less formal, almost naturalistic in their appearance, like vines swirling around columns."

Having only a passing knowledge of Kandinsky, I stood back and admired the canvas. "I like it. He's talented."

"I suppose I shouldn't be telling you this, yet," Lisa said and then paused. "Dieter's also a friend of Manfred Eickemeyer, an architect, who . . . well—let's say that without Manfred the White Rose leaflets would never get printed." She walked to the table and bent over a lumpy rectangular shape covered by a large cloth. Lisa ripped it off with a flourish like a magician performing a trick, revealing a mimeograph machine. Although I had seen one at school, I knew they were hard to come by. "We don't have to depend on Herr Eickemeyer," Lisa said in a boastful tone.

The sight of the green metal machine with its roller plate brought the task at hand into sharp focus. Lisa reached into her coat pocket, withdrew a flask filled with schnapps, unscrewed the cap, and let me smell the sweet, biting odor of the liquor.

"I could use a drink," I said, taking it from her and swigging it back. The strong taste burned my throat as I took off my coat. We took seats across the table from each other. "Where's Dieter?"

Lisa drummed her fingernails on the table. "He'd rather not

be here . . . in case something happens. He could be arrested for letting us use his studio and wants no part of producing the leaflets. He feels the less he knows about what we do here, the better."

"In other words, he's frightened," I said.

"He'd prefer the word 'cautious.'" Lisa rested her cigarette on an ashtray close to overflowing with cigarette butts and spent matches. "Shall we get started?"

Fear snapped at me. I was about to take the first step toward treason and there would be no turning back.

"What do you want me to do?" I asked.

"First read the leaflets Hans and Alex have written, and then write ours," Lisa said. "You'll be the words. . . . I know you write better than I do." She pointed to a box in the far corner of the studio. "That's my job—I'm in charge of the stamps, the stationery, and the envelopes. We address them to Nuremberg residents, mail them in Vienna and whatever we have left over, we distribute there."

She reached into her coat pocket and withdrew a letter-size envelope, unwound the thread securing its top, slid out the leaflets, and held them in her hands as if they were sacred objects.

"My God, you risked your life to bring them here!"

She smiled. "Be careful, these are the only copies I have." She read: "*Leaflets of the White Rose. I. II. III. IV.*" The words and numbers burned into my brain, and as I read through them, Lisa maintained a solemn silence, leaving me to my thoughts.

After about twenty-five minutes, I placed the leaflets back on the envelope. Lisa's mouth scrunched into a thoughtful frown, another cigarette poised in her right hand. She cocked her head so that the blonde hair that usually framed her right ear dropped in a shallow curl next to her cheek. "So . . . what do you think?"

Actually, I had few critical suggestions to offer; my nerves were in shards after digesting the words crafted by Hans and Alex.

"I can't believe what I've read." The daring audacity of the writers, the strength poured onto the pages, thrilled me but at the same time scared me to death. How was I to match such thinking? These were indeed treasonous thoughts put on paper with death assured to the writers—that was a fact. A jolt surged through my body. I was surrendering my life to something new, unknown, and deadly. The fact that I had read the words of the White Rose and didn't report Hans, Alex, and Sophie to the Gestapo made me as much a traitor, a co-conspirator, as they were.

"It turns from classical references in the first leaflet, to a full-scale assault on Hitler and the stupor of the German people in the later writings," I said. "Imagine impugning Hitler as a liar and branding him as a 'dictator of evil!' This shocks me beyond anything I could imagine."

"It should," Lisa said calmly. "Now it's up to you to put your feelings about the Reich into words, to paint a true portrait of this monster who rules us." She put out her cigarette and leaned toward me. "We must do something. Our resistance is the only course we have, the only way that can make a difference. Hans, Sophie, Alex, and Willi are the leaders of the White Rose. The leaflets talk about sabotage—a subversive act—but, as far as we know, no one has ever taken up that call."

"Then why put ourselves at risk if our words make no difference?" I asked, wanting her to confirm what I was thinking.

"Because, as Sophie says, we have a conscience. We have no other choice but to reject Hitler and his killing machine. *Our* means are nonviolent—we tug at the hearts of good German people."

I rose from my chair and paced around the studio, which had taken on the surreal atmosphere of a dream: the table, the chairs, the artwork, the bed, all tilting toward me like some fantasy from Don Quixote. "I don't know if I can do this, Lisa. We'll be executed! You know that. Everything in Germany is monitored, spied upon; every shadow, every footstep behind us would be a potential threat. What about my parents? My father is in enough trouble as it is."

Lisa sighed and brought her folded hands up to her face. After a few moments, she said, "Now is the time to back out if you must, because once the words have been written and published, they are in the world forever, unless Hitler wins the war. In that case, the efforts of the White Rose will have been in vain and the memories of our accomplishments will vanish without a trace." A deep sadness darkened her expression as she paused to collect her thoughts. "Perhaps we can help Germany come to her senses before it's too late. The decision is yours to make."

I leaned against the table and considered what this would mean. I had never been a deeply religious person, but somehow I felt as if the hand of God was lowering me into a swiftly flowing river that I couldn't escape. I would either drown or be tossed ashore battered and broken. Neither choice was appealing. And yet, when I thought deeply about the horror of Sina and her children, their tiny hands clutching at her coat, the Gestapo arresting my father, and the calm composure of Hans, Alex, and Sophie, who placed their lives in jeopardy for what they truly believed was right, what truly mattered—the correct choice sounded like a clarion call in my head.

"Let's begin," I said as firmly as I could, and noticed that my hands were shaking.

"I'm relieved," Lisa said. "I knew your heart would lead you to the White Rose, because I know the decent person you are." She offered the flask to me again, but I declined another drink in order to keep my wits about me. "There's one thing we need to do before you write a single word."

"What's that?"

"We must make a pact, swear to each other that if one of us is arrested, questioned, imprisoned, or even tortured, we will not betray the others in the White Rose. It's the only way the group can continue to fight tyranny." She put her hand over her heart. "Swear it."

I took a deep breath and put my hand over my heart. "I swear never to betray the White Rose."

"And I again swear never to betray the White Rose," Lisa said. "Let's drink to our agreement."

She got up from her chair, gripped the flask, tipped it backward, and gulped a large helping of schnapps.

She handed it to me, the hammered tin flashing in the light. I drank in honor of our agreement, knowing that I had just sealed my fate.

We struggled long into the night, searching for the right words, the expression, the nuances of thought that would put power behind our deliberations so they wouldn't appear empty and without force, like meaningless scratches on paper.

At first, I wanted to describe the awful scene in Russia, the murders, the blood spilled from innocent Russians and German soldiers, but, upon consideration, we decided that such an account would bring suspicion upon Alex and me and, thus, the rest of the group. How terrible and frightening to realize there was no path to the truth unless it ran past the possibility of our own deaths.

As the hour neared midnight, my eyes blurred, my mind slowed with the passing night, and with each advancing minute the completion of our task grew less likely. I also began to worry about waking Frau Hofstetter, and Lisa's long walk home in the dark. She finished the last of the schnapps and took out a cigarette from her case, but then put it back, forgoing her urge to smoke.

"My throat is sore," she said, clutching at her neck with her hand. "I hope I'm not catching a cold."

I shivered in the chilly air. The heat source in the studio was minimal—a single rusted radiator far from the center of the room where we sat. The coal burner, sealed away in another space behind a brick wall, had already been stoked for the evening and was of no use to Lisa and me as a source of warmth.

"Perhaps we're taking the wrong approach," I said. "I can't write like Hans and Alex—I don't know the classics, I'm not versed in Latin; my Christian ideals are less than perfect." All these various precepts had been presented by the White Rose in the first four leaflets.

"Let's finish for the night," Lisa said and yawned. "Do you have class tomorrow?"

"Yes, philosophy, with Sophie. We sit next to each other, but we don't talk about anything except what Professor Huber says. We never mention the White Rose."

"He has a way with words, I hear."

I gathered my notebook and pen and placed them in the satchel I'd carried to the studio. "He's wonderful, and the students flock to him. He becomes a different man in front of the class; it's as if another personality has possessed him, the limp that plagues him disappears and an animated power from beyond simply takes over. The ordinary man is transformed into a superman."

"Sophie tells me that he's made disparaging remarks about the Reich."

"His words are subtle, as secretive as a meeting of the White Rose, and if you aren't paying close attention, you would never know." I pictured him in front of the class, his arms lifted in broad gestures, his face displaying more emotions than an actor onstage. "I wonder what the hardened National Socialists in class say about Huber behind his back. It makes me fear for his life. Are they biding their time, or just too stupid to understand what their ears are hearing? They'd be hard-pressed to make a case against him. Professor Huber is genius enough to twist the meaning of his words before any court, if he were questioned."

Lisa smiled sardonically. "I wouldn't characterize any National Socialist as stupid—not for your own good—but they're certainly blinded by their devotion to Hitler. They can't comprehend what the man has wrought, what he's bringing down upon our beloved Germany. They follow him blindly even as the rumors of atrocities spread across the land, they refuse to believe that he could be involved, that he could do any wrong."

I lifted my coat, but alarm flared in Lisa's eyes, and I quietly replaced it over the back of my chair. She put a finger to her lips and sat stiff and silent in her chair.

The doorknob moved in a slow circle and then stopped.

My breath caught as a key clicked in the lock.

The door creaked open and a wan face peered around its edge.

Lisa, her back to the entrance, turned frantically and then sighed in relief. "God, Dieter, you scared the life out of us."

The artist, his long cloth coat draped around his body, stepped into the room. "How goes the battle?" he asked, his words slurred by alcohol.

"We were just leaving," Lisa said.

His long face, as pasty white as one would expect from a man who spent much of his time in a studio lit only by light-bulbs, turned briefly before he threw his coat halfway across the studio to his bed. His black hair was slicked back, the half-moon circles under his eyes as dark as the recesses of the room. He collapsed, boots and all, with a tumble on the mattress.

Dieter held up his hands, palms facing the ceiling. "I don't want to know what you're doing—remember?"

"Of course," Lisa said, and gave me a sly look. "Thank you for the use of your studio. Is it all right if we come back the day after tomorrow?"

"Certainly." He turned toward the wall, his body away from us, and pulled a tattered blanket up to his waist. By the time we had donned our coats and gathered our things, Dieter was snoring in soft purrs.

"Artists . . ." Lisa switched off the floor lamp. We felt our way in the dark, our only guide a thin rectangle of moonlight seeping around the door's frame.

"I'll see you in two days," I said, and hugged Lisa after she had secured the studio. The north wind pummeled us as we scurried to the street.

She waved good-bye and struck off toward Leopoldstrasse and home.

I slowed down and breathed the crisp air, observing the twinkling stars and the constant light of bright planets I couldn't identify, the sense of infinite space giving me a calm that had escaped me during the preceding hours, wondering if the professed Christianity of Hans and Sophie were guiding them as they formulated their plans to stir sabotage against the Reich. I wished I had a faith as strong as theirs that would extend not only to them but to myself. I stared into the icy night sky wondering what to write in our leaflet, since we had failed to come up with anything. The cold exacerbated my anxiety and I shivered under my coat. So much was at stake—the White Rose, my parents, my life. The pressure nearly paralyzed me as I trod the dark streets.

As the wind swirled around my body, I realized keeping secrets would now be a way of life. Alex had reminded me that we Russians were good at that.

Words.
Words are powerful tools that can cause irreparable harm when used for evil—to divide and conquer.

Joseph Goebbels, the Reich's Minister of Propaganda, knew only too well how important he was to Hitler and the National Socialist Party. His power came from words that incited, that spurred the Nazis to violent action, admonishing them to embrace a "total victory" possible only through the extermination of their opponents.

How could I produce a leaflet that would change people's thinking? The sickening thought that I might need to think like Goebbels struck me as Lisa and I sat in Dieter's cold studio, our coats wrapped around us as I grappled with the formidable foes of pen and paper. Using his malicious intelligence and cold-hearted odious personality, Goebbels was a master of invective. I couldn't stand the man, whom I had only seen from afar on a platform in the Marienplatz surrounded by his lapdog admirers. He reminded me of a rat with his thin lips, beady eyes, and receding chin; a man who spread his venom with shouted, twisted words, arms and face mimicking his tortured vocabulary. His prestige and influence were undeniable, though; the Nazi faithful adored and venerated him like a saint.

As I thought about his oratorical power, an idea flashed through my mind. The Propaganda Minister also communicated through art—his state-approved posters often showed a powerful Nazi figure smashing a "vile" opponent, usually a communist or Jew.

Two days had passed since we had been at Dieter's studio and, after another two hours, all I had to show for my efforts was a paragraph of scratched-out lines.

"Maybe I should be the one to write it," Lisa offered. Her coat was pulled snugly around her shoulders, only her pale winter face and a small section of bare neck showing above the collar.

I dropped my pen on the notebook in frustration, forgetting my sudden inspiration. "Perhaps you should—I seem to be getting nowhere. There has to be an angle that will serve us, something we both know about." I rose from my chair and felt Lisa's eyes following me about the room.

"Hans and Alex have had their difficulties writing the leaflets, but they eventually agreed," she said, reaching into her pocket for her flask. She shook it. "Damn rationing. I couldn't get a decent helping of schnapps." She stuffed it back in her coat. "Are you pre-occupied?"

I turned to her. "What are you getting at?"

Was she annoyed because I hadn't produced any words of note? She poked her fingers into her cigarette pack on the table, a nervous habit I'd seen her resort to before. "Your hair's a bit shorter than it was two days ago, and I noticed a spot of color on your nails."

She was correct. Bored with my studies, I'd trimmed my hair while sitting in front of the dresser and coated my nails with a faint pink polish I'd found in Frau Hofstetter's bathroom cabinet. The color was barely visible in the gloomy studio light, and when applying it, I had considered it so subtle I didn't think anyone would notice. Overly made-up women were frowned upon, but I'd succumbed to an urge to make myself pretty, hastened, I'm sure, by a certain man.

"Thinking about Garrick, perhaps?" Lisa prodded.

I studied one of Dieter's formalist female nudes, placed strategically over his abstract paintings, a reclining figure on a chaise, flowing drapery covering her breasts and genitals. "I haven't seen him since Hans's party—I've been too busy with class . . . and you."

"But what do you think of him?"

Seeing that Lisa wasn't going to give up her inquiry, I sat across from her. "I think he's handsome. . . ."

"And?"

"I don't know what to think." I wasn't ready to confess an attraction to Garrick, although I'd decided that if he asked me out I would go. What could it hurt? There'd be no talk about what I'd seen in Russia, certainly no conversation about the White Rose, and only casual mentions of Hans and Sophie. I gave Lisa an honest answer. "I'll go out with him if he asks me."

She nodded.

"He said things at Hans and Sophie's that made me think he was against National Socialism, but I'm not ready to share secrets with him."

"Of course not! Neither are Hans and Sophie."

"He's hard to figure out."

Lisa tapped the cigarette pack against her fist and then pulled one out. Instead of lighting it, she let it wobble on her lips, the cigarette paper stuck to the skin. "And until we do . . . good . . . with Garrick out of the way—let's concentrate on our job. Hans is eager to see what we've come up with."

"Smoke that thing or put it back in the pack," I said. "You look like a lady of the evening."

She laughed and lit the cigarette. The dry odor of burned tobacco wafted through the room. "Yes, the Reich doesn't like those women."

I pointed to the nude Dieter had painted. "Now, I remember what I wanted to say. What about art?"

Lisa blinked and exhaled a large puff of smoke. "What about it?"

"You know more about it than I. Why don't I write about the repression of artists and how the natural course of German culture is being destroyed by National Socialism? I can point out how Goebbels uses art in his propaganda to oppress the enemies of the state."

After a moment, Lisa's eyes brightened. "I think it's an excellent idea and I can edit it. Hans and Alex haven't written about that."

I grabbed my pen, moved to a new page in my notebook, and wrote the first words of *A New Leaflet of the White Rose: The oppressive government of National Socialism has strangled the creativity of all artists who would dare oppose the confining prison of what the Reich deems appropriate, and in this death grip the originality, the individuality, and the soul of the German People have been snuffed out. The Spirit of Germany has been crushed under a foul dictator's iron boot.*

I handed these words to Lisa, who nodded as she read them, her face breaking out in a smile far removed from the dispirited picture she presented earlier.

"Are things going well?" Hans asked in an obligatory manner, after I arrived at his apartment the next afternoon.

"I wouldn't be here if they weren't," I said, expecting to be dismissed at any moment like a schoolgirl from class. We sat on a small couch bathed in a feeble winter light that struggled to cut through the gloom of a dismal day.

"And how is Dieter?" he asked, this time as if my presence were a burdensome duty.

If I were a smoker, I would have lit a cigarette. Hans's distracted manner was making me nervous, as if the Gestapo was hiding in wait in another room. At any rate, it was clear that he had other things on his mind than our leaflet.

"I saw him once when he returned to the studio at midnight," I said. "Lisa talked to him—I didn't even introduce myself."

Hans placed his fingertips on his temples and massaged them with increasing force, sending the skin on his scalp and the dark promontory of his hair into a ruffling wave. "Good . . . good . . ." he muttered.

Unable to bear much more of his tense behavior, I reached into my coat pocket and pulled out the pages I'd ripped from my notebook. "This is what you're looking for." I handed him the draft, which had caused me considerable anxiety on the short walk from my apartment to his. I'd tried not to be conspicuous while carrying the pages, and, in the effort, wondered whether my excessive caution was giving me away. Every person on the street became an enemy, a subject of terror, as if I were reading some tale of mystery and imagination devised by Edgar Allan Poe, whom my father had introduced me to from a Russian translation. *Their icy breaths flowed toward me from the street, my distraught mind reeling with every step as they advanced with gelatinous eyes, glowing, and malevolent, trembling lips lined with spittle* . . . such was my frame of mind as I walked to Hans, my heart and hand ever aware of what I was carrying in my pocket.

He took his time reading it. The desk clock in the adjacent room ticked as clearly as if I had placed it next to my ear.

Finally, he looked up from the pages and said, "This is perfect, although . . ." He suggested a few changes to my copy, but nothing that insulted my abilities as a leaflet writer. "I'm pleased with the result," he added. "Where are you going with it?"

I assumed he meant where Lisa and I were planning to distribute it. "Vienna, first."

He rose from the couch and looked out the window, throwing a pale shadow in the murky light, his white shirt and gray pants indistinct, his head bowed slightly, shoulders drooping under the weight of his thoughts. Outside, the bare branches of the trees quivered in the wind, slashing in front of the window like black lightning.

For a few minutes he stood there, and I sat like a prisoner awaiting sentencing from a judge. When he turned, no smile graced his lips, no hint of happiness shone on his face. "Thank you, and God protect you," he said.

I pocketed my draft and left him. He didn't even see me to the door, perhaps because he didn't want us to be seen together. The walk home was much the same as my walk over, only Hans's sour disposition had cast a depressing pall on my efforts. I had expected an effusive outburst from him, some grand acknowledgment of a job well done.

When I turned the corner to my street, I stopped short. Garrick Adler stood in front of my apartment, leaning against the wrought-iron fence that lined the small patch of yard the Frau owned. I thought of turning away and coming back later, but it was too late. He lifted his hand in greeting, having already spotted me from his post. A shiver raced up my body as I wondered how he'd found me.

His arms were bundled across his chest as if he was clutching something inside his coat, and he smiled, his blue eyes flashing, as I stepped closer.

"I know what you're thinking," he said as I stopped in front of him.

"You're a mind reader, too, in addition to working in insurance?" I hoped my nervousness about having the draft leaflet in my coat pocket didn't show.

"You want to know how I found you," Garrick replied.

"Yes, that would be nice." I had no intention of asking him inside, although the wind was cold and sharp under the overcast sky.

"Your father's name is in the phone book," he said smugly. "Your mother gave me your address—after I explained who I was."

Heat rose in my cheeks, a blush, not from seeing him, but from my mother's temerity. "I'll have to talk to her about giving my address to strangers."

Garrick blushed in turn, his face reddening from my words as he looked down at the walk. "I hope I'm more than a stranger." Something rustled under his coat and he squirmed to keep it from moving. "Patience . . . patience . . ."

"I'd ask you in, but Frau Hofstetter doesn't like *strange* men in her house." My smile was a bit too forced, I imagined, and my heart softened a bit as I looked upon a man who had done me no harm. "What do you have under your coat?"

A muffled "mew" arose from Garrick's chest.

"A kitten?"

"Not just any *katze*—meet Katze!" He released his grip, opened a few buttons, and spread the lapels of his coat. An adorable white face with startling green eyes and orange patches of flamelike fur, streaking up from the emerald orbs to the up-turned ears, stared out at me. My heart melted as the little creature eyed me and dug his claws into Garrick's shirt.

"I can't keep him," he said. "I would if I could, but I'm allergic to cats." He lifted the kitten and held him in his hands. "Go ahead. . . . Hold him."

"I can't keep him," I protested. "Frau Hofstetter will kick me out. . . . I think."

"But you won't know unless you ask."

I took the kitten from him, and the tiny thing squirmed and mewed in my hands for a moment before settling into my palms like they were the natural place for a bed. "Where did you get him?"

Garrick opened his coat and fanned his hands across the fabric to get rid of fur. "In the neighborhood. He's a stray. His mother and the rest of the litter were killed. Thank goodness, he was old enough to get along without her."

I looked down on Katze's cute face and tiny body. "Oh, I don't know, Garrick—I appreciate the thought."

"He's no trouble—he's really very quiet and well behaved." He buttoned his coat.

As I held the kitten, I recalled the cat we had left behind in Leningrad after we fled. I had cried as my parents gave my Lotti to an old woman whom I was convinced was going to eat my pet. My father assured me that the "kind old lady" next door would do no such thing. I hadn't been convinced.

I held Katze close to my face and felt the silky warmth of his fur against my skin, and I knew the more I held onto him the harder it would be to let go.

"Well, I suppose I can try . . . for a few days," I said as the kitten purred in my ear. "But we'll have to find him a new home if I can't keep him."

"Of course," Garrick said. "I knew the moment I saw you at the synagogue you had love in your heart." His bold smile, usually so full of intelligence and cunning, showed only warmth. "Give him lots of love."

I thought of the leaflet copy in my pocket and panic needled me. "I have to be going. I have house cleaning plus biology studies to complete."

He reached out and rubbed Katze's ears. "Sure. . . . Can I visit him sometime?"

I wanted to say yes, but I also wanted to say no. Garrick left me conflicted—inviting someone into your life, into your home, was a dangerous gesture even if they had showered you with kindness—but I relented, against my better judgment. "Of course. But please don't just show up. You need to make arrangements with me . . . somehow." I had no phone, and I didn't want to tie up Frau Hofstetter's personal line with my business, let alone have Garrick appear when I was working on something for the White Rose. "Drop me a note in the letter box."

"I'll get in touch. . . . You can always come to see me." He looked at me fondly, petted Katze one final time, and told me his address again before walking away. Of course, I already knew where Garrick lived.

I found myself alone with the kitten, his home atop my bed, curled like a snail's shell in the folds of a blanket. I had no idea whether the Frau would let me keep him, but that wasn't important now. I needed to build a box for him and find food; but, for the moment, I watched the small orphan rest.

As I stroked the kitten's small frame, I thought of the perils of accepting a gift from anyone living under the Third Reich, let alone starting a relationship with someone you had known for only a short time.

CHAPTER 5

———⸻———

Paper. Envelopes. Ink. Lisa's typewriter.

"Thank God, Hans and Sophie have friends who purchase the materials." Lisa stood over my shoulder as I typed the stencil, every typewriter key striking the paper with enough force to make a deep impression in the wax coating. "They ask no questions about their task," she continued. "Imagine only one person buying thousands of sheets of paper from a stationery store, the same with envelopes. You might as well turn yourself in to the Gestapo, because the proprietor would. Hans's girlfriend has made many individual purchases."

I stopped typing, cleaned my glasses, and then looked down at my copy. "Lisa, you're making me nervous. It's hard to correct the stencil if I make a mistake." I pointed to the chair across the table in Dieter's studio, where we'd come to work a few days after I'd seen Garrick. "Smoke a cigarette for God's sake, or have a drink. Try to relax."

She sauntered to the chair with a petulant look, and taking the flask from her coat, unscrewed the top, and turned the container upside down. Not a drop poured out. "Still no schnapps," she said. "It's hard to find vodka, too." She dropped into her chair and settled instead for a cigarette.

"I'm almost done and then it's up to you to operate this contraption," I said, staring at the black cylinder of the mimeograph machine sitting on the desk. It tormented me because once the ink was poured and the stencil wrapped around the drum, the paper would be inserted for copies. The first step in the process of resistance against the Reich would have begun, and if one was cynical and pessimistic, perhaps even fatalistic, printing the leaflets was another step toward the gallows. "While you're waiting, why don't you go through the phone book?"

"That's the easiest part," Lisa said, blowing smoke toward the ceiling. The scratchy smell of tobacco filled my throat, temporarily overpowering the studio odors of linseed oil and drying paint. "I'll leave addressing the envelopes to you. Do you know anyone in Nuremberg?"

"Not a soul." I resumed my typing. The whole distribution process seemed so odd, but I understood its strategic necessity. Lisa and I would travel to Vienna to mail leaflets to addresses in Nuremberg, just as leaflets mailed to Munich were posted from other cities. We weren't sure what the SS and the Gestapo knew about the White Rose, but the whole point of making a risky trip was to allay suspicion from our home city and to make the group seem much larger than it was. If we could place a few extra leaflets at locations along the way, so much the better.

"Picking names at random is half the fun," Lisa said. "Pick out ones that strike you—it makes no difference if it's a doctor or a plumber."

I held a finger to my lips and then continued my typing. After another half hour I had finished, read through the copy, and deposited it in Lisa's hands.

She read it as well and then attached the stencil carefully to the cylinder. "My turn," she said, and reached for the handle to turn the drum, but stopped, gazing in horror at her fingers. Their tips were stained a purplish black from the ink, a clear indication to anyone who saw them that she had been up to no good. She ran to the sink, which had no hot tap, and tried as best she could to rinse off the stains with soap and cold water. After a few minutes, she returned to the table, her skin having turned somewhat bluish gray.

"Damn," she said. "I didn't even think . . . thank God it's winter and I can wear gloves."

Lisa had calculated that we needed to run off about five hundred copies of the leaflet—that number accounted for a large percentage to be mailed from Vienna to Nuremberg, a few flat sheets to be deposited at storefronts in Austria, as well as some for Hans and Sophie.

She turned the crank and the first sheets flew off the cylinder and landed on the table. I picked one up with a gloved hand and studied our handiwork, pleased with the outcome. The flat, almost odorless smell of the ink rose from the page. Lisa stopped to feed more paper to the machine, as I addressed the envelopes with the names I had chosen from the phone book. Wearing thin cotton gloves, I wrote in block letters to disguise my handwriting. It took about an hour before the last leaflet was printed. After that, Lisa left the device, rubbing her right shoulder before collapsing in her chair.

"That's harder work than I imagined," she said. It had been a while since she had smoked and I could see the urge firing in her eyes. She grabbed a cigarette and asked, "And how's Katze?"

"Fine." I looked up from my pile of envelopes. "He's a dear, actually. I keep thinking Frau Hofstetter will burst in the door one night and demand I throw him out, but that hasn't happened. No rule was mentioned about not having animals when I moved in. Who knows, maybe she likes cats. I haven't had the nerve to tell her about him yet, and Katze seems quite content to climb up on the bed or play with the pom-poms hanging from the bottom of the spread. Fortunately, his meow is so soft I don't think she would hear it unless she was in the room next to him."

"Why did Garrick give you a cat?" She twirled the hair behind her left ear with an ink-stained finger and pursed her lips, an inquisitive look I'd seen before.

In truth, I'd considered the same question and found no good answer. Was it because no one he knew would take the animal: no brother, no sister, or friend who liked cats? Maybe his claim of an allergic reaction was true, although I didn't recall seeing any redness in his eyes. Maybe he wanted to draw me out of my shell. Certainly Katze hadn't distanced me from Garrick; if anything, his gift had drawn me closer.

"I'm not sure," I said truthfully. "I never expected it, but I'm glad he did. I love Katze's company."

"Dangerous . . . dangerous . . . dangerous." Lisa repeated the words like a mantra. "He *wants* to get to you."

"Please stop." I jabbed my pen into the table. "We've been through this—yes, he's attractive; yes, I don't know him that well, but there's nothing there." As I proclaimed my innocence to Lisa and mentally freed myself of any advances from Garrick, I also knew that I had found myself thinking about him, wondering what kind of man he was, imagining us linking arms as we strolled down the street on a spring day, perhaps even stealing a kiss under an oak, but with my studies, work, looking in on my mother, and the danger of my association with the White Rose, no serious attachment seemed possible.

My mother wasn't helping matters, either, for she hoped I'd marry a husband who might help get my father out of prison before he served his full sentence. "We must fall in line to save your father," she'd told me with tear-stained eyes. "What else can we do?"

"You'll never be a Nazi!" I responded harshly, barely restraining my anger at her and at the government that had forced her into submission. We let the matter of my father drop because it was too painful to discuss.

Pointing to the pile of leaflets, I turned Lisa's attention back to our task. "The copies are done. You can help me address the envelopes."

"*You* are a wet blanket," she said, pulling on her cotton gloves. "I'll not get more out of you about Garrick. Put the phone book in the middle of the table."

Lisa had the good sense not to quiz me again, so we worked in silence until we were close to exhaustion. Midnight neared and we knew Dieter would be back soon to reclaim the studio. We still needed to stamp and seal the envelopes before scheduling our Vienna trip.

Lisa hauled out a large leather suitcase—the eventual repository of our mailings. She lifted a false bottom that, if packed properly, would conceal the letters and loose leaflets.

"What if the police check it?" I asked. "Won't they be able to tell the bottom is raised?"

"That's why we have to be precise in our packing," she said. "The envelopes have to be compressed, bound by twine, and the leaflets stacked like a card deck."

I picked up a letter I'd addressed to a Herr Weingarten in Nuremberg. I liked the sound of the name and I suspected the man and his family were Jewish, although I had no idea if that was the case. It struck me that he might no longer be in the city if he was Jewish or a supporter of Jews. The family might have fled, or, I imagined with a shudder, suffered some tragic fate.

When choosing names, I found myself looking for those I thought would be sympathetic to our cause—if not a Jew, then who? Perhaps I had taken the wrong approach. Should I have been looking for Teutonic Germanic names, traditional Bavarian families? Would their minds be changed by an anonymous letter in the mail condemning the Third Reich, or would they just be enraged or scared to death because they'd received it?

"When I sealed this envelope, I sealed my fate," I said, holding up one of the letters but knowing I'd taken that step weeks before. The cloying smells of inked paper, oil paints, and Lisa's cigarettes seeped into my head. I dropped the letter on the table, knowing that any reflection about my fate was safe in the clandestine surroundings of Dieter's studio.

A soft whoosh of air fled from the suitcase as Lisa closed the lid. "I've been a traitor since the White Rose found me . . . but when we mail our first letter our heads are marked." She ran her fingers over the top of the case. "We could burn these letters now and no one would be the wiser."

High treason.

The charge for our crimes. The sentence would be death.

Why am I doing this?

As soon as I asked myself the question, a myriad of answers popped into my head like white knights on horseback sent to vanquish my faintheartedness. First, I'd seen what the SS could do—they were cold, calculating killers exterminating anyone who didn't fit into Hitler's master plan; second, my father was in prison for reading banned books; third, rumors had begun to circulate that Germany had lost the war; fourth, a few ordinary students and military men with extraordinary courage had started a movement that I wanted to be part of. I hoped my small effort might lift the world from the hell it had become.

Those were the reasons why Lisa and I would risk our lives to travel to Vienna and mail the leaflets of the White Rose.

We worked another night at the studio, sealing and stamping the letters, binding them tight with twine (we had to hide a pocketknife to cut it), and packing the suitcase until it could hold no more. The case held all but twenty of the planned mailings. I volunteered to alter my coat's lining to hold the remaining letters, and to meet Lisa the next morning at her apartment because it was closer to the Hauptbahnhof. We planned to catch a Vienna-bound train, timing our journey to mail the letters after dark, scatter the remaining leaflets, and then catch the last train back to Munich—if all went well.

When I arrived in the early morning at the building where my parents and I used to live, Lisa was alone. Her parents had left for their jobs. She took me to her bedroom, where the suitcase sat on her bed, the brass locks facing us.

"This whole operation has been kept from my mother and father," Lisa said with pride. "My mother's a bit of a snoop, always looking under my bed for God knows what on the pretext of cleaning." She smiled. "I changed the tag. Look what's inside."

The locks flipped open with a metallic twang. A long blue dress, leather gloves, a red scarf, a fleece nightgown, an assortment of bras and underpants, all neatly folded and pressed, covered the case's false bottom. "I'm going to visit my aunt," she said, explaining her alibi. "You're going to visit your future husband."

"I'm not carrying luggage."

"*Your* clothes are already at the home of your betrothed,"

Lisa said matter-of-factly. "Give the police a shy look and they'll send you on your way—I'm certain your inconspicuous nature will win them over."

I looked down at my plain dress and shoes, feeling slighted by Lisa's "compliment." I had dressed to be bland, a normal German among many at the train station.

Lisa's proposition about my "future husband" seemed absurd, but my sincere belief in a nonexistent boyfriend in Vienna might be all that kept me from arrest and imprisonment. I pictured him: tall, handsome, with brownish-blond hair, an intelligent smile, and dimples, and realized I'd pictured Garrick. He would do.

Lisa peeled back some clothing, revealing the false bottom, a brown-silk-lined panel. "Everything's in place under here, including the knife." She returned the articles to their place, closed the suitcase, and secured the locks. "Are you ready?"

"Yes." My heart skittered in my chest as danger closed in. I swallowed hard and wiped a bead of sweat from my brow. "I have to remain calm . . . think about something besides what we're doing . . . until we get there."

"Sophie advised me to sit apart from you in the same car to avoid suspicion," Lisa said. "We can take turns hauling the case to the station, but the last few blocks I should do it myself. You follow at a safe distance. If I'm stopped, go on as if nothing has happened, and slip out of the station. Don't speak to me or look my way."

"I feel like a fool." I felt unprepared for our journey. Our mission burst into painful focus, along with the reality of what we were risking.

"Remain calm and we shouldn't have any problems," Lisa continued. "The White Rose has successfully gone before us." She lifted the case off the bed and placed it on the floor. "We'll purchase tickets separately—mine first. Let a few people go ahead of you then buy yours. Do you have your papers?"

I nodded and patted my coat pocket, my fingers brushing over the fabric concealing the twenty letters.

"All right, we're ready to go." Lisa hugged me, picked up the case, and swung it toward her bedroom door. "Whew, if we do this a few times, we'll build up our muscles."

We left the apartment and walked down the stairs. "No talking from here," Lisa ordered as we stepped away from the building. A frigid north wind stung our faces. The swirling, iron-colored clouds, and the smell of snow in the air, heightened my anxiety. I sweated through the cold as Lisa, energized by nerves, picked up her pace, carrying the suitcase as if it were a handbag.

The train ride to Vienna was a long one, seven to eight hours on a good day, but necessary to shield us from casting suspicion on our Munich operation. We hoped to have lunch on the train, and, upon arrival in Vienna, find boxes for mailing our letters as well as suitable places to drop the leaflets. The last train out would put us back in Munich early the next morning.

A couple of blocks from the station, we stopped on a side street and wished each other luck. The streets were crowded with pedestrians despite the cold, and the stone buildings stood colorless around us. Lisa disappeared in the crowd in front of the stone arches and iron girders of the Hauptbahnhof. Now and then I caught sight of her head, a blonde thatch of hair bobbing through the crowd.

Several people stood in line in front of me as Lisa, never looking my way, prepared to buy her ticket. I readied my identification papers and pulled out my Reichsmark. After purchasing mine, I, along with many others, lined up for a security check. I tried not to fidget as Lisa made her way through the gate, the unopened suitcase in her hand.

The station policeman, a middle-aged man who seemed in need of coffee, eyed my papers and me without comment. I showed him my ticket, and he waved me through with no hesitation, as if I were another "ordinary" German. The nervous fear I'd been fighting faded for a moment because I'd made it through the checkpoint without a problem. However, this was only the first step in a dangerous gamble. I cautioned myself not to get too confident.

A few meters behind, I followed Lisa to the waiting train.

She boarded, and, without any hesitation, swung the case onto a luggage rack in a passenger compartment, and then took a seat near the front of the car. I sat halfway behind her on the opposite side.

The train chugged out of the station, the wheels grinding slowly in the frosty air, the drab buildings and naked trees slipping by, the smoke from the engine spiraling past the windows in an ashen cloud.

Finally, the city dropped away and the train, picking up steam, glided through the Bavarian countryside. Someone had left a National Socialist magazine on the empty seat next to me and I picked it up, perusing the pages with little intention of reading the state-sponsored articles, it serving only as a distraction from my nervous condition. Suddenly, I found myself awash in paranoia. My palms broke out in a sweat and I craned my neck, glancing behind me. The car was half-full, apart from the compartments at the end. No one looked particularly suspicious or out of place. I took a deep breath and turned back to the magazine, *Frauen-Warte*, which gave hints on how German women could be better mothers and homemakers by using the publication's fashion tips, sewing patterns, and recipes. After a lackluster half hour of looking at happy homemakers, I turned my attention to the window and the landscape that would soon transform into the Austrian hills. Lisa appeared content to stare ahead, quietly minding her own business.

My sense of calm dissipated into silent terror when a guard, attired in his gray-green uniform and steel helmet, rifle slung over his shoulder, passed by me and stopped at Lisa's row. The young man muttered something I couldn't hear. Lisa, smiling and laughing, rose from her seat. Apparently, the guard was pleased with her attitude as well, for he broke into a smile as he escorted her to the compartment where she'd deposited the suitcase.

Lisa never turned her eyes toward me as she walked past, but she touched the guard's arm lightly. I turned, as several others did, to see where he was taking her. After several minutes, which seemed like hours, Lisa reappeared with the guard, both smiling and talking. The young man offered a slight bow and then continued his march forward to the next car. I closed my eyes and sank into my seat, preferring not to interact with anyone until we arrived at our destination. I wondered what I would have done if I had been questioned by the guard. My pulse quickened.

Having passed the security check at the Austrian border and after stopping in Linz and a few smaller cities, the train arrived in Vienna about half past three. Fortunately, we hadn't been interrupted by the threat of air raids, as many trains were. Usually those alarms turned out to be reconnaissance flights engineered by the Allies rather than bombing raids.

After Lisa's encounter with the guard, I had forgotten about lunch, so after departing the train and walking a safe distance from the station, I caught up with her and asked if we could stop for a bite to eat.

"You must tell me what happened," I whispered as we sat in a secluded corner of a café drenched with the smells of coffee and chocolate. Lisa had checked the suitcase in a locker at the station so we could walk about unhampered by the load.

"Let me get a good coffee and torte," she said, "and then I'll tell you."

We ordered and within a short time our food and drinks were delivered to us. I looked at her with eager eyes and gobbled my sausage sandwich.

"He was a sweet guard," Lisa said. "He found me attractive, which is always a help in these cases."

"Go ahead," I pleaded, trying not to attract undo attention.

"Simple really. A man who had reserved a seat in the compartment noticed that I placed it there and then walked away. Our fellow traveler reported it as suspicious." She cut a slice of her chocolate torte with a fork, popped it into her mouth, and then sipped her coffee. "Delicious."

"I wish I could be as blasé about this as you."

"The handsome young guard said, 'You've left your suitcase unattended. What was your reason for doing that?' I told him I didn't want to clutter up my seat with baggage, and I thought it would be safe there because I *can't* lock it—I pointed out that thieves don't usually travel in compartments. He wanted me to open the bag and I, of course, agreed."

My muscles tightened even though the incident was over. "Then what?"

Lisa smiled. "I was more than happy to oblige, and complimented him and the traveler on their observant eyes and sense of duty to the Reich. I pulled down the case as if there was nothing of weight in it, opened it, and offered the guard a look. I told him my story about my aunt in Vienna. He stuck his hand inside to root around, but once his fingers lighted upon my silk underwear he stopped and his face flushed as red as a cherry. Our young hero must be a virgin . . . or a suppressed Catholic. So I closed the case and that was that."

I stifled a snicker, but, amusement aside, I was astounded at Lisa's resourcefulness and courage in the face of possible arrest. "I'm learning," I said, "but I don't know that I will ever be as brave as you."

She lifted her cup. "You already are."

"I don't feel it." I clasped my hands on the table and looked at the other diners on this early winter afternoon: an elderly couple sitting in their thick coats, sipping hot chocolate at seats near the window; four students attired in colorful bulky sweaters and boots who, for all the world, looked like Hans, Sophie, Alex, and Willi, chatting and arguing over book passages, filling the café with their free and inspired laughter. For an instant, I longed to be like them—nondescript, leading a normal life, believing that the war and its atrocities were far away from Vienna. How could such a scene, a view of life as composed and common as a vacation postcard, play out in front of me when my own was filled with danger?

Lisa grasped my hands, aware of my wandering eye. "We all feel that way . . . most of the time," she said as if reading my thoughts. "The others do as well . . . but there's something greater that's driving us . . . a force that requires action."

I twined my fingers through hers and a river of strength, an unspoken camaraderie, flowed between us. "The sun will be setting soon," I said. "We should be going."

"That's the spirit."

We freshened up in the bathroom and left the café. The light faded as we trekked down streets neither one of us had traversed in our lives. Soon the city was covered in darkness, only the dimmest of lights seeping past the blackout curtains of shuttered neighborhoods. We walked past the tidy homes and businesses of Margareten and Wieden looking for likely sites and, finding a few, memorized their locations so we could return later to post the letters. Venturing into Mariahilferstrasse, the main shopping street of Vienna, we noted a few stores with recessed entries where we could drop the leaflets.

By the time we finished our walk, it was nearing six, leaving us three hours before the last train departed for Munich at nine.

I visited another café close to the one where we had our quick lunch, ordered a coffee and pastry and lingered over my small meal, as I waited for Lisa to arrive at an adjacent corner with the suitcase. We had decided that if she didn't appear by closing time at seven, I was to go to the train station and return home without her. I tried not to fidget, but found myself gazing out the window every thirty seconds or so, perusing the printed menu on the table, or obsessively cleaning my glasses with my napkin.

Most people had dispersed to their homes as the hour neared, and I clutched my cup and spoon, worried that something had happened. But about ten minutes before our pre-arranged departure time, Lisa ambled into view through the window, the suitcase swinging from her right hand. I paid the bill and joined her on the corner, showering her with hugs as if she were a long-lost relative. We wrapped our coats tighter about our throats as flecks of snow peppered our heads and spotted my still warm glasses with melting flakes.

"Sorry to give you a scare," Lisa whispered, "but I've already mailed some near the station." She looked at the case, which rested near her legs, and spoke again after a few pedestrians strolled past. "Dark streets, empty buildings, and deserted post boxes make for good mailings and a lighter load. I've cut the twine—all we need to do is open the case and drop the letters."

The snow, the biting wind, the dark and empty streets made our task easier than we had anticipated as we deposited the letters into boxes in Margareten and Wieden. Our only concern occurred in Margareten when a boy and his mother appeared out of nowhere, apparently to play in the falling snow. We turned away from their eyes, and they passed by us without looking back. Before our last mail stop, we hunkered in an alley where I cut the fabric concealing the letters in my coat and extracted them. I was grateful to have them out and in the mail, for they had shifted to one side, causing me to compensate for their weight.

Mariahilferstrasse was mostly dark as well, the stores closed and shuttered, although a few diners came and went from restaurants.

We ducked into the vacant stalls of a food market that had closed for the winter. Lisa slipped her hand inside the suitcase and produced a bundle of leaflets, which I curled into my secret coat pocket. We decided to split up and meet again at the train station about eight thirty, maintaining our distance from each other as we had done on the trip from Munich.

I strode down Mariahilferstrasse, where only a few people scurried about in the dismal night. A set of footprints had been laid in the freshly fallen snow. I followed them before they ended in scuffed tracks at the doorway of number 25, a tall stone building that even in the gloom reflected a pale yellow from its slick surface. Adjacent to the door was a jewelry store with a wonderful window display of clocks: rounded shelf clocks, nightstand pieces with glowing dials, rectangular wall clocks with swinging pendulums and beveled glass cases, and beyond those displays, in the showroom, the stately grandfathers. The sound of the many clocks striking seven thirty enchanted my ears as the sound filtered through the windows.

The entrance seemed the perfect place to drop the first of my leaflets. I reached into my coat, preparing to pull out about a dozen of them, when a deep voice from behind sent me hopping in fright.

"May I help you, Fräulein?"

I doubled over in a feigned coughing fit. Eventually, I straightened and turned to find a man staring at me. He was square-jawed and clean-shaven—that much I could make out in the feeble light—wearing a slim homburg hat, a black coat that hung nearly to his ankles, and a swastika band positioned just above his left elbow.

My mind raced with excuses as I struggled for words. "You frightened me to death," I finally replied. "Hardly a soul out on a night like this."

"My point, exactly." His lips parted in a forced smile.

I backed into the jewelry store entrance, a little closer to the door. "The weather has given me a cold. I was searching for my handkerchief when you came upon me."

"May I see your papers," he said, thrusting out his gloved hand.

"Of course, but is that really necessary?" I coughed again and then shivered from the cold . . . and my equally frozen nerves.

"Yes. Papers, please."

I reached into my coat pocket and withdrew the documents. He took out his cigarette lighter and rolled the spark wheel. The pungent odor of naphtha shifted to a guttering flame whose reflection bounced off the glass. He perused my documents quickly and then handed them back to me.

"A student from Munich," he said, firing his cigarette and then capping the lighter. "What brings you to our fair city?"

I slid my identification papers into my side pocket and drew my arms tight across my chest to keep the leaflets secure in my coat. "I'm visiting a friend's aunt," altering my alibi so I'd have an excuse to get to the train station. "We're traveling back to Munich tonight."

"It's a little late to be shopping." He turned his head and blew the smoke from his cigarette into the wind.

"My mother has a wall clock that's on the fritz." I gave him a chance to size me up as I pointed to the display windows. "She misses the chimes. I was thinking of giving her one—" I stopped, having almost said "for Christmas;" we weren't allowed to celebrate it. "My friend's aunt recommended this store." My breath caught for an instant because I had cornered myself in a trap. What if he asked for the woman's name and address? I only knew a few street names from the afternoon walk, and he could easily drag me to the street to make me prove my statement.

"The stores have been closed for hours, I'm certain you know that." He leaned closer to me, his dark eyes peering at me from underneath the homburg's brim. "Yes, this is a good store now. . . . It used to be Jewish . . . but no longer."

"I'm getting very cold and a little worried talking to a stranger," I said, trying to slide my way toward the walk, my arms still clutching my coat. "Should I call for the police?"

"They'd never hear you in this wind," he said, "besides I'm from the Oberabschnitt Donau. You're safe with me. May I escort you to your next destination?"

I knew enough to surmise that he was from the SS, although he certainly wasn't wearing a uniform like those of German SS members. I decided to politely decline his offer, hoping he would take the hint. "I'm on my way to the train station, but I don't need an escort. I can find my way."

"I wouldn't have that, Fräulein," he said with true National Socialist conviction. "A young woman out on a night like this? Might I add a *pretty* young woman behind those glasses. There's a taxi stand near the corner."

With one hand, I pushed my glasses up on my nose, hoping that he noted my innocent gesture. He extended his arm like a gentleman, but, shaking my head, I refused because of the leaflets still resting inside my coat.

I walked next to the building entrances, while he strolled to my left. The snow had begun to fall in earnest, making the coating of slush and ice already on the street treacherous. As we neared the corner, I slipped on the slushy mix, and losing my balance, thrust my arms toward a building to keep from falling. My hands flew away from my chest, and a leaflet slipped from my coat and fluttered to the ground. The SS man, more concerned with my fall, failed to notice the paper as it caught briefly in the snow and then tumbled away in the wind. I flattened myself against the façade; his hands grabbed me from behind like pincers.

I gasped, not from being saved from a fall, but in relief that the leaflet had blown a few meters down the street, and, I hoped, out of sight in the slush. I coughed again, kept my back to the man, and thrust my hand into the lining to make certain that no more leaflets would slip out. Only moments later, I turned, squelching an attack of nerves, and tottered next to his side in the chilly mess to the taxi stand.

We stood for several minutes waiting for a car. Finally, one appeared down the street, its lights fracturing the white cascade of flakes descending upon Vienna. He hailed the taxi and we got inside the warm compartment, both of us brushing the snow from our shoulders. My glasses were a mess from the moisture, but I kept my hands clutched in my lap. In ten minutes, we arrived at the station, having made only passing conversation on the short trip. I told him of my nursing service in Russia, hoping it would allay any suspicion forming in his mind. He told me nothing about himself.

"Wait here," he ordered the driver as we pulled up. The SS man sprang from the car and opened the door for me. "Here's where I leave you, Fräulein Petrovich. I'm already late for a meeting. I wish you a pleasant journey back to Munich." He stood stiffly and extended his right arm in the Nazi salute. "Heil Hitler!" I returned the gesture, attempting to muster as much enthusiasm as my escort.

After the car departed, I walked across the snowy entrance to the station. Inside, my knees buckled and a bout of uncontrollable shivering consumed me. I plopped down on a wooden bench and hoped that the few people gathered in the station wouldn't notice my anxious behavior. I looked up, head shaking, at the station clock. It was five past eight, about a half hour before Lisa and I were to meet.

After a few minutes, I wandered to a newsstand, bought a

newspaper and a cup of tea, and then looked for an open bench near the departure track. I was acutely aware of the leaflets still inside my coat, and of the one I had dropped.

But another threat emerged as I searched for a place to sit. At least twenty German SS officers stood near the track conversing with a few men who were dressed like my Vienna escort. They appeared to be headed to Munich.

A few drops of tea spilled over the lip of my cup as I quieted my shaking hands. More than anything else, I needed to warn Lisa of the danger when she arrived at the station, but it would have to be with a look, not a word. To my horror, several of the men stared at me as I sat down, raking me with their eyes. I ignored them as best I could without seeming to be petulant. A relaxing ride to Munich, which I had been looking forward to, especially after my encounter with the Austrian SS man, had suddenly taken a dangerous turn—one which caused me to wonder whether we should attempt the long journey home.

CHAPTER 6

Lisa arrived at the station on time at eight thirty, her hair damp and disheveled from the blowing snow, the suitcase clutched in her right hand. She must have noticed the congregated SS men, because she chose a seat at the entrance near the newsstand, far away from me. Other travelers had gathered, whether to escape the snow or to travel to Munich I wasn't certain.

I hoped to catch Lisa's eye, but she turned away as soon as I looked her way. I had no choice but to sit, pretending to be interested in the paper, knowing that communication was impossible.

All passengers, except the SS men, were called for a security check. As I passed through the inspection, I fought hard to control my nerves. The leaflets were a heartbeat away from being discovered. Fortunately, the guard seemed bored by his late shift and gave me a cursory look. Lisa was behind me, but I paid no attention to her.

Our train backed onto the track a few minutes later, the cars and engines coated in white, rivulets of meltwater pouring down their metal sides as the warmer air of the station struck them. This time, I boarded first, the heated car sloughing the chill from my body, as I searched for a seat away from the SS. The conductor herded us down the aisle, pointing out empty seats. "It's snowing all the way to the border," he said.

I found a spot in the middle of the car. Not long after, Lisa walked past and took her place a few rows ahead of me. She carried the suitcase, which, I hoped, contained only her clothes. I prayed that she, unlike me, had been able to drop all the leaflets.

The conductor asked for my ticket, marked it, and moved on to Lisa. After he left, I glanced back over my seat, and stunned by what I saw, turned quickly around. Rows of SS men had gathered in our car, many standing in the compartment or at the entrance of the one behind, a few smoking, one passing a flask to another. I surmised that the Reich was holding a high-level meeting in Germany, possibly in Munich or Berlin. Lisa and I were surrounded by the very men we were fighting against.

The train pulled away precisely at nine and soon we'd left the city behind for the dark countryside. With little outside light passing by, the windows turned into black mirrors. I caught sight of my reflection in the glass: face drawn, eyes gray, looking as if I needed a bath and a great deal of sleep. Sweat broke out on my forehead from the car's heat but I didn't dare take off my coat with the unsecured leaflets inside. I unfastened its top buttons and fanned myself with the newspaper, keeping the treasonous material hidden from the SS. As time drifted by, my eyes grew heavy and my head nodded to my chest several times before reflexively jerking me awake with a snap of my neck.

After one violent jerk, my eyes shot open and adrenaline coursed through my body. The same guard who had questioned Lisa on our journey to Vienna stood in the aisle beside her, the suitcase in his hand. I heard snippets of their conversation over the wheels' muffled churn on the snowy tracks.

"I thought you were staying in Vienna with your aunt," the man said.

I took off my glasses and slipped them in my pocket to present a different face, and then raised the newspaper so I could just look over it.

"Oh, you remember me," Lisa said with a laugh, trying to make light of the situation.

I, once again, offered a silent prayer that all the traitorous material in the suitcase had been delivered.

He glowered and leaned toward her. I didn't catch what he said, but Lisa answered, "My aunt . . . her sister . . . showed up unexpectedly . . . no room, so I decided to return to Munich."

His eyes swept over the car and I looked down, avoiding his gaze. "Open it," he ordered. I didn't dare look up. My palms broke out in a sweat, and, for a moment, I thought I might pass out from the car's heat.

The locks clicked. Finally, I raised my head. I couldn't keep my eyes off the suitcase.

For the second time in one day, the guard inspected the suitcase. His arms dug into it with vigor. Lisa's dress and nightgown were soon draped over the back of a seat in front of me in the course of a thorough inspection. Was he doing so for the benefit of the SS men because he wanted to show off in front of his superiors?

He asked Lisa to stand, which she did, and he ran his hands over her from head to toe. Satisfied with his search, he locked the case and withdrew a notepad and pen from his pocket.

"What's your name?" he asked.

"Lisa Kolbe. . . . You've seen my papers."

"I asked only for your name, Fräulein," he said severely. "I'd advise you to keep your mouth shut."

He wrote on the pad and then stuffed it in his pocket. "Have a good journey," he said in a cold voice. "I trust I won't see you tomorrow."

Lisa turned to him. "No, I'll be at home studying. Thank you for your diligence, Herr . . . ?"

"It doesn't matter." He turned abruptly and rushed past me on his way to the back of the car. Looking straight ahead, Lisa took her seat. I turned briefly to see the guard encircled by the SS men.

Not more than a minute had passed before one of the officers in his black coat, cinched leather belt, and chest strap, strode up to Lisa. He introduced himself, pushed his pomaded hair back with his hand as he leaned over, and then spoke loudly enough that several rows in the car could hear what he was saying. "Fräulein Kolbe. It's unusual for a young woman to make a round trip to Vienna in one day, especially one from Munich. I would like your address . . . in case I need to get in touch with you at a later time."

Lisa complied, after which, the officer stuck out his arm in the Nazi salute, turned and walked away.

We traveled past Linz and then to the border. I moved closer to the window and curled up in my seat with the newspaper partially covering my face, my buttoned coat concealing the damning leaflets that I carried.

We arrived in Munich sometime after three in the morning to a deserted station except for guards at their posts and sanitary workers pushing mops and brooms. The SS men departed in black Mercedes sedans lined up on the street; Lisa brushed past me silently without giving me a look.

I thought about dropping the leaflets in the women's bathroom, but, even at the early hour, I felt that would prove too risky. I took a taxi home, where Katze greeted me with several long meows. Fighting exhaustion from the long day, I searched for a safe hiding place for the leaflets until I could figure out what to do with them, finally placing them in an envelope and securing them to the underside of a dresser drawer. They seemed safe, surrounded by wood.

Frau Hofstetter knocked on the hall door the next morning before sunrise. Groggy from only a few hours' sleep, I threw on my robe to find the rigid woman scowling at me, the folds of her sagging face cast in shadow by the lone hanging bulb. Her ruffled housecoat and mismatched slippers indicated that she had suffered a distressing night.

She cleared her throat and then began, "Fräulein Petrovich, you have a cat in your room."

I'd been caught, and it was useless to pretend otherwise. I looked toward my bed, where Katze slept, curled in the warm, comfortable folds of my blanket. "Yes," I replied meekly.

The Frau had little patience considering the early hour. "The next time you leave that cat alone for the day, and half the night, warn me, otherwise I shall send you packing. Also, you've neglected your duties."

I sagged against the door. "I'm sorry, Frau Hofstetter. I was called away to help a friend. I'll start work as soon as I get dressed."

She harrumphed and scratched her gray, frizzy hair. "I have no problem with cats—I had one myself for many years. Herr Hofstetter hated it . . . I think that's why I liked it so much." She rubbed her hands. "At any rate, the poor thing was lonely, missing you all day, so it . . ."

". . . Katze."

"Katze never shut up. I'd be happy to feed him, perhaps even play with him, if you'd allow me to do so." Her lips formed a brief smile, which faded quickly.

"That would be wonderful, Frau Hofstetter. He was given to me—the poor animal had no home—normally he's no trouble at all. I didn't know I was going to be away so long. I kept meaning to tell you about him . . . ask your permission, that is . . . but I've been so busy."

She straightened, resuming her stern stance. "I'll expect you to honor my request." She turned, but then looked back. "You can join me for breakfast in an hour, if you'd like—and then you can wash the dishes that have piled up in your absence." She pointed at me. "I have money for you."

"That would be nice," I said. She returned to her room and I plopped on the bed next to Katze and stroked the silky white fur on his back until his purring filled my ears. "You don't know what a lucky cat you are," I said to him, and thought of Garrick for the first time in days.

Lisa and I didn't speak until we were both invited to another gathering at the Scholls' at week's end.

"I was scared on the train," I said to her when we were well away from my apartment and prying ears. "I didn't know what to think when the guard questioned you and then the SS man appeared."

"Yes, it could have gone badly, but everything was in place so

I had no worries about an uncomfortable situation," Lisa said, understating the situation in her usual manner. I took her words to mean that all her leaflets had been distributed.

"*Uncomfortable?*" I asked as loudly as I dared.

She shook her head as if no response was necessary. "What about you? How did your evening go?"

I told her about my encounter with the Austrian SS man, the leaflet blowing away in the wind, and my escorted trip back to the Vienna station. "I still have some of my literature," I added. We spoke to each other in generalities, ever aware that our words might be overheard.

"We'll have to do something about that," she said.

A full moon hung above us, showing its glorious silver face these few days before Christmas, a holiday that most Germans, if celebrated at all, kept as a private observance. The Reich had tried its best to alter Christmas for its own use, changing its name to Julfest, replacing the star at the top of the tree with a swastika, removing any references to God and Jesus from holiday carols.

When we arrived at Hans and Sophie's apartment, I was surprised to find that neither of them were there. Instead, Alex Schmorell met us at the door. I hadn't seen him in months but was immediately taken in by his engaging smile and bubbly good humor. His manner reminded me of the time we had spent in Russia. "Hans and Sophie are at their parents' home in Ulm for the holiday," he said, inviting us in with a broad sweep of his arm. Alex smiled easily, his lean form attired in a dark jacket, high-necked sweater, and pleated pants. "We're having a bit of a Julfest celebration," he said, winked at me, and then captured me in his arms in a grand hug. "It's good to see you again. Have a piece of cake—it's hard to get these days unless you know the right people."

I happened to look past his shoulders, across the room, where three men sat in a V-shaped wedge. The two at the top of the V, Professor Huber and Willi Graf, gestured and bent toward each other as if engaged in a fiery debate, while the other man, his back turned toward them, said nothing. Garrick Adler faced the door and cast a sour glance at me as Alex engulfed me in the hug.

"I hear you've been busy studying," Alex said to me as he escorted me to the table where a holiday cake, pastries, and several bottles of wine glowed in the candlelight. "Literature studies are particularly important now." He picked up a candle and lit his pipe, puffing a spicy, woody odor into the air.

I followed his coded language. "Yes, I've made a point of letting everyone know about my essay—as many as I could—even out of town."

Alex faced me and shifted his eyes back toward Garrick, who had fixed his upon mine. "He's still a new man, untested as far as Hans is concerned," he whispered. "Watch yourself." I was grateful that Alex had informed me of Garrick's standing in the group because I'd wondered whether Hans and Sophie had decided to include him.

I nodded, poured a glass of wine, and broke away from Alex, hoping to at least draw Garrick out of what seemed an uncomfortable situation. Looking into my heart, I felt sorry for him, as forlorn and withdrawn as he seemed in his chair.

"How's Katze?" he asked in a humble voice as I approached.

I pulled up a spare and sat down beside him. "He's fine— such a treasure—I don't know what I'd do without him."

"I'm glad," he said, sporting a glimmer of his luminous smile. "Has he grown?"

"He's getting bigger. Frau Hofstetter knows about him now." I clutched my wineglass, knowing I couldn't tell Garrick how my landlady had made the discovery. "Still not drinking?"

He looked down at his chest and picked at the fuzz on his heavy sweater, not saying anything for a time. "No . . . I'm not much in the mood for Julfest, or anything else for that matter."

He raised his right hand to his temple and I caught a glimpse of his eyes, which looked as if they were filling with tears. Before I had a chance to ask him what was wrong, Professor Huber rose from his chair, walked to the table, his right leg dragging behind him, and tapped a spoon against a wineglass. Everyone turned their attention to him.

After collecting his thoughts, the professor focused his heavy-lidded eyes upon us and then began a lecture on the teachings of Gottfried Wilhelm von Leibniz, a seventeenth-century mathematician and philosopher who formulated his own inventive theories on nature's harmony and its opposite, evil. I had already learned something about Leibniz in the professor's class.

Although I wasn't particularly interested in the subject—which made me feel as if I were in the university auditorium—I was certain the professor's words contained messages that only those in the White Rose could decipher had I taken the time to listen carefully. Lisa had told me that the professor had erupted after a meeting with Hans earlier in the year, shouting that something had to be done about the Reich.

Instead, what captivated my attention was the professor's personage. His small stature, pursed lips, and washed-out face belied his ferocity as an intellectual and a speaker. When the fire of oratory overtook him, it was as if a veil hiding his true personality dropped. The professor became a new man, his face contorting into agony and pleasure, his legs and arms working as one, as if the disability that plagued him had never occurred, his theatrical voice booming throughout the apartment, his skin reddening with fervor. We were all held spellbound—except for Garrick.

The professor finished his orations on Leibniz and took a small break to gulp a glass of water before tackling his next subject—Hegel. Garrick motioned for me to join him outside. I was happy to get a breath of fresh air. We walked down the stairs, and I huddled in the doorway across from him as he lit a cigarette. The smoke flared away from his mouth into the black, crystalline sky.

I leaned against the door. "What's the matter? You don't seem yourself tonight." I surprised myself because I *was* concerned about his well-being, but I also thought I might be able to get a better understanding of his personality.

"You must excuse me," he said. "My mood . . . has not been good lately, for I've seen things, heard things, that I can't believe."

His melancholy tone reminded me of the Russian secret I'd carried for many weeks before I revealed it to Lisa—a truth I didn't dare reveal to Garrick. I folded my arms across my chest and rubbed them as the cold air bit through my blouse. I studied his face, the full moon's light the only illumination to gauge the sincerity of his feelings.

"Would you like to talk? I'm a good listener."

He took another puff on his cigarette, dropped it on the stone walkway, and crushed the smoldering tip with his shoe. "I would say this only to you . . . because I know I can trust you. . . . You are my friend."

"Yes," I said timidly.

He put his hand against my cheek and the warm tips of his fingers settling on my chilled skin set me shivering.

I turned my head, not wanting to encourage his affection but, at the same time, enjoying his touch. Silently, I cursed the Reich as well as my natural timidity with men. The simple pleasure of having a relationship had become too complicated under Hitler's rule. How could I be certain that Garrick was a man I could trust, a man who could share my life? The conflicting emotions in my head and heart were too great, and, in these uncertain times, I had no clear answer to my question.

He bowed his head and whispered in a voice so low I strained to hear the words.

"I *hate* the Nazis. I *hate* Hitler."

Those words burned into me, as if they were on fire, and I shuddered against the door. "What?"

He repeated the seven words, this time looking directly at me. His sincerity, the tortured feeling that emanated from deep within him washed over me. I wanted to reach out, hold him, express my sympathy for his feelings, but I didn't yet dare for fear of revealing how *much* I agreed with him. The irony was not lost on me and I sagged from the weight of my thoughts. The truth was always hard to bear in Nazi Germany.

"Be careful," I said. "Your words are treasonous. I could have you arrested."

"I know." He collapsed against the cold wall and reached for another cigarette, but struggling to hold it in his shaking hands, he stuck it back in the pack. "You could testify against me at my trial, which might lead to my execution . . . but I don't think you will. . . . You feel like I do."

I exhaled and my warm breath formed a cloud that dissipated in a fog over my head; I felt as cold and alone as the stars that shone above. I said nothing, only stared into the sky, protecting myself from his assertion that I felt as he did.

"I'm sorry. I hoped you would understand."

"You can think what you want, but watch what you say."

He wrapped his quivering hands around mine. "I want so much to help. I want to be part of something better than I am." His eyes shifted toward the door and to the apartment above. "But *they* don't trust me. . . . I'm sure of it. Hans and Sophie haven't accepted me; yet, I've done all I can to show them I care about what they do."

I wanted to help him, but I had to keep my distance. "What have they done? I don't know what you're talking about."

Garrick released my hands as his anger and anxiety appeared to lift. "It's all right. You don't have to share anything with me."

"I have nothing to share," I said, shivering again. "Let's go inside—it's cold."

"I'm going home," he said. "Will you tell them good-bye for me?" He touched my cheek again, and this time I let his fingers linger longer than I should have because I wanted to feel their warmth. Perhaps, it gave him some comfort as well.

"Yes," I said. "Please remember what I told you." I grasped his hand gently and removed it from my cheek. "I'll pet Katze for you."

In the moonlight, a look that I had never seen in a man's eyes, a look of tenderness combined with the possibility of love, touched my heart. He turned to leave, but then added, "May I take you out to dinner on Saturday?"

"Well . . ." Something within me sprang forward despite the cold night, something that required caution. I thought of many good reasons why I shouldn't go out with him, but all of them centered on me and the monastic life I was living. Yet, it would be a chance for me to get out of my stuffy room and learn more about him. "All right," I finally said. "Call for me at six. I should be done with my work by then."

He kissed my cheek and was on his way, his newly lighted cigarette bouncing in orange arcs in the air.

I rushed up the stairs, excited to tell Alex and Lisa what Garrick had told me. I spotted Lisa first, engaged in a conversation with Willi now that Professor Huber had ended his discussion. Willi and I had rarely spoken and this evening was no different. He was as Aryan a soldier as Hitler could have wished for, with light hair, a strong chin and intense eyes, but who had confessed his hatred of National Socialism to Hans and Alex. He seemed a rock to me—a quiet, silent fighter whose expression always bordered on the careworn, but a man who would never betray his friends. We said hello and exchanged a few pleasantries, then Lisa drew me aside to the table.

"I was looking for you," she said, her mouth forming a disagreeable frown. "I didn't want to stir up trouble, though."

"I was outside with Garrick." I cut a slice of chocolate torte and popped it into my mouth.

"I thought as much."

"Don't roll your eyes at me," I said, although she hadn't done so. "He was quite kind to me. I'm going out with him on Saturday."

Her eyes widened and a look of disbelief spread across her face. "So, he *is* making advances."

Anger flared in me, but I knew Lisa was only trying to protect me and the White Rose. "It's just dinner. . . . He was . . . well, how should I put it?"

Lisa smirked, awaiting my answer.

"I guess the best word to describe it is 'romantic.'" We stood looking at each other for a moment—Lisa's eyes widened. "Look," I continued, trying to hide my irritation. "I would never betray anyone in the White Rose, but I want to go out with him at least once. All of my life, men have taken fourth place to my studies, my nursing, and my father's wishes. I know many women don't think that way—particularly these days—

wanting to be a mother and homemaker for the Reich." I gave Lisa a friendly pout. "And besides, you're not my mother . . . or Hitler."

Fortunately, she took the jibe in the spirit in which it was given and soon was laughing with me. She filled her wineglass half-full of Riesling and sipped it. "I know. Just be careful."

"I'm so damn tired of being careful—looking down the street, watching the street corners to see if someone is standing there, whispering to keep my voice from being heard, always wondering if someone is listening on the other side of the apartment wall." I threw my hands up in exasperation. "It's maddening."

Lisa started to reply, but I cut her off. "And I know it's the way we must live or we could be imprisoned, but how long can this war go on? How long must we live this way? It's almost 1943 and the United States is in it now. How long can Hitler hold out? How many people have to die before Germany is rid of this tyrant?"

A hand grasped my shoulder and I stiffened, my feet rooted to the floor.

Alex rested his head next to mine and whispered, "Thank God this is a safe place to get worked up. I could tell from across the room that you weren't happy."

I patted his head and he laughed and swung himself beside me in a playful step. "Fascinating material on Leibniz and Hegel, but it gets tiresome reading between the lines." He cocked his head to the side. "Huber is leaving." The professor, putting on his coat and scarf, appeared his rather hunched self again, having expended himself on his diatribe. He nodded in a typical professorial gesture and was soon out the door, leaving Lisa and me alone with Alex and Willi.

"Want to help me tidy up?" Alex asked. "Hans and Sophie deserve to come home to a clean apartment after the holiday."

We all pitched in and soon the dishes and glasses were washed and put back in place. Willi blew out the candles as we picked up our coats.

"I must tell you what Garrick told me," I said as we gathered at the door. Alex opened it to make sure no one was outside and then closed it. "He said he hated Nazis and Hitler." The room grew quiet, all of them fixed in their spots, as they soaked up my words. "He feels that Hans and Sophie have betrayed him by not letting him into their confidences. He *believes* something is going on and he wants to be part of it."

Willi fastened the top buttons of his coat. "I don't trust him—he's too eager to be part of us."

"What do you think, Natalya?" Alex asked. The soft, intimate tone of his voice made me think there was more to his question than a solicitation of my opinion, as if he harbored an honest affection for me.

I thought for a moment. "He sounded sincere. . . ."

"But men have a knack for sounding sincere," Lisa said. "You should be on your guard when you go out with him."

Alex nodded as Lisa spoke. "Going out? That's a different story. . . . Yes, I'd be careful."

"I will—you needn't worry about me." I pulled on my gloves, ready to end the conversation. Obviously, no one trusted Garrick.

"Following your heart could be your downfall," Willi said. "My heart leads me to one place and there's no trouble there."

Saying nothing more, I opened the door and led everyone downstairs to the walk. Alex and Willi said good-bye. Lisa agreed to accompany me a few blocks before returning home.

"What did Willi mean about a place where there's no trouble?" I asked. We walked under the etched shadows of trees, the black branches stained against the lighter colors of stone.

"He's a devout Christian," Lisa said. "He believes in God and heaven, and I think, in his own way, he longs to get there sooner rather than later." She paused. "Hans and Sophie are Christians as well. . . . We must be the two agnostics in the group."

Lisa knew my feelings about religion, about my on-and-off-again belief in God, so I kept quiet. I was ashamed sometimes that I used God when He was needed and then neglected Him; but, as far as I was concerned, being a good person and sometimes praying to get to heaven was radically different from being a martyr. I couldn't reconcile Willi's way of thinking—if Lisa was correct in judging his feelings.

We were near Leopoldstrasse when the shrill, rising cry of air-raid sirens filled our ears. I looked up instinctively but saw neither bombers nor heard the whir of engines. However, the clear sky suddenly lit up with searchlight beams crisscrossing it.

"I've got to get home." She kissed me on the cheek and sprinted down the darkened street.

I ran north toward my apartment, hoping Katze and Frau Hofstetter were safe. As I neared my room, yellow light flashed behind me, like lightning from a summer storm. I watched as the bombs fell on the northern outskirts of Munich only a few kilometers away.

After one brilliant explosion, I swiveled toward the house, and, for an instant, I saw the indistinct figure of a man standing in the bushes near my window. The light faded and the form disappeared, leaving his shadowy imprint burned upon my eyes. I wondered if I had seen a phantom, or imagined a specter.

I staggered toward my door, the bombs still exploding in the distance. I found my key and stepped inside.

"Katz . . . Katze . . ." I called out. The cat had disappeared.

I bent down, looked under the bed, and found the creature shivering on the cold floor. When he saw my face, he rushed toward my arms. I lifted him up and felt a draft surging in from the window. It was a small crack, but enough to let the winter air into the room. I hadn't left the window open; in fact, I was certain it was closed when I left for the party. Perhaps Frau Hofstetter had been in my room; after all, she could come in through the hall door, or perhaps—I didn't want to think about it—the apparition had been in my room? I rushed to the dresser, and discovered, with a sigh of relief, that the leaflets were still in their hiding place under the drawer.

A violent knock on the inside door left me gasping for breath. Frau Hofstetter stood in her nightgown, hands over her ears, tears dripping from her eyes.

"I'm scared . . . to . . . death," she stammered. "I don't want . . . to be alone."

"Come in," I said, pulling her inside my room.

She threw herself on the bed and covered her head with my pillow. I sat beside her as Katze curled up in my arms. The Frau lifted the pillow occasionally for a gulp of air until the bombs faded and the all-clear sounded. She turned on her side and I realized from her breathing that she was asleep. I didn't have the heart to wake her, so Katze and I slipped in bed beside her. I knew my father, still in prison, and my mother, were safe because the bombs hadn't fallen near them.

If the truth be known, I was happy to have the Frau's company because the image of a man standing outside my window had unnerved me. I tried to reconstruct his face from the brief seconds I had seen him, but only one made sense—Garrick Adler's.

CHAPTER 7

⟥◦⟤

I bundled up the Friday morning of Christmas Day; the wind slashed down the street, making the short walk to my mother's apartment uncomfortable. The stone streets and brick sidewalks were dry, but a coating of frost had iced the edges of the dead leaves and grass in an outline of glittering white.

Frau Hofstetter had given me half of a baked chicken—which I was happy to share with my mother—and a delicately braided silver necklace that my landlady no longer wanted. I decided to give the jewelry to my mother because there was no extra money for presents.

A rising tide of sadness swept over me as I thought of my father in prison, sitting alone in his cell on Christmas Day, with barely any light and little heat to warm his body. Tears gathered in my eyes, but the day, as it had in years past, promised something greater to my heart than grief: a serenity, a promise of life beyond the grave, the unalterable belief that good would triumph over evil, that love would ultimately conquer hate. Those holiday promises tempered my gloom as I walked in the frigid wind.

Munich observed the holiday sedately as had been the case since the Nazis came to power. Despite my misgivings about the state of the world, my struggles with religion, my fears about the activities in the White Rose, I wanted to cheer up my mother on the holy day.

When I arrived, I found her sitting on the couch in one of her black dresses. However, unlike previous years, when her immaculate demeanor mirrored the occasion, the wrinkled dress, mended stockings, and scuffed shoes revealed her true emotions. Her hair swept back from her forehead in a sloppy wave to a clip on the crown of her head. Lack of sleep and worry had turned her eyes dark and puffy. She was in no mood for Christmas because of my father's absence and the approach of a bleak New Year.

My mother had no decorations except for a paper cutout Yule tree that I had colored with red and green ink when I was a child. We had little money for extras these days with only my meager pay from the Frau to support the family. Extras like cigarettes, pastries, and wine, could be purchased or bartered on the black market, but everyday necessities were becoming difficult to find. My mother had looked for jobs but found none.

She rose like an old woman from the couch, gave me a hug, and kissed my cheek.

"How are you, Mother?" I asked, forcing joy into my voice, trying to lighten the oppressive mood.

"You know how I am," she replied, her voice barely above a whisper. "I feel as if I've aged fifteen years in a month." The antiseptic odor of vodka rested on her breath.

I looked toward the kitchen, where a pot of potatoes sat boiling on the stove—the vegetable was the only addition to the chicken I'd brought.

"Would you like a drink to celebrate Christmas?" she asked, stepping away from me.

I looked at my watch—it was only a few minutes past eleven—and shook my head.

"It's your father's—from Russia. He hid it for himself but I found it—to him it was like a treasure, a reminder of the past we fled." She surveyed the room as if she were seeing it for the first time. "It's hard to keep secrets in a small apartment."

I removed my coat, the necklace in its pocket, placed the chicken on the small kitchen table, and returned to the sitting room. My mother was standing in front of my father's book-case, which had suffered a few nicks when it was knocked over. She moved a few state-approved volumes, revealing the bottle of vodka, and reached for a glass on top of the case. She poured a generous helping and drank about half of it in one gulp.

"Mother, don't you think it's a bit early to be—"

She slammed the glass on the shelf, causing some of the liquor to slosh over the top. "Don't tell me what to do! I'm your mother!" Her hands shaking with fury, her face flushed, she pivoted toward the window.

"I'm sorry. I only meant—"

"You only meant to help me—to stop me from drinking." Her voice had quieted but she remained standing with her back to me, her figure framed in the gray winter light.

I was at a loss for words. My father's imprisonment had taken more of a toll on her than I'd suspected. Our family was struggling to get by with little money and few resources. Perhaps it *was* time for me to look for a husband. I thought of Garrick, but shook my head to rid myself of his image. How he felt about me was of little consequence at the moment, considering my current state. Marriage was a dream for another day.

I was in no mood to antagonize my mother when peace and joy should rule the day. "Whatever you'd like to do is all right with me," I said, reconciling myself to the fact that, despite my alarm, I had no control over her drinking.

Her eyes red and watery with tears, she turned to me, stumbling a little on the way to the couch. I caught her in my arms and guided her to the seat. She lay her head on my shoulder and sobbed. "I'm so worried about your father," she cried out, as I dried her tears. "I don't think he'll survive."

Suddenly, I was overcome with guilt. My studies, my work, my seditious activities with the White Rose—and, if I was honest with myself, my fear of seeing him in prison—had kept me away. I offered these words to my mother to lessen my shame. "I've been negligent in visiting Father, because I've been so busy . . . but he did tell us to live our lives as if nothing had happened."

She straightened, unmoved by my excuse. "He needs our help, Talya. We can't let him waste away."

My mother was right; I'd been selfish in my way and I made up my mind on the spot to visit him. "I'll go every week after the New Year. I promise. Perhaps, he'll be out before June."

"He'd be so happy to see you." She knotted her handkerchief and placed it in her lap.

"I'm going out tomorrow night with a man I met," I said, thinking that the news might take her mind off my father.

The skin around her temples crinkled from her smile. "A nice man, I hope."

"I don't know him that well, but he knows friends of mine."

"What does he do? He's not in the armed forces?"

"He had an injury. He works for the Reich insurance."

"I suppose that's a good job."

"Yes. . . . He gave me a cat."

"What?"

"A cat. I call him Katze."

"Oh . . ."

The pause ended our conversation about Garrick and I realized what a strain the war and our separate lives had placed upon our relationship. We barely knew each other these days.

After noon, we ate our chicken and boiled potatoes and talked about many things: my studies, Frau Hofstetter, the neighbors who had deserted my mother after my father's arrest. After we finished our meal, I presented my mother with her gift. I had no box or gift wrap, so I took the necklace from my coat and handed it to her as she sat sipping a cup of watery tea.

She ran her fingers over the fine silver links. "Oh, it's beautiful, Talya, but you shouldn't have. You can't afford such a gift."

"There was no cost," I admitted. "Frau Hofstetter gave it to me, but I thought you should have it because you've always been more fashionable than I."

"I'll cherish it," she said, fixing the clasp around her neck. For a moment, she looked like the mother I remembered before the Nazis rose to power: happy, vibrant, full of fun and laughter, a woman who sang along with the phonograph and danced with my father over the hardwood floors after dinner. The memory was brief, a flash soon extinguished; the sorrowful stoop and sad eyes returned.

I helped my mother with the dishes and we sat for an hour or so listening to the phonograph—not Christmas carols, but Schubert and Beethoven, classical music we could play without fear of being locked up as would have been the case with Mahler, Mendelssohn, or American jazz and swing.

I left soon after, wanting to get home before dark. "Remember your promise to your father," my mother said as I departed. I assured her I would.

As night descended over the city, the temperature dropped and I rushed home to find the cat, now much bigger than when Garrick had given him to me, curled up in his favorite resting place on top of the bed. Having no homework to occupy my time during the holiday break, I played with Katze and listened to the sound of the radio coming through the hall door from the sitting room. The fare was mostly Nazi military marches, but the sound at least helped the time pass. I brushed my hair in front of the dresser mirror and got ready for bed. The Frau soon turned off the radio and trundled down the hall to her room. I pulled up the covers to my chin as Katze purred against my side. I was as comfortable as I could make myself in my room, but trepidation jangled my nerves. I wondered whether my condition was from excitement or fear.

In less than twenty-four hours, I would be having dinner with Garrick Adler.

He knocked on my door at six the next evening, after I'd finished my work for the Frau. Of course, I expected him to be on time; what I didn't expect was how handsome he looked or the gift of the single red rose he carried. The irony of the rose wasn't lost on me and I wondered if Garrick knew more about the group than he was telling—also how had he managed to purchase the beautiful flower in winter?

Taking off his gray overcoat, his black gloves, and scarf, he asked if he could play with Katze for a few minutes before we left for the restaurant. I agreed, and having no vase, went to the kitchen to find a drinking glass to fill with water.

As I turned on the tap, adrenaline rushed through me. My fingers turned red from clutching the glass. I had remembered the leaflets, which were still hidden beneath the dresser drawer not four meters away from Garrick. I pictured him casually examining every item on my dresser, or opening drawers, the envelope spilling forth its treasonous contents. I calmed myself and returned to the room to find my date sitting on the bed and rubbing Katze's belly. The cat playfully bit Garrick's fingers and batted his hands with his paws as if the animal remembered who had rescued him from death.

"Thank you for the rose," I said, placing the glass in front of the dresser mirror. I pulled out my chair and sat, blocking Garrick's view of the drawer. I crossed my legs and smoothed my blue dress, the newest piece of clothing I owned, yet several years old. He wore a double-breasted blue suit that accented his blond hair and complemented his form; his shoes were two-toned, navy and black. Still playing with Katze, he leaned back on my bed, displaying the picture-perfect model of the National Socialist ideal. Had I taken a photograph or had the talent to paint his portrait, the result could have been used for Nazi propaganda posters. He was perfect—perhaps too much so. In comparison, I felt underdressed and drab.

I watched him play with the cat for a few minutes. "Where did you get the flower? They must be doubly hard to get this time of year—with rationing."

"I wanted to bring you something besides a cat." His face flushed and he turned back to the animal. "I have friends who know people—much like Hans and Sophie."

I changed the subject, not wanting to pursue that topic. I also wanted him out of my room before Frau Hofstetter imagined that something indecent was happening in her house. "Where would you like to go for supper? Nothing expensive—I'm not dressed for fancy."

He petted Katze a last time and got up from the bed. "I was thinking about Ode. It's not far from here. You don't have to worry about fancy on my salary." He showed his beautiful white teeth, that lustrous smile that lit up a room.

Although I'd never been there, I'd heard of Ode, a restaurant frequented by university students, artists, and bohemians, an establishment where a man like Dieter, who owned the studio where Lisa and I printed the leaflets, might meet friends. Others had told me the food was good and reasonably priced. I expected it might be crowded on a Saturday night, the day after Christmas, and I hoped that Dieter wasn't there, for I had no desire to explain to Garrick how I knew the artist.

We got our coats and left Katze behind to enjoy his solitary evening. He was a little better about being alone now than when I had left him to travel to Vienna. Frau Hofstetter would look in on him if he was noisy.

The city had shrugged off its holiday lethargy. Cars buzzed down the thoroughfares. Pedestrians, taking a break from the increasing threat of air raids, enjoyed the clear, crisp weather. Garrick was friendly, but not overtly so, and our walk to the restaurant was cordial and pleasant.

Ode, housed in an impressive stone building with arched windows and heavy, medieval-looking doors, stood on a corner in Schwabing. The large dining room was similar to a beer hall with its vaulted ceiling, narrow aisles, and wide tables crammed with festive people laughing, singing, and lifting beer steins to their health. A massive stone fireplace, its mantel carved with scrolled columns and gargoyles, blazed at the rear of the room. I looked around the restaurant for a familiar face, unsure whether such an encounter would elicit dread or happiness. Jovial students, some of whom I recognized from classes; soldiers with their girlfriends or wives; and a few locals, older men and women flushed from the heat and fanning themselves with the paper menus, filled the room with noisy chatter.

"Look!" Garrick grasped my arm and pulled me forward. "There's an empty spot near the fireplace." It appeared to be the only one, unless we were willing to sit at a larger table with strangers. We rushed to the seats, threw our coats over two of the four chairs, and sat down. "Is this good?" he asked. "Perhaps we'll have the table to ourselves."

"It's fine." I retrieved my handkerchief from my handbag and wiped my glasses, the lenses clouded with condensation. The birch-log fire spread its warmth over my chilled skin. The smoky odor of the burning wood cheered me at first, but then reminded me of the synagogue fire on Kristallnacht. The following morning I'd met Garrick—as Lisa and I stood horrified near the remains of the gutted house of worship. That day, our eyes had locked.

We had ordered drinks and were conversing about the menu when Alex Schmorell strode toward the table. Shurik, with his affable face and easy walk, was the kind of man one could identify from across a room. A wreath of pipe smoke flowed past his head as he approached, his black leather boots glistening in the firelight. Attired in a high-neck sweater, a smart gray blazer and dress pants tucked into his boots, he stopped at our table and said hello. I responded; Garrick gave him a curt nod.

"Nice to see you again, Natalya." Alex winked and then kissed my cheek. I wondered if he'd had a bit much to drink or was just feeling frisky. "I miss our time in Russia—with Sina," he added.

I winced—the memories and feelings that had propelled me into the White Rose were too bitter to recall, especially in front of Garrick. As charming as he could be, Alex's slight flirtation bothered me. We were friends—nothing more. Perhaps he was trying to get under Garrick's skin.

Garrick shot me a derisive look as if I had betrayed him. "I didn't know you were in Russia together."

"Oh, yes," Alex said. "Our experiences were eye-opening."

I held my breath, hoping Alex would say no more. The birch logs sputtered and popped in the fireplace.

"Do you mind if I sit down?" Alex asked. "I'm alone for the evening."

Garrick paused, but reluctantly conceded. "Go ahead." I wondered if his concession was an effort to ingratiate himself into Hans and Sophie's circle through Alex, with the intent of finding out more about them. If I flattered myself, it seemed that Garrick was a reluctant gentleman—good manners triumphing over jealousy.

Alex lifted my coat, placed it over Garrick's, and sat next to me. He ordered a drink, leaned back in his chair, and tossed his book of matches on the table while puffing on his black pipe.

For a moment, I was thrown back to the Russian steppes, to Sina's house and the first night when she'd pointed the gun at us. Later that evening, after too much vodka, we had all laughed about her mischief. Alex and I related to each other through our Russian childhoods, our parents' emigration, and the tragic connection we felt after witnessing the war in our homeland. In our short time together, Alex had become the friend I could call "Shurik."

"How is the insurance business?" Alex asked.

Garrick lowered his head. "Fine."

"I don't mean to pry," Alex said and looked to me for help.

I gave Alex a look, cautioning him not to push Garrick.

Garrick folded his hands and placed them on the table. "It's just . . . just that I can't serve . . . like you do, and I'm in no position to attend the university like Natalya." He raised his head, his eyes brightening a bit. "But I *could* do more, if people would let me aid our country."

Alex's drink arrived at a most opportune time. After we toasted to our health, Alex turned the conversation away from Garrick's implication. "Are you eager to get back to the university?" Alex asked me, and placed his right hand on my arm.

Garrick shot up from his chair, his eyes as fiery as the flickering fireplace, apparently incensed by Alex's innocent display of affection. "I'm going to the bathroom," he announced roughly and swiped the matches from the table. Alex started to object, but Garrick had already stormed off.

I attempted to speak, but Alex lifted his hand. "He seems a bit upset . . . I can get more matches."

I looked over my shoulder and saw Garrick toss them onto a table occupied by three men and a woman. From their spot, the diners glanced at Alex and me and then turned back to their food. They were unlike the others at Ode. The men wore dark suits; the woman was smartly attired in a black dress and draped hat adorned with pheasant feathers. They looked overdressed, officious, and, although discreet, I got the distinct impression they were spying on us.

Garrick disappeared into the hall and I turned to Alex. "Shurik, do you know the people at the table across the room—three men and a woman—all nicely dressed?"

Not as fearful as I, Alex studied them and then turned back to me. "No idea, but they're not here for dinner." He lifted the pipe from his lips, scrunched up his mouth, and in a stuffy voice said, "This place is much too common.... They don't serve 1934 Dom Pérignon." He dropped the accent. "I think I better leave you two alone. Garrick doesn't seem to like me. You can gauge the true measure of a man from situations like this."

"What do you mean?"

He leaned toward me, whispering, "He's not calm.... He's a loose cannon." He took his pipe and tapped it into the ashtray. "When you're in our business, you need a cool head. Hans and Sophie are the epitome of it. I don't think he's good for us." He clutched my hand in a warm grasp. "It's good to see you again—outside of our studies."

"Studies," I knew, meant the White Rose. "You as well, Shurik." I released his hand as Garrick returned to the table.

Alex got up from his chair. "I'll leave you two to your dinner." He kissed my hand. "Natalya ... Garrick ... a pleasure to see you both. Good-bye for now."

Garrick grunted.

We ordered supper and a long silence ensued until our food arrived. I didn't want to provoke Garrick's surly mood, which made me uncomfortable and fidgety during our meal. I focused on the laughter in the room, the warmth of the fireplace, and my glass of wine.

Having drunk his own wine and eaten half his dinner, Garrick finally spoke. "I'm sorry if I was rude, but after all, Natalya, it's our date ... not the three of us."

"You told me you wanted to get to know Alex and the others better," I said.

"I do, but not when *we're* out together." He sighed. "Maybe we should start over from this point."

"Why did you take Alex's matches and toss them to those people at the other table? That was rude." I looked back, but the chairs were vacant, only empty dishes and crumpled napkins on the table.

He cut into his beef and said without a hint of guilt, "They're friends of mine from the insurance service. One of my friends indicated he needed a light."

"I didn't know that," I said.

"You and Alex were pre-occupied. I'm sorry if you felt I was rude . . . Alex can get more matches."

We finished our meals, both of us uneasy in our respective roles; I had little hope of salvaging the evening. Garrick suggested we take a walk by the Isar River north of the Englischer Garten and despite my inclination to end the evening, I agreed.

We left after a cup of coffee, and as we walked, I told him what I thought of his behavior. "You're not going to get anywhere with Hans, Sophie, or Alex acting like that." I thrust my hands into my pockets to highlight my disgust. "In fact, maybe I should be home with Katze . . ." I regretted my words as soon as they slipped from my mouth. I was too harsh. Being with my cat was cozy, but it wasn't human companionship—and Garrick *had* offered me more than any other man I'd met.

His face sagged, as if he'd been struck, and he apologized again.

We came to a wide expanse of land along the river's shore-line. The broken clouds, misty and gray against the sky, swept over us in a hurried journey to the southeast. The river, whipped by the wind, lay like an obsidian ribbon except for the cresting whitecaps. The trees stood naked under the clouds and stars. Even as Garrick strolled next to me, I felt alone and mildly annoyed with myself that I had criticized him. A wave of conflicted feelings washed over me.

Whether he recognized my discomfort or a sense of masculine duty arose in him, Garrick placed my arm in his and sidled closer.

Cold gusts smacked our faces, but the air refreshed and braced me, after the heated closeness of the restaurant. I would have been happy just to be quiet, alone with my thoughts, but Garrick broke my reverie.

"May I tell you something?" he asked. He had a way of presenting his thoughts in an obsequious manner, which made me wonder about his true character—was he charming or timid?

"Of course."

"It's hard for me to talk about this because my life has been so sheltered since my injury three years ago. I thought women would consider me a freak when they saw my leg; they would think me less of a man." He paused, and looked around to see if anyone was nearby, but no one was. "The Nazis and their damn war did this to me. I don't like to talk about it, but it's true."

After what I had seen in Russia, I had no reason to doubt him. I clutched his arm and said, "Go on."

"I've been—what is the word—fascinated, I suppose—with you from the first time I saw you four years ago. You were never far from my mind after I saw you and Lisa at the café, after our chance meeting at the museum . . ."

Garrick guided me to a bench, where we sat looking out upon the river, our backs to the wind. "I'd like to earn your trust," he continued, "and, if you're willing—to let me into your life."

"Garrick—" He cut off my words with a finger to my lips.

"Don't answer—think about what I've said—but know this. I used to think there was nothing in the world to hurry for, that at my age I had all the time in the world, but I know now that's not true. Time is too precious to waste."

My heart melted a little. Garrick had his good qualities: He was handsome, a man who had shown me kindness despite his faults; on the other hand, he was a man whose swagger and disagreeable first impressions were masks for his own insecurities. Perhaps I could like him more than I did, even grow to love him, but the war obstructed such feelings—everything was so uncertain. He probably understood that as well.

"Have you gone out with other women?" I asked.

"Yes . . . but there's been no one special . . . nothing to keep me going back."

I leaned against his shoulder and the warmth from his body melded with mine. I weighed my words carefully, but perhaps not as much as I should have. "You want me to trust you, but it's hard to trust anyone these days. The Reich requires that we have one mind." That admission was more than I should have revealed; it was too easy to make the jump to the role of traitor. How easy it was to speak in riddles.

"The people at the other table—my friends—they're like me," he said, rubbing his gloved hands together. "Have you heard of the White Rose? Have you seen their leaflets?"

The blood rushed to my face; my body stiffened from his revelation. I thrust my hands into my pockets, happy that the night covered my emotions. "No," I lied. "I've never heard of it. What is it?"

"It must be a group—no one really knows—they write the truth about the Reich. My friends think like I do. They want to meet Hans, Sophie, Alex, Professor Huber, and the others."

"Do you think Hans and Sophie are part of the White Rose? What are the writings about? Who are the 'others'?" I barraged him with questions, hoping he would believe my innocence.

Garrick told me about two of the leaflets he had read. Of course, I had already studied them all at Dieter's studio.

"I didn't turn the leaflets over to the police," he said. "I should have, but I destroyed them instead. They were powerful. . . . I didn't want to be implicated or arrested because I had read them." He straightened against the bench. "I don't know if Hans and Sophie are in the White Rose—or if there are others—men and women who love poetry, music, free thought, and complex ideas that should be debated by reasonable minds. It cheers me to know there are people like that in Germany."

I remembered what Alex had said to me at the restaurant—"He's a loose cannon." I wanted to believe that Garrick was on *our* side—the side of right—but I couldn't be certain. "I should be getting home," I said after a few moments, fearing that further conversation might reveal too much. "Katze surely misses me, and Frau Hofstetter may be tired of cat sitting." I shivered to make a point.

"Let me walk you home," he said, rising from the bench, his old smile and charm returning as he extended his hand toward mine. "I hope I didn't make you uncomfortable."

We hurried back to my apartment, the wind biting through our coats, the frigid air taking our breath away.

"May I see you again?" Garrick asked as we arrived at my door.

How hard it was to be kind yet noncommittal. I took out my key and said, "Classes will be starting again; I must visit my mother more often." I discerned his frown even in the dark doorway.

"I'm sorry Alex interrupted us," he said. "He spoiled the entire evening." Garrick kissed my cheek, stepped back, and said, "I admit it—I was jealous of his intrusion, but if you'd rather go out with—"

"Give me a few days to get things done. I'm home on weekends."

He threw me a kiss and sped off into the night. I closed the door, breathing a sigh of relief. Katze jumped off the bed, ran to me, and rubbed his warm body against my legs, his white fur crackling against my stockings.

What am I going to do about Garrick? I kept thinking as I got ready for bed. *I should never have gone out with him. It's like heading toward a waterfall in a canoe, knowing that the plunge will lead to disaster. The spirit is willing, but the flesh is weak. He's too dangerous for me.*

New Year's Eve and January 1, 1943, came and went with me nursing a bad cold. I had come down with it a few days after my late night with Garrick. Katze kept me company in bed, and Frau Hofstetter, freeing me from my duties while I was sick, fed me chicken-broth soup combined with vegetables she could find.

I thanked her for her kindness. Even though I was sick, I took advantage of the Frau's absence one afternoon and burned the remaining leaflets in her woodstove. I stirred the ashes with fire tongs and flushed most of the powdery remains down the toilet.

Garrick came by twice during the week, but I only had to appear at the door in my nightclothes, clutching my balled handkerchief, for him to get the hint. "I'll come back when you're well," he said, gazing at me through the gauzy curtains covering the window.

By the end of the week, when my cold lessened, I ventured out, keeping my promise to visit my father in prison.

Stadelheim Prison, an imposing stone structure with a red-tiled roof, looked more like a government building than a penal institution. I spotted its severe edifice afer the trolley turned a corner. My heart thumped in my chest, and, judging from the rigidity in my body, I was more nervous than when I'd made the trip to Vienna. Before me was an extension of the Nazi state where many opposed to the Reich were imprisoned or executed. I feared for my father. What condition would he be in? Had he been treated well or had he been beaten in order to implicate others? I had no idea what to expect.

Several guards surrounded the gate. Visiting hours were prearranged, so I'd made sure to arrive on time. Swastika flags swayed in the breeze; the building exuding a cold, yet powerful, appearance. I walked past the guard towers, through the sterile courtyard, to the front door.

A prison matron seated behind a wooden counter and glass barrier asked my business.

"I've come to see my father, Peter Petrovich," I said.

The woman screwed up her pale, steely eyes and opened a large book, running her pen down the long pages. She made a call from the phone on her desk, talked with someone in a low voice, and then hung up. "Take a seat," she said flatly.

I sat for ten minutes on a bench, along with a few other visitors, breathing in the antiseptic odor of the scrubbed hall, listening to the muffled metallic clang of prison doors opening and closing, hearing the faint call of men's voices. A guard carrying a rifle over his shoulder appeared at the end of the corridor and motioned for me to follow.

He unlocked a door at the end of the hall. I turned into a room filled with other armed guards and rows of long tables flanked by benches. My father, wearing a drab prison uniform, his hands resting on the oak table as if he was praying, his unkempt hair falling over his ears, looked up as I entered. Another sentry hunched behind his shoulder and watched my father's every move. The guard stepped back, but not so far that he couldn't hear our conversation. His rifle was at the ready, pointed in our direction if he needed to fire it.

My father reached for my hands as I sat. The guard snorted and my father drew back.

"I'm happy to see you, Talya," my father said.

My anxiety lessened upon seeing him, and I studied him carefully. He was never a heavyset man, but no doubt he was thinner than the last time I had seen him. The uniform hung from his shoulders, deep lines creased his forehead, and gray hair had sprouted from his temples.

"I'm happy to see you too, Papa," I said. "I'm sorry I haven't been here sooner."

He waved his hands as if to forgive me for my failure. "It's all right—I've been treated well." He looked over his shoulder at the guard whose mouth formed a thin slit, silent and unmoving, then he turned back to me. "It's good for him to know that I've been well treated. I'm the model prisoner—I clean, I help the sick—I know something about drugs." He smiled, showing yellowish teeth. "They like me here."

"I'm happy, Papa." A deep despair filled me. My father was dying, his spirit taken away, his will to fight crushed by imprisonment. "I would have brought you something . . . but I'm not allowed."

Again, he unclasped his hands and waved them as if to dismiss my words. "No matter. I'll be out of here in five months and home. We can celebrate then. . . . How is your mother?"

"Fine," I said, not knowing if he was aware of her drinking.

"And your studies?"

"Fine, as well." I was melting inside with pain and horror, as if I were a candle and the flames were licking against me, removing my skin layer by layer in the bright fire. We could say nothing of substance to each other. Everywhere there were ears, listening for one word, one thought that would signal a traitor to the Reich, a treasonous subhuman who deserved to die. Even if my father had been mistreated, he couldn't have told me. I stared at his face and neck, the bare portion of arms not covered by the uniform, but there were no marks and bruises that I could see.

The guard held up three fingers to me, signaling that my time was almost up.

"Tell your mother hello and give her my best wishes," my father said.

"I will." I had nothing more to say; in fact, there was nothing more *to* say.

He leaned toward me. "National Socialism, Talya! All hail our glorious leader!"

The guard jumped forward from his post. "Stop yelling!" He pointed the rifle at my father's back.

I leaned back on the bench, shocked at my father's words. He had never been a Nazi supporter. We had fled our home in Russia under the terror of Stalin. My father hated dictators and all they stood for. The guards must have beaten the doctrine into him.

"Heil Hitler!" My father stood and pointed his arm stiffly at me.

"I said 'shut up'! Sit down, Russian swine!" The guard swung the rifle at my father and struck him between the shoulders. He crumpled on the table with a roar of pain as I screamed.

Rough hands dragged me from my seat, jerking me up from the bench, pulling me toward the door. "Papa," I called out, "what is wrong?"

Another guard pushed me into the hall and slammed the door. "That was foolish," he said. "Your father is a stupid man."

"My father is a good man." I jerked my arm free from his grip.

He shoved me down the corridor and out the entrance as the other guards watched. "Get out, Russian whore. Make sure this bitch is removed from the yard!"

The sentries looked as if they were ready to shoot, so I stumbled out the gate, its bars clanging behind me.

A few minutes later, I boarded a trolley and sat in the back away from the other passengers. Tears streamed down my face and I struggled to keep from choking. What had happened? Had he become a Nazi sympathizer, or had he put on a show for the guards in hopes of an early release? Perhaps my mother, who had visited him more often, could explain.

As the grim buildings of Munich passed by under an ashen sky, I understood again how important the White Rose was . . . *not only to Germany . . . but to me.*

CHAPTER 8

My mother was well into the bottle by the time I arrived at her apartment. I told her about my father's behavior, but she had no explanation, and, in a fit of pain and sobbing, collapsed on the couch. I didn't press her further for fear it would add too much stress to her already delicate emotional state; so, I ended our visit with, "Otherwise, he seemed fine. We had a nice talk." I spoke in platitudes without much truth to them.

As we said good-bye, my mother said, "Don't desert him, Talya." The prospect of visiting Stadelheim again made me shiver, but I promised her I would try despite what I'd seen.

Classes started soon after the New Year and I found myself involved in the busy world of the university. I spotted Hans and Sophie several times in the main hall or strolling about the grounds, but we kept our distance. Few looks were exchanged and fewer words spoken. Hans was so protective of his sister that I didn't really know how deeply Sophie was involved with the White Rose. From their standoffish behavior, I sensed that something might be planned, but I had no idea what it was— the writing of another leaflet, or some other secret activity that might be even more daring than those carried out in the past.

Garrick dropped by my apartment a few times, but only for conversation. Although he was chatty, and we laughed and smiled in our few minutes together, work and studies came first. I wanted to go out with him again, but, the occasion never arose because Lisa required me for another White Rose project—a second leaflet.

A few days after classes started, Lisa and I found a secluded spot on the university grounds as night was falling. The air was cold and a light snow fell lazily on our shoulders from a sky more benign than threatening. I was glad to get out of the stuffy classrooms, despite sitting on a chilly stone bench underneath an oak's bare branches.

"Are you ready to write another?" she asked, searching her coat pocket for cigarettes. "I'm dying for a smoke."

"Yes," I said, "but what will I write about this time?"

"Maybe you can talk about Stadelheim," she offered.

"Too dangerous. It might be traced back to me."

"Dieter's offered his studio again," she said, finding a cigarette. "I think Hans and Alex are writing another leaflet, but I'm not sure. I get the feeling . . . you know how that is."

I nodded. "Yes, I do."

"This time we'll be going north—mail from Nuremberg. What if we meet on Wednesday night, the thirteenth, to start?"

I had no commitments for that night, so I agreed to meet Lisa at Dieter's.

But that day, something unexpected occurred. All the university students were ordered to the Deutsches Museum—to celebrate the 470th anniversary of the founding of the university. Rumors circulated and tongues wagged as we trooped to the museum, which was located on an island in the Isar River.

"I suppose they've canceled classes because of our defeats in Russia," Lisa and I overheard one male student say. I turned to see him wipe his eyes. "All of us men will be sent off to war, there'll be no escaping it," he added, turning his gaze to the street.

I was impressed with his frankness, but his friends disagreed, for they urged him to keep quiet. "The National Socialists want to see who supports them . . . or to the point, who doesn't," another man said. "This gathering isn't about the war."

When we arrived at the fortresslike building with its rotunda entrance, Lisa and I, along with most of the other university students, were herded up the stairs to the large auditorium's balcony. I recognized a few friends of Hans and Willi sitting among us, as well as a couple of Professor Huber's students. No members of the White Rose—at least those that I knew—were in attendance. Quietly, I asked Lisa about their absence.

"They're snubbing rallies, even when ordered to attend, as a matter of conscience," she whispered. We'd made no such pledge.

The purpose of the assembly soon became clear to me.

A cadre of SS men, grim and smirking, stood guard at the exits. Important Nazi officials, from the student association and Bavaria, all shining and puffed-up in uniform, sat on a platform at the front of the auditorium, which was festooned with a banner trumpeting the occasion. I leaned over from my seat to survey the chattering crowd below: Wehrmacht soldiers; students soon to go to war; and veterans—many injured, on crutches or in wheelchairs—occupied the seats along with robed university faculty, including Professor Huber, whom I recognized from the elongated shape of his head. This was a Nazi rally in full force, but for what purpose? This assembly was called to celebrate more than the founding of the university.

The crowd hushed when Paul Giesler, an important regional Gauleiter, strode to the stage like a bull charging out of a gate. He was an imposing figure in uniform—his hair slicked back revealing a high forehead, piercing eyes, large Roman nose, but with a Cupid's mouth a bit too small and sweet for his arrogant personality. From the start of his speech, Giesler intended to take no prisoners—no one was immune from his venom.

He began by praising the university and its place in German life, but soon reviled it for fostering "twisted intellects" and "falsely clever minds." He bellowed, "Real life is transmitted to us only by Adolf Hitler with his light, joyful, and life-affirming teachings."

Those who were about to go to war or worked for National Socialism received his praise while those who studied "without talent" or "seriousness of purpose" garnered his revulsion.

The university, he said, was no refuge for "well-bred daughters" who neglected their roles in the Reich.

A nervous agitation fell over the crowded balcony. Feet scraped against the floor, a signal that the speech was not going down well with the students. A catcall erupted in back of me and several more soon broke forth. I looked over my shoulder at the SS guards, whose expressions had shifted from satisfied smiles to scowls of sinister apprehension. Lisa nudged me and smirked, feeling the rising resistance to the Gauleiter.

Giesler, not to be outdone by mere students, fed on the growing restlessness. "The natural place for a woman is not at the university, but with her family, at the side of her husband," he shouted to the balcony. More catcalls erupted, including those from Lisa and me. The scraping of feet against the floor nearly drowned out his speech.

To cap his point, he yelled that women should present a child every year to the Führer. With a mocking grin, he finished his tirade with these words, "And for those women students not pretty enough to catch a man, I'd be happy to lend them one of my adjutants. And I promise you *that* would be a glorious experience."

A maelstrom arose in the balcony, drowning out Giesler's words, sending the students into a frenzy of pounding feet and derisive shouts. Women behind us jumped from their seats and rushed to the exits, only to be captured in the arms of the SS and the brownshirts.

"Time to get out of here," Lisa said.

I looked toward the exit. "They're arresting those women."

We didn't have long to wait, for another SS man plowed down the row in front of us, shouting for us to get out or be hauled off to jail.

A group of university men, none of whom I knew, shoved the SS men making the arrests and soon fists flew and blows were landed. Bone cracked and one of the male students fell backward into the balcony, clutching his bloody nose. A roar arose from below and I peered down to the orchestra level. Fistfights had broken out there as well. Several of the professors scattered around the fighting groups, thrusting their arms into the fracas, but to no avail. Professor Huber's voice boomed above the others, calling for calm, but no one seemed to listen.

Somehow, the arrested women managed to free themselves during the melee, and Lisa and I fled down the stairs with them and out into the courtyard, where several scuffles were taking place. Sirens blared in the distance, signaling the arrival of more police and military squads. We knew when to make an exit.

The students had broken into several smaller groups and we joined one, trekking down the street back to the university, holding hands, uniting arms, and singing. Despite the turmoil, Lisa and I were flooded with a lightness of spirit, sensing that all we had done, or might do, was worth the struggle.

"It feels good to resist, to be a traitor," I said, for once not caring who heard it.

Lisa smiled and placed her arm over my shoulder.

Soon we arrived at Ludwigstrasse on our march to the university, but the police were waiting for us with batons drawn. Swinging their weapons, they rushed at us, forcing us to break apart. We dispersed under their onslaught, but the smiles from other students, the feeling that we had *done something* remained with me for days, even as a state of emergency was declared in Munich.

Lisa and I went our separate ways, still intending to meet that evening at Dieter's studio. However, on my way home, a chilling sight dampened my enthusiasm. Under the Siegestor, the triumphal arch marking the entrance to Schwabing, Garrick stood with his group of young insurance friends we'd seen at Ode. I didn't know what to think. Had they attended the assembly, or were they observing the police, or us? I didn't remember seeing them in the auditorium but the building was crowded and I could have missed them.

I pretended not to see him and walked on the other side of the street past the arch. Despite that, I was fairly certain Garrick had spotted me. Yet, he made no effort to come my way. He and the others seemed unconcerned about what had transpired, their faces lacking the students' smiles or any sense of jubilation.

They reminded me of elegant upper-class Germans, attired in their dress coats and ties, the woman wrapped in brown fur and wearing a stylish hat.

Garrick lit a cigarette, shielding the lighter with his hand. The smoke billowed around his face before dispersing in the wind.

I hurried, on edge, to my apartment.

That evening, Lisa and I worked with a renewed sense of energy. In the few hours we had been apart, she had discovered that Hans and others in the White Rose had no idea what had happened at the auditorium. Their response was to get to work on their next leaflet. That was our task as well.

I wrote the text in under two hours, leaving the subject of the Gauleiter and his offensive remarks alone—a subject too close to us—and wrote of the "blindness" of the German people, those who followed like sheep as the country teetered on the brink of destruction. Such "defeatism" was punishable by death; but, with each line, I saw Sina and her children falling to a bloody death in the hollow near Gzhatsk, I heard the crazy words my father had spoken in prison.

By eleven, we had completed our work, including printing five hundred leaflets and addressing one hundred of them to names picked out of the Munich phone book. This time we didn't seek Hans's approval, and we included several university professors in the mailing whom we felt might be swayed to our way of thinking. We agreed to meet the following evening to finish the task of addressing the envelopes. Lisa would bring the suitcase, and we would plan our trip to Nuremberg as we had planned our trip to Vienna. Dieter, looking sleepy, arrived as we were leaving.

As I walked home, pre-occupied with thoughts of our upcoming journey to Nuremberg and the dangers it presented, I paid less attention to my surroundings than I should have.

I jumped when a voice called out as I inserted my key into the lock.

"You're late tonight." I recognized the timbre, somewhat

raspy and slurred, and the lean, muscular figure as it slipped out of the shadows in the Frau's yard.

"God, Garrick, you frightened me." I collapsed against the door and looked at my watch. "It's nearly midnight. What are you doing here at this hour?"

He sauntered toward me, his feet sliding on the frosty grass. "I could ask the same of you." He reached the door and leaned on the frame. His normally smoothed-back hair ruffled in the wind and his eyes took on the color of night.

"Come in . . . but be quiet," I said. "I don't want to wake Frau Hofstetter. I need to feed Katze."

"Thank you. That's very nice of you." His breath was heavy with liquor.

I opened the door and turned on the desk lamp.

Katze greeted us, and Garrick swept him up in his arms. "What a good little puss he is," he said, trying to rub the struggling cat behind his ears. Katze pushed his claws into Garrick's coat and launched into the air, landing on all fours by my legs. Garrick dusted off his coat. "Damn, he must be hungry."

I removed a small tin of food from the drawer, an extravagance the cat rarely received, and spooned some on a dish. Katze meowed and waltzed around the room like he'd never been fed in his life.

Garrick collapsed in my chair. I took off my coat and threw it on the bed.

"So, what are you doing here?" I asked.

"I've been celebrating and I thought I'd drop by."

"Celebrating what?"

He opened a few buttons on his coat and leaned back. "What did you think of Giesler's diatribe today?" His head swayed, and he blinked as if the light from my lamp was painful to his eyes.

I didn't want to fall into a trap of revealing my feelings on the subject, so I answered with another question. "What did you think?"

"I thought it was won . . . der . . . ful." His words drifted through the air in a hazy blur.

"You've had too much to drink, Garrick. You should go

home." I was astounded at his condition—I'd never seen him drunk.

"You noticed," he said, and then patted his legs. "Come sit on my lap."

"No," I said, resisting his offer. The advances of an inebriated man held no attraction for me.

Katze finished his meal, and I picked him up and listened to him purr like a motorcar on a winter's morning.

Garrick leaned forward to the point that I thought he might fall off the chair, but he righted himself and said, "Okay then, go out with me Saturday night. We haven't been out in three weeks."

"If you can recall, I was sick." It was after midnight now, and I wanted him out of my room. I was willing to agree to a date just to get him to leave. "I'll go out with you if you promise to go home and sober up." I could always change my mind later.

"Yes . . . yes . . . today was wonderful. I thought everyone should celebrate."

He rose on wobbly legs and Katze and I escorted him to the door. "Be quiet when you leave."

Garrick put a finger to his lips and then kissed me on the cheek. "Saturday," he said and ambled down the walk like a leaf in the wind.

I closed the door and speculated on what had prompted his overindulgence. His unusual behavior didn't endear him to me, and reinforced my feeling that nothing should get in the way, not even Garrick, of my work with Lisa.

Katze and I jumped into bed, both of us ready for a good night's sleep.

Lisa reminded me that our travels to the medieval city of Nuremberg would be much like Daniel entering the lions' den. The city had an old and storied history, not the least of which was its recent distinction of holding huge Nazi rallies during the Party's formative years.

The night after Garrick showed up at my apartment, Lisa and I finished our work and planned our trip. We modeled it after

our successful journey to Vienna: parting at the Munich Hauptbahnhof before boarding the train, joining forces in Nuremberg
after we could meet safely, locating the best post boxes to mail
the leaflets, distributing the leaflets that remained, and then
returning home. Lisa would carry the suitcase and, if asked,
provide the same explanation she had used before—an overnight stay with her aunt. I, of course, was on the way to visit a
friend—a memorized name and address taken from the Nuremberg phone book to bolster my alibi—a sounder tactic than I
had used in Vienna. We both hoped that nothing about our trip
would lead to that level of scrutiny.

We boarded the train mid-afternoon on a dull, cloudy Saturday, with our scheduled traveling time to Nuremberg considerably shorter than that to Vienna. We planned to be finished with
our task an hour or so after sundown, and back in Munich by
nine that night.

Getting aboard was much the same, although my nerves vibrated like plucked piano wire when we arrived at the station.
I followed Lisa, watching with one eye as a guard pulled her
aside for a random check. I held my breath as she opened the
suitcase and held up several articles of clothing; but, my fears
were unfounded, and the satisfied guard closed the case after a
brief inspection. Another waved me past after a cursory look at
my papers. We took our seats on opposite sides of the car. Lisa
kept the suitcase nearby on the floor but covered it with her
coat. Shortly after we left, we were checked by a third guard,
who called for our papers. The young man looked us over but
didn't ask Lisa to open the suitcase. We glanced at each other
with relief as he walked to the next car.

The northern Bavarian countryside was wooded and monotonous, not nearly as interesting as the landscape to the south,
and I found myself fidgeting in my seat, my still-tense nerves
jolted by any loud noise or grating voice. By the time we arrived in Nuremberg, the sun was setting and long shadows had
already spread across the city.

We checked the suitcase in a locker and set out to find what
we were looking for. Having been in Nuremberg only once

when I was a child, I was taken with its charm: the towering Gothic Frauenkirche in the city center, the castle turret rising in the distance, the rows of shops and restaurants constructed in traditional Bavarian design with angled roofs and colorful painted walls trimmed with wood. Even in the dark, the city seemed to glow with a charm from ages past.

Having found several isolated post boxes, we stopped for coffee and a pastry at a shop, but didn't talk much, the mailing of the leaflets heavy on our minds.

Lisa returned to the train station to pick up the suitcase. We agreed to meet near the doors of the Frauenkirche in about an hour.

The hour passed, along with another half hour, and I paced in front of the church, my stride quickening as much as my heartbeat. The city center was empty, except for a few evening strollers, and as time dragged by, my thoughts darkened like the sky. Had Lisa been arrested? Had something provoked police suspicions at the train station? Was Lisa—I dared not think it—dead?

I brushed away that terrible notion and looked at my watch; it was nearing seven. We had agreed that if anything went wrong, we'd make our way back to the train station, separately if necessary, to catch the eight o'clock train.

After another five minutes of frantic pacing, I walked around the corner of the church, near a long block of shuttered businesses, to the first post box we'd identified.

The cobbled street was deserted and Lisa was nowhere to be seen.

With time running out, I ran to the next location nearer the station, crossing the bridge over the inky waters of the Pegnitz River, passing another church with two large spires, stopping in front of the box on Marienstrasse. I breathed heavily, the cold air carving into my lungs. I looked to my left and right and behind me; again, no sign of Lisa. I whirled on my heels, wondering whether I should go back to the meeting spot in front of the church or head for the train.

Where are you? Please, God, let her be safe.

I walked slowly away, knowing there wasn't enough time to get to the third box and back before the last train departed. I'd resigned myself to making the return trip to Munich alone, when I crossed a dark, narrow alley between two buildings and out of the corner of my eye caught something moving.

I peered into the gloom. A man and woman were wedged in the dark recess of the alley, writhing in a frenzied movement of arms and legs. I stopped, taken aback. Had I stumbled upon a couple's secret lovemaking?

Then I spotted Lisa's suitcase a few meters away from the entrance, its cover flipped open. Lisa's robe lay half in the case, the other half spread across the damp stones.

I sprinted down the alley to aid my friend.

"Tell her to get out," the man said roughly to Lisa after hearing my footsteps. His hand covered her mouth. Lisa uttered a few muffled cries.

"This is what we do to whores wandering the streets of Nuremberg." The man turned his body toward me while holding onto Lisa's arms with one hand, the other still covering the lower half of her face. He was young—I could tell from his voice—and he wore a uniform under his unbuttoned coat, his pants stuffed into his calf-high boots. SS, I thought.

"A friend? Tell her to leave or she'll be next." He removed his hand from Lisa's mouth for a second.

"Go!" Lisa yelled. "Leave!"

I stopped, my feet rooted to the ground, my hands and arms shaking with fear and fury. "No! Let her go and I won't report you to the SS."

He arched his head back and roared with a hideous laughter that echoed down the alley. "I *am* the SS."

Lisa bit into his hand.

Screaming, he shoved Lisa against the stone wall and reached for the gun at his side.

We both rushed for him, she from the front, I from the side. I hit him with as much force as I could muster. As he grappled with us, the gun flew from his hand, landing with a metallic thud on the stones, sliding between my feet until it was behind me. He pushed me away, and I toppled backward toward the weapon.

Lisa kicked at his legs and groin.

I grabbed the weapon by the barrel as Lisa lunged for his arms.

He was about to encircle Lisa's neck with his hands, when I smashed the gun's butt into the side of his head. Moaning, he slid down the wall to the damp cobblestones.

I stared at the man's splayed body. "Oh, God, I've killed him."

Gulping in cold air, Lisa steadied herself against the stone wall. "I doubt it, but it's fine with me if you have. One less Nazi rapist in the world."

With outrage and disgust surging through my body, I kicked the man's legs. The blows bounced harmlessly off his boots. I looked at the weapon in my gloved hand, wondering if I had drawn blood. A nervous chuckle gushed from my throat as I dropped the gun to the ground.

"Quick, while he's out," Lisa said, recovering her composure and pointing to the suitcase.

We ran to it, removed the letters and flyers, and threw the clothes back inside. We stepped out of the alley to find the street deserted. Luck was with us. Lisa stuffed the envelopes into the box as I concealed the leaflets under my coat.

As we hurried to the train station, I dropped them in the doorways of lifeless homes and businesses, making certain that no one was watching or following us. An exhilarating sense of freedom came over me as I placed them on the doorsteps. I had proven my worth as part of the White Rose and defended my friend against an attack.

Our only concern was getting out of Nuremberg before the attacker could alert the police. We cleaned up in the women's room before boarding the train to Munich.

My nervousness broke out in unrestrained giggles as I looked at the solemn guards who paced the station with their rifles swung over their shoulders.

"I could take them on," I whispered.

"Don't let your heroics go to your head," Lisa said in a shaky voice.

"Did he see what was inside the suitcase?" I asked.

She shook her head. "I don't think so because he only saw it coming toward his head as I tried to hit him with it. Fortunately, only my clothes fell out."

A few minutes later we boarded the train. Because the suitcase was empty except for the clothes, we felt no need to travel apart. As I settled back in a seat next to Lisa, a disturbing thought entered my mind. If the man wasn't dead, he'd notify the authorities as soon as he could. If the Gestapo was thorough in its thinking, which was usually the case, one phone call to nearby trainmasters, including the one in Munich, would put two women traveling together in jeopardy. We'd be questioned, and most likely arrested, as soon as we arrived.

We decided to get off the train at Dachau and find our way home, even if we had to walk.

Lisa told me what had happened as we sat in the back of a nearly deserted trolley on the outskirts of Munich. The SS man had followed her; so, deciding not to endanger us both and hoping to lose him, she had walked for a long time before ending up at the post box near the train station. She hoped that I might find her there. The thug was more taken with her looks than the contents of her suitcase—a fortunate occurrence—but his unbridled Nazi superiority led him to assault an unaccompanied female. I arrived only minutes after he had dragged Lisa into the alley.

In the course of a few hours, I'd metamorphosed from nonviolent resistance to physical assault, but I took solace in the memory of Hans, Willi, and Alex attacking the guards who'd bullied the prisoners.

Exhausted and happy to be free, we said our good-byes at the Marienplatz. Yet another surprise awaited me as I arrived home a few minutes before ten.

The tip of a cigarette flared orange near my door. I knew immediately what had happened.

I ran to him with open arms, hoping to smooth over his hurt feelings for standing him up on our date. "I'm sorry, Garrick," I said, and I was sorry, but moreover I was ashamed of my stupidity for making such a mistake. I attempted to embrace him, but he stepped away.

"Where have you been?" he asked, anger bubbling beneath his restrained voice. His tone was clear, sharp, focused, unlike the last time we'd met, when his words were slurred by liquor. "I've been waiting for hours."

His building rage frightened me, but unlike my encounter with the SS man in Nuremberg, my body urged me to flee, not fight.

"I was at Lisa's," I said, thinking as fast as I could under his malignant gaze. "She's not feeling well and wanted company. I'm sorry I forgot—I'll make it up to you."

He stepped away from the door, threw his cigarette on the walk, and grabbed my arm. "That's a lie. I went to Lisa's tonight. She wasn't at home and her parents had no idea where she was." His grip on my arm tightened. *"Where were you?"* He shouted the question so loudly I feared he might wake Frau Hofstetter and the neighbors. Katze bawled behind the door, aware that something was wrong.

"We went to see a movie."

"Which one?"

"Garrick, let go of my arm." I tried to pull back. A cold, paralyzing fear coursed through my veins. I felt that he might strike me; indeed, he might do something worse.

He released me, and I stumbled backward on the walk, preventing a fall by clutching the bare branches of a bush.

"You're like all the rest," he said bitterly. "Like Hans, Sophie, and that Russian you like so well. All your fancy meetings and airs, only letting in those you approve of—like some childish secret club."

"That's not true," I said, hoping to defuse his anger.

A warm yellow light appeared around the edges of the blackout curtain; soon the gauzy figure of Frau Hofstetter peered around it, her features flickering in the glow of an oil lamp. "Is everything all right?" she asked after opening the door. "I heard voices and the cat is yowling like a tiger."

Katze sprinted out of the door and rubbed against my legs. I lifted the animal and cuddled him in my arms. "Yes, everything is fine, Frau Hofstetter," I said. "Garrick was escorting me home. I guess we were having too much fun."

Calm settled across Garrick's face, which was what I hoped would happen. Placating his anger seemed the only way out of a tense situation.

The Frau scowled at Garrick. "It didn't sound like fun to me. Come in, Natalya, or you'll catch another cold."

Garrick stared stone-faced at my landlady. I grabbed his hand and said, "Come by tomorrow afternoon and we'll talk." My fast-beating heart calmed, and, to make a show of it, I leaned over and kissed his cheek. "See you."

"Good night, Frau Hofstetter," he said, and turned on his heels.

I followed my landlady inside and put Katze on the bed. For once, I was happy that the Frau had treated me like I was her daughter.

"He *seems* like a nice man," she said as she left my room, but from her sarcastic tone, I knew she didn't mean it.

"Yes," I replied halfheartedly.

She ambled to her bedroom, the oil lamp in her hand, patches of light moving down the hall, like sunbeams flickering through a train window.

I made sure my front door was locked, never so glad to be safe, warm, and at home. Garrick's angry face haunted me for most of the night.

PART 2

TRAITORS

CHAPTER 9

February 1943

Garrick stayed away for several weeks, and frankly, after our last encounter, I didn't miss him. His outburst had frightened me and, in effect, added clarity to my feelings about our relationship. My newly formed resolve strengthened my concern about getting involved with him—or any man.

I continued my life as usual, attending class, visiting my mother, and working for Frau Hofstetter. My mother encouraged me to visit my father, but I had not gone to Stadelheim since the ugly experience there. My mother said my father's behavior was a ploy to get out of prison early; but, my deepening allegiance to the White Rose kept me away. Nazi salutes and cheers surrounded me daily and I didn't need to hear more of them from my father.

Lisa and I talked about the White Rose when we could. Her few conversations with Hans and Sophie convinced her that something was about to happen, but she had no idea what it was. Hans was his usual inscrutable self, as he preferred to keep secrets to himself. Lisa told him what had happened in Nuremberg—noting that the mailing was successful, but the danger was greater than even she'd imagined. Her encounter with the SS man had made the peril all too real and it showed. Her usual smile was muted and I found that she shifted the conversation away from men anytime it turned toward them; and, she showed little enthusiasm for more White Rose missions. We decided to let our efforts cool for the moment, certain that the SS was looking for "two women traitors."

On February first, a Monday, I walked home after a morning class, made a small lunch in Frau Hofstetter's kitchen, and was eating it at my dresser when a harsh knock interrupted me.

My spirits fell when I recognized Garrick's figure through the window. He had finally decided to pay me a visit. I had better things to do than spar with him—my biology and science classes were in full swing and I needed to study for upcoming tests; my mother wasn't feeling well and wanted me to go to the market for her; the Frau's dishes needed to be washed. And yet a small part of me missed the man I'd thought I'd known.

His grim expression prompted me to open the door. His double-breasted tan coat was pulled tight against his body, his matching homburg tilted upon his head at a jaunty angle. I felt the *need* to smile, as if it was required of a woman to welcome a man, a grateful response for the good fortune of a visit. I stared at him, unable to make out what he was thinking.

"May I come in?" he asked in a formal tone.

Again, the *need* to be polite struck me. His awkward courting had shifted from flattery to mild annoyance. After my encounter with the SS man in Nuremberg, a growing anger and suspicion had soured me on all but the most benign of men.

Still, I invited him in. "Of course—if you're kind."

He spotted the half-eaten cheese sandwich on my dresser. "Naturally. I apologize for my behavior." He looked distractedly around my room. "I won't disturb your lunch. I only have a few minutes."

Katze ran to him and rubbed against his legs, but Garrick brushed him away with his foot. He took off his hat and sat on my bed. The winter light filling my room gave him a ghostly look, his face made even paler by his tan coat. Katze jumped up on the bed beside him, but he paid no attention to the cat.

"I don't know how to say this without upsetting you," he

finally said. He planted his hands firmly on the bed and stared at the door. I sat rooted to my chair.

"Upset me? What's wrong?" My mind immediately went to my parents, my father in particular, but Garrick knew so little about them that I discarded the thought.

He turned his head somewhat, his lips rendering a rather sharp disdain. "I think it's better if we don't see each other."

Despite our ups and downs, the finality of his words startled me. In truth, we hadn't seen that much of each other, but his attention was flattering; and, sometimes my thoughts drifted to what our relationship might be like once the war was over—if we both survived it.

I wiped the sandwich crumbs off my fingers and put my hands in my lap. "I thought we could be friends but you've been so angry lately. Frankly, I've been frightened of you."

"I don't like to be excluded," he said firmly.

"What do you mean?"

He jerked his head toward me, his nostrils flaring. "You know exactly what I mean—you and the rest of them!"

There was no need to dig deeper into this professed wound and the truth behind it; he was right, I knew exactly what he meant.

"This is about Hans and Sophie and those silly meetings where we eat pastries, drink wine, and *pretend* to have intellectual discussions, isn't it?" I asked, attempting to soothe his ruffled self-esteem and proclaim the innocence of the White Rose. "There's no reason to get upset about that. We're just students getting together. Most people wouldn't want anything to do with Hans and Sophie anyway—they would find them extremely boring."

His eyes softened. "I don't find them boring," he said, his voice trembling. "I find them rude, selfish, and insufferable. They have no idea what I've gone through. I tell them what I've suffered and *still* they want nothing to do with me."

"What do you think they can do for you?"

"I've told you how I feel about the Reich." He lowered his gaze. "Must I practice the indignity of repetition?"

"No," I said, shaking my head.

His intense blue eyes locked on me and behind them I saw something frightening, something that sent me shuddering in my chair—a flash of unadulterated hate.

"Something terrible is happening with Hans and Sophie—I know it and I can't be part of it, and, I hope you won't be part of it, either."

My breath caught in my throat. How much did Garrick know about the White Rose? What was he getting at, or hoping to find out? My only recourse was to deny his words.

I opened my arms in a plaintive gesture. "I haven't seen Hans in weeks and I only see Sophie in class. The three of us haven't talked." That was the truth, and I hoped my admission would finish the conversation. Any further discussion would drive me into lies.

His anger faded, and a spot of warmth flickered in his eyes.

"I do care for you, Natalya," he said. "Please understand my feelings, but it would be better for both of us if we went our separate ways." He picked up his hat, placed it on his head, and patted Katze, who had settled next to him. "Good-bye, Katze. I know you'll be well taken care of."

He rose from my bed and started toward the door. His parting words had touched me and, impulsively, I hugged him.

Underneath the tan coat, a pistol butt stuck into my ribs. Not expecting my embrace, he pulled away in surprise, as if I had struck him. In that brief instant, I saw the outline of the weapon, holstered from his shoulder. It wasn't against the law for German men to carry certain weapons, but its presence shook me to the core. I thought of the gun I'd smashed into the head of the SS man.

Garrick was out the door before I could say good-bye. With mixed feelings, I watched as he raced down the street, and, I believed, out of my life.

Two days later, Frau Hofstetter screamed at me from the sitting room. "Natalya! Come into the sitting room. Quickly! Quickly!"

I rushed from the dresser, where I'd been studying, and flung open the door to find her bent over the radio next to her favorite chair. The oil lamp sputtered on the table beside it. The stove's fire had waned, and I shivered in the chilly air.

"A few days ago, the radio played the *Adagio* from Bruckner . . . announcing the defeat. Rumors have been circulating." She fiddled with the volume, turning up the sound until it boomed throughout the room, her shawl falling in gentle folds from her shoulders.

I had no idea what the "rumors" were.

A bright fanfare of trumpets followed the slow pounding of drums; then, a solemn male voice intoned through the speaker: "The battle for Stalingrad has ended. The Sixth Army, under the exemplary leadership of Marshal Paulus, true to its oath to fight to the last breath, has succumbed to the enemy's superiority and unfavorable circumstances . . ."

I pictured the bodies, Russian and German, and my thoughts retreated to the grounds of war.

Snow, deep enveloping snow. So cold you can't feel your hands or your feet, then your body turns warm, almost boiling hot, before the dark destroys you. Coats buried under crested waves of white, blood frozen upon the glittering crystals, crimson turning to black in the bitter winter cold. Bodies piled upon bodies, row upon row, like stiff carcasses hung in a butcher's shop. Stunned, I stood rooted in place, and a lump rose in my throat culminating in sobs and tears for the dead. I cried not for the Wehrmacht, not for the Nazis who were shot and killed, but for all the dead, no matter the side, in a world gone mad. I thought of Sina and her children again and the others slaughtered that day, along with the thousands, the hundreds of thousands, the millions dying because one man believed *he* could conquer the world. *He* was the monster that had created this destruction, a modern Hydra striking at all within his serpentine reach.

Frau Hofstetter shuffled to me, placing her arm around my waist, tears glistening in her eyes.

". . . However, one thing can be stated—the sacrifice was not in vain . . ." The radio droned on, the words barely registering with me. ". . . the hardest fighting and most bitter hardship . . ."

Munich hushed in the winter silence. We Germans had never heard such news during the years of victory after Nazi victory. A bombing raid would have been nothing compared to the psychological damage coming from the radio. Were these deaths in vain? Perhaps this loss would turn the German people against Hitler; these German deaths might give added strength to those of us who resisted, the people who wanted the tyrant's despicable rule to end.

I wondered what Hans, Sophie, and Alex were thinking at this moment. Were they celebrating a defeat? Probably not—perhaps they were angered, furious, Hans working on his next leaflet or poised to take an even more daring leap into resistance, the others plotting their own form of treason.

The sorrows of Russia. A mother's tears as she held onto her children's hands, the rifles poised behind her back. An apartment long ago in Leningrad, a cat that loved to be petted; the possession I adored more than anything in the world. Russia burst with pain, the people stoic in their misery, a country filled with woe from the hands of a leader as authoritarian and tyrannical as the one we lived under now. My father shook from fear, worried that somehow he would be the next to disappear under Stalin's rule; my mother ill from too many tears. They had no choice but to give up everything, suffer the long and bitter journey to Germany. As a child, I was unaware of the depth of their sadness. Only after a trip that never seemed to end, until we arrived in Munich, did any joy return to our battered lives. Germany's deliverance left us laced with bittersweet smiles. As a child, I had loved my homeland. I was sad to go. My journey to the Russian Front had revived melancholy memories among the tragedy on the steppes.

I left my landlady and returned to my room as the strains of a military funeral march, *Ich hatt' einen Kameraden*, played on the radio.

Truckloads of people never came back from the forest. Now thousands upon thousands of German soldiers are dead.

Later that afternoon, we were told that all forms of entertainment in Germany would be closed for three days, even restaurants and cafés.

After the announcement, I had no doubt the "true" Germans
would rise from their seats wherever they were, sing the anthem,
and extend their hands in the salute. Their cries would echo
throughout the land, but not for the same reason as mine.

I returned to my dresser and tried to study, but the pen
slipped from my trembling hands. I looked to the street, the
world as still as a Christmas Eve night, no one passing by on the
icy walk, the trees as naked as the raw emotions filling my body.
I closed my book.

"Did you hear the news?" Alex threw his coat on my bed
and patted his arms with his gloved hands to stave off the cold.

I hadn't expected a visit from anyone the evening of the Stalingrad announcement but considering my bleak mood, I was
happy to see a friend. He paced like a horse in a pen, stepping
back and forth from my dresser to my bed as Katze's green eyes
followed him about the room.

"Sit down, Shurik. You're making me nervous." I offered
him my chair, but instead he sat on my bed after taking off
his gloves. "If you're referring to Stalingrad . . . Frau Hofstetter
and I heard it on the radio."

"Is she here?" he asked.

"Of course," I said. "It's after seven. She's usually in bed by
nine." The radio had filtered through the hall into my room all
day, although the Frau had lowered the volume after the announcement.

"I don't want to be overheard." He leaned back, unbuttoned
his jacket, and loosened the pale tie around his neck, which
streamed down the length of his white shirt. "What a day—I
can't decide whether to laugh or cry."

"Most Germans are crying," I said.

"Professor Huber is furious. He was incensed by the news of
the deaths. I'm sure he'll have much to say—as far as his words
can take him."

He cracked a smile, and I understood what he meant. We could only say so much about the Reich; our public conversations would remain a series of coded words and innuendo as long as Hitler was in power. He combed his fingers through his hair and a bluish-white burst of static electricity popped from the tip of a finger to his head. "Ouch!"

I laughed and put my hand over my mouth, hoping that Frau Hofstetter hadn't heard my outburst.

Alex slipped from the bed and settled at my feet, much as he had done at Sina's hut. The fleeting memory brought back a pleasant feeling of warmth and kinship with our Russian host. I wished for another bottle of vodka to share.

"How are you—really—tell me the truth?" he asked softly, his long legs folded beneath him, his face filled with melancholy longing. "How is Garrick?"

"I haven't seen him in days. He told me we're through."

His eyes widened. "Really. Why?"

"He thinks Hans and Sophie are planning something—something terrible—he wants to be part of it, but he feels excluded because they haven't welcomed him into their inner circle. It's as if he's obsessed with them."

Alex clucked his tongue. "He's guessing, and it's a good guess, but his eagerness makes us all suspicious and on edge. We must keep an eye on him." He tilted his head and the light from the desk lamp cast a golden glow on his hair.

I leaned toward him. "I won't be watching him."

He clasped my hands. "Despite what we've seen and suffered, I look back with fondness on our time in Russia. I wish we'd had more time to get to know each other."

I'd never heard such sadness in his voice, as if he expected, or *knew*, some disaster was about to befall us. I withdrew my hands from his and touched his face.

"Is everything all right, Alex? Are you, Hans, and Sophie keeping something from Lisa and me?"

"I dream of Russia, the grass rippling in waves across the wide land, the sun ripening the golden wheat in June, the snow covering the earth in endless white in December. I wish we could ride together over the steppes." He paused and tried to smile, but failed. "No, the White Rose is keeping nothing from you—nothing that can't be told."

His face brightened and his eyes twinkled in the lamplight. "But something is happening tonight—a response to the news." He leaned closer, his voice no more than a whisper. "We're going to paint the town."

"What?"

"Hans, Willi, and I will be painting slogans in response to the senseless murders perpetrated by the Führer."

"Where?"

"Anywhere we can . . . as many as we can."

A chill raced over me as I pictured the men racing from building to building, corner to corner, always one step ahead of the authorities. "That's madness. Out in the open? If you're not shot on the spot, you'll be arrested and executed."

"It's a risk we're prepared to take—for the truth." He looked at his watch. "I should be going. I'm meeting them at the studio to gather the paint and the brushes."

"You'll need someone to keep watch."

He shook his head and got up from the floor. "You said it yourself—it's madness. Don't worry, we'll be armed."

The chance to do something after today's news, to make a statement, for our voices to be heard, filled me with joy. My pulse quickened in anticipation; I wanted to go despite the danger. The memory of Nuremberg arose in my mind, but this would be different. In Nuremberg, I'd been alone with Lisa. Here, in Munich, a city I knew, I'd be with three men I trusted.

I'd made up my mind. "I'm coming. I'll make a nuisance of myself if you put up a fight."

He kissed my cheek and then his face lit up with a smile. "You are a crazy Russian, but like all from our homeland you know what it's like to fight and suffer." He grabbed his coat and gloves from my bed. "Let's go."

I grabbed my winter apparel, and we hurried from my apartment. Down the street, a match flashed and the silhouette of a man disappeared behind a tree. I alerted Alex and both of us stopped, Alex even stepping to the other side to get a better view. The man wasn't Garrick, as I suspected, and we continued on our way to the studio where Hans had printed his leaflets.

As conspirators in the night, we plotted our movements around the city. To say our actions were intricately planned would be false; however, our impulsiveness generated an excitement that filled the studio of Manfred Eickemeyer, not far from Dieter Frank's in Schwabing.

When Alex and I arrived, Hans skulked away and sat scowling at the table. Alex went to him and for several minutes they sparred with each other over whether I should join in the operation as a lookout. Alex was for it, Hans against, but in the end Russian stubbornness won out after Alex reminded his friend that this evening was "my idea." Indeed, Alex had also crafted the large stencils to be used for the paintings. Willi, attired in his army uniform, sat by, saying little, but I could tell from his grim face and tense body that he was eager to get on with the task.

The stencils read *DOWN WITH HITLER* and *FREEDOM*; yet another branded Hitler as a mass murderer. Alex concealed the stencils in a bag. Hans, armed with a pistol, was selected as the main lookout. Willi was to carry the paints, and I the brushes. The primary paint was a greenish-brown mixture with a tarlike consistency—hard to scrub off and whose color would attract a great deal of attention in the morning. We also carried red and white paints. Alex had the idea to paint white swastikas and deface them with a slash of brilliant red.

Hans informed us of the strategy: "The night will be our ally—the streets dark and empty, but we'll make the most of the late hour, painting our slogans where they will be seen by the masses."

He leaned against the table, his arms propped behind him for support, his black hair tussled, his handsome face coloring like blush wine in the dim light. He seemed like an unlikely young army general thrust into battle, directing his troops for the first time. The electricity in the room, the rush of adrenaline, thrilled me, but I knew the risk—our lives were in danger.

"I'll use this pistol only if I'm forced to," Hans continued. "Remember our purpose. If we're spotted or approached the best tactic will be to split up and run. Let nothing drag you down, either person or matériel." He put on his coat. "Get home safely if the worst happens."

I gathered my courage at the door. As we stepped into the night, Alex and Willi led the way. Hans drew me aside. "Sophie knows nothing of this. She would be upset if she knew you were here in her place."

His words did nothing to encourage me and I wondered if Sophie, when she found out, would be angry. Hans locked the door and, saying little, we followed the others.

We stopped first at an apartment building near the university. I stood watch with Hans, his hand on the pistol concealed in his coat, as Alex and Willi painted. They worked in quick strokes, slapping the paint across the stencil until *FREEDOM* was freshly painted upon the stone. Alex then drew a white swastika next to the slogan, which Willi marred with a bright red slash. The two then stuffed the wet stencil and brushes into the large paint bag. We repeated the process at another nearby building, grateful for the quiet streets and the lack of police.

"We should go to the Feldherrnhalle," Hans suggested.

"No," Willi replied. "Too many guards."

Of course, Willi was right. An around-the-clock armed vigil was held at the Feldherrnhalle, a Nazi shrine for those fallen in the Beer Hall Putsch. I found it hard to believe that Hans would even suggest such an action, considering the risk. Perhaps he was getting too cocky, too smug in his thinking.

At a corner formed by two large buildings, Alex and Willi

painted *HITLER THE MASS MURDERER* as Hans kept watch on the street. I focused on the blacked-out windows of nearby apartment buildings. As we finished, a man in a sable-colored coat turned the corner a few blocks away. We quietly packed up our materials and left, the man still well away from us.

We came to the university library, where Alex and Willi painted *DOWN WITH HITLER* in green paint on the wall. Despite our frayed nerves, our luck held with no sightings of police or pedestrians. Long after we began our task, we ended it at that site.

We returned the stencils and paint to the studio, and were thankful for a job well done. Alex escorted me back to my apartment and then headed to Hans's, where the men planned to celebrate with a good bottle of wine. Their high spirits, however, were sure to awaken Sophie, who would soon learn what we had done.

My gleeful mother phoned the next morning. I took the call in Frau Hofstetter's sitting room but kept my voice to a murmur. My landlady was preparing her breakfast; the sizzle and smell of fried eggs drifted in from the kitchen.

"The slogans are everywhere," my mother said, her excitement mounting with each word. "Have you seen them? Everyone is terrified, yet thrilled beyond belief." She paused to catch her breath. "I know the people are happy, Talya! To *see* such words on the walks and buildings written about . . ." She stopped, unwilling to say "Hitler."

Mother, I wanted to say, *watch what you say because your phone may be tapped. Your husband—my father—was arrested for reading illegal books! Whether he's a Nazi now makes no difference to the Reich. Who knows, the Gestapo may be listening to the Frau's line.*

"Say no more, Mother. I just woke up." She had no idea I was involved in the action. "I'm headed to class soon." She ignored my warning.

"The police are everywhere, hovering over the workers trying to scrub off the paint. The guards are giving them a hard
time and the poor ladies are working as if their lives depended
on it. The paint won't come off without a fight."

We hadn't planned on there being consequences for poor
scrubwomen. "Let me eat breakfast, get dressed, and I'll see
what the furor is about."

"I wish your father were home," my mother said. "I'm count-
ing the days."

"So am I," I said, and wondered if my father would return
to his normal self when released from prison. I hung up and
dressed for class. Frau Hofstetter asked me if everything was all
right with my mother.

"More than all right," I replied. "For the first time in months,
she's in a good mood."

In less than an hour, I was at the university. A crowd had
gathered around the entrance, but the students in it moved, circled, and shifted like a line of travelers catching a train. I inched
closer, cleaning my glasses with my handkerchief as I pushed
forward to see what everyone was staring at. Of course, I knew.

As I came into sight of the still readable words *DOWN
WITH HITLER* on the wall, I saw the familiar face of Sophie
Scholl, her shoulder-length hair now longer than it had been in
the fall. She wore a heavy gray sweater and a plain skirt and
her gaze centered on the frantic scrubbing of the two Russian
women whose brush-laden hands worked in broad mechanical
strokes over the painted letters—slave workers captured by the
Reich in the recent campaign.

I crept up behind her. No guards were in place, just students
who took a look, most in surprised horror, a few showing smug
distress for the affronted Reich. To my dismay, Sophie remarked
to the women as students passed by, "Leave it, so it may be read.
Why else would it be there?"

I clutched her shoulder and pulled her out from the jostling
crowd. I doubted whether the Russian women understood her
German words or even knew what they were trying to erase.

Sophie's hair flipped in the breeze, and she shot me a look that would break glass. We stopped near the end of the building, far away from the distraction, so we could talk undisturbed. For a time, we stared at each other, me wearing my dark coat, she in the sweater, as if we were two boxers sizing each other up for a match.

"It should have been me rather than you," she said in a tone very near a scolding. "What if something had happened—there's no need to involve two families. I told Hans that I would go the next time—I will stand as lookout. He tries so hard to keep me out of things."

I couldn't blame her for being put out; on the other hand, I had been willing to take the risk and Alex had come to me, either by plan or coincidence.

"Be careful of what you say," I said with a touch of anger in my voice. "The crowd has ears." I immediately felt like my words were misdirected at someone who knew the obvious. Didn't she care who heard her words? She was getting as brazen as her brother. I shook my head and took a step backward. "I'm sorry. I shouldn't be telling you what to do, but what you said might get back to the Gestapo."

Sophie stared at me, her gaze cutting past me, as if she were looking toward the gossamer landscape of a far-away country. "My brother, Alex, and Willi were drunk with excitement when they came home last night. We shared a bottle of wine, but I want to share more than drink—there's so little to make us happy these days. This morning, Germans, all over Munich, were stopped in their tracks by the slogans. The police had to break up traffic jams. What an achievement."

"Just be cautious," I said.

She looked over her shoulder at the women scrubbing at the words, the students taking peeks and then slinking away as if too much attention paid might link them to the crime.

"The time for caution is over," she said, turning back to me. "Someone had to start this, and now it will continue."

The wind ruffled the collar of her sweater. She blinked and turned away.

I followed her to the university entrance, only minutes from the start of my class. As Sophie disappeared in the crowd, I couldn't help but wonder how far she and her brother would go; how far they would let caution fall from their lives to bolster the reputation of the White Rose.

I was soon to find out.

CHAPTER 10

No one in the White Rose knew what Hans and Sophie had planned for February 18, 1943. Not Alex, not Willi, and certainly not Lisa and me.

When I thought about it later, the decision to drop leaflets at the university seemed rash, one borne of impetuous youth, an act of hubris, of self-importance gone awry, but that was me trying to make sense of their actions, surely not the thinking of Hans and Sophie. The White Rose had managed to evade the authorities, but Hans knew he was being followed, and he may have suspected that time was running out. Perhaps that was why he and his sister were so determined not to involve others in dropping the last of the printed leaflets.

Before that fateful day, Alex told me that the men had journeyed out on two other nights to paint slogans in Munich, including DOWN WITH HITLER at the Feldherrnhalle, which Hans had suggested the night I was with them. How they achieved it, within eyesight of the guards who kept vigilant watch over the Nazi shrine, I never found out because the events of February 18 thwarted our actions.

A warm sun greeted me that morning as I stepped from my apartment. Katze had jumped onto the windowsill as he usually did when I departed for class, and I blew him a kiss. The air thrummed with a pleasant breeze, wafting the rich smell of the thawing earth over me. Winter's end seemed imminent and the promise of an early spring assured. I had no premonition, no

sudden fear about the day; in fact, the bright sun fed my good
mood as I walked to the university. My optimistic disposition
continued on my journey, despite the bare poplar trees lining
the street, and the cool air still lingering in the shadows.

Lisa and I exchanged greetings in the Lichthof, the grand
atrium of the building, with its open gallery and grand staircase, and then headed to our respective classes housed next to
each other on the second floor. I sat through a particularly un-
interesting biology lecture, more concerned about getting a taste
of the good weather than listening to the professor talk about
animal zygote formation. When the bell rang and the classroom
doors opened, I met Lisa in the gallery corridor along with the
other students, who in a bustling crowd pushed to their next
lecture.

A rough bellow rose above the general commotion as we
neared the balustrade. "You're under arrest!" The man shouted
his words again as an electric shock raced through my body.
Lisa clutched my hand and we looked across the gallery to the
staircase. What I saw sent me into a tailspin that made my stomach turn over. Lisa must have felt the same—feelings that we
had to conceal from the other students. A custodian, whom I'd
seen before in the building, pointed and screamed at two people
who stood immobile on the stairs.

We watched with dread as the man directed his rage at Hans
and Sophie Scholl.

Hans carried a large suitcase; Sophie was close by his side. As
far as Lisa and I could see, our two friends remained calm, pro-
claiming their innocence in muffled voices, their bodies erect,
yet somehow relaxed, as if they had practiced the posture in
case of their arrest.

"The hall is locked," the man yelled. "You can't get away—I
know what you've done. Come with me." He picked up one of
the many leaflets spread across the Lichthof floor, which I assumed had been tossed from the gallery above, and clutched it
in his hands.

Muted conversations broke out among the students as the
custodian herded Hans and Sophie up the stairs to the Chancel-

lor's office. The door closed and our two friends disappeared from view.

Lisa shuddered and we looked at each other, fear bubbling in her eyes—but we knew we *couldn't* speak, *shouldn't* speak for fear of incriminating ourselves. Saying nothing, we made our way through the crowd to the atrium floor, where we gazed upon the scattered papers. One student picked up a leaflet, read a few lines and then dropped it as if it were on fire. Others kept their distance from the strewn papers, which also had been deposited outside classroom doors and in the laps of the marble statues decorating the hall.

I read the first few lines of the tract in silence: *Fellow Students! Shaken and broken, our nation is confronted with the downfall of the men of Stalingrad. Three hundred and thirty thousand German men have been senselessly and irresponsibly driven to death and destruction by the inspired strategy of our World War I Private First Class. Führer, we thank you!*

I read no further because the doors burst open and a flood of police and Gestapo agents poured into the hall. Lisa nodded at me and then broke away, assuming it was safer to be apart than together.

The agents brushed past each of us with unflinching eyes, scrutinizing us from head to toe with neither a sneer nor smirk, but with enough of an inspection to make me feel guilty beneath my skin. I supposed they did this hoping that someone other than Hans and Sophie would admit to the crime, but no one broke, no one came forward. Their presence quieted the milling crowd. Two of the agents methodically gathered the leaflets in their gloved hands: from the floor, from the laps of the statues, from around the classroom doors. "Turn over any you have to us," they shouted to the students. A few came forward with sheepish looks and handed the papers to the agents.

Panic overtook me and I tried with all my might to squelch it. My hands tightened and my fingers reddened from the fists I had unintentionally made. A hundred questions, or so it seemed, raced through my mind. What would happen to Hans and

Sophie? What would happen to me? If I was arrested, would the agents come after my mother and father? I imagined the Gestapo dragging my mother from her apartment; my father being beaten by the guards so he would confess the guilt of his treasonous daughter. What of Alex and Willi and even Professor Huber? What would happen to Garrick and the others involved with the White Rose, no matter how minor their roles?

These black thoughts were too much to bear and I struck them from my mind. I took careful breaths to calm myself and turned my face away from the other students.

As I fought back tears, the police and agents continued their work, until the Chancellor's door opened, and I watched, stunned, as Hans and Sophie stepped out, both handcuffed. My friends, surrounded by long-coated Gestapo agents, were pushed forward through the crowd, their eyes fixed straight ahead, neither of them glancing at anyone they knew. They were ushered out the door and into a waiting car.

That was the last time I laid eyes upon Hans and Sophie Scholl.

Much later, we were released from the hall. I stepped over the tiled head of Medusa encircled by stars, through the doors of the Lichthof, past the stone arches and into the sun. The warmth felt strange against my skin after the chill that had shaken me inside. Students had gathered outside as well, unable to get into the building, unintentional observers to Hans and Sophie's arrest. Lisa, without a look or word, passed by me and turned south on Leopoldstrasse, certainly headed home to brood about the arrest, as was I, both of us stupefied by what had happened.

I spotted Alex Schmorell on the edge of the crowd, standing tall and aloof. He apparently had watched as Hans and Sophie had been taken away. It was dangerous to draw attention to each other, so I kept my distance. He vanished like the sun blotted out by a cloud and I was left with the memories of Russia, Sina, our times together at Hans's apartment, the confrontation with Garrick at Ode, and the tempestuous night of painting anti-Nazi slogans, wondering if I would ever see him again.

Despair filled me. As much as I hated to think it, as much as I wished for everything to return to the way it had been, those times were over.

The White Rose was crumbling around me.

I spent a fitful night, barely sleeping at all, comforted only by Katze. Every brush of wind against the door, every shadow that managed to creep around the blackout curtains chilled my blood. I expected the Gestapo to knock on my door at any moment. The thought of escaping crossed my mind, but to where? I couldn't in good conscience leave my mother; travel was difficult in the winter despite the springlike weather; my friends would be of no use—it would be better if I stayed away from Lisa. My closest relatives were in Russia and a journey to Leningrad was impossible—even if they were still alive to welcome me.

In the morning, I looked at myself in the bathroom mirror. What greeted me was the image of a woman older than her years, black hair disheveled, plumlike circles showing under the rims of her glasses, a frown that couldn't be undone by mere good wishes and prayers.

I said nothing to Frau Hofstetter at breakfast except for a few sentences that I'm sure made little sense to her. "It's possible I may be away for a time. Would you please look after Katze while I'm gone?"

"What?" Her face puckered. "What's this about? You can't leave me with your cat. How will I get along with all the work that needs to be done around here?"

"My mother's not well," I said, making up an excuse. "I'll be back when I can."

"Well, you'd better, or you'll be out on your ear with no money."

I reassured her that I wouldn't walk out on her, but I'd planted the seed in case I needed to leave Munich.

I dressed and returned to the hall for my class with Professor Huber. He skulked about the auditorium with a scowl on his face, showing much less animation and enthusiasm than in previous lectures. I wondered what must be going through his mind now that Hans and Sophie had been taken away. After class, students murmured in the hall about the professor's physical and mental condition. I was not alone in noticing the change in his demeanor.

I walked back to my room as despondent as I had ever been in my life. I put the key into the door and was surprised to find it unlocked.

I grasped the knob and pulled it toward me.

He was sitting in my dresser chair at the foot of my bed, his booted feet resting upon my spread. The blackout curtains had been lifted, and when I opened the door fully, the light struck his blond hair. Katze was nowhere to be seen, but something dark and metallic on the sheets caught my attention. It was a Luger, which I recognized from its distinctive curved handgrip.

I closed the door. My nerves fired in unison and limbs tightened when I surveyed my room in shambles.

"How was class?" Garrick asked, casually, with no emotion. He pushed back in the chair, so it rested on its two hind legs, and lit a cigarette. "Do you have an ashtray?"

"You know I don't smoke."

"That glass will do," he said and pointed to my dresser.

The one I'd used for the rose he'd given me still sat there. I walked to my dresser, shocked by what I saw: the drawers had been pulled from the case, their contents dumped on the floor; my school notebooks and papers had been ripped apart, their pieces lying scattered beside clothes and toiletries.

I picked up the glass and handed it to him. My bed was in an equally deplorable state, the sheets wadded, crumpled, from a thorough search, the pillows ripped open, feathers lying in wispy piles on the floor.

"Where's Katze?" I asked, thinking that the worst had happened. Shaking, I took off my coat and sat on my ransacked bed within an arm's reach of the Luger.

"He's safe with the Frau." He smiled and crossed one leg over the other. "I hope you don't mind if I smoke, but I suppose at this point it doesn't make any difference. The Frau had no objections." He puffed on the cigarette and pointed to the pistol.

"You don't know what I had to go through to get that cat for you. I must have searched fifteen alleys before I found a mother and kittens." He lifted his right hand and formed the outline of a gun with his forefinger and thumb. "Boom, boom, boom, boom, boom," he said, his fingers repeating the action of each word. "One was still alive when I finished. I wondered whether I should finish Katze off today—put him out of his misery. He must have been a very unhappy cat living with a *traitor*, but I suppose you weren't able to fill his head with too many seditious ideas. I considered skinning him alive and leaving his carcass hanging from the door—but even I'm not that cruel."

"You . . . didn't," I stammered, a horrible understanding dawning upon me. "You . . . couldn't . . ."

"Couldn't what?" Garrick swung his legs from the bed to the floor and leaned toward me, parallel to my right side. "Couldn't kill a cat? Couldn't love you?"

I grasped my chest, unable to breathe for a moment.

"Relax. You'll have plenty of time to consider your betrayal of the Reich. I suppose you're wondering whether Hans and Sophie turned you in. I'll get to that in a minute, but first there's some unfinished personal business." He crushed his cigarette into the glass and lit another. "The real irony of the situation is that I really do care for you, but we got off on the wrong foot from the beginning. I told you the truth when I said we couldn't see each other anymore. I didn't want to get involved in something that might *disturb* my sleep."

My hand crept toward the Luger. Was I crazed enough to use it, fighting for my life like an animal in a trap?

Garrick looked at my hand. "Go ahead—shoot me." He picked up the pistol and wrapped my right hand around the grip, positioning my forefinger on the trigger. "One clean pull is all it would take." He guided my hand toward his head until the muzzle was positioned in the middle of his forehead. "Kill me, but if you do, you'll surely die. I'm of much better use to you alive than dead."

I sighted down the barrel. How easy it would be to put a bullet into his brain, but I knew he'd already declared himself the winner of his game. I'd be hunted down and exterminated if I played on. My mother and my father might die as well. The situation was hopeless. I released my grip on the weapon, and it fell harmlessly upon the bed.

"A wise choice." Garrick patted my hand, and then resumed his relaxed position in the chair. "Hans and Sophie told us everything."

"Us?"

"The Gestapo, of course. Don't play dumb, Natalya. The moment you walked in the door, you knew."

"I knew, but didn't want to believe it."

I also wanted to say, *I don't believe you. Hans and Sophie would never betray their friends,* but even saying that would be enough to incriminate me. I looked toward the door, thinking I might run away.

"Don't bother," he said. "There are two more agents outside—waiting." He drummed his fingers on his thighs. "God, how I hate this. I wanted things to be different—in all the months I tried to infiltrate this group, I hoped you'd be the one I could turn to, an informer who would turn them in for their traitorous activities. Imagine Hans and Sophie and Christoph Probst writing and distributing those terrible leaflets! Probst was an outsider. No one suspected him until Hans and Sophie were arrested. Lies told by Germans who took advantage of all the opportunities generously given by the Führer—our education, our welfare." He lifted the glass with the cigarette butt in it and studied it in the light. "If you look closely, you can see a rainbow. Sunlight broken into its component parts. *Broken*—just like Hans and Sophie and, I suppose, Alex. He's involved, too, I'm sure—but he's disappeared. He can't escape any more than you can. The White Rose is a house of cards about to fall."

"I don't know what Hans and Sophie have been doing," I said. "They haven't told me anything. And who is Christoph Probst?" Words failed me; my protest was weak and insignificant for I suspected the evidence must surely be mounting against Hans and Sophie.

"So you claim not to know Probst? When he was questioned

at the university, Hans tried to tear up and eat Probst's next diatribe. He failed and we matched the handwriting." Garrick sneered. "Even your defense is pathetic. You might as well tell me everything—or save it for the judge—but if I had the choice, I'd much rather confess to me than to him. He has a reputation for getting the truth out of those who come before him."

Katze meowed in the sitting room across the hall. His call was the only noise in the house.

"Why don't you arrest me?" I asked, my hands trembling as I spoke. "Get it over with, if that's what you want."

"It's not what I want," Garrick said. "It's what you've made for yourself."

"I have nothing more to say."

"But I do." He rose from the chair and pushed it across the floor to the dresser. "I hope the Frau doesn't mind what we did to her furniture. She can clean up the mess; it will give her something to do as she readies for a new tenant." He crushed his cigarette inside the glass and replaced it on the dresser. "How will your mother cope when she finds out that the two people she loves most are in prison? It'll be hard on her, so hard she might break."

I pushed myself off the bed and rushed toward him. "Leave my mother alone! She's suffered enough. She knows nothing of this."

He shoved me away, and I stumbled backward. Garrick crept toward me, inching closer to my face. "And still you know nothing? Well, here's what I know."

I fell back on the bed, fearful that he might strike me.

"There was an incident in Nuremberg, not long ago, where leaflets were distributed and an SS guard was assaulted by two young women. They knocked him silly, actually. He was lucky to wake up with nothing more than a bad cut and a headache. He put together a description of the women and sent it off to Berlin and Munich, along with the leaflets he found."

My throat tightened, tongue dry against the roof of my mouth. Garrick leaned over me, his mouth forming a cruel smile.

"I remember that night vividly despite having too much

schnapps," he said. "We had a date and you didn't show up. When I saw the leaflet and the description of the two women, it wasn't hard to figure out, especially when you lied about your whereabouts with Lisa Kolbe."

"I didn't lie," I said.

He grabbed my shoulders and shook me. "You're lying now!" He let go, stepped back, and pointed to the door. "Two agents are standing outside ready to take you to headquarters. They won't be as kind to you as I've been. Talk! Save yourself."

I stared at the floor, unable to speak.

"Lisa Kolbe's been arrested. She's on her way to Stadelheim Prison."

"I don't believe you. You're trying to get me to confess to something I didn't do."

He turned to me, his face flushing with rage, his body puffing up from his own sense of power like a man whipping a beast of the field. "Do you know a man by the name of Dieter Frank?"

Any sense of hope, any feeling that I might escape the Gestapo's clutches evaporated with his question. Of course, I knew the artist whose studio we used to prepare our leaflets. I realized I couldn't defend myself against his accusations; Lisa and I and the rest of the White Rose were finished. I shook my head, not looking at his face.

He grabbed my arm roughly, pulling me toward the door, my feet sliding over the floor, my gaze sweeping across the room that had been my sanctuary since I'd moved away from my parents, my studies and possessions strewn across the floor like chaff. I sobbed as he pushed me out into the arms of the two waiting Gestapo agents, one of whom slapped handcuffs on me.

I looked back briefly. Garrick picked up the pistol from the bed but said nothing to Frau Hofstetter, who stood near the open hall door with Katze in her arms, the cat's green eyes focused on me. The Frau's eyes were red and swollen.

The men led me down the walk, pushed me into the seat of a waiting sedan, slammed the door, and within seconds, I was on my way to Gestapo headquarters.

The house, Frau Hofstetter, and Katze faded away.

*   *   *

I had never been inside Wittelsbacher Palace, the Gestapo headquarters in Munich on Brienner Strasse, until the time of my arrest. Nothing stirred me in the car as we wound down the avenue toward the immense redbrick building with its arched cathedral windows—neither heat, nor cold, nor the cigarette smoke from one of the agents. The radio crackled, but none of the words made any sense. The world drifted by like I was in a small boat on a river, observing the shores through a smoky lens.

One of the agents, a man I knew only as Rohr, grabbed my right arm as we exited in front of the building. The other agent sped away in the car—Garrick had stayed behind. If the Renaissance-style structure wasn't formidable enough, the crowds who swarmed around the endless parade of criminal suspects intimidated me as well. Perhaps these people were part of a Gestapo plan, a tactic used to humble their prisoners. There were no boos or hisses, only suspicious eyes marked by intense stares and the desperate feeling that one could be attacked at any moment for an offense against the Reich.

We entered the headquarters. I was rushed up the steps to the second floor, where I was instructed to sit on a wooden bench until Rohr was ready to see me. A soldier stood guard, although he showed little concern for anything except his rifle, which he was polishing to a gleam with a handkerchief. My hands throbbed in my cuffs; my back ached and the unpleasant hall air pressed cool against my skin. To my left, on another bench, a group of young men and a woman sat in a daze. I didn't recognize any of them, but I wondered if the net thrown to capture the White Rose had been tossed over a wide sea. Most sat with their heads bowed, saying little or nothing to each other, with disquieting expressions on their faces.

Uncomfortable, I sat for about twenty minutes before a tall woman with a pad and pen opened the agent's door and escorted me inside. Rohr had taken off his coat and seated himself behind his large oak desk. His Nazi Party pin, affixed to the lapel of his brown suit, shone in its glory. He was a man of moderate size with black hair and oval face, not unpleasant in look or demeanor, but with the pinkish skin of a newborn, a florid characteristic innate to many native Bavarians. I had trouble analyzing him, a most inscrutable man who showed little emotion. Rohr, like me, wore glasses, but he had the annoying habit of putting them on and taking them off absentmindedly, as if they were a prop for his ego and official status.

He fumbled with his glasses, pinched his nose, and said to me, "Take a seat." The woman, a secretary, took her place in a dark corner and began recording our conversation on her pad. She would be a witness to all that went on in the room.

"What are the charges against me?" I asked impulsively, although he had not permitted me to speak.

He picked up a pen and tapped it on the large pile of documents in front of him. "I will ask the questions. You answer."

I nodded.

"How long have you known Herr Adler?"

I thought back to Kristallnacht, when he'd stood next to Lisa and me at the remains of the smoldering synagogue. Garrick's voice seeped into my head, a distant memory. "The SA set it on fire with gasoline, and then tried to throw the Rabbi in the flames. He wanted to save the Torah scrolls. They're dogs, all of them. They had the Rabbi arrested. He'll end up in Dachau for sure. Pigs." At the time, I thought he was referring to the SA— now I realized his hateful words were meant for Jews and the Rabbi. I had been blinded by a handsome man whom the Nazis used to good benefit.

"We met four years ago," I said, "but we've been acquainted for only a few months."

"Herr Adler has informed me of his investigation into the White Rose and his *association* with you." He stuck the pen cap in his mouth and sucked on it for a moment, then took off his glasses. "I believe you know more than you're telling . . . and we will sit here until the truth comes out."

I sat upright in my chair, hunger gnawing at my stomach, aware that Rohr intended to make this a long process.

He picked up a file from his desk, opened it, and shifted two brilliantly white sheets of paper under his desk lamp before returning his glasses to the bridge of his nose. "The charges against you are: attempted murder upon an agent of the Reich; treason by subversive acts, including the writing and distribution of seditious material, specifically in Nuremberg; *and* consorting with traitors and misfits. Do you have any idea what this means for you and your family? Your father has already been sentenced to prison for sedition. If you're lucky you might get an adjoining cell." His lips parted in a shallow smile.

"I have visited my father once since his imprisonment. He has sworn his allegiance to the Führer." I hoped the agent didn't hear in my voice the disappointment that filled my head. "He knows nothing of these charges levied against me. I am innocent."

He stared at me as if I were a disobedient child. "You didn't answer my question. Do you know what these charges mean? A *Sippenhaft*, a collective punishment"—he turned the lamp toward my face and suddenly the room became warm and uncomfortable—"and something far more lethal might be in store for you—execution. Do you know how the President of the People's Court doles out his ultimate penalty? By guillotine." He paused to let his words sink in. "However, it would be up to him to sentence you, or dispense leniency if he sees fit."

I twisted in my seat, trying to ease the pain of the handcuffs while imagining the flashing metal blade positioned above my neck. A violent tremble racked my body.

Rohr took note of my discomfort and turned to his secretary. "Unlock these, please, so we can get on with it. She's not going anywhere."

The woman rose, left to get the key, and returned after a few moments. She bent over me, grasping my hands, turning, twisting, until the cuffs clicked open and fell away. Relief poured into my arms and shoulders as the pressure subsided. I massaged the raw skin on my wrists while she returned to her seat.

"I'm sure we can have a civil conversation without fear of an escape attempt, can't we, Fräulein Petrovich?" He slid an oak box carved with Nazi insignia across his desk so it rested in front of me. "Cigarette?"

"I don't smoke."

He smiled. "Neither do I, but I find it relaxes some people—opens them up. Cigarettes can be hard to find these days." He returned the box to the corner of his desk and leaned back in his chair; his face disappeared in the glare. "Tell me the facts about the charges I've read. I caution you, I'll know if you're lying."

I squinted into the light. "They are false. I was in Nuremberg when I was a child. I passed through it on the train from Berlin when I returned from my nursing duty at the Eastern Front."

"Now I know you're lying. Your friend Lisa Kolbe tells a much different story. You accompanied her to Nuremberg."

I looked into the glare, determined not to show the tight fear that constricted my body. I was certain Rohr was bluffing, hoping to get me to admit to the crimes. Lisa would never betray me. We had taken an oath to protect one another—all those in the White Rose had sworn to do the same. Still, part of me wondered if she had been tortured; perhaps she had broken under the powerful blows of the Gestapo.

Sweat broke out on my brow from the heat. I thought of summer days, roses in bloom, and picnics with my parents in the Englischer Garten on the banks of the Isar, anything to take my mind off the shadowy figure of Rohr and his questions. I remained silent.

"All your friends are here or on their way to prison." His hands appeared from the halo and rested on the table, his fingers threaded together. "Hans Scholl, Sophie Scholl, Christoph Probst, Willi Graf. We know there will be others . . . your friend Alexander Schmorell."

"None of them have done anything—"

He leaned forward past the light; his pink face shining scarlet with anger. "How do you know that? I'm losing patience! There is a limit to my generosity when it comes to traitors! Your head will soon be on the block. Think on that for a time—while I eat my lunch."

Rohr lurched from his chair, shoved the file into his desk, and locked the drawer. The secretary followed him out, closing the door behind her.

I was alone in the locked room, and, for the first time since my arrest, my resolve began to crumble. What if Rohr's words were true? If Hans and Sophie and the others were under arrest, subject to Gestapo interrogation, what hope would there be for me? The *Sippenhaft* Rohr spoke of would come to pass and my mother, already of fragile mind because of my father's imprisonment, would be questioned and possibly sentenced to prison because her daughter was a danger to the state. I shook in my chair; my stomach ached and my head swam from lack of food.

Rohr had given me no orders to remain in my seat, so I got up and walked to the window. It was barred and at least ten to fifteen meters above the street, so escape was impossible. The clouds had thinned, throwing splashes of sun on the crowds below. Shivering, I sat down and studied the formal furnishings of the room: the grand oak desk, the green-felt ink blotter, the wall calendar with each day marked off by a red X, the rolled blackout shades, the unassuming draperies that hung from the top of the tall window to the floor, the chairs, some in red leather, others in gold fabric festooned with black swastikas. The room befitted the Gestapo and gave me no comfort in its opulence. I was alone with no one to help.

I hung my head and sobbed, trying desperately to keep my voice from rising to a pitiful scream. I tried my best to hide my tears by wiping my eyes on the hem of my dress.

Two hours passed before Rohr returned, accompanied by his secretary. He sat in his heavy oak chair, but this time lowered the lamp shade so the light wouldn't shine in my eyes. The afternoon was growing long and my stomach was tied into knots; my hunger had turned to apprehension. "It looks as if you've been crying," he said. "Are you ready to talk?"

I shook my head.

"Very well," he said. "You've had your chance. Your silence

is a testament to your guilt." He turned again to his secretary. "Take her away."

The woman approached me with the cuffs but said nothing as Rohr held my hands behind my back. A female guard escorted me to a basement cell containing a small window. She took off the cuffs and told me that another guard would be back soon with paperwork for me to fill out. I would have no visitors, she added.

Orders were given: change into a prison dress; complete paperwork giving name, address, and other personal facts; don't make noise; the lights will be on all night. A guard brought a small meal of bread and cheese, the sun set, and the lights blazed on in my cell. I crawled into bed and pulled the blanket over my head, trying to block out the constant illumination. It took me several hours to fall asleep, after which I dreamed of my parents, Lisa, and the White Rose. The nightmares were horrible visions of death and blood, screams before the guillotine blade fell, lopping off heads into a metal bucket—sights too terrible to envisage, too terrible to sleep through. Many times I woke up during the night, sopped with sweat, my arms and legs numb with tension, convinced that I was going to die.

CHAPTER 11

———»·o·«———

Rohr questioned me for hours on Saturday and Sunday, even telling me how much the Führer had suffered under the negative onslaught of those who didn't believe in his vision of Germany under the Reich.

"You have no idea how our gracious and kind leader has suffered from those who try at every turn to undermine his authority," he spouted, his voice brimming with indignity. "To restore the heritage of our people, to rid our land of those who would pollute it; these goals are what our benevolent Führer seeks. Only through his voice and wisdom can we build a better Germany."

Over and over he questioned me about the White Rose, informing me that the trial for Hans, Sophie, and Christoph would be held on Monday. Late Sunday afternoon, he announced with glee that Roland Freisler, the President of the People's Court, would be presiding over their trial. He slashed a finger across his neck in a quick stroke. "It's dark and I'm tired," he said. "You're going back to your cell to think about all I've told you. I'll be busy tomorrow at the Palace of Justice. You and Lisa Kolbe will be tried on Tuesday unless you confess to your crimes." He picked up my file and placed it under his arm. "I wish you a good night. Because you've had nothing to say for yourself for three days, I can't imagine you'll have anything to add tomorrow." He took off his glasses and squinted at me. "Your trial will go forward. . . . Believe me."

He and his secretary left the office, leaving me in the company of a female guard who handcuffed me and then led me back to my cell.

Exhausted and numb, I tumbled onto my cot, hoping that I might soon eat the cold soup and stale bread that had been served to me the last two nights, hardly fit to eat but better than starving. Despite the feeling that I was somewhere other than on earth, perhaps on some distant planet fabricated from a dream, I was proud that I had not bent under Rohr's questioning. I'd remained mute for most of those hours, wondering if Lisa had done the same, while knowing nothing of the fates of my other friends in the White Rose.

Rohr was correct. Only guards and servers visited me on Monday. I had hours to contemplate the warm February day, while standing in the shafts of brilliant sun that poured through my small window. Of course, I wasn't able to leave my cell to enjoy the early spring weather, and as the sun moved on and sank in the west, anxiety built up in my head and chest, pressing my ribs against my side and causing my skull to feel as if it might explode. The crushing duress turned to depression as night fell.

About six in the evening, a woman I had never seen before entered my cell after being let in by a guard. She was of medium build and height with chestnut hair, somewhat pretty, but what struck me most were her eyes. A kind softness emanated from them despite the fact that they were raw from crying. Her gaze looked as if it had been prescribed from heaven, but I knew from her clothes that she was a prisoner too.

"I'd like to sit with you, if you don't mind," she said, and seated herself on the edge of my cot. "The guards will come back for me in twenty minutes."

Immediately, my defenses went up. Who was this woman and why would she want to visit me? Was she really a prisoner or was she a Gestapo agent attempting to coerce a confession from a defeated inmate?

I scooted back on my thin mattress, my back to the cold

stone wall, much too tired to spar with this woman. "Who are you?" I asked.

"I'm sorry." She took a handkerchief from her sleeve and dabbed her eyes. "It's been a trying day for many, including me—not everyone here is bad." She extended her hand. "I'm Else Gebel. I work in administration, processing, filing—those are the tasks given to a political prisoner."

Not knowing if her story was true, I had no desire to shake her hand.

She withdrew hers. "I'm here to look over your cell . . . to make sure you can't commit suicide."

"You needn't worry," I said, and tugged at the blanket and sheet. "I can't hang myself from the window."

"No, you can't and I don't think you will. . . ." She lowered her gaze to the cold stone floor. "Over the past four days, I got to know Sophie Scholl." She paused and her body sagged, as if her words had drained her strength.

"What makes you think I know Sophie . . . Scholl? Is that the woman's name?"

She raised her head, her gaze still radiating the kindness I had observed. "Agents talk. Rumors circulate at the headquarters. Sophie was hardly more than a child, but one of immense maturity and unyielding courage."

I slumped in the corner, pulling the blanket over my legs, as I waited with dread for her to continue.

"She's dead," Else said, her eyes filling with tears that rolled down her flushed cheeks and fell in black streaks on her gray prison dress.

"Dead . . . Sophie dead. . . . It can't be true. . . ." I moaned, my cry small and guttural from the pain that knotted my stomach.

Else, trembling with sorrow, bent toward me and clutched my hand. "Cry. . . . It's all we have. I've cried for hours now."

Be strong, be strong, I kept repeating to myself, resisting the temptation to give in to agony, forcing myself not to break down in a heap upon the bed. I breathed deeply and attempted to calm my agitated soul. "It's too fast . . . too soon. . . . Convicted and executed in one day?"

Else released my hand. "Convicted in hours, not a day. No one escapes from Hitler's 'hanging judge.' The others are dead too."

I capped my hands over my mouth and stifled a scream. If only Else Gebel was a dream, an apparition, an angel of death with kind eyes come to tempt me and fill me with lies. If I closed my eyes, would she be gone? I did so, but when I opened them she was still there, her face and hair frozen in the cell's garish light, her shadow creased across the bed and floor.

"Who are the others?" I asked weakly.

"Hans Scholl, Christoph Probst . . . all guillotined this afternoon." She wiped her eyes. "The prison seems deserted today. Instead of the sounds of many coming and going these last days, there is silence. After two o'clock we received the frightful news from the headquarters: all three sentenced to death!"

"Did you talk with Sophie?"

"I was her cellmate, placed there to keep her from killing herself. . . . And now she's gone."

We sat with our sorrow, but Else's time was growing short.

"Sophie made me promise to tell her story, and I will honor that promise," she said. "She had a dream last night: On a beautiful sunny day she brought a child in a long white dress to be baptized. The way to the church was up a steep mountain, but she carried the child safely and firmly. Unexpectedly there opened up before her a crevice in the glacier. She had just enough time to lay the child safely on the other side before she plunged into the abyss. She interpreted the dream this way: 'The child in the white dress is our idea; it will prevail in spite of all obstacles. We were permitted to be prisoners, but we must die early for the sake of that idea.'"

My heart rejoiced at the prophetic power of the dream. The idea, our work, would prevail despite our deaths, the deaths of countless thousands; the vision of the White Rose would outlive the Reich.

"The agent who interrogated Sophie was shaken by the experience," Else continued. "I saw him about four thirty; he was still in his hat and coat, white as chalk. I asked him, 'How did she take the sentence? Did you have a chance to talk to Sophie?' In a tired voice, he answered, 'She was very brave. I talked with her in Stadelheim Prison. And she was permitted to see her parents.'

"Fearfully, I asked him, 'Is there no chance at all for a plea of mercy?' He looked up at the clock on the wall and said softly in a dull voice, 'Keep her in your thoughts during the next half hour. By that time she will have come to the end of her suffering.'"

Else balled her fist as if it were a bludgeon and struck it on the cot. "Three good, innocent persons have to die because they dared rise against an organized band of murderers, because they wanted to help end this senseless war. I should like to scream those things at the top of my lungs, and I have to sit here silent. 'Lord have mercy on them, Christ have mercy on them, Lord have mercy on their souls,' is all I can think."

The cell door shuddered from a heavy knock, and a woman's harsh voice rose above the sound. "Else! Time's up! You're needed in the receiving room."

She rose from the cot and pulled me into her arms. "I have been here for more than a year and don't expect to be out until the war is over. Let me give you a hug. God be with you. Remember these thoughts—the same I had for Sophie. 'You have returned to the light. May the Lord give you eternal rest, and may the eternal light shine upon you.' I'll bring you sausages and butter and real coffee in the morning. Try to sleep. Tomorrow will be a hard day."

The door opened and Else hurried from my cell into the hall. The door thudded to a close behind her and once again I was alone. Shaken and dazed by her words, I fell upon my mattress and curled up in a ball. I wanted to cry but no tears came. All I felt was an overwhelming sense of hopelessness caused by an oppressive combination of depression, grief, isolation, and hunger.

My trial was scheduled for the next day, and I would plead my innocence. However, Freisler's ears wouldn't hear "not guilty," when he had the chance to snuff out the White Rose or anyone else he deemed an enemy of the Reich. Else was right, tomorrow would be hard, but out of kindness she'd made no mention that Tuesday, February 23, might be my last day on earth.

Else's words about Sophie comforted me.

I wondered if I had been visited by an angel.

Else returned at seven the next morning, proving she was a real person. Other than a brief conversation about how I slept, and my fawning over the sausages and real coffee she'd managed to gather for me, we had little time to talk.

We were interrupted by my attorney.

He thrust out his arm in the Nazi salute before he even introduced himself. A guard brought in a chair so he could sit. Else smiled sadly, said good-bye, and left my cell.

"I am Gerhart Lang," the man said coldly, a sneer creeping into his voice. "I have been appointed by the court to handle your case."

He was nothing like his name, Lang—he was short rather than tall—a man who I judged had a fondness for rich food and good wine—confirmed by his ample belly and thick arms and legs. His oversize coat barely came together over his stomach. However, his face showed none of the typical floridness of the Bavarian character; rather, his complexion was pale and bloodless as if he spent most of his time in the company of books and ill-lit offices, while nurturing a healthy disdain for people—particularly traitors.

"We only have a few minutes," he said, planting his fat palms firmly on his thighs. He carried no briefcase, no files, giving me an indication that I was, in fact, already guilty. "What do you have to say for yourself? How will you plead?"

"Not guilty, of course."

He clicked his tongue against his teeth and shook his head. "My dear girl, why prolong the agony? I've seen the court papers, heard the confessions. The President of the People's Court may go easier on you if you plead guilty."

My breakfast grew cold by my side, adding to my irritation with Herr Lang. "*You* have no use for me, do you?"

He leaned toward me, his face flabby and pale, and I wondered if he might topple from his chair. His lips quivered in subdued rage. "I have no use for *traitors!*" He inched closer, his warm, acidic breath spreading over me. "You didn't see them go to their deaths, did you? What good boys and girls they were, as assured in their walks to the guillotine as they were in their traitorous convictions. Mere children with twisted, perverse ideas they thought they could get away with. Imagine toppling the Reich! The whole concept is laughable.

"Their resistance did them no good, yet their actions hurt the Fatherland's war effort. Traitors! Cowards! That's what they were. How they paid back the land that bore them, comforted them, and supported their educations and soldierly dreams. Well, the Reich had the final say over their treasonous acts. You should have seen the blood spurt from their necks when their heads rolled from their bodies."

I cringed at the image he had thrust into my head and shuddered on my cot. Tears built behind my eyes but I was uncertain whether they were fomented by fear or rage.

"I see you do have *some* sense," he said, pushing back in the chair. "Don't waste your tears on scum."

"Get out," I said, restraining my anger. "I have nothing to say to a man who has already made up his mind about my guilt."

He barely gave me a glance as he rose from the chair. "I'll see you at trial." He paused as he headed out and, with a quick look back, added, "May the judge have mercy on your soul." He knocked on the cell door.

A guard moved in swiftly, removing the chair, and allowing Herr Lang to exit. The door slammed behind them.

The plate of sausages, spread with a dollop of butter, and the tin coffee cup sat on the end of my cot. I looked at the food, a plate of sustenance which I would have relished on any other day, but now the meal mocked me as the Last Supper must have mocked Jesus.

My resolve crumbled and I burst into tears—all hope was lost. I buried my head in my thin pillow and cried until another knock sounded at my door. These raps sounded different—they spoke of compassion and concern—if sounds could transmit such feelings.

The door opened slowly and a man in a tattered black suit entered my cell. His sympathetic smile gave my crushed spirit some hope as I blinked back tears.

"I'm here to help you," he said, kneeling in front of me. "I offer you sustenance for your spirit."

"I think you're too late . . . Father . . ." I had no other name for him, although he wasn't dressed like a priest or, for that matter, any pastor that I had ever seen.

"Neither Father . . . nor Rabbi . . . nor Pastor . . . I'm all religions. Whatever you need, I am. Call me a chaplain."

"Thank you," I said, wiping my eyes with the edge of my blanket. "I need to eat."

"Go ahead. Your trial will begin in a few hours, maybe sooner if the judge wishes." He pointed to the sausages. "Those look good. Eat. I can talk or I can listen—whatever you'd like."

I picked up the plate. "Talk." I bit into a link and chewed; the warm meaty juices flowed down my throat and I blessed Else for getting this food.

"How much do you know?" he asked.

"That they're dead."

The chaplain bowed his head and uttered a prayer so quickly and softly I couldn't hear it.

"Pray for me," I said, feeling that God was closer to me than ever before, easier to feel His presence now that Death was marching toward me.

"I've been praying for days now—first I prayed for their bodies, now I pray for their souls." He broke from his kneeling position and sat on the stones by my cot.

"Please, sit here," I said, and patted the end of my mattress.

"I'm fine, Natalya," he said. "In fact, I prefer it. I'm used to the cold hardness of the church rather than luxury. In recent years, the cold has seeped into my soul and I have fought hard against it." His smile was filled with a sadness that mirrored the tenor of his soft blue eyes. He scratched the top of his head, stirring the thinning strands of black hair. "Your position is precarious—I'm sure you know that—but I'll do everything I can to aid you, which may not be enough to save you from death."

The chaplain bowed his head again, unable to look at me. No longer hungry, I put down my plate and took a sip of coffee. The pain emanating from the man seated near me was palpable. It felt as if the sorrow in his soul was flowing into mine. I wanted to lift his chin gently with my finger like a mother tending a hurt child.

"Sophie, Hans, Christoph—all dead," he muttered, lifting his head. "Hans tore apart the draft of a leaflet he carried when he was arrested at the university. The Gestapo pieced it together and matched the handwriting to Christoph. It was only a matter of time until he was captured. Willi has been arrested too, but so far is alive." His voice dropped to a whisper. "The Gestapo and the SS want to get every bit of information they can out of Herr Graf. The Reich is in the business of arrest and execution. Any word, any phrase that doesn't please them leads to an arrest. Impeding the morale of our troops is an executable offense. There's no room for negativity in the Reich."

I placed my cup next to the plate of unfinished sausages. I wanted to ask him if Alex and Professor Huber had been arrested. Every fiber in my body wanted to trust the man who sat at my feet, but I could never betray anyone in the White Rose. Perhaps the Gestapo sent this "man of the cloth" to me as a trick, a guise to get me to incriminate others. I wouldn't tell him any secrets, although my heart ached to know if my friends were still alive.

His pale blue eyes burned a hole in my soul.

"Hans and Sophie took communion from me," the chaplain said. "We prayed together before they were taken away. Christoph was baptized as a Catholic by a priest and given his first Holy Communion and then Last Rites. God was filled with irony yesterday . . . humor, some would say.

"Sophie was the first to enter the building where they keep the guillotine. A few minutes after five o'clock yesterday her life ended. They took her first because she faced her trial and execution with a calm face; she had accepted her fate with a dignity that even her captors admired. Then came Christoph, who had told Hans and Sophie that he would see them in eternity, and also that he didn't know 'dying could be so easy.' Then, finally, Hans. The worst part must have been the waiting, watching the others go before him. Perhaps that's why they saved him until the last. Before the blade came down, he shouted, '*Es lebe die Freiheit!* Long live freedom!' Then it was over. Stadelheim was quiet once again, but always on watch like the jaws of a shark waiting for more prey."

"Please, don't torture me with their deaths," I begged. "My own weighs on my mind."

He rose from the floor and straightened his body. "You deserve to know that they met their fate with dignity and grace. The whole world deserves to know their story when it can be told. Would you like to pray with me—receive communion?"

I shook my head, feeling somehow unworthy of His attention, as if it would be an affront to God, whom I had ignored, relegated to the back of my mind for years. "No. I haven't been in church in some time."

"A building is never the answer, Natalya. Your faith will get you into heaven."

"I'm glad you told me about Hans and Sophie," I said, "but I want to be alone now—to consider what I have to say to the People's Court."

"Have courage," he said, grasping my hands. "If you are lucky, if you are sentenced to prison, perhaps they will forget about you. Sometimes it takes a year or more for prisoners to meet their fates. Languishing in a cell may not be pleasant, but at least you'll be alive." He turned toward the door. "I'll pray for you and hope to our Lord that I don't meet you today as you walk toward God."

"If we do meet, we can say a prayer together."

He knocked on the door and slipped through the narrow opening before it closed.

I was left alone in the glaring light.

*   *   *

Shortly after nine in the morning, a guard escorted me out of Gestapo headquarters and into a waiting car for my journey to the Palace of Justice. The handcuffs were on again as I stepped from Wittelsbacher Palace for the first time in more than three days. The air chilled my skin, but my body and soul reveled in my temporary freedom. The pleasure of release was tempered by what I was about to face.

After a short drive, the Palace of Justice rose before me, a massive stone building adorned with classical statuary, Corinthian columns, arched doorways, and a prominent dome. The structure looked down upon me with cold indifference, its façade as bleak as my mental state.

My guards ignored me, possibly because I was only one of many prisoners they had to transport. They yanked me from the car and whisked me up the stairs past the interior columns and arches at breakneck speed. One of them, a sleek man with dangerous eyes, shoved me onto a bench and told me to "be quiet" as he stood over me. Muffled voices seeped from behind a wide door a few meters away—the murmurs of men I didn't know, men who would sit in judgment of me. I sat for ten minutes listening to the click of footsteps on the stairs, the hollow echo of doors closing and opening, the rushed steps of a prisoner as he was led away.

Finally, I entered the hall where I would be tried. An armed policeman, attired in a blunt Prussian hat and stiff uniform decorated with gold buttons and medals, led me to a bench. Row after row of uniformed, high-ranking Nazi officials sat in the room, casting their severe officious judgment upon me. I took my seat next to someone I hadn't expected to see.

Lisa Kolbe and I locked eyes for a few seconds, enough time for her to whisper, "I told them nothing." She smiled and looked away as the policeman slid between us to keep us from talking. The glance I'd gotten from my friend showed that she'd been treated badly. Her blond hair, sheared to a thumb's length, reminded me of the Polish women POWs I'd seen from the train. Purple bruises dotted her cheeks and a cut under her left eye had scabbed over. Why had I been spared such treatment? Did the Gestapo feel that Lisa knew more about the White Rose than I, or was my incarceration at headquarters somehow softened by Garrick Adler? My bottled-up anger turned to despair, causing my body and spirits to sag as I pivoted from Lisa. Any measure of rage, any inclination to unleash fury upon the gathered policemen, the Nazi officials, and the Gestapo agents would have been dealt with severely had I attempted any angry display.

The men sat in the gallery to our right, the judge's bench was positioned to our left. Not one person in the crowd was there for Lisa and me—no friends, no relatives, no allies to speak on our behalf. We were alone against a force much stronger than a cult or a tribe; we stood against the German State, the Third Reich. The men who persecuted us were having a fine time at our expense, chatting about the weather, laughing at our predicament, preening in their starched uniforms, admiring their medals and swapping war stories, comparing their invitations to a trial they were privileged to witness, the coveted summons from Hitler's "hanging judge," as Lisa and I feared for our lives.

The door at the far end of the hall, to our left, swung open and Roland Freisler made his entrance. Others followed him in, but his presence, his swagger, shifted all eyes toward him. He swept into the room like an actor onto a stage, his scarlet robes billowing around him, a winged Nazi eagle pinned over his right breast. An oval hat of the same color sat upon his head. The President of the People's Court reminded me of a character from a Wagnerian opera. I had seen Nazi officers for many years, but this man trumped them all in style and form. Sadism seeped from him in the form of his bird-of-prey stare, the cruelness of his face.

The gathered sycophants stood when Freisler entered. He gave the Nazi salute, which the crowd returned. He seated himself in the middle chair behind the bench and gazed around the hall. The oval facial lines leading from the top of his nose to his jaw enhanced his dour, sinister appearance, which his hawk-like eyes accented. In the feverish pageantry of Freisler's entry, I failed to notice that my attorney, Gerhart Lang, along with a second judge, a court recorder, and another man had taken their places in the hall. I assumed that the man who took his place next to Lang was Lisa's attorney.

Freisler raised his hands to quiet the court. "This should only take a few minutes," he said, and smiled to general laughter from the audience. "Let's dispense with formalities, for you witnessed the same perverse show yesterday when the other traitors were convicted." He pointed a thin, long finger at the men sitting in the gallery. "We know what the outcome will be, don't we?"

A chorus of "Ja" rose in the room. Lisa and I looked at each other in dismay. I'd known that my fate was sealed before I stepped into the courtroom; those who had warned me of a judicial travesty were right.

Freisler opened the file in front of him. "The defendants have both told their attorneys that they will plead 'not guilty.'"

Many of the gathered Nazis snickered and hissed, while others booed. The judge dismissed them with a wave of his hand. "Despite what we all know to be true, let's not get too far ahead of ourselves. Defendants, rise."

The policeman lifted us from the bench. All eyes turned from Freisler and settled upon Lisa and me.

"Lisa Kolbe and Natalya Petrovich—how do you plead?"

"Not guilty," we replied in unison, my voice a little stronger than Lisa's.

"Ridiculous! Sit down!"

We sat as ordered and those gathered turned their gaze again toward the judge.

"The charges against you are: attempted murder upon an agent of the Reich; treason by subversive acts, including the writing and distribution of seditious material, specifically in Nuremberg; and consorting with traitors and misfits." He closed the file, lifted it, and then slammed it on the bench. "Traitors and misfits, indeed! Look at them! We have rooted them out like an evil plague. They must pay for their crimes, their disservice to the Reich!"

Affirmative calls for justice resounded in the hall, until the judge pounded the gavel for silence.

Freisler then read a prepared document listing the crimes and the investigative reasons for the charges. He droned on for thirty minutes, with flourishes of bombast and anger, until he stopped to collect his strength for his next emotional outburst. After a brief pause, he read more pages outlining the accusations against me, with the same outrage that he had used in describing Lisa's charges.

After an hour, the duplicating machine, the printing stencils, and copies of our two leaflets were hauled onto a court table and taken into evidence. All those on the bench, except Freisler, took a few minutes to examine the objects; most of the men, including our attorneys, gazed at the leaflets and then looked upon us with disgust in their eyes. A horrible thought struck me as I considered what fate must have befallen Dieter Frank, the artist whose studio we had used to produce our treasonous material. Had he been taken to Gestapo headquarters as well, or was he in prison or, perhaps, dead? What lead had the investigators followed that brought them to the studio and the evidence? I didn't know if I would ever have the answer to that question.

The full weight of what lay ahead for me and those associated with the White Rose pressed upon my shoulders. I struggled with my emotions as I thought of my mother, who now had a daughter in circumstances more dire than her husband's. When I joined the resistance, I knew this day might come; however, one lives with the hope that the unthinkable will never occur. An untold number of faces appeared in my head: Sina and her children massacred in Russia, the Rabbi of the burned synagogue, the Jewish victims of Kristallnacht, the "subhuman" prisoners tortured and beaten by German troops, Wehrmacht soldiers frozen in the snow outside Stalingrad. All had died upon the orders of a madman. Those faces mattered more than mine.

"Have you anything to say on behalf of Lisa Kolbe?" Freisler asked her attorney.

The middle-aged man squinted, stood, and said, "President, Lisa Kolbe pleads 'not guilty,' but one can plainly see from the evidence that the Court has proved its case. I ask for clemency because the defendant is young, only twenty years old, and has obviously been hypnotized by the seditious actions of others."

"Hypnotized!" Freisler raged, his face turning as scarlet as his robes. "The woman is a traitor! Her guilt is as plain as the nose on my face. What would you have her do—walk out of here with her freedom?"

The man bowed his head. "Life in prison," he said in a voice hardly above a whisper.

"Ha! The insolence and the stupidity . . ." Freisler scowled and pointed to Lang, my attorney. "Do you have anything of substance to add to the mockery these defendants have made of these proceedings?"

Lang wrested his meaty frame from his chair and faced the President. "If it pleases the Court . . . no," he said smugly, and, turning to me, forced a smile upon his lips.

"A wise man," Freisler added as Lang sat again. "The defendant Lisa Kolbe may speak, but only if she vows to tell the truth."

The policeman led her to the gallery floor, where she was told to stand directly in front of the President. He stared at her, his raptor eyes surveying her like a bird swooping down upon a rodent.

Lisa started slowly with little feeling in her voice. "I have been beaten to force the 'truth' from me."

Boos echoed throughout the hall. "Let her speak!" The President hammered his gavel until the men quieted. "Nonsense! You, a lowly traitor, accuse good men, who have taken your wretched body into custody, of abusing you? More likely your wounds were self-inflicted for sympathy from the Court." He placed his hands on the bench and smiled. "Let her tell her lies."

"I learned what the others who have gone before me said in this hall—that someone had to begin—that the White Rose is only echoing what many in the Reich are thinking, but no one dares to say."

Freisler rose from the bench, the gavel poised in his hand as if he was about to strike my friend. "You dare utter such words in this court? You *are* the traitor and will be dealt with severely when the sentence is given."

Lisa stepped forward and the policeman lunged, tugging her back from the bench. "*You* are the guilty one! *You*—the President of the People's Court who kills with vengeance in his heart. As Hans Scholl said before he died, 'Long live freedom!'"

Freisler thrust his robed arm toward Lisa's attorney, the red folds falling like drapery. "Shut her up, now! Shut her up before I have her executed in this hall!"

The gallery erupted in cheers, and over the commotion, Lisa shouted, "If it is guilt you want, then I *am* guilty! I was responsible for everything."

Freisler waved his arms frantically in an attempt to stir up even more outrage than had broken out from his words. I was uncertain if he had even heard her "confession."

Buoyed by Lisa's courage and my own anxious push of fear, I stood and shouted at the men, "I am guilty." None of them seemed to hear me over the uproar, but I couldn't let Lisa be brave alone.

The President dropped his arms to his side and the hall quieted. All the men who had stood to shout objections returned to their seats—except for two who stood near a door at the rear of the hall. They strode toward the bench with measured step. One I recognized immediately, and soon the face of the other burst into my memory and added more dread to my already frazzled nerves.

Garrick Adler, his coat draped over his arm, blond hair glinting in the light, eyes never leaving the gaze of the President, passed through the gallery. The man accompanying him, the SS officer who had attacked Lisa in Nuremberg, strode by Garrick's side.

Freisler recognized Garrick and called him forward. "You have something to say to the Court, Herr Adler?"

Garrick bowed to the President, paused, and then said, "Lisa Kolbe, as she has declared, is guilty of all crimes. She was responsible for everything. Untersturmführer Sauer of Nuremberg will testify that what I say is true. Natalya Petrovich is 'not guilty.'"

No one moved in their seats as a stunned silence descended upon the hall.

Freisler's eyes narrowed, his lips drew tight, and he pointed to me. "Adler, you're asking this court to believe that this sub-human, this *German*, of *Russian* descent, is innocent?"

"I am guilty," Lisa said again. "I acted alone."

"Lisa Kolbe tells the truth to the Court," Garrick said.

I wondered what game he was playing and kept silent for the moment.

The President frowned and called the two men to the bench. "See what a distraction you've created, Adler. The Court will take a private recess with you to consider this matter."

Everyone rose as Freisler, Garrick, and Sauer left the hall for the President's chamber. The policeman instructed Lisa to sit in a chair near the bench; she glanced my way now and then with no expression on her face but for her eyes, which instructed me to keep quiet, to not say a word about "guilt." Upon Lisa's urging, I was willing to grasp my slim chance of survival.

For an hour, I watched the Nazi officials mill about the hall, inspecting the duplicating machine as if it were the latest secret weapon devised by the Wehrmacht, reading the leaflets with expressions of horror or sarcastic glee, whispering about the proceedings. I imagined those hushed conversations were directed at Lisa, me, and Garrick Adler.

A short time later, the President made his entrance, followed by Garrick and the SS officer. All stood.

When everyone was seated, Freisler commanded, "Defendants, rise."

Lisa and I did so.

He angled the transcript pages in front of his face and read, "After careful consideration by this court, in the Name of the German People, Lisa Marie Kolbe, on this date, February 23rd, 1943, pursuant to the trial held this day, you have been found guilty of assault upon an officer of the Reich, of writing and distributing leaflets in a time of war, sabotaging the war effort and calling for the overthrow of National Socialism, having given aid to the enemy, weakening the security of the nation: on these charges you are to be punished by . . ."

He paused and stared with gleaming eyes at Lisa, who stood before him. "Death. Your rights and honors as a citizen are forfeited from this day forward." Whispered approvals of the sentence rippled through the room. "Because you have been found guilty, you are ordered to pay court costs."

Lisa lowered her head but didn't turn to me. Before I could say anything, a policeman grabbed me by the arm and led me to the front of the hall. My friend was whisked out the side door by the officer who had stood next to her. That was the last time I saw Lisa Kolbe. I faced Hitler's judge alone.

"Natalya Irenaovich Petrovich," Freisler began. "In the Name of the German People, on this day, February 23rd, 1943, you have been found *not* guilty of all charges except for that of consorting with traitors and misfits, which has led to propagating defeatist lies as well as a terrible cost to the war effort, giving aid and comfort to the enemy, and calling for the overthrow of National Socialism . . ."

His stern eyes bored into me. "Therefore, on this account, you are to be punished by five years in prison to be served beginning this day. Because of your guilt, you are ordered to pay court costs." He smacked the gavel once more. "This trial is adjourned."

I have little memory of what occurred after his pronouncement because my confused mind went blank. I struggled to make sense of what had happened in the hall, and only upon reflection did I realize that Garrick and the SS officer had swayed Freisler in his decision. I was horrified that I had seen my friend sentenced to death; and, what should have been elation for my five-year prison sentence turned to guilt and shame as others died for the resistance. Five years in a young life is a lifetime; yet, I was to live. A whirlwind of emotions coursed through me, and my head reeled, while the world stood still momentarily after the President's judgment.

The policeman held my arms in a pincerlike hold, slapping

handcuffs on my wrists, although I had no desire, or even the strength, to struggle. There would have been no escaping the Palace of Justice. For a brief moment, I caught sight of Garrick and the SS man leaving the hall by the door they had entered, without a word to me.

A boxy police wagon awaited me on the street. The day had turned gray, colder, the air smelling of rain. How long would it be before I was outside again? Where would I be taken? The absurd thought struck me that I should be transported to my mother's apartment so I could let her know where I was being taken.

"Where are we going?" I asked through the wire mesh that separated me from the driver. The guards had told me nothing.

"Stadelheim," the driver said, keeping his eyes on the road ahead.

I was to be held in the same prison as my father.

CHAPTER 12

Stone upon stone, square windows with descending triangular caps at their tops, rain dripping from the red-tile roof: These were the features of Stadelheim the day it became my home. While some fortunate prisoners were confined in cells with windows, I was unlucky in that respect. After my indoctrination, I was taken to a cell without a window, belowground for all I knew, and tossed into it, separated from my father and Lisa Kolbe.

Alone.

Instead of lamenting and crying over my misfortune, I tried as best I could during the long days to stay positive, to remind myself that instead of a death sentence I had received a prison term. But in the lonely dark, far after midnight, fears crept into my head, slowly at first like the descent into a nightmare, before they exploded in terrifying visions that tormented me.

How different would the world be in five long years? Would the Allies triumph over Hitler and National Socialism? Would Munich, the birthplace of the Nazi movement, still be standing? But these questions were global issues. What of my life? I lay awake nights wondering if I would survive my prison term, knowing that any moment I could be whisked away to the guillotine. I heard nothing of Lisa's fate, or of my father, and still wondered what Garrick and the SS man had said to Roland Freisler that had saved me from death.

As the days and nights dragged on, I drew some solace from

the chaplain's words at Gestapo headquarters: "Perhaps they will forget about you." Languishing in prison was preferable to death, he had told me.

I had no idea what life in prison would be like, because I had no experience here other than my visit with my father. Golden moments in the sun faded as the dark days and nights marched in a methodical procession—time seemingly slowed to a slow tick of the clock.

When I arrived at Stadelheim, I was given a new prison dress of plain gray cotton, replacing the one I'd been given when I was arrested. This dress held something different for me—a red triangle, which pointed up rather than down. This badge, the matron explained in the same matter-of-fact tone as if I were trying on new clothes at a department store, was issued to spies or traitors. She also handed me a worn brown coat, which was of great comfort in my cold cell. When asked what jobs I could perform, I told her that I had some experience as a nurse. "Medical" was no place for prisoners, she said, because of access to equipment and drugs; therefore, I was dispatched to the kitchen to prepare food and wash dishes.

At least in the guarded kitchen, I was with other prisoners, although no talking or exchanges of any kind were allowed except for the transmission of orders between a guard and inmate. Once an order was given, we were expected to perform our duties in a timely and precise manner. Any failure on our part would generate a slap on the head with a hand or with something harder, usually metallic. Many women wandered the kitchen with bruises on their faces, cradling their ears because they couldn't hear from the damage done by repeated beatings.

Our day began at dawn, when we put out the toilet bucket. Once the door was locked, we were fed dry, dark bread and weak coffee. Then, we were taken outside, where we marched in lines around the compound. Those that fell were not seen again.

Next, we went to our jobs. Some prisoners worked outside Stadelheim on Mondays and Thursdays. In the beginning, I thought those men and women were the lucky ones, but at the end of the day only a few would return. The whisperings in the kitchen told of more beatings, transfers to other prisons, or executions. These murders of prisoners, for reasons unknown, usually occurred on Tuesdays and Fridays.

A small piece of sausage or other meat was thrown into the soup on certain days. Some of the prisoners said that we were eating the flesh of those who had been killed by the Nazis. Because I worked in the kitchen, I suspected this wasn't true, although I was never sure where the meat came from.

After a few weeks of solitary confinement, I craved conversation with anyone—guard or prisoner. One day in the kitchen, I attempted to talk to a slight young woman whose dress fell around her thin frame like a potato sack. The one distinguishing characteristic of the worn fabric was the shiny, new black triangle sewn to the fabric. I had seen this woman on duty before. From the slight smiles she directed my way, I hoped she could be trusted. Of course, I knew the risk of talking to another prisoner and the danger of exposing others to such a forbidden action. It didn't matter to me—I was desperate not only to talk, but for information about the prison.

We stood over the sink peeling turnips, which had been stored through the winter. This vegetable was to be prepared for the officers and guards, not for the mouths of prisoners.

A sentry sat on a chair a few meters away, an older woman whose hair was pulled back in a severe bun. She made it quite clear she had no objection to killing prisoners who might wield kitchen utensils as weapons.

"What's your name?" I whispered to my compatriot as I kept my gaze focused on the turnip in my left hand.

Her head turned slightly and her eyes, the color of brandy, flickered, taking in as much of the room as possible without being obvious to anyone but me. Perhaps she had been in prison for a long time; she seemed adept at being secretive.

"Call me 'Reh,'" she said quietly, tilting her left shoulder toward the armed woman. "Be careful of Dolly—she's a mean one."

I continued my peeling, cheered by the sound of another human voice talking to *me*. However, once our conversation had begun, I wasn't sure how to proceed. More information about the prison would suffice, I thought.

"How long have you been here?" I asked.

"Almost two years."

I shuddered at the thought of being held in Stadelheim for that long. What a trial my father had endured for a sentence of only six months—two years seemed an impossible time—and I had three years added to that figure. I'd learned to pray every night for an Allied liberation.

"And you?" Reh asked. Her name meant "deer" and she reminded me of a fragile doe, with thin legs and body, liquid brown eyes, and graceful, attentive movements.

"Just over a month," I answered. "I've been sentenced to five years."

"You got off lightly. I'm in for ten." She dropped a peeled turnip into our bucket and grabbed one from the counter. "What's your name?"

"Natalya." I finished peeling mine as well, dropped it into the container and reached for another. "What does the black triangle mean?" I felt awkward asking what the symbol stood for.

Reh uttered a short laugh.

Startled, I looked at Dolly. She leaned forward in her chair, placed her finger on the pistol's trigger, and stared at us with blazing eyes.

"Quiet now," Reh whispered as I returned to my task. We worked in silence for several minutes before another group of prisoners appeared in the kitchen and brushed us aside so they could wash dishes in the sink. The smell of leftover beef stew and sausages rose from the dirty bowls and plates. The clatter allowed Reh and me to continue our talk farther down the counter.

"I like men," Reh continued, "and peach schnapps."

I wasn't sure what she meant.

"I was deemed 'asocial,' by the court because I was addicted to both. I got five years for each of my trespasses. I used my best feminine wiles to entice the judge, but that didn't work—damn him, the old Nazi."

"Do you ever think of getting out of here?" I asked.

"If you mean escaping, don't ever talk about that with any-one." She lifted a hand and brushed back her short brown hair from her forehead. "It's impossible, anyway. You'd never make it out, and those that do, don't last long. That's what I've heard. No, I'm resigned to my time here . . . unless a miracle occurs . . . or I die."

I dropped my peeler and massaged my right hand, which had cramped from the repetitive motion.

"I don't think I can last for five years," I said, after working out the knots in my fingers.

Reh dropped another turnip in the bucket. "We all think like that in the beginning, but imagine what life would be like on the outside—on the run—every Gestapo agent, SS man, every local policeman combing every hill and valley, knocking on doors, just to find your poor, tired body. And where would you hide? You can't go to your parents, your relatives, or your friends." She looked at my red badge. "They'd be in danger as well, sus-pected as traitors. The only way you'll get out of here is time served, or dead on a gurney. Now that my delirium tremens have passed, I have it pretty good in here: food, a place to sleep, and I don't have to worry about being blown to pieces. The Al-lies don't bomb prisons. Believe me, they know where they are."

She paused. "Some women I've known have gone mad and been transferred to an asylum. Maybe it's better there."

I picked up one of the three remaining turnips, thinking I might make a bold move and ask Reh where the entrances and exits of the prison were located, and was blindsided by some-thing hard that crashed against my head. I saw stars. When I'd recovered enough to know where I was, I found myself splayed against the counter. My glasses had flown into the turnip bucket.

"Don't you think you've talked enough, *traitor*?" Dolly's voice bubbled with subdued rage. "Keep talking and you'll get more than keys smacked against your head."

She glowered at Reh and then stalked off while I rubbed my right temple, my head throbbing, blood trickling down my fingers.

Reh handed me my dirty glasses. "Don't cross her," she said under her breath. "She hit you because you're new. I've had plenty of whacks."

I washed the lenses quickly, returned them to my face, and winced as the right earpiece scraped against a cut. My head thudding, I continued my work, but said nothing to Reh for the rest of the afternoon.

Despite Dolly and the other guards, Reh and I whispered when we could; however, as I experienced more of Stadelheim life and the efficient Nazi organization running it, the less an escape seemed possible.

Between my cell confinement and structured duties, my life had become limited in a way I'd never imagined possible. Spring turned to summer and the kitchen heat became unbearable: a torture chamber of fetid odors, hellish humidity, and sweat. Several of the women who worked with me passed out from the ovenlike temperatures and never returned to their duties. Whether they were transferred or killed because they had simply become useless, I never found out. They were replaced by incoming prisoners.

At night, alone in my cell, my thoughts devolved into a festering playground of disturbing images, most of which centered on my captivity and the impossibility of escape. I knew that Freisler could change his mind at any moment because of "evidence," real or manufactured, and that possibility did nothing to thwart my growing depression. The occasional walk around the garden compound, gulping in fresh air no matter the weather—hot or cold—bolstered my spirits briefly, until I was remanded back to the kitchen, or my lonely cell. Yet, I prayed that I'd indeed been forgotten by the court—the choices being death or wasting away as the chaplain had explained—an insane paradox. These thoughts drove me mad, and the frayed nerves unraveling beneath my skin aggravated my state of mind.

One blistering afternoon in late summer, a visitor arrived at my cell.

Garrick Adler had come to honor me with his company. For my own sanity, I thought of refusing to talk to him, but Garrick might answer questions that had plagued me for months.

He was dressed in an SS uniform, a clear statement of his allegiance to the Führer, and a departure from the less militaristic Gestapo style. He looked *well kept*; those were the words that came into my head when I saw him. His jacket and pants were neatly pressed, his black boots polished to a brilliant shine. A guard brought a chair and then left the cell.

He took off his cap and sat down.

I sat on the edge of my bed, facing him.

His expression was thoughtful, curious, no smile, no frown, as if he wanted to know what conditions were like in prison. I wondered what he thought of me slumped on my bed, in a prison dress as bedraggled as I felt. When he spoke, an immediate loathing rose from my gut.

"I suppose this is a surprise," he said, as if he had invaded my solitary confinement.

I stared at him, unsure what to say, anger lifting from my stomach into my throat.

"If you don't wish to talk, I'll leave," he said, "but I bring news you may want to hear."

My lips quivered along with my voice. "I am surprised that you even *care* enough to be here. What do you want?"

He looked at me and I knew what he saw: my rough hands, the prison cut of my hair, my stained dress, and dirty glasses. I wondered if he was as ashamed of and embarrassed for me as I was of myself for ever thinking of trusting him. Garrick, who had declared his affection for me, now sat within arm's reach, as handsome as ever in his vile uniform.

"Are they treating you well?" he asked.

I laughed out loud, then I spit at his feet. He moved his polished boots away from my spittle. "How dare you!"

He removed the cap from his lap and held it in his hands. "I didn't ask to offend you. If you're being treated badly . . . perhaps I can pull a few strings."

"Leave me alone," I said, lowering my head. "I don't want your favors. Didn't you get what you wanted—the destruction of the White Rose?"

He raised my chin with his finger and then pointed to the death's-head, the skull and crossbones on his cap. "I took an oath to the Führer and the Reich. Do you think I can ignore that pledge without consequences for everyone who knows me? My family, others I know and love—even you—would be in grave danger if I renounced my vow to the Reich." He put the cap back in his lap. "I *saved* you."

So, he'd confirmed what I'd thought for months. Garrick admitted that he'd saved me from the death sentence. The question I needed to ask was, Why?

He knew what I was thinking. I took off my glasses, wiped the lenses with my sleeve, and nodded—my acknowledgment that he had saved me.

Garrick stared at the wall behind me, his gaze focused on the stones as if he could see past them into the earth, into the garden compound, into the blue heaven and the fiery sun. He clenched his cap so hard I thought he would crush it in his grip, and then, with a shudder, he released it. "Because . . . because I thought . . ." He could go no further.

I had my answer—I still held power over him, which he'd admitted long ago. "What did you want to tell me?" I asked with less antagonism. "I see you've been . . . promoted?"

He cocked his head. "Yes, a promotion of sorts. I'm SS now—out of the Gestapo. I don't do as much investigative work as I used to." He glanced at me. "Your father is at home—he was released as scheduled—I had something to do with that—I put in a good word."

Relief flooded me. I'd assumed that he'd been set free, but I was unable to confirm it through prison gossip or by any other means. The guards were notoriously tight-lipped about anything to do with prisoners, especially after they vanished.

"Thank you. I didn't know. My parents haven't come to see me."

"You can't have visitors. You're to talk to no one but me." He arched an eyebrow. "But you can talk to *others* in Stadelheim."

My thanks turned to indignation as I grasped the meaning behind his words. "You want me to spy on other prisoners, don't you? You want to know what others tell me."

"It's a small favor—tit for tat. Yes, tell me."

"That's why I'm still alive, isn't it—because you want me to root out other traitors? That's why I'm in solitary confinement—so I'll relish the opportunity to talk with anyone."

"The White Rose has been broken by the People's Court, but the Reich is concerned that the resistance isn't dead. The Gestapo, the SS, are always on the lookout for those who undermine the Führer. If you help me find them, bring them to justice, perhaps things will go easier for you and your family."

Never. Never in a thousand years will I betray others for the sake of the Reich. Too many have died or been murdered for the grandiose dreams of a madman. I am just another who has taken a stand. I sagged against the cold stone wall.

He frowned as he rose from the chair. "That's enough for today." He put on his cap and knocked on the cell door. It creaked open.

I turned away, not wanting to look at him.

"Natalya," he said, "your time is running out. I've given you a warning that I hope you'll heed. You must find others who would betray the Reich or your usefulness will be over. President Freisler agreed to this at your sentencing, but he doesn't have unlimited patience—as you've seen. Your cooperation is the reason your father is out of prison, at my urging, and your mother is safe. It's an unfortunate state of affairs, but one that is now out of my hands."

I refused to look at him. "Your leg was never injured, was it?"

"No. The Gestapo protects its own . . . if you need to speak to me, notify one of the guards. They have their orders."

The door closed behind him, but his voice carried through the hall as he walked away. "The traitor Lisa Kolbe was executed by guillotine the afternoon of her trial—don't suffer the same fate." He paused as if he was expecting me to cry out in rage against his words. "Alex Schmorell, the Russian, and Professor Kurt Huber died on the thirteenth of July after their April trial. Willi Graf, the soldier, is still alive for a reason you can understand."

I held in my tears as his footsteps faded. When the hall was again silent, I buried my face in my thin pillow and cried.

CHAPTER 13

Garrick Adler came to see me a few months later near the end of October 1943, still hoping to arrest the traitors I'd failed to discover. I had nothing to report, but I pressed him for details about how Alex, Professor Huber, and Willi, who had been executed a few weeks before, had been captured.

My friend Alex, whom I'd last seen at the university when Hans and Sophie were arrested, had fled Munich in an attempt to conceal himself in a POW camp for Russians in southern Germany, with the eventual goal of traveling to neutral Switzerland. He carried forged papers, but a planned meeting in Innsbruck disintegrated when his contact for the camp failed to show up. He retreated to Mittenwald, where someone recognized him, forcing him to flee over the mountains, but bitter winter storms stopped him. He had neither the food nor the appropriate clothing for such an arduous journey. Regretfully, he made his way back to Munich only to take cover in a bomb shelter in Schwabing during an air raid on February 24. There, he was identified by an old girlfriend, and as a man on the run, as exhausted as an antelope pursued by lions, was arrested by the Gestapo.

Professor Huber was arrested at five in the morning two days after Alex. Three agents swarmed past his twelve-year-old daughter, who had answered the door, and dragged him from his bed. His wife was away and, thankfully, spared the terror of that early morning. Because Professor Huber had composed the leaflet that Hans and Sophie had dropped at the university, his death sentence was sealed. All the professor's efforts to burn books and incriminating evidence before he was arrested came to naught.

Of the three men, Willi's capture was the least dramatic. The soldier arrived home the evening of the day Hans and Sophie were taken into custody. He and his sister were talking when they were arrested. He was unaware of what had happened to his friends, and the Gestapo knew where to find him.

The second trial of the White Rose was held on April 19. Fourteen men and women were judged. Of those, Alex, Professor Huber, and Willi received the death sentence. The derisive Freisler had shrieked at Alex, calling him a traitor, before sending him back to his seat. Willi was the second to appear before the President of the People's Court, who was somewhat lenient with the soldier, telling him that he "had almost gotten away with it." Freisler reserved most of his invective for Professor Huber, whom he called a "bum," and excoriated him for his political diatribe against the Reich.

Alex and Professor Huber had been executed by the guillotine a few months after their trials. Willi was held in prison in hopes that he would give the Gestapo more information about other traitors. On October 12, 1943, his life ended after he revealed no new information about seditious activities within the Wehrmacht. I felt as much sorrow, without tears, as I could for all of them, but I had little emotion left to give.

"Willi's silence ended his life," Garrick said. "Keep trying, Natalya, for me—for what little we had."

"We had nothing," I replied, a pitiful creature attempting to retain my dignity.

"But I felt something—there could have been something between us."

"You stand with Hitler and I do not."

He closed his eyes and his face tightened. "I know your political convictions, but think of your family, think of the difference you could make for them. One clue, one lead, one step that might lead to another is all I . . . *we* . . . need."

"I'll try," I said, and sighed. I didn't mean my words any more than I believed that Garrick and I would ever be together. It was a ruse, a ploy to buy time.

"You'll go mad here, Natalya," Garrick said. "Do you want me to transfer you to an asylum?"

He left me with that question, convinced that finally he had gotten to me.

After Garrick's visit, I expected that Death might touch me at any moment in my solitary and monotonous routine. The fall turned to winter, and winter transformed into spring, but I saw little of the seasons. Reh, who had become frail during the cold months, disappeared one day never to return, as did many others. I subsisted on potato and turnip peelings as additions to my meager meals, always aware that if I were caught stealing them, I'd be beaten. As the months dragged on, I knew an escape from Stadelheim was impossible. I would die here, forgotten, or by my own hand.

Garrick's question about the asylum had stuck with me and I remembered what Reh had said about prisoners being transferred to such institutions. Perhaps it would be easier to escape there. As a last resort, I decided to go mad—a plan concocted out of desperation.

Nearly all of us at Stadelheim went mad in late April of 1944, when the Allies launched heavy air attacks on Munich. All daily operations at the prison halted and I, for once, was happy that my cell was belowground. Still, the earth shook around us and although the bombs fell close by, the prison suffered no direct hits. The smell of scorched earth and burning wood filled the air and filtered down into the prison depths. I dipped the corner of my blanket in water and put it over my mouth so I could breathe. At points during the attack, which carried on overnight and into the next day, screams echoed down the halls and I feared that prisoners were being executed under the cover of falling bombs.

I worried for my own safety, but I also thought of my parents, and even Frau Hofstetter and Katze, wondering if they'd been driven from their homes or had died in the onslaught. The thought was too horrible to contemplate, but I had no choice but to cower in the corner and muddle through the thudding explosions.

The relentless attacks made it easier to fall into insanity.

No pen. No paper—nothing on which to record my thoughts, so I lie in bed and concoct voices in my head. It's easy to go mad; it's harder to convince those who oversee my fate that I'm a lunatic. I'll try very hard to make them believe I'm insane, but what if I succeed in my madness? Will they send me to an institution, or will they classify me as an expendable "undesirable." Perhaps they'll say I'm making things up and just lock me up tighter.

God, the nights are long, and the days are dreary, and often I've thought that death would be preferable to spending another hour in this cesspool, but then I think of my parents and the slightest flicker of hope appears that I might see them again. Even Katze with his bright green eyes appears before me, and I stroke his warm fur down to the pink skin; my ears drink in his purring. What I wouldn't give to spend a morning with Frau Hofstetter, enjoying a warm breakfast in her kitchen, washing her dishes, doing her laundry, or even listening to military marches on the crackly radio in her sitting room.

But, by all that's good in heaven, I despair to think of men like Garrick Adler—free, alive, breathing in the fresh spring air, plucking a new blade of grass, savoring the aroma of a lilac. He betrayed me and left my heart wounded. Why was I forsaken, Lord? Why have my family and I suffered while brutes roam free? Where is the justice in that?

But if I dwell too much on my sorrows, I will disintegrate and my madness will be real.

Think, Natalya, think. . . . Remember your nursing training. . . . What psychological conditions would serve you best? What disorder of the mind will get you transferred from Stadelheim?

*Depression, anxiety, antisocial behavior aren't strong enough.
Psychosis? Too strong? A break with reality . . . schizo-
phrenia?*

*I have weeks to think about it, months to plan—unless they
remember I'm here.*

"What the hell happened to you?" Dolly asked, her teeth
bared in a vicious grin.

I grabbed the butcher knife from the counter and twirled it in
my hand, making a flashing circle under the glare of the kitchen
lights.

"Put that knife back." Dolly withdrew her pistol and pointed
it at my head.

"What's the matter? You always liked me before." I put the
knife back on the counter and walked to the kitchen sink, where
I slouched over a pile of dirty dishes.

"I never liked you, you traitorous bitch," she shot back.
"Come look at what's happened to the double-crossing back-
stabber." Dolly summoned the other guards, two women and
one SS man, who came to her side and studied me like I was a
freak at a circus show.

She and the others had been slow to notice because the
change had been gradual over a few days. I didn't want the process to happen all at once—that would have been too obvious.
I had pulled hair from my scalp, a horrendous, painful process
that had brought me to tears so many times that I'd stuffed
my blanket into my mouth to keep from screaming. Patches of
bleeding scalp, small at first, were exposed. The strands, the
tufts, which had come out I'd kept under my mattress for another purpose. I'd woven a cross of hair. Religion was always a
safe choice for madness, either one way or the other—devil or
saint. I chose the route of saint, thinking it might appeal to the
latent religious feelings of suppressed Nazis. That tactic was
safer than summoning Satan. What I needed was a credible
vision of the Virgin or the Apostles to complete my religious
hallucinations.

I'd ripped my dress carefully with my fingernails, fraying

the weave so I could insert bits of detritus into the fabric. Hair, dirt, scraps of paper, shards of a stray leaf, broken glass, a piece of wood, toilet paper, anything that I could patch onto my dress, I did. The effect transformed me into a walking garbage bin. I scraped myself with glass, making sure I'd cleaned the sharp edge. The cuts were shallow but drew a thin film of blood, which quickly coagulated. When I caught sight of myself, the effect scared me. I was the walking picture of an asylum inmate. The transformation had taken days, piece-by-piece completed when it was possible; it seemed that only now, when the picture was finished, had my horrendous metamorphosis struck them.

"I don't want her near me," one of the other inmates complained. "She's crazy and she stinks. Can't you hear her moaning at night?"

Dolly laughed and the other guards joined in. "We can't hear her and we don't want to." The plump guard approached me, her blonde braids jiggling as she sauntered over with a pronounced swagger. Clearly, she was the boss of the group, even lording over the SS man. She held her nose when she came within an arm's length, spit at my feet, and glared at me as if I were the lowest of vermin. "You disgust me." She paused and studied me from head to toe, her eyes moving over me in a slow sweep. "I wonder if you're really crazy at all—maybe you just want us to think you are."

"I saw you last night," I said, and picked at my scalp.

She slapped my hands away from my head. "Saw me where?"

"With us—at the table."

She shook her head and lifted her hand as if she was going to strike me. "Make sense, you Russian whore! What table?"

"With Jesus and the Apostles. We were having supper."

Titters from the other guards erupted into full-scale laughter. Dolly lowered her hand.

"See, what did I tell you," the inmate who had spoken against me said. "She should be locked away."

"Shut up," Dolly said roughly, and pushed the woman back.

"This is going to be *your* last supper unless you pull your weight around here," she told me. "No laziness, no idleness! I won't stand for it. If you're crazy, you won't care if they send you to the guillotine. That'll be the true test."

"You ate a lot at supper—Jesus had to hold you back."

I saw the slap coming, but I couldn't avoid it. She struck me hard across the cheek and I fell back toward the sink, cutting my hand on the knife I'd placed on the counter. I thrust my hand toward her face, blood trickling down my palm. "See what you've done. I thought you liked me. You had supper with me."

"Damn Russian bitch—"

The SS man interrupted the volley of curses that Dolly was prepared to unleash. "Listen!" He signaled the guards to gather around the radio at the back of the kitchen. It was always on low volume, a constant drone I tuned out after hours of listening. What the announcer was saying was unclear to me, but the guards' eyes widened and they looked at each other with a dismay that quickly turned to something bordering on horror.

It was late on the afternoon of June 6, 1944. The invasion at Normandy, France, had begun.

My attempts at feigning madness failed for the most part—not because I didn't try. The administrators and guards at Stadelheim wouldn't put up with it. I supposed they had seen such behaviors before. I remained in prison because Garrick and the Gestapo wanted me alive, as they had Willi, until I no longer served a purpose.

I kept the insanity in my head and most days the feeling was easy to hold. In fact, it scared me how easily I fell into the darkness, resulting in an emotional battle to keep the madness from overtaking me. That balancing act between sanity and delusion exhausted me.

If I was moody to the point of silence, Dolly or one of the other guards would slap me for their entertainment until I was forced to talk, even if the words that came out of my mouth were nonsense. When the blows came faster and harder, the pain would roar through me, and eventually I spoke rather than be beaten to death.

If I sat in my cell, refusing to move, the guards hauled me out. That scheme failed as well; the slaps to the head, the fists to the back—unrelenting until I stood erect and cheerful at my kitchen station.

My life was stagnant; yet, the world moved on. The feeling that I'd accomplished nothing more than peeling turnips and occupying a prison bed was the worst of all.

Garrick's visits ended.

The court had forgotten me.

Escape was impossible. I kept my eyes open, always searching for the right time and place to break free, monitoring the kitchen doors when I could, studying the patterns of the guards, holding in memory the placement of the halls and windows, always looking for an opportunity, but the armed presence was too strong, too determined, and thwarted any attempt at freedom.

I scaled back my madness, the charade having little effect other than causing me additional pain from the guards' bullying, and isolating me from fellow inmates. I even disposed of my "cross" of hair because Dolly and the others had ignored it. The buxom guard, on most days, let me pass with barely a look. I'd become a ghostly presence after Reh's departure, forced to eat, work, and sleep as if nothing on earth mattered—not even the war, which seemed far removed except for the Allied bombings. I got used to living like a specter. My parents, still unable to visit, never came to Stadelheim. The terrible thought struck me that they might have perished in their bombed-out apartment.

The prison officials shifted their attentions toward the radio as the summer faded and the mood in Stadelheim turned as morose as the encroaching fall weather. The orange and brown leaves dropped in abundance in the courtyard, the wind sharpened into a biting chill, and the first snowflakes flecked the air in mid-October. I wrapped up in the brown coat I'd been given when I entered prison. I would have frozen in my cell during the long nights, if not for it.

I noted a distinct change as the fall of 1944 took hold, a change I could only attribute to Germany's declining fortunes of war. Although nothing was said to me, and we inmates weren't allowed to listen to the Nazi broadcasts, I assumed things were not going well for the Wehrmacht. Dolly and the other guards managed to make our lives a model of compartmentalization and discipline, but their moods would alternate between hope and despair depending on the war news of the day. Apparently, the Reich's propaganda machine was failing to bolster the country's sagging spirits.

One particularly bleak day, when the cold seemed to have penetrated even the warmth of the kitchen, and the guards were poised over the morning broadcasts, a high-ranking SS man in full uniform appeared at the door. Such an official presence was rare and the stiff rhythm of his military walk sent chills racing over me. I wondered if my last day on earth had finally come.

The man drew Dolly aside, whispered something, and handed her a folded piece of paper. The stout woman smiled and curtsied in her obsequious way before opening the paper and reading it. Her overzealous display made me sick, but I couldn't look away. After reading the notice, Dolly shifted and pointed to me.

The officer spotted me, and I averted my eyes, a defense too late and surely noticed by him. His heels clicked across the stone floor as he approached. The inmates gave him a wide berth—I turned, closed my eyes, and uttered a quick prayer for deliverance. As Hans, Sophie, Alex, and others in the White Rose had learned, I now believed my time had come.

The overt power of his body fell upon me, although he merely had come up from behind. I'd never felt this kind of power, and the sensation of his all-encompassing supremacy terrified me.

"Fräulein Petrovich?" he asked in a tone that sounded more like an indictment than a question.

I turned, saying nothing. His cold gray eyes took me in. Disgust crossed his face before being replaced by his dictatorial demeanor. "You are to come with me."

He grabbed me by the arm and pulled me past the guards—Dolly smirking, the others somewhat shocked by my removal—and out the kitchen door.

"Where are you taking me?" I asked.

He said nothing, but retained his firm grip on my arm. I cried out in pain as he dragged me up the stairs to a well-lit room overlooking the prison's walls. An armed guard closed the door behind us as the officer pushed me inside. The space was stark, unfurnished except for a small wooden table and four chairs. The room's only redeeming feature was the bank of windows that let in the ashen light. On a spring or summer day, the sunlight pouring in the room would have been enough to cheer any prisoner.

"Sit," he ordered.

I did so and took a seat facing the window—the slightest opportunity to look out upon the day brought me some relief—while trying hard to keep the guillotine out of my mind. We sat for several minutes, he saying nothing, studying me like I was a medical specimen or some new species, drawing a cigarette from his coat pocket, lighting it with a flick of his gold lighter, and blowing smoke down to a round crystal ashtray on the desk.

The time dragged by and finally the door opened. I turned my head to see my mother stepping into the room, her face pale and careworn, her white hands clutching her black purse in front of her like a shield.

My heart leapt in excitement, though my mother appeared to be a shadow of her once vibrant self—a woman who used to dress to the nines to go shopping but now looked like an ordinary housewife in her worn dress and frayed hat. I wanted to rush to her, but the SS man, sensing my joy, clutched me by the arm and held me fast to my seat.

She shuffled toward the table. The officer released my arm and signaled that my mother should sit in the chair next to him. Once seated, she looked at me with distress, tears trickling from her eyes.

"It's good to see you, Talya," she said. "Your father and I have worried about you for too long a time."

Shaken by this surprise, I slumped in my seat, mortified by my appearance. My hair had begun to grow back, but patches of bare scalp still remained. My dress was dirty and bore the remnants of the trash I had inserted into the fabric. Shame reddened my face. I was in no way presentable to a mother who had raised me in a fastidious manner.

I started to reply, but the officer held up his hand. "We have no time for pleasantries. Say what you came to say, Frau Petrovich."

My mother wiped her tears and then looked down as if she suffered from her own shame. "Herr Adler has come to see your father and me," she began, her voice trembling. "He has presented our family with a kind offer from Gestapo headquarters in Munich." She raised her head and studied me with her sad eyes. "It's one we would be wise to accept. Herr Adler told us you were sick and that if you didn't get treatment, you might be . . ." She shook violently and her body, in turn, was wracked with sobs.

"In fact, Herr Adler insists upon it," the officer interrupted, impatient with my mother. "I come as an intermediary for the Gestapo. What your mother is trying to say, Fräulein Petrovich, is that you are to be committed to Schattenwald at daybreak tomorrow. There, you will be treated for your mental disorder until it is deemed that you are fit to return to society." He crushed his cigarette in the ashtray, leaned toward me, and clasped his hands on the table. "There is one stipulation for the Reich's generous level of care, however."

I studied the SS officer's cold, unyielding face and wondered if Garrick had convinced the Gestapo that I would be useful rooting out more traitors—this time at an asylum. I'd heard of Schattenwald, which had a reputation before the Nazis as a kind and restful place. I was certain that emotional serenity had vanished.

"Am I schizophrenic?" I asked. "Psychotic? Simply mad? What if I choose not to go?"

"You know better than I how sick you are," the officer replied, his brows shifting upward. "It's interesting that you have a background in nursing. You, more than others, *could know* how these mental conditions manifest—what their symptoms are. But, aside from your knowledge, there is another more important issue to consider. You have not fulfilled your commitment—your promise to the Reich—according to Herr Adler. Who do you suppose has been keeping you alive since February of 1943? After all, you know the punishment meted out to the other members of your traitorous organization." He turned to my mother. "As do your parents . . . but time is running out."

I shook my head, unwilling to say or acknowledge anything that might incriminate me.

"The stipulation is that you *serve* the Reich by revealing its traitors," he continued. "You will from tomorrow forward be on a constant lookout for the infiltrators, frauds, and foreign agents who fill the halls of Schattenwald and wish the failure of the National Socialist war effort. Herr Adler believes you have the capacity to do so, despite your . . . illness. And once you have done your duty there, you will be assigned to other . . . places. Do you think the Reich has an endless supply of money to kindly support those who take advantage of our state, who live in a manner that is unproductive?"

I wanted to spit in his face because I had seen firsthand how the Nazis manufactured the disappearances and deaths of those who couldn't work or didn't produce to the level the state expected. Of course, I had no intention of betraying the residents of an asylum, traitors or otherwise. The idea was preposterous—my friends had sacrificed their lives in our fight against tyranny.

"I will ne—"

Before I could finish, my mother reached for my hands, terror etched on her face. "I implore you, Natalya, think before you speak. What you say will have long-lasting consequences for your father and me as well. It is so hard to *live* these days."

"Frau Petrovich speaks the truth," the officer said. "There are consequences for every action and . . . *inaction*."

My anger, as it had so many times in the past year, mutated into what felt like a brick in my forehead, thrusting me into the throes of depression. If I wanted to save my parents' lives, I had no choice but to agree to the Gestapo's demands. The Reich had turned the tables, after I had attempted to outwit them, trapping me in my mad ruse. How long could I survive in Schattenwald? How much time did I have? If I didn't betray anyone, my days surely would be numbered. What little resolve I had left wavered as I considered how to deal with this terrible situation.

"Your answer, Fräulein," the officer demanded. "My time is valuable." Smiling, he removed my mother's hands from mine.

I nodded, unable to mount an objection; my mother stared at me with wide eyes. "I will do as you ask," I said.

"Good," the officer replied. "See how easy it is to remedy difficult circumstances? One only has to bend . . . and honor a pledge."

He got up from his chair, momentarily leaving my mother and me alone at the table. She whispered "Thank you" and then added "Your father offers his love and regrets. . . ."

I put her fingers to my lips and kissed them.

The officer rapped on the door. "Frau Petrovich—it's time for us to leave your daughter. I sincerely hope she completes her task to our satisfaction. It will not go well for you—or for her—if she doesn't." He stared at me. "You will be transferred to Schattenwald at dawn tomorrow."

My mother tottered past me as a guard appeared. She and the officer disappeared at the end of the hall as I was led back to my cell. I marveled at how quickly one's fate could change under the Reich, how expectations and one's dream of life didn't matter for those who opposed Hitler. After my skimpy meal that evening, I tumbled into bed knowing it would be my last night at Stadelheim. I lay awake for many hours knowing that an asylum was my last chance at life.

The following morning, a guard herded me to the prison showers. I enjoyed the cleansing water despite its chill. I was issued a new dress that was in considerably better shape than the one I had altered, but my red triangle had changed to black, signifying my "mental illness." The guards let me keep my brown coat.

The police wagon taking me to Schattenwald arrived as the sun glinted on the eastern horizon, another tribute to timely Nazi efficiency. I took a last walk through the barren courtyard, a final glimpse of the prison walls and gate, before I was shoved into the wagon. No one came to say good-bye as I left—not even Dolly had come to see me off—and any reason to continue my "insane" act abated as I left Stadelheim behind. The Reich knew the truth behind my behavior, and I suspected that if I didn't perform at the asylum as expected, my death would come within months, if not sooner. Bouncing along in the wagon, I formulated a plan to keep quiet and submissive, to keep to myself, until I figured out how to escape from Schattenwald—if that was possible.

The trip to the asylum took less than a half hour, the imposing structure situated in a wooded area near Karlsfeld, south of Dachau. I'd learned about the Dachau camp from Lisa, although it was nearly impossible to confirm any of the rumors we'd heard; still, I suspected that there was a connection between the "business" of Schattenwald and the nearby concentration camp.

After weaving through the outskirts of Munich, the wagon passed villages and woods before arriving at the asylum's main gate, which was guarded by two men, one outfitted in a doctor's laboratory coat, the other in a standard Wehrmacht uniform. The wagon stopped at the guardhouse, and after the army man talked briefly with the driver, the gate opened and then closed behind us. All these details I noted with the grim determination of a police detective, hoping they would serve me in the future.

The gate was mechanized and heavy, probably four meters tall, with no break across its spiked top. Despite the early morning sun, the woods surrounding the asylum cast dark shadows, giving me the odd feeling that we were passing through a tunnel. The thick stands of oak and beech were a blessing and a curse: They would be easy to hide in, but their dead branches, brambles, and weeds would make an escape more difficult. Glancing through the wagon's window, as flashes of light and shadow swept past me, I spotted a stone fence, at least three meters high, encircling the property. My spirits sagged as I took a hard look at my fading chances for freedom.

After three minutes on the winding lane, the wagon arrived at Schattenwald, a baroque building whose exterior consisted of decorative pillars, arched windows, and domed turrets that reminded me of a cathedral. I suspected that at one time it was the home of a rich family. The sunlight reflected off its stone exterior in a rosy-pink hue, giving the structure the false perception of a cheery façade. Two large three-story wings extended east and west of the main building and spread to the edge of the dark woods. They appeared added to the original structure.

Leaving the wagon's motor running, the driver alighted from the cab and opened its rear doors. A rush of cold air struck my face, amid the vehicle's exhaust fumes. Two burly men grabbed my arms and pulled me from the wagon. "I can walk without your help," I told them, but they paid no attention to my objection.

"Good luck here. . . . Are you as mad as you claim to be?" a man with thick arms taunted me. "The doctors will take *good* care of you." He laughed aloud as he and his partner forced me through the door, past the faded grandeur of the lobby with its gold-flecked wallpaper and tarnished chandelier, and into an office to the right of the entrance.

The odors of disinfectant and ammonia faded, only to be replaced by the scratchy smells of aging paper and tobacco smoke. The men instructed me to sit in a red leather chair in front of one of the largest oak desks I'd ever seen. A gigantic arched window, barred with filigreed scrolls of vines, looked out on the spacious grounds verdant with grass. Bookcases, loaded with medical volumes and files, lined each wall except for the one behind the desk; there, an unused fireplace sat, its blackened stone firebox and marble mantel streaked by smoke.

But the focal point of the room was a grandiose painting

that took up half the space above the fireplace. I was unsure whether the scene was to inspire horror or awe, but I judged it to be a painting of Prometheus, who, in mythology, found himself bound to a rock while a large eagle ate his liver each day, only for the organ to regenerate and be eaten again—his punishment from Zeus for giving mortals the gift of fire. The half-naked Titan writhed in agony as the bird pecked at his flesh.

The artist and date of the painting were florid enough, but I couldn't make out the inscription even with my glasses. I wondered if it had been repainted or "doctored" recently, for a swastika had been applied to each wing of the eagle. Did Prometheus symbolize Hitler's conquests or, more to the point, the patients at Schattenwald?

A shadow appeared behind the opaque glass that made up most of the office door. A distinguished man I judged to be in his early fifties stepped into the room, his black hair, graying at the temples, slicked back across his head. He wore dark pants and a starched white shirt, accented by a black bow tie, and carried a pipe and leather-bound notebook. He would have passed for a professor, had it not been for his white lab coat.

His eyes took me in as he rounded the desk and pulled out his chair. A slight odor of rubbing alcohol wafted past me as he sat down. He struck a match, lit his pipe, and puffed on it, spewing a few embers on the desk, which he extinguished with his fingers. Opening his notebook, he said, "Fräulein Petrovich, I am Dr. Werner Kalbrunner. Welcome to Schattenwald."

I squirmed in my seat, unsure how to respond to his formal greeting, undecided whether I should remain mute or talk. I looked down at my chapped hands and said nothing.

My reluctance didn't stop the doctor from observing me. His gaze swirled in an endless sweep from my waist to the top of my head. His scrutiny made me so uncomfortable I wanted to order him to stop; however, I was in no position to do so.

"I know your history," the doctor said in an authoritarian voice free from emotion. "I also know when someone suffers from a mental deficiency." He paused while I continued to stare into my lap. "Look at me," he ordered as if he were talking to a child.

I obeyed. He leaned back in his chair and puffed on his pipe, sending balloons of smoke sailing over his head toward the unfortunate Prometheus.

"Good," he said. "Let's have a talk—bring everything out in the open."

I looked into his eyes, trying to judge his character, and found myself unable to get past his stare. His brown orbs appeared incapable of displaying feeling. "What would you like me to say—that I'm mad? That I'm guilty of my crimes?"

"Are you—on both counts—or not?"

Again, I feared any wrong word would send me to the guillotine, faster than I'd anticipated, so I said nothing.

He opened his notebook and rustled a few papers. "You can relax in this room, Fräulein. Many rooms at Schattenwald are monitored by listening devices, but this office and the operating rooms are not. Dr. König and I made sure of that. We need rooms with privacy to conduct our interviews." He rested his pipe in the large ashtray on the desk and then looked out the window. "It looks as if the weather will be beautiful today. Days like these are a blessing before winter sets in."

I gazed upon the lawn as well, the sun high enough above the trees to send spears of light shooting down to the frosty grass. A few orderlies in white uniforms strolled the grounds, taking advantage of the warmth. I turned back to him wondering if there was any sincerity in his view of the weather. A sliver of hope crept into my head. "Tell me what you know about me."

He opened a drawer, pulled out a pair of reading glasses, and positioned them on his face. "You are Russian, from Leningrad; a citizen of the Reich, you served as a volunteer nurse on the Russian Front; your parents live in Munich, current address unknown because of the Allied bombings." He ran a thin finger down the page. "An associate, Lisa Kolbe, was executed for assaulting an officer of the SS, writing and distributing seditious literature, consorting with the enemy—the White Rose." He looked over his glasses at me. "Stadelheim authorities report 'serious mental problems,' but are uncertain of their validity. You seem sane to me."

Apparently, I hadn't fooled this man with my ruse.

The doctor took off his glasses, tossed them on the desk, and chuckled. "Stadelheim is useless . . . they're prison administrators and guards. What do they know about the mental state of their inmates? The fact is they drive more people mad than they rehabilitate. Most of the time the Stadelheim cure is the chopping block."

"You know a great deal about me," I said, "but how do you know I'm sane?"

"First, no one who's mad would ever ask that question," he replied. "Second, by looking at you . . . but then, certain men in the Gestapo *never* considered you insane. Those men were smart enough to figure out that you were trying to get yourself committed to an asylum. Were you looking for an easier way out of your captivity?"

I sighed and turned back to the window.

"Believe me, Fräulein Petrovich, I have the greatest respect for you because you survived Stadelheim, but an escape from Schattenwald is just as difficult, if not more so. As you can see, we are in the forest—so to speak—far from any apartment buildings in which to seek cover, far from any shops, restaurants, churches in which to find refuge. Believe me, there is no way out."

"What do you want from me?" I asked, resigned that my last days would now be played out quickly, with no need of ever reporting to the Gestapo.

"I believe you've been given a formidable task, one that if not completed successfully might lead to your death . . . but Dr. König is my equal here. . . . We make joint decisions based on our diagnoses."

He smiled as a ray of sun fell through the window onto the parquet floor. "Schattenwald can be so cold during the winter. Would you like a cup of tea?"

I considered his offer. "Yes, I'd like that." Tea would take the morning chill away, and it would be my first sip of the brew in more than a year.

"Good. I'll call for it. Then I'll introduce you to the duties you'll be performing while you're here."

"Duties?"

"You were a nurse, were you not?" He picked up the phone on his desk to call for the tea.

"Yes." A shiver overtook me as I sat back in my chair.

"Well, then . . . you'll be helping me as we treat the insane."

CHAPTER 14

Because Schattenwald was filled with patients, I shared a room with a young woman who spent most days and nights curled in a ball on her cot. Dr. Kalbrunner told me she was mute, deaf, and unresponsive to most treatments, so her days at the asylum were most likely numbered. He had volunteered this information clinically, matter-of-factly, as if I were a member of the staff. "You will benefit from rooming with a patient who can't talk or hear," he explained. "There is less need to hide one's feelings . . . one's secrets."

"We don't often get trained patients who can assist, so we should use your knowledge for our benefit," he continued. "You're still a prisoner, however, and I would caution you not to grow fond of the other residents."

He needn't have reminded me. His attitude toward me was oddly discomforting or soothing depending on the day. By some measure, I was a "member" of the staff, and I felt I was being "groomed" by Dr. Kalbrunner. For what, I wasn't sure.

From the first day, the doctor had taken me to the treatment rooms, as they were called, at the rear of the main building, where "needed" medical procedures were performed. He had pointed out where supplies were kept under lock and key, escorted me to the common rooms, and one in particular, where men and women, young and old, all looking tired and haggard no matter their age, wandered about in what must have been a grand ballroom or sat in chairs staring through barred windows to the great lawn. I knew nothing of their histories—only that some seemed medicated; others, with shaking limbs and trembling voices, appeared manic. The squirrels and birds that cavorted on the lawn on their way to the woods were the only company these fellow residents enjoyed in their mental confinement.

The patients ate in a common room that looked out on another bank of woods—the food was not prepared badly, but the amount on your plate or bowl was measured by the servers. I soon realized that patients in the worst shape were given smaller portions containing fewer calories; their gruel was thinner and less nutritious than those of us with hopes of being "cured"; in other words, the "lucky ones" held some particular role or benefit for the Nazis.

My duties, as prescribed by the doctor, were numbing and mindless and consisted mainly of scrubbing operating floors after surgeries, emptying bedpans, and cleaning up messes created by the most excitable patients. At times, I was called on to help restrain a resident or even help with feeding, but never did I witness a medical procedure or make use of my real nursing experience. My days and nights were as long and protracted as those spent in prison.

Early in my stay, I wondered why Dr. Kalbrunner was showing me such "kindness." I had no immediate answer to that question, but I suspected his concern might be a trick.

The other Nazi staff members were perfunctory, obligatory, and punctual in their duties and seemed less threatening than the guards at Stadelheim. At Schattenwald, people appeared and disappeared, but the crowded conditions made it hard to judge. Most patients couldn't talk because of their illness or the effects of medication; others, like me, had been warned to keep silent. Schattenwald appeared to be a staging ground for the end of one's earthly journey, an institution outside of Munich somehow forgotten and spared from the Allied bombings. The doctors, nurses, and orderlies must have sensed this finality, known their roles, and carried out their duties accordingly.

Dr. König was equally inscrutable. He was somewhat older

than Dr. Kalbrunner, and looked like a grandfather with his gray beard, bald head, and spritely blue eyes. He almost danced around the room, light in step, a smile gracing his face whenever I saw him, showing great agility and dexterity, and unusual strength, for a person I judged to be in his sixties. His Nazi Party pin was proudly displayed on his suit lapel. Unlike Dr. Kalbrunner, Dr. König rarely wore a lab coat.

As my time at Schattenwald lengthened from a few days, to a week, to a month, and winter deepened, my concern grew about the time I had left. I chuckled out loud in my room one night as I thought about my "stipulation" of finding traitors and conspirators among these patients. As far as I could tell, every man and woman who worked at the asylum was a dedicated National Socialist, and residents had no head for politics or the slightest comprehension about the war that raged around them. I grew nervous and agitated about my numbered days, unable to sleep nights, even in the total darkness provided by the blackout curtains. Escape plans shot through my half slumbers but always ended in a nightmarish jumble instead of a carefully executed strategy.

I found a piece of chalk in an operating room and used it to mark the passing days by scratching marks underneath my bed. My silent roommate slept across from me, mostly unaware of my comings and goings.

Fourteen days had come and gone in December 1944, when Dr. Kalbrunner opened my door shortly after midnight the morning of the fifteenth. My roommate stirred, giving the doctor a drowsy glance before returning to her sleep. He stood in shadow, the hall lights behind him framing him in garish white.

"I need your assistance, Natalya," he said.

I threw off my blanket, rose from my cot, and rubbed my temples in an effort to rid myself of my weariness. "My assistance? For what?" My limbs were heavy and I wondered if I'd heard him correctly.

"Come with me . . . and be quiet. I don't want to disturb others."

I put my coat on over my dress, for the corridors of Schatten-wald were cold during the late fall nights. No one stirred in the sterile hall with its rows of white doors lining each side. Behind them, patients slept—some restrained, some deep in dreams in-spired by their drugged state, others moaning softly for free-dom. Without saying a word, Dr. Kalbrunner led me down the staircase. An orderly and an armed guard stood talking at the bottom of the stairs. They nodded at the doctor but said noth-ing to him, apparently used to seeing high-ranking staff escort-ing patients in the middle of the night.

The doctor picked up his pace after we passed the men, and we moved swiftly through the large common room until stop-ping in front of a locked door on the far wall—the entrance to the operating rooms I had seen before. Making use of his key, we stepped into a long hallway lined on each side with small compartments. Each entrance contained a small window allow-ing a visitor a look inside. The rooms were sterile, like laborato-ries; white tiled, with stirrups and restraints hanging from the walls; syringes, scalpels, and other medical instruments placed neatly on silver trays alongside metal slabs sturdy enough to hold a human body.

The smell in the corridor reminded me of the operating tent on the Russian Front but without the benefit of proper ventila-tion. The cloying odors of sour linen, medicinal alcohol, and wounded flesh hung heavy in the air. I fought back the urge to gag.

"Are you all right, Natalya?" the doctor asked, noting my discomfort.

I placed my hand over my mouth and nodded.

"We're stopping at the last operating room," he said. "No one is allowed inside unless Dr. König and I give permission. You'll see why in a moment."

We had come to yet another doorway at the end of the hall. The doctor produced a second key from his pocket, the lock clicked, and he pushed the door open.

The space was dark except for a bulb that produced a fan-tastical blue light from a lamp positioned high above our heads.

The room was twice the size of the ones we had passed and held racks of medical equipment, containers of powdered and liquid drugs of various sizes and colors, and a slab large enough to hold two bodies side by side. Much of the wall space was covered by padded cloth to limit the noise from the operations conducted here.

On the slab, glowing silvery blue under the light, a young woman, secured by hand and ankle straps, lay faceup. Her complexion had the ghastly hue of the dead, her short hair raven black in the strange illumination, her fingers and toenails fluorescent in the light. Except for her arms and feet, her body was covered by a sheet—the sight and the cold dampness of the room sent my head and stomach spiraling.

I clutched my abdomen and cried out, "I'm going to vomit."

The doctor pointed to a wall where a porcelain sink abutted from the padded surface. "If you must."

I ran to it and retched up the thin soup I'd eaten for dinner. My back heaved several times until there was nothing left to expel.

The doctor's cold fingers crept across my shoulder. "It *will* get worse. You must steel yourself to such horrors. Are you well enough to walk?"

I gasped. "I need a minute . . ."

"But only a minute," he said, and walked toward the slab.

A sharp pang hit me again, and I leaned over the sink but only a bubbly froth came out. I turned on the tap; icy water poured from the spigot. I splashed it on my face and drank a little, attempting to calm my gut. After a few moments, my breathing relaxed and I was able to face the doctor.

"I'll show you how you can assist me." He walked to the wall and flipped a switch. The blue light went out, plunging the room into total darkness before an overhead bank of white lights came on in its place.

He returned to the table and picked up a syringe filled with a clear liquid from the medical tray by its side. "This is filled with phenol. Inject it into her heart and she will die." He handed it to me.

"She's not dead?"

He walked behind me and placed his hands on my shoulders. "No, she's been given a sedative. She'll never know what you've done—she'll die peacefully in her sleep."

My hand trembled and the syringe bounced in my palm.

"Be careful," he cautioned. "You don't want to waste a drop of this precious medicine." His grip tightened so much that I had no strength to turn on him. The thought of thrusting the needle into him passed through my mind, but such an attack would have destroyed any chance of escaping Schattenwald. The guillotine would be waiting.

He guided me toward the body. I could see the woman's face clearly now under the white light. She was pretty with short black hair, and dark-lashed eyes closed in her induced slumber.

"Go ahead." His voice taunted me, like a hunter encouraging a novice to slaughter a beast, urging me to kill the young woman in front of me.

"What's her crime?" I asked. "What's she done to deserve death?"

"She's a Jew and a communist—she's scum—the Reich must rid the world of such vermin."

I struggled in his grip, hoping to wrench myself away, but he was too strong. His fingers dug deeper into my shoulders.

"Is this how I pay for my crimes against the Reich—by committing murder?"

I thrust the syringe backward, toward the doctor, but he caught my wrist and shoved me toward the slab. I faced him. "I'll never kill a patriot who stands against a murderous dictator." I tossed the syringe onto the slab. "*You're* the brave doctor. Go ahead! I want to see you kill her so you'll be sent to hell with the rest of them. Then, you can *kill* me."

A hand clutched my coat. I screamed and jumped away as the young woman rose up on her elbows.

Dr. Kalbrunner eyed me coldly, judging my reaction as the woman eased out of her restraints and swung her legs off the table. "I'm sorry I had to do this, Natalya, but I . . . we . . . needed to know that you didn't share the Nazi fondness for killing undesirables. If you did, your time here would have ended tonight." His eyes shifted to the woman, and his clinical gaze transformed to one of relief. "It's all right, Marion. There'll be no execution tonight."

The sheet slipped from her body, exposing her thin legs and sunken chest. As frail as an old woman, she walked toward me, extending her hand in greeting. I clasped her icy fingers as she clutched at me like a feeble person grasping a cane.

"I'm fine, Doctor," Marion said, "as long as I can lean on Natalya."

I unbuttoned my coat, opened it, and Marion huddled against me.

My confusion prompted the doctor to speak. "This room is safe from others, Natalya, but you must listen and listen well. What I'm going to tell you can only be said once—there will be no going back if you want to live. Marion and I felt you should know our plan because it won't succeed without you. Our resistance—your resistance—is too important to let die. You must carry on."

Marion shivered and her bony back pressed through her thin dress into my ribs.

The doctor picked up the syringe and replaced it on the tray. "You may be correct in your assessment about my going to hell—for I am a murderer, but only of those who are suffering, who have no hope of escaping the condemnation of the Reich." He paused and looked down at the slab. "You must understand that I have no choice, like all of us who live under Hitler. . . . I save those who can make a difference. You and Marion are worth saving."

"Every life is worth saving," I said.

"If you truly believe that, you are as out of touch with reality as the Nazis." He approached us in measured steps, a man as confident in his convictions as Roland Freisler of the People's Court. "Think, Natalya—come down from your rosy castle in the sky. I, too, have a family I love. The formal order to kill those who are mentally deficient has been dropped—the Aktion T4 program came to an end in 1941, but Dr. König and the others—make no mistake about it—the Gestapo, the SS—they *expect* it to continue. Your loyalty is questioned if it *isn't* done. So . . . I kill those who are nearly dead—but not because I want to. . . . I'm selfish. . . . I want to save my family's life and my own, and in doing so I can save others." He bowed his head as if his spirit had broken. "I suppose what I've said makes no sense, but if you were in my position you'd understand."

"Dr. Kalbrunner is saving me," Marion said, still huddling inside my coat. "I'm a Jew and a communist—once a member of what the Gestapo calls the Red Orchestra. They imprisoned me and then sent me here because I was related to someone in the group. They didn't have enough evidence to send me to my death; but, I have more connections than the Nazis suspect, and I'm eager to continue my resistance against the Reich. Dr. Kalbrunner is our savior. König knows nothing of this—he stands with the Nazis."

"What we've planned is complicated, Natalya," the doctor continued, "and we trust you because of your association with the White Rose, but we had to know that your very being—your soul—opposes the Nazis. You didn't *want* to kill, but before this war is over you may have to." He pointed to the far end of the room. "Let me show you what remains of Schattenwald."

Marion slipped from my coat as we followed the doctor to a large metal door. "It is always locked, but there's an extra key on the shelf under this box of linen." He lifted it and metal glinted silver in the light. "Only Dr. König and I and a few SS photographers are allowed into this room. The reason will become obvious once you enter." He unlocked the door.

The cold struck our faces as we entered a large, industrial space with no windows, the walls lined with shelves. A pale bulb burned overhead, leaving most of the room in shadow. There were no medical supplies or medicines in this room. Instead, the treasures of the dead awaited us. Although no bodies were in sight, the room had the distinct putrid odor of death. The doctor pulled a box from a shelf, opened it, and I gasped. It was filled with gold fillings—hundreds, perhaps more. An equal number of boxes storing the same dental work spanned from floor to ceiling. He proceeded down the rows of shelves, each case holding its own bounty from the dead: watches, rings, bracelets, necklaces, hair—until we arrived at items too large to be held in boxes. Violins, guitars, flutes, books, small paintings, gold picture frames, expensive suitcases—the trappings of those who had clung to what they could carry from their homes at the last minute, the possessions of men, women, and children snuffed out by the Nazis.

"What happened to the bodies?" I asked.

"There's a crematorium at Dachau, not far from here," he responded. "Usually, it's their own dead, but they take ours as well." He led us to the end of the room. "This is Schattenwald's southernmost point. Go through this door and you're on the grounds. It's only locked from the outside, but escape is not as easy as that. The door is armed and guards make the rounds of the building, so your timing must be perfect."

Overwhelmed and exhausted, I leaned against the shelves holding the musical instruments. "What do you want me to do?" I pulled Marion close, her thin body resting against me for warmth.

The doctor stood next to the door, studying it, before he spoke. "Give us your allegiance—don't betray us. It was no accident that you were placed with the mute. Marion will be executed, her file falsified, the woman in your room will take her place in death. We've planned her escape by the route I'm showing you."

"This is madness," I said.

The doctor straightened. "You don't understand. I *need* a body. The body has to be *dead* to be delivered to Dachau. Marion will take the place of the patient in your room until she can be safely moved out. You may have to smuggle food to her, aid her when help is needed, because she'll have to stay in bed. You'll be next—exchanged for another patient. Do you understand how this must work?

"Marion's life shouldn't be sacrificed for a woman who rarely leaves her bed, who never speaks, who can't hear a spoken word. The cards were against her in the first place. Her parents wanted her to die from the moment she was born because she was *defective*. They are avid Nazis and, under the regime, they found a way to fulfill their wish."

Marion looked at me with desolate eyes, all the more sunken in the dim light. "I would never ask this of you, if I couldn't make a difference, if I couldn't fight the evil that has consumed Germany." She put her thin hands on mine. "Natalya, I know that I will die sooner than later, but I beg you to let me spend my last days fighting . . . not rotting in this place. Let me die with honor and at peace with my conscience because I tried, because we have to resist . . . as your friends did."

Her words crushed me. How was one life worth more than another? Didn't the people the Nazis considered "freaks" deserve to live as well? Despite these questions, mounting an argument against the doctor and Marion was difficult, for I understood what lay ahead for the woman in my room. Her death, like mine, was looming large, her days growing short. If I could save someone like Marion who might help bring down the Reich, then, perhaps . . . my life wouldn't have been in vain. I shuddered at the *choice*. Hitler had masteredminded such choices for his people—always a matter of life or death.

After a brief consideration, and with a sinking heart, I consented.

"Unfortunately, there is no other way." The doctor's eyes flickered impatiently. "All right, let's proceed, for we don't have much time—I don't want to generate suspicion. If our plan fails for any reason, you must save yourself. Remember what I've told you. I've placed an electric torch behind this suitcase." He lifted the leather case and showed me the lamp. "You'll find it necessary in the dark woods."

He pointed to two wires that snaked around the door from a metal box on the wall, one was red, the other blue. "Remember blue. The blue wire connects the door to the alarm box and must be pulled out, snapped, or cut by any method you can devise, perhaps a scalpel from the medical tray. The alarm will sound if it's not disconnected.

"Schattenwald is shaped like a cross," he continued. "Think of this room as being at its apex, or like twelve on a clock face."

I nodded, surveying the room's hideous contents.

"Go south into the woods about one hundred meters. A small stream runs there—it may be frozen—follow its banks until you reach what would be the hour of nine. A large stone outcropping rises a few meters to the east of the stream. Look for a split in the boulder—clothing has been hidden there to replace your prison dress. Keep your coat because you will need it."

My head was swimming with information, but still the doctor continued.

"On my walks around the grounds, I make sure these measures are in place." He leaned against a shelf while Marion and I stood across from him. "This door isn't guarded as heavily as the others because only doctors have access to the room." He looked at his watch. "Food and supplies arrive at seven in the morning through the main entrance. The guards are busiest and more distracted at that time. However, getting past the gate to the outside is the trickiest part—sometimes the guards have dogs—particularly in the winter, when the dark prevails. Travel upwind, if you can, so the animals won't catch your scent.

"The shift changes at eight in the morning, about the time the sun rises this time of year. Your only escape route is through the gate. The fence around the grounds is unbroken and topped by electrified wire. Don't even consider climbing it."

"It sounds impossible," I said.

"Difficult, but not impossible," the doctor replied.

"There's another thing to remember," Marion said. "The number one hundred."

"Yes?" I asked, unsure what she meant.

"Memorize this combination: thirty-two, fifty-six, twelve. The numbers total one hundred."

I repeated the numbers until I had them firmly fixed in my head.

"They're the street numbers of safe houses in Munich. They may save your life, so don't forget them. Blumenstrasse, Uhlandstrasse, Steinstrasse—BUS." Marion nodded as I repeated the names several times.

"We've taken long enough," the doctor said to me. "I'll take you back first and then come back for Marion." He put his hands on her thin shoulders. "You should take your place on the table in case someone makes an unexpected entrance." He addressed me again. "Act like you're drugged. Stare at the floor, look no one in the eye, limp occasionally as I take you back."

We returned to the operating room where the slab waited for Marion. She climbed onto it. Dr. Kalbrunner placed the restraints on her wrists and ankles without locking them and covered her with the sheet. He handed me the syringe filled with phenol. "In case it becomes . . . necessary."

"For murder?" I asked, securing it in my coat pocket.

"No." His eyes dimmed. "Suicide."

I said good-bye to Marion and wished her well. On the way back, we passed the guard, but not the orderly who had been standing with him. I followed the doctor's instructions and said nothing to the guard; he never spoke as I limped up the stairs. The doctor left me in my room and I hid the syringe under my mattress. Whether it was the presence of the needle or the burgeoning hope of escape, for the first time in many weeks I fell into a deep sleep.

The doctor had revealed his plan for Marion early Friday morning. By the break of day on Monday, no word had come from either him or Marion. I found myself pacing my small room, nerves taut to the breaking point, the young woman next to me unaware of my anguish regarding her imminent demise.

Regardless of their whereabouts, I had to carry on at Schattenwald as if nothing out of the ordinary had happened. This included being called to breakfast on Monday with the rest of the patients who were lucid enough to eat their own meals. We ate in a large room opposite the common room. The day was overcast with pearly gray clouds sealing the sky. An occasional sunbeam burst through the clouds only to be sapped away by the wan billows.

I was chewing on a hard crust of bread and drinking weak tea when I spotted two SS officers strut onto the lawn from a door leading into my wing of the asylum. Four of these bellicose men eventually left the building, escorting Dr. Kalbrunner and Marion in the middle of their formation, the doctor wearing black pants and an open white shirt, Marion hobbling along as if her right leg had been injured.

My heart thumped; clearly something had gone wrong. The doctor turned his body toward the windows as he passed, displaying the bloody shirt, red welts, and purple bruises on his face and chest. One of the officers shoved the doctor forward with a blow from his palm as if he didn't want to soil himself by touching his prisoner.

Marion stumbled forward toward the woods, head down, eyes fixed on the ground.

Soon they disappeared into the forest shadows. I dropped my bread on my plate, my nerves twitching in horror. The time, if ever there was such a moment, had arrived when I could plead insanity—I was slipping into a darkness like none I had ever felt, even more so than at my trial. I covered my face with my hands and trembled over the bread plate, forfeiting all hope for my friends.

A nurse poked me in the back. "What's wrong?" she asked roughly.

Now was not the time to draw attention from the staff. "Nothing," I said, uncovering my face and straightening in my chair. "I felt the need to pray."

She frowned. "No praying here. Do it again and you'll be reported." She whacked the back of my head with her hand for good measure. "Eat!"

I lifted my cup to my lips. In the distance, muffled gunfire echoed through the woods—four shots fired in rapid succession. There could be no mistaking the sound.

A few minutes later, the four SS men emerged from the woods, smiling and laughing as they passed the dining room window.

I couldn't hear what they said, but I knew what had happened. Dr. Kalbrunner and Marion were dead, and the SS officers had left their bodies on the ground—like Sina and her children. A short time later, four male orderlies left the building and walked casually by the windows, two of them carrying body bags in their gloved hands.

I finished my bread and tea and listened to a Schubert string quartet that someone had put on the record player. I think it was *Death and the Maiden*. A few of the patients rose from their chairs and moved in time to the music. One could hardly call it dancing, but it was the most affirming vision I'd seen since my stay began. A crippling inertia settled across my body and I stared through the window at the pearly sky and the thick woods.

I shook the numbness from my brain, knowing that no one would notice the ravings of a "lunatic."

Death stood in the corner leering at me, laughing with frosty breath, and I could feel his cold hands around my neck.

Now, any escape from Schattenwald would be one of my making.

CHAPTER 15

I didn't have to wait long to find out my fate.

About six o'clock in the morning on the twenty-first of December, the winter solstice, Dr. König came to my room.

When the key settled into the lock, I had barely enough time to extract the syringe from its hiding place and secure it in my coat pocket. I said nothing to the smiling doctor, and he was equally mute—except for an order to follow him. I asked if I might put on my coat because it was cold in the building. He agreed and led me out of the room.

We traveled the same route that I'd taken with Dr. Kalbrunner: down the stone stairs, through the common room to the door at its end, passing the long row of operating rooms until we arrived at the chamber where I'd met Marion. Two orderlies stood in the corridor, and one opened the door, allowing us to enter.

Lights blazed in the room. Dr. König released my arm and told the men to shut the door and "wait outside until called." The padded space loomed large in my memory, as I fought the fear that threatened to swamp me. I breathed deeply, hoping for calm; I didn't want to break down in front of this Nazi doctor.

The memory of the two-person slab that held Marion also was burned in my mind and set my pulse thumping. A middle-aged woman lay splayed on the metal, her wrists and ankles bound by the leather straps.

I took quick note of my surroundings. Everything was much

the same as before, but the medical trays on both sides of the slab grabbed my attention. A bloody scalpel and forceps lay on the tray nearest the woman; on the other side, by the empty slot, the same equipment, unused, glinted in the light. A brown bottle on that tray caught my eye.

The doctor grasped my arm and led me around the slab, allowing me to see the woman from another angle. Gray streaks ran through her hair, but I had no idea if she had aged naturally, or if Schattenwald had drained her youth. The skin on her exposed arms and legs spread in fleshy pools on the slab as if she had lost a great deal of weight.

Her thin medical gown was bunched at the groin in a bloody V, the precious fluid from her body flowing in rivulets down her legs to a trough at the bottom of the slab. There, her blood drained into a pipe that disappeared into the floor.

"It *is* cold, but you won't need your coat," the doctor said, stroking his gray beard. "Please relax. Schattenwald is a model of efficiency and exemplary medical practice, our sanitation and hygiene are benchmarks for other institutions." He paused. Unlike Dr. Kalbrunner who was tall and thin, Dr. König was of medium height, but decidedly more muscular. For his age, he was a strong man; his powerful arms swelled underneath his suit jacket. "Hang your coat on the hook." He pointed to the wall across the room. "Then take your place here." He tapped his fingers on the unoccupied part of the slab.

I shuffled to the wall, turning my left side toward him, palming the syringe from my coat. I cupped it in my hand so it remained hidden from him, the needle extending a few centimeters past my curled fingers. I prayed that the smug doctor wouldn't notice it as I drew closer.

"I'm sure you've heard the unfortunate news about Dr. Kalbrunner," he said as I returned. "I'm your doctor now. Make yourself comfortable on the table."

"What have you done to her?" I asked to distract him. I slid onto the table and concealed the syringe in the folds of my dress. The sting of the cold metal seeped through to my skin, causing me to shiver; I felt as if I was climbing into my coffin.

"Take off your shoes and lie back," he said. "What I've done to *her* is immaterial to you, but it is in the best interest of the Reich to ensure that all unfortunates are unable to bear children."

He had sterilized her.

"Is that what you have planned for me?" I dropped my shoes to the floor and then lay back on the slab, making sure the syringe was within my grasp. I wanted to stab him in the neck then, but the orderlies stood outside the door.

"No, my dear, we have something else in store for you. It's all written in this little book." He held up a slim volume bound in red leather and then opened it to a particular page. "Your name is Natalya Petrovich, isn't it?"

He knew my name—this was a game. "Yes."

"You were associated with the White Rose, I believe?" He placed the book on the equipment tray.

"Yes." I scooted my fingers over the syringe.

"You were ordered to find those at Schattenwald who might betray the Reich, is that correct?"

He leaned over my body, his strong hands fastening the straps to my right wrist and then my right ankle. The jugular vein popped from his neck, the vein, strong, filled with flowing blood that if injected with the phenol would cripple and kill in an instant. The warmth of his body, the medicinal smell that emanated from his clothes, filled my nostrils. Still, the men stood outside.

"You've had no success rooting out these traitors and conspirators against our glorious Führer?"

"None. It appears that the SS have succeeded where I've failed."

He positioned the equipment tray until it was within a thumb's reach of my left arm. "I like your sense of humor, Natalya, but there is important business to be done—"

A knock interrupted him. "Don't go anywhere," he said with a sly smile as he turned from me toward the door.

I knew he'd be gone only a short time. A chance for survival presented itself. I stretched my free arm as far to the left as I could in an effort to clutch the tray's rim—it remained a finger-nail's length away. I jerked hard, wrenching my right arm and leg in the straps so violently I nearly cried out, but I was able to budge the tray with my fingertip and move it to within my grasp.

The orderlies informed the doctor they had been called to attend other patients. Dr. König directed them to remove the woman who lay next to me and return in an hour.

While the doctor and the men went about their task of removing her, I lifted my head and peered at the open book. Two columns divided the page, one of them marked *Tod*. My name was at the bottom of the death list. My time at Schattenwald was over. I lay back. The terror filling me brought clarity: *The syringe is useless unless I can get it into his heart or neck. The brown bottle may be ether, but the stopper needs to come out.*

The orderlies lifted the woman's limp body and placed it on a gurney.

The doctor accompanied them back to the door. "Make sure she is delivered to the correct room," he said as he watched them leave.

Barely moving my body, I grasped the top of the brown bottle, loosening the stopper with my fingers. I settled back on the frigid slab, afraid to take my eyes off Dr. König. He locked the door and turned toward me with a macabre grimace. The mint-like odor of ether drifted toward me, a smell the doctor surely would notice as well.

I had only seconds.

Everything shifted into slow motion; my limbs, even those unbound, seemed glued to the slab. The doctor moved toward me, his grimace widening to a smile as he rounded the slab, the movements of his arms and legs precise, like those of an automaton. The smile faded as he neared the tray, sniffed, and reached for the brown bottle.

I grasped the bottle before he could reach it and flung its contents toward the stunned doctor.

The stopper flew off, and streams of the clear liquid landed on his face.

He cried out, a scream unheard because the room was constructed to obliterate such noise. He clawed at his eyes, unable to see, and staggered toward the tray, knocking it against the slab.

He collapsed in a heap on the floor, moaned, and then lay still.

I held my breath to keep from breathing the fumes. I had to act quickly. The restraints were tight, but a scalpel was within reach. I cut into the strap securing my right hand. The leather fell away. I shot up and unfastened the ankle strap.

I leapt from my deathbed and fumbled for a surgeon's mask still on the tray. I positioned it on my face and breathed, filtered air filling my lungs.

I picked up the syringe that had rolled to the bottom of the trough.

Dr. Kalbrunner had warned me that I might have to kill to stay alive.

Dr. König lay curled on the floor on his left side, his knees folded like a sleeping child, the inviting jugular once again exposed. I took my eyes off him briefly, looked around the room, and thought about what had gone on in this terrible place. I remembered Lisa, Hans, Sophie, Alex, Willi, and the others who had died opposing the regime. I'd watched as Dr. Kalbrunner and Marion were executed. The boxes of gold fillings, the jewelry, the personal possessions plundered from those killed by Dr. König would never leave my memory.

I jabbed the needle into the doctor's neck and pushed the plunger, injecting the phenol. His body shook for a second, then his chest constricted, a hiss left his mouth, and his breathing stopped.

The time for nonviolence and passive resistance had ended.

I'd killed a man. A hollow numbness washed over me, but I felt no remorse. Any such emotion was obliterated by my will to live.

Everything that Dr. Kalbrunner had told me about escaping Schattenwald flooded into my head.

I raced across the room, grabbed my coat, and put on my shoes, every second precious. The silver key to the last room lay under the linen box just as the doctor had shown me. I opened the door, retrieved the electric torch, and shined it on the exit.

Blue . . . remember the blue wire.

I placed the torch on the floor, grabbed the wire, and using my body weight, leaned back on my feet. The wire snapped and I tumbled to the cold floor, half expecting to hear an alarm. However, no sound blared.

Cold air rushed past me as I opened the door and peered around it. No guards were in sight. The winter night was still and deep, the stars obscured by the clouds, spits of snow salting the air. I closed the door and darted toward the woods.

Dr. Kalbrunner had said to go one hundred meters into the woods and I followed his instruction, soon finding the stream that he had described. I switched on the torch briefly, making sure that it was pointed away from Schattenwald. The water ran clear and cold, with patches of silvery ice reflecting the torch light. I turned it off and closed my eyes, allowing them to adjust to the void—when I opened them again, the stark black figures of tree trunks, limbs, and bushes came into view.

I'd been in the room about a half hour, which gave me another half hour before the morning supplies were scheduled to arrive at Schattenwald. The orderlies Dr. König had commanded to deal with the sterilized woman, I was certain, would arrive promptly back at seven, as instructed. Most likely, they would wait outside the room until their curiosity got the better of them, allowing me enough time to make my planned escape through the gate.

I turned left and followed the stream, the brambles clutching at my legs, my feet sliding over the exposed tree roots. As I neared nine on the clock face, a boulder rose from the darkness. There, on its east side, I found the crevice that held two dresses, a scarf, and gloves. I pulled off my prison dress and stuffed it inside the narrow split of rock. The frigid north wind poured through the trees, rattling the naked branches, sending shivers over my body as I put on the new dress—a color as dark as the night. I huddled against the side of the rock, out of the raw air, pulling on the scarf and gloves.

When I'd arrived at Schattenwald, I'd made a point of memorizing details about the entrance. The shrubs, barren in winter, grew thick and close to the gate. If I could hide myself within a few meters of it, I might have a chance. Fortune was on my side in terms of the north wind—perhaps shielding me from a German shepherd's nose—my brown coat would blend in with the naked branches.

I left the electric torch behind and struck out from the boulder, following the stream until its bubbling icy waters disappeared into a tunnel shielded by an iron grate. I shook it but the bolts didn't budge. My foot slipped and I almost tumbled down the bank into the cold water.

The path I'd been instructed to take curved toward the entrance. I crept through the trees, hearing the purr of engines a short distance away. The woods thinned, forcing me to take refuge behind the bushes that lined the interior walls. Wrapping my coat tightly around me, I ran to the wall, crouched, and scooted across the frosty earth with my back to the cold stones.

In a few minutes, I had come close enough to see vehicles— trucks, vans, a military ambulance—entering and departing through the illuminated gate. My life was now at the mercy of Fate and the one guard manning the entrance. His leashed dog, a black shepherd, seemed fixated on the equipment that rolled in and out in a constant stream. The wind poured in from the north, blowing the engine exhaust toward Schattenwald in large white puffs.

An Opel Blitz, much like the one that had carried the Russians to their deaths, lumbered up the road from the asylum. A wooden wagon bed was fitted behind the driver's compartment. Three metal stanchions crossed over the bed, supports for a tarp to protect troops from the weather. The wagon was empty, but I was much more interested in the vehicle's footboard.

A large van pulled up to the entrance as the Opel sputtered up the side of the road nearest me. Both would be stopped.

This was my moment.

When both vehicles halted, I waited for the guard to inspect the Opel. The driver turned toward the guardhouse and spoke with the man.

No time could be wasted.

I bolted from the bushes, ran to the back right tire, and crouched against it. The slim footboard under the door would be my salvation. I edged toward it, keeping low to the ground, lifting myself silently onto the metal runner, grasping the door handle with my gloved hands.

A few seconds later, the driver said good-bye and we chugged off down the road. The vehicle turned left, toward Karlsfeld, shielding me from the guard's eyes.

For the first time since I'd been taken to Stadelheim Prison, freedom beckoned. The cold wind, heightened by the truck's speed, clawed at my body but I didn't care. The stars lingered in the inky dawn sky and the road was free of traffic behind us. The driver stopped at an intersection on the outskirts of Karlsfeld, to turn right toward Dachau. I jumped from the runner, crossed a gully, and stepped into the sanctuary of a gloomy thicket. All around me were woods and the winter silence broken only by the occasional roar of a passing vehicle.

BUS came to mind, along with the number one hundred, given to me by Marion. If only I could remember the numerical combination. The streets were fixed in my head, but I couldn't remember the numbers. I had to get to Munich, twelve kilometers away, without being spotted. I had no money for transportation and I was cold and hungry. It would be a long journey to a safe house, but one that pushed me forward with an invigorated step.

I watched as the Opel disappeared, stepped from the thicket, and crossed the road, keeping as close to the tree line as possible in case I needed to take cover. In the gray predawn, I came upon a rural road that led south toward Munich. About eight o'clock the sun broke the eastern horizon with brilliant shafts of red.

As I walked, I imagined the scene at Schattenwald: The orderlies had opened the door to the operating room, finding the body of Dr. König near the slab. An intensive search of the building and grounds would be conducted in hopes of finding the perpetrator—Natalya Petrovich.

She was now a dangerous enemy of the Reich—not just a traitor, but a murderess as well. A message to my parents was imperative. Would the Gestapo arrest them, or wait for me to show up at their apartment? Either way, my mother and father were in danger.

A call for justice would be issued by Hitler himself.

My shoes had worn thin during my stay at Schattenwald and weren't meant for a long journey. Blisters formed on my feet and each step became agony as the skin scraped against the rough fabric. To keep my mind off my pain, I recalled each word uttered by Marion, certain that the last street number had been twelve and reconstructing as best I could the other numbers.

The woods that had shielded me thinned as I entered the outskirts of Munich. The trees were replaced by homes, apartment buildings, and bustling streets, which, in their own way, provided shelter. I avoided people when I could. My only meal came from a man who had abandoned half a sandwich on a park bench.

I arrived at Fifty-Six Uhlandstrasse about four in the afternoon, my feet sore, legs trembling, my glasses spotted and dirty. The sun was close to setting when I rang the bell of a rather ordinary apartment building of gray stone and dark windows, certain that this was the right address. The woman who answered studied me with eagle eyes and then frowned. Her distaste was apparent as she curled her long fingers around the door's edge.

"This is Fifty-Six Uhlandstrasse?" I asked. The address was marked in brown numerals bolted above the door.

"Yes," she replied. "What do you want?"

"I'm looking for Dr. Kalbrunner," I said, giving a reason for my intrusion.

Her eyes glittered, and she shifted on her feet. "There is no doctor here—be on your way."

"Is Marion here?" I asked, desperate for safety, hoping that the name would spark the woman's recognition.

The glitter turned to flame as she grew agitated with my questions.

"No!" She pushed the thick oak door toward me. "You have the wrong address. Never come back here again."

Stunned, I stepped back as the door slammed in my face. Had I given myself away? I had no other choice but to go to the next house, Thirty-Two Blumenstrasse. Seeking my parents or Frau Hofstetter was out of the question.

Although the distance was short, and nightfall gave me some comfort, a heavy weariness weighed down my body. My stomach growled, the cold cut through my coat with impunity, and my concentration faltered. I was surprised when I found myself at a compact but solid stone building whose arched entryway was surrounded by Doric columns.

Bombings had spotted the roof with holes and peppered the structure's white walls with craters. No light shone through the blackout curtains, but I knocked on the sturdy door anyway.

No one answered. Frustrated, I sat on the stoop and rubbed my temples, at the point of surrendering to failure, when the door creaked open. A man peered around it.

Not wanting to give myself away, I rose and asked the same question I had at the previous address. "Is Dr. Kalbrunner here?"

Darkness fell across his face, preventing me from seeing more than a shadowy figure. He wagged his finger, inviting me inside, and I found myself in a cold foyer.

"Who are you?" he asked, his breath ballooning in frosty bursts.

I collapsed against a wall as he stood in the semi-darkness. The buttery light from a distant lamp seeped toward us. "I can't tell you who I am, only that I have come at the instruction of Dr. Kalbrunner and a woman named Marion."

This answer seemed to satisfy him and he moved closer. "How are they?"

I delivered the tragic news. "They are dead."

He inhaled sharply and lowered his head. "I'm sorry—how did you know them?"

"At Schattenwald."

"I see," he said, and retreated into the shadows.

"I'm in need of food, clothing, and a safe place to stay."

He leaned against the wall opposite me and lit a cigarette. The flash of light revealed an expressive face: long, lightly bearded, and dark of eye. I judged him to be in his thirties. "Across the street at Thirty-Three. This number is given as a deception . . . in case . . ."

"Thank you. Thirty-Three." At last I'd found someone who knew about the safe houses. "Who are you?" I asked, wanting to confirm my feeling about the man.

"My name's not important, either," he said. "Beyond these open doors"—he pointed to entrances I could barely discern in the gloom—"lies the stage of one of Munich's greatest treasures—a puppet theater more than a hundred years old."

I'd never been inside; my father considered theater an expensive frivolity.

"I'm not supposed to be here," he said, his voice resonating with a sweet melancholy. "The government has forbidden me to perform as a puppeteer because of my politics. I travel Germany making a living any way I can. Sometimes I come here when I need shelter."

He puffed on his cigarette and held out his hand in friendship. "Ask for Gretchen. . . . Tell her that you've come from the theater, but don't mention me. . . . Forget that we've ever talked." He moved like a stealthy cat to the entrance. "Good luck," he whispered as the door closed.

I walked across the street to the entrance of a three-story apartment building. A list of printed names adjoining individual call bells lined the side of the stone entry. Looking for Gretchen, only one made sense—G. Geisler. I rang the bell.

I shuffled on my feet and looked up at the windows facing the street—all were dark, the building quiet in repose. Like the puppet theater, it took time for the door to open. When it did, a slender woman in a gray house dress stood before me showing none of the scorn that I had found at the first address.

"Gretchen?" I asked.

She kept her rigid, but cool, stance, neither nodding nor speaking.

"I came from number Thirty-Two."

Without a word, she led me up the stairs to her apartment, on the front of the building. A lamp, muted by a purple glass shade, stood atop an old upright piano positioned against a wall in the sitting room. It spread its strange light a few meters. A small kitchen stood to the right, a somewhat larger bedroom to the left, both shrouded in darkness except for the soft candle glow in each.

Gretchen pointed to a couch covered with large Oriental scarves that rested in the center of the room.

I took a seat, happy to be off my feet. She settled on the piano bench, the light casting a purplish glow around her.

We looked at each other, my apprehension acute because I couldn't break through her inscrutable demeanor. I had no idea whether she was pleased, displeased, or couldn't care less that I had showed up at her door. I needed her help desperately.

"The bombs fall now and then—there's a shelter down the street," she finally began. "The block manager escorts us to safety." She thrust her fingers into her dress pocket, removed a pack of cigarettes, lit one, and tossed the matchstick into an ashtray sitting on top of the piano. "How long do you plan to be here?"

"I suppose that depends on you." I shrugged out of my coat and leaned back against the couch, the silk fabric cool against my arms, the cozy feel of the apartment relaxing my frayed nerves, but failing to ease the pain in my feet. "I need food and shelter. . . . Anything you can provide I'll welcome. I also need to alert my parents that I'm alive and that they are in danger."

"We're all dancing with death, biding our time until our name is called." She puffed on the cigarette, the smoke settling around her like a gray wreath. "What's your real name?"

I hesitated, but I'd already put my life in her hands. "Natalya Petrovich. I come from Leningrad, but I'm a German citizen and have been in Munich since I was a child. I was a volunteer nurse for the Reich—"

She stopped my chatter with her raised palm. "I don't want to know more than your name. You can't be Natalya. . . . The Nazis . . . know who you are. Take another name and then I'll transform you into another person—different hair color, a change of complexion. Can you see without your glasses?"

I took them for granted so much, I'd never thought of them as an identifying marker. "I need them to read and to see close up. I suppose I could take them off when I walk."

She crossed her legs and leaned forward, the cigarette balanced between the index and third fingers of her right hand. "You won't be walking anywhere until we've changed your identity. The rule here is 'be quiet and save lives.' That means staying inside until the process is completed." She took another puff and blew the smoke toward me. "I can try to change the frames, but it might be better off if you use them only in the apartment."

I had many questions. I wondered whether she would like to question me about Dr. Kalbrunner and Marion, but from her reluctance to talk I imagined the less said the better.

"There's some soup left on the stove. Heat it up, take a bath, and tend to your feet. I'll get you another pair of shoes. The bed is mine—you sleep on the couch. There'll be no questions—I don't want to know your business, and you don't want to know mine. If there's an air raid, cover your face as much as possible until I'm through with your disguise. Make use of your scarf—it's cold weather, after all."

She stubbed out her cigarette. "There's not much room in this hole. Once you've changed identities you can find your own place and go about your work. New identity papers will be forged and given to you. . . . After that, we're strangers."

Gretchen walked past me to her bedroom, and then turned. "One other thing—remember that you're not the only person suffering under Hitler. If someone who matters more than you comes along, you'll have to move along." She paused. "It's a pecking order, really; nothing is personal when it comes to war."

She went to her bedroom and closed the door.

Her harshness irritated me after what I had been through, but I understood her reasoning. I ate my soup, treated my aching body to a bath, collapsed on the couch, and dreamed about my parents.

In the span of a week, I walked downstairs once to get a breath of fresh air on a mild winter day. I savored the cool breeze brushing down the street for a short time and then hurried back upstairs, not wanting to call attention to myself. Over the days, my feet healed until I could walk without much pain.

My body, however, crumpled from the strain of my previous incarcerations. For the first time in nearly two years, I felt safe enough to sleep without fear of death. Many days, I curled up on the couch and slept for hours. Often Gretchen would wake me up as the sun was setting, telling me that I had missed one or two visitors as well as lunch. I'd eat supper and then fall asleep again.

My first concern was my parents, and I made that clear to Gretchen. She was equally adamant that I stay away from them until my identity had been changed, or until I was out of the safe house and on my own. She didn't rush me, but it was obvious from her curt replies that she wanted to put no one in danger, least of all herself.

Christmas 1944 and New Year's 1945 passed with little fanfare—no presents, no tree, no decorations. Our only festivity was a nip from a bottle of French brandy that Gretchen had stashed in her closet. Other than that, there was little to celebrate because survival was foremost on everyone's mind.

Gretchen disappeared some days for hours and then came back to nap. Our conversations were limited to the weather, air raids—which came with deadly regularity—and about the men she seemed fond of. Over the course of the week, she disappeared for a night or two only to return in the morning looking bedraggled.

However, over time Gretchen accomplished a small miracle—my transformation. Her own hair was as dark as mine and swept back from both sides of her face in a beautiful wave. My hair was still short from Schattenwald and we kept it that way. Her answer to my prison look came in the form of a blond wig fashioned in the latest style. She dyed my eyebrows to match the wig and taught me the best technique to powder my face for a lighter skin color. I practiced walking without my glasses.

A new set of identification papers arrived under the name of Gisela Grass, a common surname for Germans. Because of my age, I remained a university student studying my old major—biology. That way, if questions arose, I'd have some idea what I was talking about.

When Allied bombs fell on the city, we found ourselves in a basement shelter for an hour or two. I heeded Gretchen's advice and introduced myself only to the block manager. The rest of the time I kept to the shadowy corner, my face partially covered with my scarf.

Eventually, I adopted the mannerisms of my newfound identity, changing the way I walked to a more relaxed and breezy style; smoking occasionally; downplaying my shy, studious nature; flirting with men; and enjoying life as best I could under the terrible circumstances. As part of my new public persona, I saluted Hitler, praised the Führer when I could, all the time hating myself, but watching for those people who in an instant revealed their disdain by the curl of their lips, the cynical flash of their eyes, that I might revive the promise of the White Rose. Finding those like-minded people and communicating with them proved more difficult than I imagined, partly because of my own paranoia about being taken again as a prisoner. Caution tempered my movements toward the resistance, my efforts hampered by bad memories. Still, my parents were never far from my mind.

But other factors were coming to the fore in early 1945. Many people whispered about the end of the war, the failure of Hitler and the Wehrmacht. Rumors multiplied. Men and women grew restless and tired of the constant bombardment, the poverty, the starvation rations, and most of all, the killing of innocents. Every family, it seemed, had suffered a loss in the war: a father, a son, a brother in the Wehrmacht; women, children, and parents from the Allied bombings. Those deaths didn't include the executions and the murders committed by the SS and the Gestapo. Germany was eating itself alive under a madman's rule.

Near the middle of January, Gretchen told me that her work with me was done and a man with access to high-ranking Gestapo members was going underground. I would have to leave to make room for him. She said nothing about the newcomer's plans, although such a man would be invaluable to the resistance. I accepted my fate, knowing I couldn't stay forever under her roof, although I had no idea where to go.

"I'd like one favor before I leave." I sat at one end of the couch, Gretchen at the other with her usual cigarette in hand. "It's part of a plan I've had since I returned to Munich."

"Yes," she said in her reserved tone.

"I want to see my parents . . . if they're alive . . . and I hope you'll make the contact, or send someone, since it's impossible for me."

She laughed—one of the few times I had seen her do so. "Impossible. If they *are* alive, the Gestapo will be on them like a flea on a dog. And please, don't argue that you're the only one in Munich who has suffered a loss. The city is brimming with tragedies." She countered any objection I might have with a wave of her hand toward the window.

"I understand," I said, "and I even know who that flea would be, but I can't deliver a message to them. *You* might be able to . . . with your contacts."

"Your parents are dead."

I slapped the couch with my hand. "No, I won't be satisfied until I find out! I *need* to know." I took a breath. "Please. . . . I appreciate everything you've done for me, and I've done everything you've asked, but I only want to know if they're alive. They may have been killed because of me." I stared at her. "You've made me a different person, but I'm still the same girl who loved them."

She eyed me coolly. "You're a sentimental fool, but in some ways I envy your resolve and your devotion however misguided they may be. I have no one to love—only those to remember. They're all gone. Dead because of one man—who I hope will spend eternity in hell. I honor my parents and two brothers with the work that I do." She paused and tilted her head to the side, leaving half her face looking bruised in the purple lamplight. A tear ran down her cheek before she spoke. "There is a German, from Russia, who might know. I'll contact him."

Knowing that my time at Gretchen's was ending, I spent several days looking for a new apartment.

One afternoon, after long hours on my feet, I found her in the small kitchen frying up a potato and a carrot. Gretchen had one hand on a spatula and the other on a book, bound in expensive leather. It looked as if it had come from the Gestapo headquarters where I'd been detained.

I sat in one of the chairs at the table. "It's not easy finding an apartment—so many have been damaged or destroyed."

She nodded and continued her reading. "It's good you're looking. Your successor will be here in a couple of days." She put the book on the table and I reached for it. "Please don't," she said, pointing the spatula at me. "You're better off not knowing this business."

I withdrew my hand as she continued to fry the vegetables. "I strolled through an empty market today and went past the Old Botanical Garden. The air is cold. The benches were empty." Gretchen faced me. "Nothing's been spared—the churches, the Hauptbahnhof looks like the remains of a child's stick fortress, people are huddled against bare walls in their shattered homes."

"Little to see now," Gretchen said. She turned off the stove, letting the food simmer in the hot grease, and walked to the patches of pale winter light that seeped through the windows onto the floor.

I joined her and observed the bundled men and women walking on the sidewalk below. We were lucky that the bombs had spared this building.

"Munich is a shell of its former self," she said. "Everything that was beautiful is gone."

"Not everything," I said.

She tilted her head in her usual manner, gray eyes flickering. "Your parents are alive."

I froze, stunned by her news.

"My contact found them—they've moved from Schwabing to an address near the Englischer Garten."

"Thank you," I said, barely able to speak. "I'm so pleased."

"It's amazing that anyone's still left alive," she said, addressing the meandering throng. "Look at them, miserable fools— they venture out during the day trying to find food, shelter, and the necessities of life only to retreat in the darkness to wretched nights of bombs. It's as if we've gone backward in time, become cavemen or insects, easily stamped out by those who wish us dead. . . . I take that back. . . . That's an insult to Neanderthals and ants—we're like germs on the cusp of eradication."

I understood what she meant and clutched her hand for a moment before she drew away.

"Don't be a fool, Gisela," she said. "The war isn't over despite what we hear. Rumors mean nothing. There will be more deaths and yours will be counted among them if you don't use your head rather than your heart."

"I have nothing to live for except my heart."

"A nice sentiment, but . . ." She paused, as if any discussion about love was unnecessary. "Tomorrow, your parents will be sitting near Schwabinger Bach in the garden, across from Leopoldpark. They will be there for a half hour, from noon to twelve thirty, no longer, possibly less. Don't talk to them, don't follow, do nothing to compromise them. Their lives, and yours, depend on it in case the Gestapo is watching. Walk past. . . . Glance at them. . . . That's all you can do."

"Do they know what I look like now?"

"They've been told."

I nodded.

"Once you've seen them, our time is over. I expect you to be gone by the end of the week."

Gretchen left me alone at the window, walked back to the kitchen, and placed two plates on the table.

The day was blustery with the threat of a stinging rain tamped down by broken clouds. Wrapped in my coat, scarf, and gloves, I left the apartment, my body prickling in nervous anticipation. Wariness set in, for I couldn't exclude the possibility that the SS, even Garrick, or another Gestapo member might be following my parents. Despite my fear, I trusted Gretchen and her contact; nevertheless, the danger still existed.

I had written a note in Russian telling them of my love and the hope that somehow, sometime, we would be able to escape Munich together. I offered no specifics, only my honest effort to formulate a plan. I secured the note in my pocket and wondered, as I walked, if my father had disavowed the hateful words he had spoken to me in prison.

The threat of foul weather had thinned the normally crowded streets. I'd left the apartment five minutes before eleven thirty, giving myself extra time to make the half-hour walk to the Englischer Garten.

The Munich that I loved, the city I'd known since I was a child, was different now, even more so than before my capture and trial. The vibrancy, the thrum of life, had disappeared in smoke and ash to be replaced by desolation. Despondency filled the air and we, the living, breathed it every second of our lives. The all-too-familiar shops and restaurants seemed worn and drab under the January sky.

As I got closer to the park, I wondered if I'd made a mistake. In the spring, the garden would be swarming with people enjoying the sun. In winter, the branches were bare, the grass brown, the benches deserted. If my parents were being followed, this would be the perfect opportunity for the Gestapo to observe suspicious activity and make an arrest. Gretchen perhaps was right—perhaps the best I could do was view them from afar. That thought alone set my heart racing with want and trepidation.

I passed the university, the Siegestor, and turned right on

Ohmstrasse until I came to the narrow waters of the Schwabinger Bach. I crossed the footbridge near a bend in the stream and looked to my left and right for a bench. I gazed at the wristwatch that Gretchen had given me. I was five minutes early.

To the north, an elderly couple appeared on the footpath. I faced them, thinking it must be my mother and father, although their dress and shambling walk made them seem older than my parents, both of them moving at a slow pace. Furtively, they found a bench, facing away from the water, and folded their arms, as if waiting for time to pass—or someone to make an appearance. I wondered if it was even safe to glance at my mother and father.

I strode toward them and then slowed, for another figure appeared ahead—a man who looked familiar. I wrapped my scarf around my nose and mouth, covering most of my face. He was dressed in a long coat, one I recalled. Underneath his hat, I recognized the somewhat older face of Garrick Adler. Fear prickled through me. He passed by my parents without a look and then headed toward me.

I focused on the horizon; redirecting my gaze to Garrick would betray me. I prayed that he would pass me by as he had my parents, and that my blond wig, makeup, and lack of glasses would hide Natalya Petrovich.

We breezed by each other. He gave me a sideways glance but then continued walking.

I kept my pace, eyeing the path, taking in my parents' profile, until I was even with the bench. My parents had aged considerably since I had seen them last, the lines in their faces deeper, my father's hair thinner without a hat to keep him warm, my mother's bony legs protruding from her coat.

Obviously, any conversation, a wave, a smile, the passage of a note, was out of the question. The only concession given was a quick turn of my head. Both of them caught my gaze, my father's sad eyes rimmed with tears, my mother's face pleading for a hug or a kiss on the cheek. The meaning of her look was clear—she had lost her only daughter and each day apart was killing her. But at least they knew I was alive.

"Natalya," my father said, leaning forward on the bench. "I love you. . . . I said those things to save us. Please forgive me."

I looked over my shoulder quickly. Garrick was out of earshot, his body partially turned toward my parents and me. My mother grabbed my father's arm and held on to it as if he were a life preserver keeping her from drowning.

"I will get you out of Munich," I said, and hurried away, knowing that such words were easy to say but harder to fulfill.

The elation I'd felt when Gretchen told me that I'd be able to see my parents faded in the cold wind. I stole a quick look to my left as I crossed another footbridge back to the city. My parents had gotten up from the bench and were walking toward Garrick Adler.

He stood, smoking, his back flat against a willow tree.

When my parents walked past him, he followed.

CHAPTER 16

So many homes had been destroyed by the bombings, my efforts to find an apartment fell short. Gretchen had given me some cash to carry me over until I could find a job, but everything I owned I carried in a small bag. All the while, I was looking over my shoulder for the SS and the Gestapo, always dancing on the edge of the cliff, trying not to make a *mistake*. My life was ruled by secrecy and distrust. Normalcy might return if the Allies won the war. If Germany was victorious, my days would be damned forever.

In a moment of panic, I considered seeking shelter at the Frau's, but I knew that arrangement would be too dangerous. Instead, air-raid shelters and the ruins of bombed-out apartment buildings became my homes. Money and food were scarce all around—a few nights I lived on scraps cooked over barrel fires, as did the other unfortunates of war.

One day, I decided to walk by the Frau's house just to see the old neighborhood. Many of the surrounding blocks had been leveled or severely damaged. Her residence still stood, looking much worse, with its cracked walls and boarded-up windows, than when I'd lived there. However, a pair of friendly eyes peered at me as I passed—Katze, now fully grown, gazed at me from the windowsill of my old room. I doubted that he recognized me, but it cheered me to see his brilliant green eyes and distinctive white and orange markings. The Frau was nowhere to be seen.

The next day, I returned to Gretchen's, desperate for a hot meal and a bath. Grumbling about my "stupidity," she served me days-old bread and leftover meat for breakfast. My situation seemed hopeless. There was little I could do to help my parents, my money was nearly gone, and I had no home.

I was sniffling at the kitchen table when someone buzzed the apartment. A man walked in, the one who had taken my place, or so I thought. He was older than I, probably in his mid-thirties, with a kind oval face topped by a full head of black hair, not especially handsome like Garrick, but with deeply set tender eyes and an innate kindness that drew me to him. He wore the work clothes and boots of a tradesman.

I left the kitchen for the couch, so they could have a private conversation. When they returned to the sitting room a few minutes later, I still was considering what to do next.

I tapped my bag. "I've only got a few days of makeup left—there are no jobs or apartments to be found."

Gretchen frowned, showing little concern for my situation. "What about Twelve Steinstrasse?" She looked at her watch—a sign that I'd taken enough of her time.

It had never occurred to me to visit the last safe house that Marion had mentioned.

"I'm headed past there on my way to work," the man said. "I can take you."

"Is our business done?" Gretchen asked with a bitter tinge to her voice.

"Yes," the man answered. "I'll be back in a couple of days if everything works out."

He walked to the couch, clutching a key in his right hand, and beckoned for me to get up. Having nowhere else to go, I accepted his offer, apologizing to Gretchen on my way out for interrupting her day.

We walked to a battered truck parked near a pile of rubble that had tumbled into the street. The vehicle was much like the Opel I'd commandeered during my escape from Schattenwald, but without the wagon bed. He opened the passenger door for me, and I took my place on the cold leather seat. He slid behind the steering wheel and turned on the ignition.

"Let's wait until the cab warms up," he said somewhat shyly. "It's a waste of petrol, but this wreck is drafty."

I pulled my coat tighter and shivered, wondering how long it would take to get to Steinstrasse. "I suppose I shouldn't ask, but are you the man who replaced me?"

His forehead crinkled. "I don't think so. I've been a friend of Gretchen's for several years. We communicate when we need to. . . . She doesn't talk about her other business." He rubbed his gloved hands together, looked at me, and asked with a frosty breath, "You have no place to stay?"

I wondered how much I could tell him, but I suspected if he had dealings with Gretchen he was a friend of the resistance. "No. I've been looking, but rooms are hard to come by. I also don't have much money—well, none, to be exact. I've been living on the street like so many others."

He nodded, thrust out his right hand, and shook mine with a powerful grip. "I'm Manfred Voll. I'm pleased to meet you."

"How do you know Gretchen?" I asked.

He gazed through the windscreen at the shadowy beings that moved through the street like ghosts in the winter day, the collapsed buildings around us, the city's fabric of life disintegrating each hour that Hitler remained in power. "The same way you do—working for a just cause against an unjust one."

I hadn't expected his blunt words in so short a time, but perhaps he recognized the same qualities—strength, resilience—in me that I believed were part of him. My liking, my trust of him, was immediate, but with everything that had happened, I still found it hard to speak truthfully.

"I'm Gisela Grass," I said.

"That's not your real name," he said, aware of Gretchen's tactics.

"No, but you know we can't be—"

"—Of course." The cab had warmed and he put his hands on the steering wheel. "Do you need a job too?"

Surprised, I turned toward him. "Yes, do you know of one?"

"Where I work—Moosburg—an Allied POW camp north of Munich. We need help with the prisoners." He paused. "That's how I know Gretchen, if you put two and two together."

The connection became quite clear. She managed a safe house, helping those who opposed the Reich. If Manfred worked with Allied prisoners, he would have connections to many people hostile to Hitler. From the prisoners, he could cultivate those most useful to the resistance. However, I was uncertain about his personal relationship with Gretchen.

"Would you like to give the job a try?" he asked. "The pay is meager, but you'll have a safe place to stay—the Allies won't bomb a POW camp—and you can ally yourself with those making a difference. I'm a supervisor, so I can put your papers through without much trouble."

It didn't take me long to make up my mind—the choices were finding transitory shelter in a safe house, living by my wits on the street, or making a little money at a POW camp. I only hoped that Garrick, and the SS, anticipating that eventually I would come for my parents, would keep them alive.

"I'll give it a try," I said.

"Good." He turned the wheel away from the curb and the truck wheezed through the streets until we were out of Munich and on our way to Moosburg.

Manfred told me about Moosburg as we drove through the countryside. I, like so many others, had no idea that Stalag VII-A, as it was named, even existed within an hour's drive of Munich.

The camp had opened six years before and held the Poles taken prisoner after Hitler's 1939 invasion. Since that time, soldiers from around the world had gone through its gates, primarily officers and enlisted men and women, who were processed and then sent on to other camps, often to their deaths. British, French, Russian, Greek, Yugoslavian, Belgian, Dutch, South African, Australian, Italian, and American prisoners had been housed there in addition to other nationalities. The number of barracks and the prison count had increased significantly as the war progressed. Initially, only ten thousand prisoners were to be housed at the camp.

"I don't know how many there are now," Manfred said, "but many of them are sleeping in tents, some even taking shelter in sewer pipes that haven't been laid."

We passed checkered farmlands and taller stretches of pines and spruce molded against the hills. The sun had burst forth from the clouds, spreading glorious warmth through the truck.

"The influx of prisoners seems to have slowed, but so many were captured in Allied advances . . ." Manfred continued. "The SS and the camp Commander are struggling with the sheer number of men."

"Tell me what you know—I've been away for so long," I said, feeling gratitude for Manfred's company, the sun's heat, and the blessing of another day.

"You must tell me your story."

"Later. The tale is too . . . painful." The sun's rays fell in patches on my shoulder and I reveled in the light and color flooding my senses. I felt more alive than I had in years, even though Manfred and I were traveling to a prison camp.

He told me of the advances made by the Allies, of their setbacks, rumors of a nasty battle being fought in the Ardennes with terrible casualty numbers on both sides, a last gasp of the German military.

"Every time I think he's finished, Hitler comes up with some new surprise," Manfred explained. "But I sense the end is near. We can only pray."

"I hope you're right." A more immediate concern than the end of the war came to mind. "What will I be doing at the camp?"

"My staff and I keep the water lines flowing, the electricity humming, especially for the guards' barracks a short distance from the main grounds. They send us where we're needed, but with the influx of prisoners, everyone is complaining about the amount of work they have to do, including the kitchen staff, cooking for so many men. The workers are civilians like me— many of them National Socialists, others are not so fond of

Hitler. You must find your friends and keep them close. I can guide you in the beginning, but take your time getting to know people."

There were certainly worse things than cooking and washing dishes for Allied prisoners. Considering the horrors of my life over the past two years, a period of relative stability seemed like manna from heaven. However, my notion of resurrecting the strategies of the White Rose appeared unlikely in Stalag VII-A. There would be too many people around, no safe area to write and produce leaflets, and no time to distribute them. There was no need to drop them in the camp—the readers were already on my side.

"Where will I be housed?" I asked.

"There may be room at the guards' barracks, or with one of the women who live near Moosburg."

"That would probably be better," I said, considering the cosmetic preparation I still needed to keep my identity a secret.

"Or you could stay with me," Manfred said offhandedly. "That way you wouldn't have to hide."

His surprising offer tempted me. The risk of discovery would be less if I stayed with Manfred, and it was much better than struggling on the streets of Munich. Despite that, I was still uncertain. "I know nothing about you. I don't even know whether you can be trusted."

"You can ask Gretchen about trust," he said with a smile.

I returned the smile, feeling that this man was telling the truth.

We passed over the Isar River on our way into the village, the water sparkling blue and clear beneath us, the naked trees along the river swaying in the wind, the twin towers of what I presumed to be a church rising in the distance.

"It's beautiful," I said as we drove past.

"We're lucky. We've been spared."

The truck sputtered through town and headed north along the few remaining kilometers of road to the camp. As it curved around a bend bordered by flat farmland, the Stalag watchtower came into view. I grabbed Manfred's arm in a sudden panic. "Stop!"

He jerked the truck to the side of the road and turned off the ignition.

I opened the door, slid out of the seat, and collapsed on a brown patch of grass near a gully. I tried to speak, but only spittle came out, followed by the remnants of my breakfast at Gretchen's. I spit out the remaining bile and then wiped my mouth on my coat sleeve. Everything I'd endured over the past two years had come rushing back to me: my arrest, the trial, my imprisonment at Stadelheim, my brush with death at Schattenwald, the murder I'd committed.

Manfred bent over me, concern etched in his eyes. "Are you all right?"

I struggled to catch my breath, swallowing drafts of cold air, placing my hands over my chest to calm my racing heart. "I think so. . . . The watchtower . . . reminded me of prison and then the . . ." I looked again at the wooden structure rising in the distance.

He lifted me to my feet from the frosty patch of ground. "Don't look at the camp. Look toward Moosburg—it's a pleasant view. Remember—you aren't a prisoner."

I leaned against him. He smiled, an expression born of care and concern, if I was to judge his character. He was right about the view: The town, its towers resting behind us, lay in profile on the horizon, inviting me to remember a time when I'd gazed in wonder at the Frauenkirche in Munich with its stunning spires that split the sky. A feeling of peace swept over me as I viewed the tranquil buildings. Munich and the bombs seemed far away.

"I can't be late," he said, looking at his wristwatch. "It's almost noon and the Nazis will use any excuse to question us."

He guided me back to the truck. I took my seat and then rolled down the window because the warm air in the cab, once comforting, roiled my stomach.

"We'll enter through the main gate," he said. "Try to relax when we pull up. I'll introduce you to the guard. They all know me, but he'll ask to see your papers. Thank him and give him what you have—don't offer more information. If he asks you a question, answer in a calm and pleasant voice.

"After we get through, I'll introduce you to the kitchen manager. She'll be happy to have the help. I'd say she's with us, but you know how people are. They grumble under their breath about Hitler and the war, but when stirred up by the Propaganda Minister they're ready to take up arms against the Allies."

I took a deep breath and steadied myself in the seat. The gate was coming up fast. We passed over a brook and soon arrived at the main entrance. The truck rolled up to the barrier; the tower guards watched over us as an armed sentry approached from a hut.

Manfred gave a modified Hitler salute, lifting his right hand, palm up, to the guard. I did the same as the two men exchanged greetings.

"Who is she?" the guard asked. "You've never brought a woman here."

"Gisela," Manfred said. "She's going to work in the kitchen. They desperately need help—everyone here's told me so, even Colonel Burger."

The guard smiled, showing teeth stained by cigarette smoke.

"She's pretty," I overheard the guard whisper, "but I have to . . ."

I opened my purse, took out my forged papers, reached across Manfred, and handed them to the man, thinking that I was anything but pretty with my grubby face, dirty glasses, and blond wig that needed washing and combing.

He leafed through the documents for a short time before handing them back. I leaned against Manfred, hoping to make a point.

The guard looked at us, ordered us to step out, and then checked under the seats. Satisfied with his inspection, he said to Manfred, "Ah, I see. A woman from Munich—a student too." He hitched his thumb under his ammunition belt. "Better here than there. The pickings are slim in Moosburg."

"The pickings are slim everywhere these days," Manfred said with a laugh.

We got back in the truck, and the guard motioned us through the gate. The camp had been constructed on a large plot of swampy land between the Amper and Isar Rivers, a consideration when it came to making it hard for POWs to escape. A rail station bordered the west side of the camp where prisoners could be unloaded for processing, or, just as easily, transferred to other camps. What struck me first about the Stalag was its size—it stretched to the wooded hills to the east and then so far to the south that it looked as if Moosburg were included within its confines. More barracks stood under the sun than I could count.

The truck lumbered down a long lane called Lagerstrasse, running between rows of austere barracks, where groups of men walked the barbed-wire corridors in their worn-out military uniforms; others strolled in flight jackets with nothing covering their bare heads. The clothing hung on their emaciated frames. Despite their thin bodies and dour faces, the men took advantage of the rare January day. Many prisoners sunned themselves against the barracks' walls.

Manfred rolled up his window and told me to do the same as we crept down the lane. "You did the right thing—leaning against me. I wish I'd thought of it." He slowed the truck to a crawl. "I didn't mean what I said about 'slim pickings.' I had to humor him."

"Yes, I've seen better days," I replied in jest; however, we couldn't afford to lose time talking about trivialities like beauty. "With so many prisoners, how hard would it be to start an uprising and overpower the guards?"

"Not as easy as you might think," he said. "These men catching a glimpse of sun—what, a thousand, if that?—they, along with the other prisoners, are an illusion of force. They're officers from many countries, not a cohesive unit.

"There are plenty of sick men here, too, but you can't see them. This place is a hellhole despite what the Nazi brass might claim. I can't help the prisoners as much as I'd like because I'm assigned to guards' barracks, where conditions are better. Here, the food is lousy and there's not much anyone can do about it considering the supplies. Malnutrition is rampant, the men are covered with lice and fleas—the only thing that helps is the cold. I've seen men strip their clothes off and bury them in the snow to kill the lice. Then, after an hour or so they put their uniforms back on and return to their cold barracks. The latrines are dreadful with a gut-wrenching stench and pits near to over-flowing. The brass doesn't care whether the slops are cleaned—the unsanitary conditions only spread disease."

"I was a nurse. Maybe I'd be of better use in the hospital."

Manfred frowned. "You'd betray yourself—it's too easy to look into the past of a nurse who shows up unexpectedly at a camp hospital. Besides, they don't want civilians in those positions. They're using French and Polish assistants under the supervision of German doctors. Stick to the kitchen."

"And no one can escape?"

He pointed to the rows of high barbed-wire fences stretched between barracks, and strung in a double row on the camp's distant perimeter. "More than seventy thousand men—maybe more—share your desire to see freedom, but if you have a realistic plan for breaking out of here, let me know. There are two thousand armed guards on patrol, an equal number on the outside, with weapons more than a match for an unarmed man."

We came to a stop near a wooden canteen in the center of the Stalag. Manfred leaned back against the seat. "Did you hear what happened in March of last year? The rumor made the camp rounds."

I shook my head. I'd heard little about the outside world while in Schattenwald.

"POWs built a tunnel at Stalag Luft III. Seventy-three of the prisoners were recaptured within days and fifty were executed under direct orders from Hitler, in violation of the Geneva Convention. Later, posters went up in all the camps saying that 'escape has ceased to be a sport.'" He bowed his head. "I've talked with Gretchen and others about smuggling in weapons, but vehicles are searched regularly like we were today—the only weapons we could hope to smuggle inside would be a few pistols and their capacity won't stand up to an MP 40 that can fire off thirty-two rounds with lightning speed.

"I've helped three officers escape—two of them later died at the hands of the SS. They never spilled a word about who helped them. They were honest, decent, honorable men. The odds of escaping Stalag VII-A aren't good; yet, I've risked my own life to stand against tyranny." His eyes locked on mine. "The men earn money, some of them work outside the camp; they have a life they believe will go on until they're liberated. Why take on the Wehrmacht, the Gestapo, and the SS, with the possibility of getting yourself and your men killed, when the slim promise of liberation fills your mind? And even if many men escaped, where would they hide in a war-torn country? These men remember what happened at Stalag Luft III."

Everything that Manfred said made sense. "If escape is impossible, what's your connection to Gretchen? What do you offer for those who resist Hitler?"

"I make sure high-ranking intelligence officers get out of Stalag VII-A. When I'm not doing that, I do everything in my power to make sure that prisoners don't die. The men and women who fight for freedom deserve to live. That's why you're with me now."

He opened the truck door. "Let me introduce you to the manager. She's a tough old bird, but fair. She'll give you good food. I'll pick you up after my shift is done at eight."

The compacted earthen road crunched underneath my feet. The camp, its barracks spread to the four corners, was huge in comparison to the small canteen. I followed Manfred to the door, where, once opened, the pleasing smells of baked bread and fried sausages made my mouth water.

"Thank you for bringing me here," I said, as he closed the door.

"This way." He pointed to a long counter filled with pots and pans.

* * *

Inga Stehlen, short and stocky, was as tough as the meaning of her surname—steel.

Her gray hair pulled back in a bun, legs descending from her plain skirt like tree trunks, her agile feet springing about in black shoes, she lorded over every detail in the kitchen. Inga reminded me of Dolly at Stadelheim, but without the obvious cruelty that my former tormentor was so quick to display.

Manfred made a quick introduction and then left us, saying he would return at eight to pick me up.

Not one to slow down operations with formalities, Inga got right to the point. "What can you do?"

"Most anything," I said, not wanting to disqualify myself from the kitchen work.

"You'll start over there," she said, pointing to a sink and washing counter. "You'll have your hands in hot water ten hours a day to start—scrubbing pots, pans, and baking utensils. If you're good, I might let you get your hands out of the sink, but we'll see." Her brows furrowed. "I don't imagine we'll have these jobs much longer."

I wasn't sure what she meant. Was she hinting that an Allied victory was all but assured, or that Germany would somehow conquer its enemies? I was in no position to debate the question. I started for the counter, but she pulled me back. "You're a friend of Manfred's?" A hint of deviltry glinted in her eyes.

I nodded.

"He's a good man. He deserves a good woman."

"Yes," I replied, unwilling to discuss her romantic notions about a man I'd just met.

She brushed by me and I took my place at the sink. I worked beside another woman who barely gave me a look until she announced it was time for her break. "Inga doesn't like us to talk," she said.

Night fell and I scrubbed and cleaned dishes, heavy pots and pans, until I was dead on my feet, but I didn't complain because I watched thousands of men with their cups and tin cans stand in line for food as the temperature dropped. They were served a weak barley soup, a few small boiled potatoes, black bread, which I noticed had been supplemented with sawdust, and tea. Some lucky ones got to sit on the kitchen floor, while most ate outside in the cold.

At eight, Manfred walked in the door. Other workers had arrived to take my place, and as I left, Inga informed me that I was expected at eight the next morning for a shift that would last until six. My only day off would be Sundays, she said. It hadn't taken me long to discover that she was the driving force behind the kitchen and canteen operation. She ruled with an iron fist and no one crossed her.

"May I take you home?" Manfred asked as we walked the short distance to his truck.

"Yes," I said, my voice breaking with fatigue. "Anywhere there's a warm bed."

We left the camp through the Lagerstrasse gate after checking out with the night-duty guards, and drove in silence for many kilometers. I relaxed in the seat, the mild bounce of the truck nearly putting me to sleep after the long day on my feet. The road took us around Moosburg until we arrived at a small farmhouse south of town near the Isar. Manfred shifted the truck into neutral, and it coasted to a stop in front of a wire gate.

"I suppose I should ask the question," I said, as Manfred put his hand on the door handle. "Are you married?"

"No," he said flatly.

"A girlfriend?"

He shook his head. "Well, maybe one." He got out of the truck and stood in front of the gate, his body framed in the headlights. "Schütze! Come here!"

A dark blur bounded from the back of the house and jumped and whirled against the fence with great joy. "She's been outside all day—she's happy to see me." He opened the gate and the dog vaulted past it and into the truck, slathering me with kisses.

I got out and the eager dog jumped after me. I stood in the frosty air, grateful, yet wary of relying on a stranger's hospitality. What was I getting myself into? Schütze circled me as I waited for Manfred to park the truck near the house and close the gate.

He strode up with key in hand. "It's not much."

The dwelling was constructed of stone and wood, with an overhanging slanted roof to slough off the Bavarian rain and snow. Once inside, Manfred lit a lamp and then the wood-stove. I could feel the generations of spirits that had resided in this modest house, their pictures hanging in black cigar-box frames on the wall, the fancy embroidered pillows and furniture covers—not of a man's taste but left untouched as a sign of respect for the women who had lived here before him—resting in their designated positions as they had for years.

Manfred hung his coat on a door hook and called the dog into the kitchen. After being fed, Schütze pawed the hooked rug in front of the stove into a comfortable bed.

I collapsed in a chair, shed my wig, and ruffled my hair so it wouldn't look as awful. The kettle boiled on the stove and Manfred returned with tea mugs for both of us, his left hand still gloved.

"How did you get this?" I asked. Tea was difficult to obtain.

He sat across from me on a small sofa with the dog between us. The pleasant sitting room, the dog, the warm fire, made everything comfortable—too comfortable—and I suddenly had the urge to run from the house into the night. Why had he opened his home to me? The losses I'd suffered made it difficult to trust anyone.

He eyed me with concern, sensing my discomfort. "So you're not a blonde. I suspected as much. You're pretty with short hair."

He smiled and I blushed, as he tapped his mug. "I get tea from the camp black market. Red Cross packages come to the officers. I can get coffee, sometimes chocolate, cigarettes as well, if I want them, in exchange for goods baked outside the camp; in other words, loaves of bread free from sawdust." He took a sip and then placed the mug on a small wooden table to his right. "You don't trust me, do you? What if I told you I know about the White Rose?"

His blunt questions caught me off guard. I looked at Schütze curled in a ball in front of the stove. "If I'm honest with you—no. Why should I? We only met today and other than knowing that you have some kind of relationship with Gretchen, I know nothing about you. You could be a Gestapo agent, a member of the SS, for all I know. Perhaps you even worked at Stadelheim or Schattenwald. Many people know about the White Rose leaflets."

He removed the glove from his left hand and rolled up his shirtsleeve, exposing his arm. The top of his hand was pitted and scarred as if it had been charred by fire. Chunks of flesh, revealing skin turned pink from the lack of pigmentation, had been removed on both sides of his arm up to the elbow.

"This is what happened to me in the Reich's French invasion. I was never one for war, never a Party member, never a supporter of Hitler, but, of course, I was forced to serve, and to take a shell that nearly blew my arm off. The wounds took months to heal because of operations and infections. After that, the Wehrmacht was through with me and then the Party tracked me down, offering me the kind stipulation that I work at Stalag VII-A."

Had I been a nurse in France, I would have tended him with care.

"I have no feeling in my left hand, my fourth and fifth fingers don't work because the tendons were severed. Luckily, I'm right-handed." He lifted the injured arm. "This is pretty useless except for balance and resting a beer glass on it. . . . I can grip a shovel and pliers if I need to." He reached down to pet the dog. "I was surprised that France was taken so easily. Hans Scholl said the same thing to me one day."

I gasped. "You knew Hans Scholl?"

"We served together—he was a good man—perhaps too good for this world. He would have been an excellent doctor."

"I knew his sister, Sophie, as well . . . and Alex . . . and Willi."

"The White Rose," Manfred said.

A log popped in the stove's belly and a thin plume of smoke

spilled into the room from a crack in the firebox glass. Schütze started and raised her head, inspecting Manfred and me with her alert brown eyes.

"She's true to her name," Manfred said. "The best guard dog I've ever had." He rolled down his sleeve and leaned back on the sofa. "So, you might as well trust me; otherwise, it's going to be a long winter. . . . Who are you?"

I closed my eyes, which were heavy from the relief that flooded my body. The thought that I might be able to trust someone again warmed my soul. I lifted the wig from my lap and stared at it—disgusted by what it signified. "I'm Natalya Petrovich, a Russian living in Munich who served as a volunteer nurse on the Eastern Front . . . who was arrested as a traitor . . . who survived Stadelheim and Schattenwald and now has a job at Stalag VII-A thanks to the kindness of a stranger." My eyes fluttered, and I fought to keep myself awake. I'd sleep indoors, warm and safe, for the first time since leaving Gretchen's—a wonderful feeling that fed my drowsiness.

"I'll wait for the rest of your story . . ." Manfred said. "Would you like to go to bed?"

His words woke me up. "I'll be fine on the sofa."

"It's small, lumpy, and, when the fire dies, very cold," he said. "I'll take it."

"No, I'd rather be here . . . with the dog. I'm used to sleeping by myself—besides you're too tall."

"All right," he said, his soft blue eyes taking me in. "I've fallen asleep on it before."

"We are *friends* tonight," I said.

"Yes—for as long as you want."

Manfred made up a bed with comfortable pillows and blankets and within seconds I was asleep.

I awoke to a gray dawn light seeping around the blackout curtains. Manfred was standing at the kitchen stove preparing breakfast, but soon he came to me bearing a smile, and a warmth in his eyes.

However, we were running late and I wanted no questions

from my new boss at Stalag VII-A. I wrapped myself in the blanket and headed for the bathroom.

By the middle of March 1945, my routine at the Stalag was firmly established. Inga moved me around the kitchen like a chess piece, first from my position washing dishes, to mopping and scrubbing, to cooking and even to baking the dreaded black bread "fortified" with sawdust. The local women used caraway seeds in their breads, making them much more palatable to the prisoners and profitable on the black market.

As rumors swirled about the Reich's ultimate downfall, the camp POWs kept a reasonably high morale. The non-commissioned prisoners often worked in Munich, so I heard stories about the state of the city—now mostly in ruins. They cleared rubble from the street, filled bomb crater holes, and re-paired damaged railroad tracks. The work was hard but not un-bearable and they seemed to be treated well, primarily because the guards were old men recruited for the job.

With Manfred, I slipped into an easy, friendly relationship and after a few weeks I called the farmhouse my home. At first I denied any attraction between us because the war made every-thing so uncertain. I finally gave up the couch, with no coax-ing from Manfred, and we slept together in his bed but never made love. Often I found myself nestled in the mornings against his bare chest, unsettled at first, but soon growing more com-fortable as we got to know each other. When we were apart, I missed him and looked forward to our time together.

Our evening talks, when they occurred, allowed our bond to deepen. I recounted my history, including my volunteer service in Russia, my work with the White Rose, my imprisonments, and my stay with Gretchen.

"What about you?" I asked Manfred one night from my chair.

"Oh, I've had a very exciting life." He removed his boots, placed them on the floor in front of the stove to dry, and took his usual seat on the sofa. He leaned back, content, and stretched his left arm across the fabric. "I was born on this land—there are easier ways to make a living than farming—especially since the Nazis took over. My father died about ten years ago. I think the hardships of running the farm and Hitler's rise to power killed him. My mother died a few years later about the time Germany invaded Poland."

"She missed your father?" I asked.

"Yes, the war didn't kill her. She died of grief—she wanted to be with her husband—at least delivered from her misery and loneliness."

"She lived alone here?"

"I had a job in Moosburg and rented a small room behind a house. I'd come out to the farm to help when I could, but it got to be too much for both of us. Eventually, we had to sell off the livestock and what few crops we grew, mostly potatoes. The Nazis felt they could help themselves to everything we had anyway. Once the war started, and after I was deployed to France, I returned here to live—by myself."

The oil lamp's wick popped and flared, then settled into a steady flame.

"I worked the farm and also did odd jobs—electrical, woodworking, plumbing—things that needed fixing. When the Nazis came knocking for workers, I told them that's what I could do, and that's how I ended up at the Stalag. I had no choice. Later I connected with Gretchen and I decided to aid the resistance while working in the camp."

"Did you and Gretchen ever . . . ?" I didn't finish my question, certain that Manfred knew what I was asking.

He chuckled. "No. Gretchen is much too cautious to become involved with someone who works with her." He rested his hands on the sofa. "She sees men who don't want a relationship—and there are plenty of those." He looked at me, the lamplight flickering in his eyes.

I squirmed a bit in my chair, not from discomfort, but from the fondness building in me for this man, a sensation quite unlike one I'd ever experienced.

He pointed to the bedroom. "My family is Catholic, but

everything about religion is hidden in that room, including my grandmother's rosaries, the family Bible, and the crucifix. Those trappings can't be on display. What about your family?"

"Eastern Orthodox, but not practicing of course. My parents dropped religion a few years after we arrived in Germany—they fell away from the church. I pray now and then."

Schütze rose from her resting place in front of the stove, apparently too warm from the fire, circled the room, and settled in front of Manfred.

"Have you had girlfriends?" I asked.

"A few—one serious affair for a time, but she wanted more than a poor farmer could offer. After my injury, she left me and got engaged to a Wehrmacht officer. He was shipped off to Stalingrad. I suppose he's dead. I haven't seen her again."

"What will you do when the war is over?"

He looked at me with a faint longing. The oil lamp's amber light mixed with the red glow of the firebox. "I suppose I'll stay here. This house is all I own, and I can't imagine giving it up for anything." He glanced at the dog, napping at his feet. "Schütze's happy here. . . . What about you?"

In a way, I dreaded talking about the future. What was there to look forward to? Even if you found happiness, how long would it take to put lives back together, how long would it take to find my parents, how long to rebuild a city and find a paying job? The more I thought about it, the more I realized that I *was* thinking about the future, and Manfred was a participant in my silent hopes and dreams.

"I might go back to the university—finish my degree—but before that I want to find my parents . . ." I couldn't finish because of the pain tearing at my heart.

He got off the couch and kneeled in front of me. "I'll help you find them—I've never met a woman as loyal and brave as you—a beautiful woman who stands behind her convictions." He grasped my hands. "All of us who resist are trying to survive. I'll give you anything you need. You've kept me company . . . given me a reason to think about love. . . . I'll be there whatever you decide, but I hope you find it in your heart to love me."

I leaned over and kissed him.

He rose and pressed against me, kissing me, stroking my face and neck with his hands.

The warmth I'd felt for him had turned into a desire that burned in my heart. "There's so much to think about," I said, gently ending a kiss. "Everything is still up in the air. I care for you so much, but we need to wait . . . until this is over."

He backed away and petted Schütze, who rolled onto her back and wagged her tail.

I could tell Manfred was disappointed, but his smile showed hope. "I was working on a leaky faucet today," he said, lightening the mood. "Did you see the bomber?"

"No." I'd been in the kitchen all day.

"Several have passed overhead recently—American and British. They aren't bombing us. The word's still out about Moosburg. I think we'll be safe until it's over."

"That's good," I said, unsure whether our luck would hold out.

"I've heard rumblings about Commander Burger," Manfred continued. "He's not in step with other Nazi officers, which makes it dangerous for him but better for us."

"What do you mean?"

"What will happen to the camp when the Allies get here?" He went back to the sofa. "Prisoners from other camps have been marched here because Hitler doesn't want them to fall into the hands of his enemies. If Hitler's pushed, he might direct his staff to institute a 'scorched earth' policy—everyone and everything would be destroyed."

The horrible recollection of the truck pulling into the Russian forest jumped into my mind—the execution that could never be blotted from my memory. Could these exterminations happen here and at the other camps being evacuated?

I had no answer, but I was terrified at the thought.

Three weeks later, the SS instituted a surprise inspection at Stalag VII-A on a rainy day. All the men and women on the kitchen staff were told to fall in for a roll call, with Inga heading the line. I had become careless about wearing my wig around Manfred's house, but I still styled it and wore it to my job.

Four SS officers, all looking stern and forceful in their damp field coats, worked their way down the line from right to left. I had taken off my glasses, which I needed for work, and put them into my dress pocket. I was in the middle of the line, my hands at my side, trying to remain calm and at attention as each man stopped and studied me.

The last officer turned his gaze toward me and I froze in terror.

I stared into the face of Garrick Adler.

CHAPTER 17

My heart felt as if it had stopped, but somehow my legs stayed steady.

Garrick stared at me, his blue eyes cloudy and dull like those of a dead fish, his mouth turned down in a scowl. He'd aged since I'd studied him closely a year and a half ago at Stadelheim. We'd all grown older, and perhaps no wiser. His dazzling smile had disappeared; his face, if only for cruelty's sake, fractured by furrowed lines.

He blinked and then moved on, inching his way down the line, looking back at me every few seconds. Perhaps my disguise had held.

After the inspection, the four SS men gathered near the center of the room and talked. We stood in our line, awaiting our dismissal, not daring to disturb the officers' conversation.

After a few minutes, Garrick called Inga forward and spoke with her as the other officers filed out of the building.

Inga pointed to me and dismissed the others in line. "The officer standing near the door wants to talk with you," she said with raised eyebrows.

Garrick, the brim of his SS cap shading his face, let me pass by.

A cold rain pattered down, so we took shelter under the overhanging roof, Garrick bundled warmly in his gray coat, me shivering in my work dress. The frigid wind sent gooseflesh rippling over my arms and legs. Garrick scrutinized our surroundings; a few prisoners smoked while huddled against the wall of a nearby barracks.

He pulled a pack of cigarettes from his pocket, thumped it against his left palm, withdrew one, and lit it with his silver lighter. The smoke curled away in the wind, but not before he was able to take a deep draft into his lungs. He studied me, his eyes losing their dullness a bit as the smoke curled from his nose. The other SS officers made a brief appearance on Lagerstrasse and then disappeared into a barracks.

"What is your name?" he asked.

I was certain he had recognized me, but I continued my charade on the slim chance he hadn't. "Gisela Grass."

"Gisela . . . Gisela . . . that name doesn't sound familiar." He touched a curl on my wig. "You remind me so much of someone I used to know. . . . Do I remind *you* of anyone you used to know?"

My instincts told me to stare at him the way he was staring at me, not to drop my gaze or display my fear, but I felt myself slipping, the ease of surrender being less effort than the constant strain of hiding. Yet, an urgent voice inside my head, pushing me to stay alive, kept me from giving in.

"No," I said. "I don't know you. Is that all you wanted—my name? It's cold and I'd like to go inside where it's warm."

"I'll tell you when you can go inside, Natalya."

I shuddered and wrapped my arms around my chest, refusing to give him more information, my body shaking under the dripping roof.

He fingered my scalp and lifted the wig, which was pinned to my own hair now that it had grown out from the severe cut I'd been given.

"The hair and the powder to lighten your skin can't hide who you are," he said, leaning against the wall, his face taking on a blank look of resignation. "I've searched for you for months and, now that I've found you, I don't know what to do with you."

I half expected him to strike me or drag me off to a waiting car, where the guillotine or the hangman's noose would be next.

"That doesn't sound like you, Garrick," I said, acknowledging his discovery. "You killed a mother cat and helpless kittens to infiltrate the White Rose—why would I expect any less punishment. Go ahead . . . take me away." I held out my hands.

"I have a surprise for you, Natalya." He puffed on his cigarette and looked out on the rain collecting in large puddles on the muddy road. "I didn't kill those cats—they were already dead—except for one—Katze. I'd hoped to scare you into a confession. I actually had the absurd idea that you might join me in rooting out other traitors . . ."

"I don't believe you," I said, lowering my hands. "You wanted me dead—everything you said to me was a lie, even your professions of care and concern."

He slaked the water from his coat. "On the contrary, I wanted you alive because I did care for you—a silly fascination, I see now, because it's a tricky maneuver ridding yourself of a painful unrequited love. Obsession can be deadly, particularly to the one who holds it in his heart. I don't care whether you believe me. I'm telling the truth." The bright, laughing smile I'd seen so often remained hidden; the flare of the blue eyes muted by the slow burn of despair and resignation. "The war is over, Natalya. We all know it, but we'll fight to the last man." His lips curved upward in a thin smile. "I really would like to know if Katze and Frau Hofstetter are alive."

"Are my parents alive? I saw you with them at the park. I passed by you."

He laughed. "Oh, so it was you. I saw your father lean forward on the bench, but I couldn't hear what he said. He lied, of course, when I asked him. I don't know if your parents are alive. Others have taken over the case." He puffed on his cigarette. "I didn't think you that brazen—to seek them out—but now I know better. You've done far worse. The SS wants you because you killed the *good* doctor. You are a powerful woman, Natalya. A powerful woman wanted by the Reich."

I lowered my gaze and huddled near the kitchen door hoping

to find some warmth from the room. "Why the change of heart, Garrick? Has your transfer to the SS softened you?"

"Is that all you have to ask?" He flicked his cigarette onto the road, where it landed in a puddle with a smoky sizzle. "The Reich assigns you where it feels you're needed. I was the one who kept you alive, just as Willi was allowed to live those extra months after his trial, the authorities hoping there would be more betrayals, followed by more deaths. In your case I was wrong. You remained stubborn to the end.

"By the time Dr. Kalbrunner was executed, I had no say in your case. You had failed to root out the traitors—Kalbrunner being one. I could no longer save you. My own loyalty to the Reich came under suspicion. Dr. König was ordered to end your life . . . I objected . . . every ploy I could think of, every argument I presented, was rejected by those in command. I was outranked and outnumbered. I had to let you escape my heart . . . and my mind."

"I had no choice with Dr. König," I said.

"I know . . . I admire your resourcefulness, Natalya." He drew closer to me. "I don't know if I could have made it out alive under such circumstances, but you *persisted*." He shook his head. "König wasn't a big loss—the sterilizations and euthanasia were supposed to have ended years ago, but some doctors have an itch they can't cure when it comes to their power over others. I understand that now. König never proved anything except how easy it is for humans to die. However, the SS was not pleased by his murder."

"What are you going to do with me?" I asked, knowing he held my life in his hands.

He chuckled. "The other officers and I came for an inspection . . . to size things up. I'm not even sure they know or care about you." He flicked the rain from his cap. "I'm going to let you remain here at Stalag VII-A. In a way, I guess it's as much like being in prison for you as for these POWs residing on Lagerstrasse—you *have* to be Gisela, don't you, Natalya? There is no going back."

I sighed with relief that Garrick was going to let me live, but he was right. I couldn't flee the camp, because I had nowhere to go except Manfred's; I couldn't reveal my true identity because I might be recognized by other Gestapo and SS officials; and, perhaps most telling, I didn't want to leave the man who had taken me into his home and heart.

"Thank you for letting me stay," I said.

"Don't thank me. Thank the Allies. They'll be here in two months, maybe sooner. We all know that. Hitler doesn't believe it. He rails against his generals and his staff thinking his ravings will somehow turn the tide of a war he can't win." He shook out another cigarette but didn't light it. "Before you think I'm too generous, that I've gone soft, I do have one more thing to tell you."

I stiffened, bracing for some terrible revelation. The rain lashed the roof in a sudden downpour from the blotchy clouds.

"I'm tired of death," Garrick continued. "When we met, I wouldn't have believed such words would ever come from my mouth, but they have. I've seen death where I least expected it, and I've marveled at those who resisted—the traitors—who went to their graves with such calm dignity and grace. They didn't shudder, they didn't fall into a heap; they shed a few tears for their loved ones and called out for freedom. Their strength comes from the heart . . . and from the soul. I felt that kind of courage from you the first time I met you at the synagogue."

I felt little sympathy for him, despite his admission. "You deceived me, Garrick—you took advantage of me, and you betrayed my friends. The White Rose and I have paid the price over and over for letting you into our lives."

He grasped my hands. "I won't say I'm sorry because you wouldn't believe me. . . . My parents are dead. When I saw their bodies blasted and burned by the bombs, I knew that I'd been wrong—and weak, while others had been strong like you. They were good Germans, Natalya." He sighed. "So, go your way. Hide, live, until the end of the war, but know that the SS wants this camp destroyed and every prisoner in it dead before the Allies arrive. We will fulfill that duty if we can. We're here today to formulate a final solution for the problem of Stalag VII-A."

I withdrew my hands from his and leaned against the door, shocked by his words.

He stepped out from under the eave, into the lane, and looked toward the sky, the drops splashing on his face. "It's glorious to live in your time, to know the moon and the stars, sunrise and sunset, good weather and bad. I treasure every day because my time is running out. I'll be back when the SS returns to the camp." He turned to me, his coat spotted with rain. "Perhaps I'll see you again. Do what you must to protect yourself."

He raised his hand in the Nazi salute and stalked off to find his comrades.

I pressed myself against the door and stood for a few minutes, watching, waiting, for Garrick to change his mind and return with the other SS men. However, a short time later, the sleek black sedan splashed down Lagerstrasse toward the camp entrance. Their time at the Stalag had ended and I cried as I watched them go.

I returned to the kitchen and warmed my hands in front of the baking stove, while swiping the rain from my damp dress. Inga and the others said nothing, but gave me odd looks as if I had risen from the dead. In a way I had.

Garrick had left me with the knowledge that the SS was sworn to destroy the camp. What could I do?

That night, I told Manfred what had happened with Garrick. He was seated on the floor in front of the woodstove, next to Schütze, and I could tell from his stunned expression that my news had caught him off guard. Despite the warmth of the house, the gleam of the oil lamp, his back and shoulders sagged under the weight of my revelation.

"I'm astonished that he let you go," Manfred said.

"He still harbors some kindness—love, if you want to call it that—in his heart for me, but, more than that, he knows the end's at hand. There's nothing more the Wehrmacht can do." I left the chair and settled on the floor next to him, running my fingers through the dog's warm fur.

"Love . . ." He rested his hand on mine. "Some days I think

love has fled from the earth, leaving only evil behind. Today is one of those days."

"We're safe and warm . . . for the moment."

He placed his right palm gently on my face. "Moments are all we have . . . only moments." His voice broke and he choked back sobs.

I cradled him in my arms and Manfred collapsed against me. I was glad to offer comfort when he'd done it so often for me.

"I'm grateful for you, Natalya. I didn't want to tell you the bad news I heard from another contact—a man I barely know—but after Garrick's visit I must. Gretchen's been arrested—taken to Stadelheim. Perhaps that's why the SS was here, because they found something in her apartment . . . who knows. If they connect me to her . . . and then to you . . ." His head drooped and the words sputtered out, "If I'm arrested, I'll never talk. Your secrets will die with me; but, you must take care of Schütze and the farm."

I kissed him on the cheek for being as quietly courageous as my friends in the White Rose. "Of course I would, but let's not predict the future. It's just as likely that they will come for me."

We sat in silence, listening to the logs pop in the stove, watching the gentle rise and fall of Schütze's breathing, mourning with mute voices what the Third Reich had destroyed. In my time at Stalag VII-A, I'd seen prisoners explode in rage, shaking their fists at God because of their imprisonment and the constant specter of death. Their anxiety and terror were palpable. All but the most hardened Nazis, who, like Hitler, believed that Germany would win the war, lived with the same suffocating apprehension. Now, the pressure was mounting with the Allied approach. No one knew what would happen to the camp.

My mind ran in circles, trying to think of a way to survive the SS extermination. Finally, a desperate thought struck me.

"I've never met the Commander, Colonel Burger," I said. "What if we tell him what the SS has planned? Do you think he'd stand to see the camp destroyed and thousands of men killed? If he has any shred of decency, any kindness in his heart, he'd want to make sure his prisoners were spared."

Manfred considered that. "Burger might stand up to the SS. . . . I can't say for certain, but I don't have a better idea."

"Arrange a meeting—it's worth a try."

He broke from my grasp. "He'll never believe me—a worker who *happens* to know that the SS is planning to destroy the camp and execute the prisoners? He'll think I'm insane."

"Make him believe—tell him that I overheard them talking—I'll go with you."

He tapped his forehead. "Good . . . good . . . yes, you should be there. He'll want to know how I got this information."

"Then it's settled."

He drew me close and kissed me. "I'm afraid, I've fallen in love with you," he whispered, resting his head against my cheek.

I returned his kiss. "Don't be afraid. Let's make the most of the time we have . . . make love to me."

He rose from the floor, extinguished the oil lamp, and led me to the bedroom. We undressed and slid under the covers.

I was hesitant at first, even though I'd slept in Manfred's bed for weeks. I had to force my father's voice from my head— chastising me for having sex before marriage. But Manfred's strong hands gathered me in with an extraordinarily gentle touch, and my body shivered as he ran the tips of his fingers from my head to my feet.

We moved from friends and partners to lovers in one night, knowing each other's bodies in a way I'd never experienced. He had been with women before; I was a virgin. Of course, I knew anatomy, having studied it and worked with men in the field hospital. In that respect, sexual characteristics were familiar.

As he entered me, I grasped his back and forced his body down upon mine. A sharp jolt in my groin shifted swiftly from pain to pleasure.

Making love, the intimacy of being close to a man I cared about, reinforced how precious life could be, especially in this time of war. We were in love and consummating our union—an act, an emotion that transcended our pasts. *Now* was all that mattered, for the future was an uncertainty.

I raked my fingers across his back and kissed his shoulders, face, and lips. Every nerve in my body fired in unison and the dark, colorless bedroom, exploded into a shower of stars and blue electric waves that rocked me until, spent, I sprawled across the bed.

Manfred captured me and snuggled against my back, our chests heaving until our breathing subsided.

After a time, I turned to face him.

He put a finger to my lips before I could speak. "We have each other. No one can take that away."

I believed his words—no matter what happened—no matter that I was wanted by the Reich—we had become one and our love could never be ripped apart.

I held his face in my hands, kissed him, and reveled in every second that we had together.

Our love deepened as the hours passed, and the night lasted forever.

Three days passed before we could get in to see Colonel Otto Burger. Meanwhile, life at the camp continued on as it had since I'd arrived. Prisoners were transported to Munich to clear the streets of debris and repair the rails; the black market thrived, especially for baked goods from farmers' wives; prisoners bathed at the cold-water spigot at their barracks, huddled against the rain, took in the sun when they could, and passed the time by walking the barbed-wire lanes.

I never told Inga about my conversation with Garrick, although she and everyone on staff who had seen the SS officers were intrigued by what had happened. More than a few eyebrows rose when Manfred arrived to take me to the Colonel's office.

"Are you prepared?" he asked as we left the kitchen.

"Yes." My stomach fluttered with nerves.

"Let me start the conversation, but if he asks you questions answer them. I'll try to put him in a good mood." He tugged my hand. "Be sure to give the salute like a good Nazi."

I gulped deep breaths as we walked down Lagerstrasse, passing through a secondary security gate, traveling past the food storage and equipment sheds until we arrived at yet another checkpoint. A work area and the Commander's headquarters stood nearby.

Manfred announced us to a guard who scratched our names from a clipboard and then opened a waiting room door. Nazi banners and slick photographs of high-ranking Reich officials hung in this long, narrow space, making it the most pompous room I'd seen since my transport to the Palace of Justice. For a few minutes, we sat in comfortable chairs until another guard opened the Commander's door and motioned us in.

Colonel Burger didn't look up when we entered. Writing, he sat behind a large walnut desk, papers and books spread across its top. A desk lamp provided what little light there was in the room, because heavy red drapes covered two slender windows. He was a stern-looking man with thin lips, slick-backed hair, and eyelids that turned down at their corners, giving him the appearance of someone always on edge, or peering over their shoulder for the next bit of trouble—much like spies portrayed in films. A framed portrait of Hitler hung behind his desk, which I focused on once and then ignored.

Two red silk chairs had been pulled in front of his desk. We gave the Nazi salute to the Colonel and then sat, as the guard had told us, until the officer officially recognized us. Burger kept us waiting for several minutes, his pen scratching across the open ledger, his eyes shifting over the work in front of him.

Finally, he looked up and said, "Voll, isn't it?"

"Yes, Commander," Manfred replied.

Burger closed the book, put down his pen, and waved the guard out of the room. "Do you have any idea how difficult it is to run a camp bursting with prisoners—most of them officers who believe they deserve special treatment—and, at the same time, figure out how to feed the additional thousands this camp was never intended to hold, while operating under the strict guidelines of the Reich?" His eyes flickered in the light, his gaze piercing us with its studied intensity.

"No, sir, I don't," Manfred said, "It must be a difficult job, but I know the prisoners appreciate all you do for them."

He pushed his chair back from the kneehole so he could stretch his legs. "Funny, I'm never the recipient of those good feelings. All I hear about are problems—the plumbing isn't working, the food is slop, the black market is inflating or devaluing the camp currency, depending on the day. It's not an easy job, Voll." He smiled and leaned back, the epaulets on his uniform flashing silvery green. "But you didn't come to discuss my problems. I've been told by my adjutant that you have information you'd like to share with me—about the SS?"

Manfred clutched the chair's armrests. I sent him a silent wish of encouragement.

"Yes, I'd like to report what was overheard when the SS officers toured the camp four days ago."

"I'm aware of their visit. Proceed."

"This is hard to put into words, sir."

"Out with it, Voll. Believe me, I've heard it all since I began armed service in 1914."

Manfred drew in a breath. "The SS intends to destroy Stalag VII-A and execute its prisoners, rather than have it fall into Allied hands."

The Colonel rubbed his jaw, picked up his pen, and scribbled on a piece of paper. "Why would the SS tell you this? How are you privy to their dealings?"

Manfred started to answer, but I placed my hand on his arm. "I overheard them, sir. I know what they said."

"And who are you?" Burger asked.

"I'm Gisela Grass. I work in the kitchen."

He bit into the end of the pen and considered what I'd said. "You were close enough to hear them—there can be no mistaking their words?"

"No, sir, I heard them distinctly. That's why they were here—to survey the camp and find the best way to carry out the extermination."

"Did they know you were listening?" His pale features reddened as if he were either embarrassed or outraged by my claim. "This cannot be true."

"They spoke the truth because they were unaware I was listening."

The Colonel rose from his chair and strode to an easel that held a large map of Germany. Like most high-ranking Nazi officials, he embodied the perfect picture of power and conformity in his uniform, the wool smoothed to a sheen, his boots polished to a gloss. He stood in front of the map with his back to us. "The Allies are closing in. It's no secret these days. All you have to do is look to the skies." He turned to us and pointed to the map, his eyes burning with fiery vindication. "The Red Cross knows about Stalag VII-A because *I* made the decision to inform them that more than seventy thousand prisoners are held here. Why has Moosburg been spared from bombs?" He poked a finger into his chest. "Because *I* had the courage to speak."

Manfred leaned forward. "I told Gisela it was because of you, sir, that we had been spared. You can stop this planned slaughter if you put your mind to it. Thousands would be saved."

The Colonel sat on the edge of the desk, his shoulders sagging under the weight of his thoughts, his eyes dimming, I supposed, from the realization that all might be lost no matter how many objections he raised, no matter how hard he tried to save the camp.

"I can only do so much," he said. "In the meantime, we must carry on." He pushed himself off the desk and walked toward us. "I think, young woman, it would be wise for you to keep out of earshot of the SS. They don't tolerate spies."

I rose from my chair. "Yes, but I will always be on the side of right."

"A noble thought, but easier spoken than done," the Colonel replied, unaffected by my effrontery. He shook hands with Manfred and then with me. To keep up the ruse, Manfred and I saluted the Hitler portrait before the Colonel escorted us to the door.

As we walked back to the kitchen, I asked Manfred, "Do you think he believed us?"

"I don't know," he replied. "The Colonel may know more about the SS's plans than he's letting on."

At that moment, the faint whir of aircraft sounded and we looked up to see waves of American bombers flying in straight lines overhead like black locusts. Everyone in the camp stopped what they were doing and stared at the sky. All we could do was pray that the day would come soon when we would be liberated.

CHAPTER 18

Late April 1945

The camp turned a dismal gray during the spring rains that transformed the frozen ground to mud. Everything and everyone were soaking wet and miserable. When we could see past the clouds into the sharp-edged blue sky, it was almost always filled with American fighter planes and bombers. Manfred identified the tiny shapes from his knowledge of "enemy" aircraft: P-15s, P-47s, B-17s, in the air above us. These numbers meant nothing to me, but after his careful instruction, I was able to identify the planes as well.

At times these pilots would buzz the camp and greet the prisoners with a friendly tip of their wings, sending the Nazi guards, too late, scurrying for their weapons. The kitchen help often raced to the window to see what was happening.

As rumors about the approaching American and Red Armies spread daily throughout the camp, the guards seemed torn between exacting revenge upon prisoners for the Wehrmacht's failure or simply escaping while there was still time. For their part, the prisoners remained cloaked in misery and deprivation, but instilled with a faith for their release that lurked underneath their melancholy smiles.

In the weeks after Garrick's visit, I made an effort to talk to as many prisoners as I could who understood German. I established a rapport in the serving line that led to conversation and personal sharing. The men told me what they were going through—although Stalag VII-A may have been better than other camps, the prisoners still suffered under deplorable conditions. Malnutrition, disease, depression, and malaise haunted the camp and no one was certain what the future might hold.

On Saturday night, April 28, the rumble of military equipment shook the farmhouse despite it being a half kilometer away from the main road. Manfred, Schütze, and I walked past the gate and down the lane until we spotted a convoy of German trucks and tanks, with their lights out, pouring down the road away from the camp.

The dark form of an American fighter plane streaked overhead and we retreated to the house, afraid that we might be the inadvertent casualties of a bombing run, but no shots were fired, no bombs dropped.

The house was mostly dark, the blackout shades had already been pulled, the sitting room lit only by the oil lamp.

Dread filled me. A nervous itch crawled over my body. I sat on the couch as Manfred nestled against me.

"I don't like it, either," he said. "It's like a summer day when the heat paints the clouds black and the world seems destined to end in a barrage of thunder and lightning."

"That's very poetic," I said, surprised at his choice of words.

"My mother used to talk like that now and then," he replied. "She loved poetry and would recite it when she was feeling happy or sad." The dog circled at our feet. "My feelings don't come out often—but whose do these days? We're all stoic, afraid to admit that we were taken in by Hitler." He took my hand in his. "I never made it to the university."

The thrum from the military vehicles continued, upsetting Schütze as well, who finally sat down before us, her tongue hanging out in a nervous pant. I looked at Manfred, he looked at me, and the dog looked at both of us, all feeling helpless against the tidal forces of war.

"We should stop feeling sorry for ourselves," Manfred said.

"There's nothing we can do. Maybe the German forces are evacuating—that should give us hope. Do you want a beer?"

I shook my head.

He got up, walked to the kitchen, and returned with a glass filled with the amber liquid. "Have a sip," he said.

I declined.

"Homemade."

"No." A thought burned in my brain. "We must go to the camp tomorrow. If the Allies are that close, the SS will move in. What—"

My words were cut off by the buzz of planes streaking low over the farmhouse and then zooming away. Bewildered, I looked at Manfred. He pushed me to the floor and positioned his body over mine.

"Two—one American, one German—I can tell by the sound of the engines."

His breath tickled my neck. "Get off." I pushed hard against the floor in an effort to dislodge him from my back. "I'm not going through this war without you."

Schütze, thinking this was some kind of strange human game, licked our faces. Manfred pushed her away and rolled off, still embracing my back with his arms.

Shells burst in the distance with thundering force. One exploded perhaps a kilometer from the house, the fractured light flashing blazing yellow beyond the shade, the dust drifting down from the shaking walls and roof. Schütze yelped and scampered away to hide under the bed.

The artillery fire lasted only a few minutes before fading into an eerie silence. The convoy continued on its way as the fighters vanished from the air.

We lifted ourselves from the floor, brushed off our clothes, and returned to the couch.

"It's been a long day," Manfred said. "I'm tired."

"You can sleep through this?" I asked.

"We have to be up early if we're going to the camp—I'll sleep fine with you beside me." Manfred drained his beer and set the glass on the floor. "There may be a battle—you should stay here."

"No." I took his hand. "We'll be there together."

We secured the house and trundled off to the bed. I lay awake for hours while Manfred slept beside me, and I wondered if he was dreaming or had dropped off into the peaceful oblivion of a deep sleep.

After a few hours of rest, we both awoke with a sense of apprehension. Manfred lifted a plank in the bedroom floor and withdrew a bundle wrapped in cloth. It contained his father's pistol, which he intended to smuggle into the camp. "I have a feeling we might need this," he said as he concealed the weapon in his coat. "They're more likely to search the truck than me."

The road that had been so heavily traveled the night before with retreating German troops was deserted in the predawn darkness. As we drove, the sky lightened, the rising sun splitting the early morning clouds.

"You're to keep safe and out of sight if war comes to Stalag VII-A," Manfred said, his hands clutching the steering wheel. "My pistol isn't much of a weapon against automatic fire, but it can drop a few SS."

A mixture of exhilaration and alarm rocked me. Garrick had said he would return to the camp. Would he be the "enemy"? Maybe the Allies would secure the camp before any bloodshed, but I doubted that would be the case.

"You stay safe as well," I said. "Don't take on the SS."

"Don't worry about me. Hide in the kitchen if you have to. We'll meet there if we get separated."

When we arrived, Manfred and I exchanged greetings with the somber guards. The men, whom we knew, seemed preoccupied with other things besides camp security. They waved us past the entrance, although we hadn't been scheduled to work on Sunday. Several guards stood on the highest level of the wooden watchtower, weapons poised to the west, as if that direction held the key to the camp's fate.

Manfred stopped the truck a short distance past the secondary gate on Lagerstrasse, and we waited, fidgeting in the cab for a few minutes, Manfred resting his hand on the pistol in his coat, I wondering if we had made a tragic mistake coming to the camp.

"Look," Manfred said, his eyes focused on his side-view mirror.

I peered into the side mirror in time to see two white vehicles marked with red crosses roll past the gate.

"Wait here," Manfred said, and leapt from the driver's seat. I watched as he ran to the Red Cross cars. Two POW officers exited the vehicles and were immediately surrounded by an inquisitive pool of guards and prisoners. The officers talked to the prisoners for a brief time, and then everyone broke apart in haste.

Manfred sprinted back to the truck. "The Americans have rejected the German proposal for an armistice and neutral zone around the camp," he reported breathlessly. "War is going to break out. The SS is dug in at the railroad embankment."

"I must warn Inga and the kitchen staff," I said.

Manfred kissed me. "I'll remain here. Take cover there if fighting breaks out."

I jumped from the truck, buoyed and terrified by the news Manfred had reported. I flung open the kitchen door, my heart hammering in my chest. "The Americans are on the way, and the SS is ready to engage them," I shouted. "The war is here!" Whether a hardened National Socialist or a foe of Hitler, every staff member reacted to my words. Most of the workers took cover under the sturdy counters while others fled from the building like startled birds. Inga was nowhere to be seen.

I turned, intending to scurry back to Manfred; instead, I found a Luger pointed at my face.

"You didn't take my advice, Natalya." Garrick lowered the gun and motioned for me to step out of the kitchen. "Let's enjoy the morning air before it gets heated."

Once we were out the door, he held the gun to my head and dragged me by the arm to the northeast corner of the building. Garrick shoved me against the wall, stepped back, and lit a cigarette. "I warned you to protect yourself."

"The war's coming to an end, Garrick. It'll be over soon. Why don't you surrender?"

He inhaled and turned his head briefly, looking at the low-hanging sun, and then laughed. "For what, prison time; execution for the crimes I've committed against the citizenry? That's what they'll say—that's what they'll charge me with—if *their* judges are anything like ours."

"You told me you were tired of death." A strange calm filled me as I looked into his eyes, a broken man if ever I'd seen one. All the life, all the energy that had been Garrick Adler had vanished, vanquished by the fall of the Third Reich. The sagging shell of the man who had once laughed and courted me in an effort to get me to betray myself and others stood before me. I was the traitor who had beaten him at his own game. Did he hate me for that?

"You'll testify against me, won't you, Natalya, and sign my death warrant. They'll have no mercy for a man who betrayed the White Rose."

The pistol trembled in his hand. His normally spotless uniform was rumpled and spattered with mud. I wondered if he had already built his foxhole at the railroad embankment, waiting for the Americans to arrive.

"I will tell the truth," I said calmly.

On Lagerstrasse, the prisoners rushed in a crowd toward the camp entrance, not one looking our way. Garrick raised the pistol and pointed it at my head.

"I'm the SS," he said. "The SS can do no wrong—it's our duty to rid the world of subhumans." He repeated those words, eyes closed, as if they were a prayer, his finger resting on the Luger's trigger.

"Give up, Garrick," I said softly. "It's over."

"Stop." The voice was firm, calm, as it floated through the pale morning light. "I'll kill you where you stand."

Manfred, having circled around one of the barracks, glided behind my attacker with his pistol raised.

Garrick turned his head toward Manfred, lowered the gun

slowly, and then dropped it to the ground. He turned back to me and asked, "Is this the man who's won Natalya's heart?"

"Yes," Manfred answered, "the one who will put a bullet in your head if you don't let her go. If you want a fight, let's do it like men."

Garrick, shoulders drooping, kicked his gun aside and turned to Manfred. "I told Natalya several weeks ago that life was full of surprises. I have another that's astonished even me." He puffed on the cigarette he still held and looked to the sky. "I told her how wonderful it was to experience life and how I thought at one time she could love *me*. I held on to that strange hope for too long—it ruined me. Duty got in the way of love." He pointed to me. "Today, I hoped she would crumble in a heap and promise not to send me to the gallows. But she didn't. . . . She's braver by far than I."

He flicked his cigarette upon the damp ground. "*I'm* the traitor because I don't want to die for my country—the way our Führer demands. Life is easy when you hold the power of life and death over others, when they cringe before you. Natalya Petrovich has more courage than I'll ever have." He stepped toward Manfred, arms outstretched. "How could I end the life of one who is so brave . . . when I'm so weak? I suppose that's no surprise to anyone except me." Garrick lowered his arms and sighed. "Let me fight one last time for the country I believed in, the country that's sealed my fate."

Manfred stood without speaking, the pistol still aimed at our adversary.

"Let him go," I said, feeling pity for a broken man.

"Leave us," Manfred ordered. "I'll keep your pistol."

"Good-bye, Natalya," Garrick said, giving me one last look. He sulked away, skirted around the kitchen, and disappeared into the throng of prisoners.

I picked up the Luger and collapsed in Manfred's arms.

The woods around the camp broke out in gunfire about nine that morning, sporadically at first, but then increasing in wild bursts as the firepower increased on the Allied side. The blasts rocked our ears as prisoners ran for cover, diving behind barracks, some climbing to the roofs and even the towers to get a better view of the fighting, others frantically digging trenches with their hands to flatten themselves against the ground.

Manfred and I, clutching our weapons, ran down Lagerstrasse until we could go no farther. We joined a group of British officers sheltered on the east side of a barracks. As we stood there, bullets zipped past us, thwacking into the wood and splintering the guard towers. We lay flat on the earth as shots pinged over our heads.

"Keep down," Manfred told me—an instruction he needn't have expressed. I covered my head with my arms and pressed my face into the muddy earth. A shot buzzed over us and an officer yelped in pain. I looked behind me to see a man clutching his left arm. Despite Manfred's objection, I crawled to the officer and, with his aid, ripped his shirt apart, and applied a tourniquet to the grazed skin, which was bleeding heavily. As more bullets flew, I dropped back to the ground.

The SS was outgunned and outmanned from the beginning, if the battle noise was any gauge. The grind of American tanks filled our ears, along with the sporadic fire of heavy artillery away from the camp, and, not so far away, the screams of wounded and dying men. Manfred and I huddled with the British officers for more than an hour before the shooting abruptly stopped.

A deathly silence followed, as if nothing on earth had survived the combat. No birds sang and the air fell fallow and stagnant, as if God had stopped the world to make His final judgment upon the war.

The POWs lifted themselves from the ground, peering around the corner of the barracks; others crawled from their hastily dug trenches, wide-eyed and full of wonder like children at Christmas.

And then a beautiful sound rolled down Lagerstrasse: the rumbling, churning, crushing thrash of tanks was unmistakable. The British POWs, Manfred, and I ran to the street and watched as three American tanks crashed through the Stalag gate. One of the tanks nudged the main watchtower, its heavy gun abutted against the structure. One blast and the tower would have been obliterated. The German guards put down their weapons and raised their hands.

The other tanks growled down Lagerstrasse and then halted, unable to press forward through the crowd of cheering, weeping men. Manfred and I wept along with them and watched as they climbed over their liberators like ants swarming over a piece of sugar.

Pandemonium broke out, prisoners screaming for joy, holding on to each other while they cried openly, shouting welcomes to the men who had set them free.

"Get off my tank, you blighters," one of the drivers yelled in jest at the British officers.

"Damned bloody Yank," one of the prisoners yelled back. "Let me kiss you."

One of the American POWs kissed the muddy tank track like it was a long-lost love, hugging the metal with tears pouring down his face.

As the American forces took charge, the guards surrendered, were disarmed, and transported from the camp as prisoners themselves. Manfred and I wondered what might happen to us German "civilians," but in the excitement and chaos surrounding the Stalag's liberation, no one paid much attention to two people in civilian clothes. We wandered about congratulating the prisoners and breathing in the spring air that refreshed our souls with newly found freedom.

The American flag was raised on the camp pole to cheers, and some hours later another American flag flew from a church steeple in Moosburg. As the flag waved over the town, the American prisoners, their days, months, and years of captivity at an end, came to attention and saluted. I watched with tears as the sobbing men saluted.

I flung my wig to the ground and put on my glasses.

The long night of tyranny and oppression was over.

*　*　*

"I must find him," I told Manfred. "I want to know."

I'd watched as the German guards and the SS were hauled away, but Garrick was not among them. If he fought, he would have been at the railroad embankment where the firefight had been intense.

Light-headed with joy, I grasped Manfred's hand as we walked past the smashed Stalag entrance, across the Mühlbach brook toward the shallow depression on the east side of the tracks. How wonderful it was to be free—to walk without fear of death. Soon we came upon the embankment.

Before us lay the bodies of three SS men sprawled across the new spring grass, their blood flowing into the damp earth.

Manfred held me back. "Don't look, Natalya."

"No," I replied.

The first two men were strangers to me. Their field jackets were spotted with blood, their weapons by their sides. I looked away, not wanting to dwell on, or celebrate, the deaths of these misguided soldiers.

The third face I knew.

I wanted to look away but couldn't.

Garrick's body lay faceup, against the embankment, his right hand clutched in a fist near his heart, his face purple and lifeless, his blue eyes cold and open and staring toward heaven. Blood pooled on his coat from a wound in his chest and seeped from bullet holes in his neck and head. He had been struck at least three times by Allied fire. His cap lay overturned in the grass not far from his body.

Standing over him, I shed no tears. I muttered a prayer for the dead as Manfred watched from the embankment's rise.

"He didn't have a weapon," Manfred said as we walked back to camp.

I didn't respond, for I knew in my heart what had happened to Garrick Adler. He had waited with the other SS men for the Allied approach. When the battle had begun, he had stood, opening himself to the bullets that would end his life. It was his way of showing he was brave enough to die.

I remembered a younger Natalya Petrovich, who never believed she would die, who'd been willing to offer her life to the White Rose, who had killed a man to save herself. The Natalya who'd looked upon the body of Garrick Adler was not the same woman of those years ago. She, the traitor, was wiser now and aware of the fragile beauty of life. She wanted to live.

Manfred and I walked under the sun and puffy clouds until we came to the camp and joined in with the laughter and cheers. The celebration of freedom had spread throughout the camp.

The Reich was dead.

CHAPTER 19

—————➤◦≺—————

Manfred and I were eventually cleared by the Americans, who intended to turn Stalag VII-A into an internment camp for civilian Germans suspected of Nazi war crimes.

When I told the American officers the story of my association with the White Rose, my trial and imprisonment, which they were able to confirm in a few days through captured records, I was released. Manfred received the same treatment after those who knew Gretchen testified on his behalf. She was found in prison, having narrowly escaped the guillotine, and was released along with many others.

A kind American Major procured papers for Manfred and me to travel into Munich, past military checkpoints to look for my parents. I'd pleaded my case to an army man who looked favorably upon my activities with the resistance.

We left the farm on an overcast and windy May morning that held the promise of warmth. Schütze jumped against the fence, unhappy that we were leaving her alone for the day. Before we got into the truck, Manfred rubbed her ears and assured her that we'd be back soon.

The road to Munich was lined with refugees and American troops. All signs of the Nazis had disappeared. My stomach tightened as we neared the city, for I was plagued with questions. Were my parents still alive? How difficult would it be to resurrect the Natalya Petrovich who'd lived before her trial and imprisonment?

"Are you all right?" Manfred asked. "You look pale."

"I don't know what we're going to find—if anything."

We traveled past the villages and towns, some looking burned out, others as if the war had not touched them at all.

"I want you to be happy," Manfred said. He shifted his gaze briefly to me, and then stopped the truck on the side of the road. We sat under the leafy branches of an oak near a swiftly flowing stream, its waters flashing greenish white over the rocks. Had it not been for my nerves, the rushing sound would have lulled me to sleep.

Manfred took my hand and looked squarely at me. "Will you marry me?"

His timing surprised me somewhat, but the question didn't shock me; in fact, I had suspected that it might come after the war was over. I touched his shoulder. "Well, it's a bit sudden," I said in jest and snuggled against him. "Do you think we know each other well enough?"

"I do," he said.

"Yes," I said, and kissed him. "I'd love to be your wife."

He smiled and pulled the truck back out on the road. We had traveled only a short distance, before we stopped again to let a ragged flow of men and women cross in front of us.

"How long is it going to take Germany to recover?" he asked. "How long will the world hold us in contempt?"

I didn't answer, but I knew Germany wouldn't be forgiven of her sins for generations—if ever.

We made it into the city and through the checkpoints, delayed only by one inspection. The papers the Major had given us expedited our journey.

Munich was in ruins, the devastation total except for the random buildings that had survived the bombings. The many hollow frames, as charred as wooden matchsticks, looked out upon us with blackened windows like empty eyes. Stone and brick had tumbled into the streets, making some impassible, others open only to one lane. The Siegestor's columns still stood, although pockmarked and jagged from the shelling. The smell of smoke and ash, and leaking petrol, carried in the air along with the smell of death, the stench of rotting corpses.

As I viewed the destruction, the hope of finding my parents faded; yet, I wasn't ready to give up.

"Schwabing first," I said to Manfred, and directed him through the clogged roads to a spot where we could park near Frau Hofstetter's home. We got out of the truck and walked the litter-lined streets, climbing and jumping over the rubble, lifting the broken branches of the stripped trees, until I spotted my former apartment.

The back of the house had been reduced to a blackened shell, the façade charred from the fire. Part of the front wall had collapsed and under it, which served as a lean-to, we found the Frau.

She was huddled under a pile of blankets, her back propped up against a pillow resting on the remains of a tree trunk. Her eyes narrowed into a squint when we approached, clearly unsure of who we were and what we wanted; but, as I leaned into her makeshift home, her eyes lit up and she reached for me.

"My dear one," she said as I bent to kiss her. "You're alive. . . . You're alive. . . ." She hugged me with her frail arms.

"Frau Hofstetter," I said. "You've survived. . . . We've all survived."

"I would welcome you into my home, but, as you can see, I have none." She patted the bottom of a blanket, inviting me to sit. "Who is this young man?"

"Frau Hofstetter, this is Manfred Voll. . . . We are to be married."

Her eyes sparkled with happiness. "Oh, I'm thrilled for you. We need more joy, more life after what has happened." Then her eyes dimmed.

"How is Katze?" I asked, unable to ask the same question about what might have happened to my parents.

"That cat?" She raised her hands in disgust. "He's doing better than I am. He has delectable mice and birds to choose from. He's around here somewhere—he always comes back to keep me company. Cats are hunters, you know. I, and the neighbors who are still alive, have only scraps. I hope the Americans don't starve us to death."

I shook my head. "No, Frau Hofstetter, I don't think they will."

"Natalya, ask her," Manfred said from his position outside the lean-to.

My throat constricted. "Frau . . ."

She thrust out her hands. "I understand your reluctance. . . . I have news."

"Go ahead," I said with trepidation.

"I'm sorry to tell you, Natalya Petrovich, but your father died several months ago. Your mother is still alive. She lives with two other families not far from here. But, be warned, she isn't well—the war has taken its toll on us all.

"The Gestapo pursued you like mad dogs for some reason—without let-up. The agents swore they would kill your parents if they didn't find you. They beat your father and threatened your mother. He never recovered from the beatings and the intimidation, but she managed to live through her heartache. She's a strong woman."

The war had hardened me to some extent, but my emotions were thawing as the days of freedom progressed. The rough, serrated edge of pain cut across my heart for my father's death, but I didn't cry—I was relieved that he was suffering no longer.

The doctor's murder and my escape from Schattenwald had killed my father when I could offer little help—and Garrick, who might have stepped in, had been removed from the case. The rage I felt against the Nazis during my time with the White Rose ignited again.

A meow and a heavy purr reached my ears. Katze emerged from the ruins of the Frau's house and rubbed his body against me in the twisting motion that all cats do. I turned, picked him up, and snuggled him against my chest.

"Please take him," the Frau said. "It's hard enough for me to feed myself. Consider him a wedding present."

I looked up at Manfred, who knelt down to pat Katze's head. "Do you think Schütze will put up with him?"

"She's been around cats before—she's not too fond of them, but in this case . . . yes."

"Thank you," I said, and leaned over to kiss the Frau's cheek. "Can you tell me where my mother lives?"

She explained how to get to the apartment building several blocks away. Apparently, the top half of the building had been rendered unlivable, but the lower floors remained standing. Manfred shook the Frau's hand, telling her that he would return to help with the rebuilding of her home. He assured her he was good at such things.

We left with Katze in my arms. The cat, apparently recognizing me, settled against my shoulder and made no attempt to squirm out of my hold.

After a short walk, we found the building. A large hole in the roof let light filter through it; cracks ran through the stone walls from top to bottom.

"You go to the door," I told Manfred, afraid I might collapse upon seeing my mother. "I'll hold the cat."

Manfred stepped forward as I waited. He knocked, the door opened, and he asked for Mrs. Petrovich. The man who answered disappeared and, soon, my mother, in a plain black dress, stood at the entrance, staring at a man she didn't know.

"Mother," I called out. "It's me."

Her eyes widened and she sagged against the door. Manfred captured her in his arms and supported her swaying form. She broke free, and, with cries of joy, we rushed to each other, nearly crushing Katze between us.

EPILOGUE

———◆———

Many years passed before my family and Germany recovered from the pain of the war. Manfred and I felt vindicated by our views about the Nazis, although we never expressed them publicly. Emotions were too raw and people were more concerned with surviving, building new lives for themselves, not dredging up the memories of a terrible past.

My mother lived at the farm for a time until we found her a small apartment in Moosburg. She was never as happy in the village as she'd been in Munich, but we wanted to be closer during this time of reconstruction. More than that, she missed my father. My mother died in 1949, four years after the war ended, a woman who never quite recovered from the horrors of the Nazi regime.

Manfred and I were married in December 1945, after all the world's hostilities had ceased and we Germans were attempting to build some kind of normalcy. Our wedding, on a cold and cloudy day, was small, with my mother and a few of Manfred's neighbors attending, as well as Gretchen, who no longer needed to hide, and Frau Hofstetter, who appreciated Manfred's weekend work on her house. We drank toasts in front of the woodstove from a black-market bottle of champagne. By that time, even our animals, Katze and Schütze, had settled into their neutral corners—peace through avoidance.

Sometime after my mother died, I had an occasion to travel to Munich by train. The rails were up and running on a decent schedule, and, quite by accident, I ran into a woman at the Bahnhof I thought I knew. Like all of us, she had aged, a bit more stooped in her walk, her hair grayer than I remembered. She was Lisa Kolbe's mother.

I spoke first and she turned, her eyes wide with wonder, bordering on shock, as if she had seen a ghost. I didn't blame her.

We talked about life in general, even speaking about the weather, before we came to the subject of death. She told me that her husband had died after the war ended. I never mentioned Lisa's death and she didn't bring it up, either.

"I want to show you something," she said. "I look at it every day."

We walked through the streets, now cleared of rubble, but with bombed-out ruins still plainly in view. We came to a building not far from the one that the Kolbes and my parents had lived in when our families first met. We climbed the stairs to her apartment, which looked out on a tree that had survived the war and was now in full leaf in the late spring. On days like these, the memories and the war seemed far away. The window was thrown open, letting in the fresh air now cleared of smoke and ash, the rumble of construction sounding in the distance, the light dancing off the leaves into the room.

There, the object she'd wanted to show me sat on a small wooden table. It was Lisa's typewriter, the green metal faded and pockmarked in spots from age and use.

"I typed our leaflets on this machine," I said. Sadness swept over me as I thought of our thwarted efforts.

"Yes," she responded. "Lisa admitted to us what she had done hours before she was arrested. We were fortunate enough to get it out of the house and hide it with trusted neighbors before the Nazis could confiscate it."

She sat at the table and caressed the keys. "Her father and I taught her to be independent, to think for herself, but we never believed that putting thoughts into words would lead to . . ."

"Everyone in the White Rose knew what the risks were," I interjected. "I'm sure that doesn't erase your pain, but we were naïve enough to think we wouldn't be arrested."

"I grieve for her every day." She looked at me with glistening eyes and sighed. "I feel better now that Hitler and the rest—the evil lot of them—are captured or dead."

I touched the keyboard and remembered the cool feel of the metal against my fingertips, the nights spent in Dieter's studio working on the leaflets. The memories came flooding back, and I shivered despite the spring warmth. It was a miracle that I was alive.

We parted with assurances to keep in touch.

As I walked back to the train station, I breathed the air deep into my lungs, savoring every breath, lightness in my step, as I considered a future I hoped would only get better. I was thankful for Manfred, our home, our dog and cat, and that we had both escaped being one of the millions of deaths caused by Adolf Hitler.

But my joy was tempered by the deaths of those in the White Rose, especially Alex, Hans, Sophie, Willi, and Professor Huber.

Countless others had followed them to the guillotine, the gallows, and the firing squads. Had their resistance been worth the price of their deaths? Some would say we failed to change history's course with leaflets and slogans painted on walls. I even wondered myself as I looked at Lisa's typewriter. But had it been so?

We had stood against tyranny when few did and many more should have taken a stand. The final White Rose leaflet that Hans and Sophie had dropped at the university, smuggled out of Germany, had been copied by the millions and dropped by the Allies over German cities. Surely one German who looked up to the sky, expecting bombs to fall, had taken the leaflet in hand and thrilled to the words he read. Words of resistance, struggle, and hope.

Had we failed? That question was answered when I remembered the bravery demonstrated by those in the White Rose as they took their final steps.

As Sophie Scholl told Roland Freisler, the President of the People's Court, at her trial, "Somebody had to make a start."

She and Hans did.

I followed—forever proud—with a promise to never let the world forget.

AUTHOR'S NOTE

The White Rose has been the subject of numerous non-fiction books, university studies, papers, essays, lectures, and even a critically acclaimed German film: *Sophie Scholl: The Final Days* (2005). In fact, the number of books, the astounding amount of file material kept by the Nazis, which, in this case, survived destruction by the Gestapo, makes writing a book about this particular resistance movement all the more difficult from a fictive standpoint. The volume of written words and historic research is staggering. My task would have been monumental indeed if my goal was to compare and contrast these differing accounts.

Then why attempt this novel? As I pointed out in *The Taster*, my novel about a food taster for Adolf Hitler, published in 2018, I've always found World War II a tragic, terrifying, and humbling subject. Despite those daunting parameters, the war fascinates me along with many others. A recent article I read pointed out that some of the war's appeal may lie in the nature of the conflict itself. It was perhaps the last combat situation in which America entered and exited as a hero nation, unlike the wars that followed and continue to this day. In the opinion of some, it may have been the last war in which good and evil were clearly delineated.

However, the White Rose had more than just war appeal for me. The story of this resistance movement is truly one of courage, a David and Goliath story that would end in sacrificial tragedy for most of its members. Questions arise: Why would the members attempt the distribution of incendiary, treasonous leaflets under Hitler's dictatorial regime when there was little chance of success? Did they cling to the hope that they would succeed—that their leaflets would change the course of Nazi Germany and the war? Did they realize that every day they lived with the prospect of death as they plotted and wrote their words? These were some of the fascinating and troubling questions that drew me to the White Rose.

The story of Hans and Sophie Scholl is well-known throughout their native land, less so in America. On a recent trip to Germany for research on *The Traitor*, I noted a few observations. I wouldn't quantify these in the realm of unqualified truth, but others who have been to the country have echoed similar impressions. They are:

- The Scholls and those in the White Rose circle have become national heroes (almost folk heroes) and an integral part of Germany's World War II history.
- Germans don't mince words about National Socialism and the terrible effects the Reich had on the world and their country.
- Reminders about Nazi horrors, ranging from plaques to memorials, are abundant, particularly in those cities most adversely affected by the war.
- School children are taught about the Reich and its crimes. History has not been forgotten or replaced by a false narrative. In Munich there is a museum dedicated to the rise of National Socialism as related *to that city alone*. It is a terrifying and bitter story to tell, but it is *told*—on the former site of Hitler's Munich headquarters.

I can safely say that fewer Europeans outside of Germany, and most Americans, particularly young people, know little of resistance movements like the White Rose and the Red Orchestra. Their only exposure may be a mention in passing during a history class on World War II. This is another reason I wanted to write *The Traitor*. We should *never* forget.

Those acquainted with the White Rose know the story: Hans Scholl, and his sister Sophie Scholl, and Christoph Probst were executed on the same day in February 1943; Alexander Schmorell and Professor Kurt Huber were felled in July of the same year, followed by Willi Graf in October, only because the Gestapo was hoping Willi would expose more of the group. He didn't. The core of the White Rose was snuffed out in less than a year. Many others were given prison sentences of varying length for their participation in and sometimes unwitting aid to the group.

On April 22, 2009, George Wittenstein, a surviving member of the White Rose, presented his personal account of the group at a Holocaust Memorial Week program at Oregon State University, and asked the question of the gathered students and faculty: "What would you do (have done) about the Nazis?" Several students suggested answers, but Wittenstein always had a rebuttal. Telephones were tapped; the press was controlled by the state; work permits were needed; it was almost impossible to leave Germany because money and resources were scarce for those who needed to flee—if you could find a country that would take you. In fact, those who resisted during those years had little choice but to conform to the Nazi standard; thus, the birth of the underground, nonviolent resistance group.

Wittenstein explained that communication was key for resistance groups, but under the regime it was nearly impossible to achieve. According to him, there were more than three hundred resistance groups in Germany, but "they didn't know about each other." He also stated that the White Rose did not have "members." There was no membership card, no membership number—the participants were a group of "friends." Relationships drew them together.

At least eight hundred thousand Germans were imprisoned for active resistance during the war years. Roland Freisler, Hitler's high-profile "hanging judge," whose task was to rid the state of its enemies, ordered more than twenty-five hundred executions, including those of Hans and Sophie Scholl. His preferred method of execution was the guillotine. Ironically, he was killed in his courtroom during an Allied bombing raid on Berlin late in the war.

Rather than take the Hans and Sophie Scholl story, about which volumes of non-fiction have been written, I decided to concentrate on three fictional characters who, in the novel's world, became "satellites" of the group.

I did this for a number of reasons.

I have too much respect for the Scholls and the White Rose to put unnecessary words in their mouths. Their own diaries and the resistance leaflets speak for themselves. Both Hans and Sophie were literate and forceful writers, Sophie's writings often filled with poetic rhapsody. When a real person from the White Rose appears in *The Traitor*, I made every effort to stay true to their character and feelings. I didn't want to spoil the legacy of the White Rose by placing Hans, Sophie, and the others in situations that never would have occurred.

As in my other books, I try as best I can to marry fiction with history. No action—nothing that happens to these characters— is outside the realm of possibility in this horrifying time of Nazi rule. The scenes with the White Rose, as a group, have been created as they most likely happened. Of course, dialogue is invented by necessity, but I've made every effort to honor the person. I took this task seriously.

Readers often want to know what books I have read for research. One only has to surf the internet to find a wealth of material on the White Rose, but I'll mention a few of the sources that were instrumental in my writing:

- *Sophie Scholl and the White Rose*, Annette Dumbach & Jud Newborn, revised, updated edition, Oneworld Publications, 2018.
- *At the Heart of the White Rose, Letters and Diaries of Hans and Sophie Scholl*, edited by Inge Jens, Plough Publishing House, 2017.
- *The White Rose, Munich 1942–1943*, Inge Scholl, (Sophie and Han's sister), Wesleyan University Press, 1983.

- *A Noble Treason, The Story of Sophie Scholl and the White Rose Revolt against Hitler*, Richard Hanser, Ignatius Press, 1979.
- *We Will Not Be Silent, The White Rose Student Resistance Movement That Defied Adolf Hitler*, Russell Freedman, Clarion Books, 2016.
- *The White Rose*, a publication of Weisse Rose Stiftung e.V., Munich, 2006.
- *Every Man Dies Alone*, Hans Fallada, Melville House Publishing, translated by Michael Hofmann, 2009 (A superb novel about a married couple's resistance in Berlin).
- *Sophie Scholl: The Final Days*, Zeitgeist Films, 2005.
- *Alone in Berlin*, IFC Films, 2017 (Based on *Every Man Dies Alone*).

Three fine museums in Germany are must-sees for anyone interested in the subject:

The Topography of Terror, on Niederkirchnerstrasse in Berlin, is an indoor and outdoor history museum on the former site of the main Reich Security Offices. The site also includes a large section of the Berlin Wall.

In Munich, on Brienner, is the Cradle of Terror, a four-story museum dedicated to understanding the origins and ideology of National Socialism in the city where its beginnings flourished. Lest anyone think otherwise, this museum is not a celebration of fascism, but an educated look at the past and a warning for the future.

Also, in Munich is a small museum, the Weisse Rose Stiftung (White Rose Foundation), at the Ludwig-Maximilians-Universität, where Hans and Sophie were captured distributing their final public leaflet.

As always, thanks are due to my beta readers, Robert Pinsky and Michael Grenier; my editor at Kensington, John Scognamiglio; my agent, Evan Marshall; and my manuscript editors, Traci Hall and Christopher Hawke of CommunityAuthors.com.

And not to be forgotten, I want to thank my readers who have been with me for four Kensington books. You give me the courage to go back to the keyboard—to create fiction based on history that I hope will not only entertain but tell stories that need to be told.

APPENDIX 1

———◆———

White Rose Leaflet—I have chosen the **third leaflet** of the White Rose to include in this book because it, of all the writings, concerns a subjective and reasoned approach to passive resistance against National Socialism. I believe it displays the true thoughts of Hans Scholl and Alex Schmorell during this time and their feelings about the Nazi state.

Leaflets of the White Rose, III

Salus publica suprema lex*

All ideal forms of government are utopias. A State cannot be constructed on a purely theoretical basis; rather, it must grow and ripen in the way an individual human matures. But we must not forget that at the starting point of every civilization the State was already there in rudimentary form. The family is as old as man himself, and out of this initial bond, man was endowed with reason, creating for himself a State founded on justice, whose highest law was the common good. The State should exist as a parallel to the divine order, and the highest of all utopias, the *civitas dei*, is the model which in the end it should approximate. We do not want to pass judgment here on the many possible forms of a State—democracy, constitutional monarchy, and so on. But one matter needs to be brought out

———————————————

* Public safety is the supreme law

clearly and unambiguously: every individual human being has a claim to a useful and just State, one which secures the freedom of the individual as well as the good of the whole. For, according to God's will, man is intended to pursue his natural goal, his earthly happiness, in self-reliance and self-chosen activity, freely and independently within the community of life and work of the nation.

But our present "State" is the dictatorship of evil. "Oh, we've known that for a long time," I hear you object, "and we don't need to have it brought to our attention yet again." But, I ask you, if you know that, why do you not bestir yourselves, why do you allow these men in power to rob you step by step, openly and in secret, of one domain of your rights after another, until one day nothing, nothing at all will be left but a mechanized State system presided over by criminals and drunkards? Is your spirit already so crushed by abuse that you forget it is your right—or rather your *moral duty*—to abolish this system? But if a person no longer can summon the strength to demand his right, then it is an absolute necessity that he should fall. We would deserve to be dispersed throughout the earth like dust before the wind if we did not muster our powers at this late hour and finally find the courage which up to now we have lacked. Do not hide your cowardice under a cloak of prudence! For with each day that you hesitate, failing to oppose this monster from hell, your guilt will keep growing as in a parabolic curve.

Many, perhaps most of the readers of these leaflets are not quite sure how to offer effective resistance. They see no chance to do so. We want to try to show them that everyone is in a position to contribute to the collapse of this system. It won't be possible through individualistic enmity, in the manner of embittered hermits, to prepare the ground for the overturn of this "government" or even bring about the revolution at the earliest possible moment. No, it can be done only through the cooperation of many convinced, energetic people—people who have agreed on the means they must use to attain their goal. We don't have a great deal of choice. There is only one means available to us: *passive resistance*.

The sense and the aim of passive resistance is to topple National Socialism, and in this struggle we must not recoil from any course of action, wherever it may lie. We must attack National Socialism *wherever* it is open to attack. We must bring this monster of a state to an end as soon as possible. A victory of fascist Germany in this war would have immeasurable, frightful consequences. The military victory over Bolshevism must not become the primary concern of the Germans. The defeat of the Nazis must *unconditionally* be the absolute priority, the greater necessity of this latter demand we will demonstrate to you in one of our forthcoming leaflets.

And now every convinced opponent of National Socialism must ask himself how he can fight against the present "State" in the most effective way, how he can strike it in its most vulnerable places. Through passive resistance, without a doubt. It is obvious that we cannot provide each individual with a blueprint for his acts, we can only suggest them in general terms, and each person has to find the right way for himself to attain this end.

Sabotage in armament plants and war industries, *sabotage* at all gatherings, rallies, and meetings of organizations launched by the National Socialist Party. Obstruction of the smooth functioning of the war machine (a machine for a war that goes on solely to shore up and perpetuate the National Socialist Party and its dictatorship). *Sabotage* in all the areas of science and scholarship which further the continuation of the war—whether in universities, technical colleges, laboratories, research institutes or technical bureaus. *Sabotage* at all cultural events which could potentially enhance the "prestige" of the fascists among the people. *Sabotage* in all branches of the arts even the slightest bit connected with National Socialism or rendering it service. *Sabotage* in all publications, all newspapers in the pay of the "government" that defend its ideology and aid in disseminating the brown lie. Do not give a penny to street collections (even when they are conducted under the cloak of charity). For this is only a disguise. In reality the proceeds benefit neither the Red Cross nor the destitute. The government does not need this money; it is not financially dependent on these collections.

After all, the printing presses run continuously to manufacture any desired amount of paper currency. But the people must constantly be kept in suspense; the pressure of the curb must not slacken! Do not contribute to the collections of metal, textiles, and the like. Seek to convince all your acquaintances, including those in the lower social classes, of the senselessness of continuing, of the hopelessness of this war; of our spiritual and economic enslavement at the hands of the National Socialists; of the destruction of all moral and religious values; and urge them to offer *passive resistance*!

Aristotle, Politics: ". . . and further, it is part [of the nature of tyranny] to strive to see to it that nothing is kept hidden of that which any subject says or does, but that everywhere he will be spied upon, . . . further, to set all men against each other, friends against friends, the people against the nobility, and even the rich among themselves. Then it is part of such tyrannical measures to make the subjects poor, in order to be able to pay the bodyguards and to keep them occupied with earning their livelihood so that they will have neither leisure nor opportunity to instigate conspiratorial acts . . . Further, such taxes on incomes as were imposed in Syracuse, for under Dionysius the citizens had gladly paid out their whole fortunes in taxes within five years. The tyrant is also inclined to constantly foment wars."

Please copy and distribute!

APPENDIX 2

Permissions

Leaflets of the White Rose, number III; a written entry from August 28, 1942, by Hans Scholl regarding the burial of a Russian; and the first paragraph of the sixth leaflet, all copyright, 2006; *The White Rose* (booklet), Weisse Rose Stiftung, Munich, used by kind permission, pages 65–67, page 54, and page 71, respectively. The third leaflet appears as Appendix 1; Hans Scholl's entry, page 31 in the novel; sixth leaflet, page 170.

Hans Scholl's words on pages 32–33 taken from a letter to his parents, September 18, 1942, from *At the Heart of the White Rose, Letters and Diaries of Hans and Sophie Scholl*, used by kind permission (Walden, NY: Plough Publishing House, 2017), page 242.

Excerpts of Gauleiter Paul Giesler's speech on 138–9, reproduced with kind permission of the Licensor through PSLclear, from *Sophie Scholl and the White Rose*, Annette Dumbach and Jud Newborn, copyright 2018, Oneworld Publications, page 131.

Excerpts of pages 146–47 from *The White Rose, Munich 1942–1943*, copyright 1983 by Inge Aicher-Scholl. Published by Wesleyan University Press and reprinted by kind permission. (Pages 187–8 in the novel, reference to Else Gebel's letter to Inge Scholl from the White Rose, Munich, 1942–1943).

Stadelheim Prison description on pages 204–5 based on the testimony of Roy Machon used by kind permission of the Frank Falla Archive at (www.frankfallaarchive.org).

The description of Stalag VII-A at Moosburg, beginning on

page 276 and thereafter, used by kind permission of The Hawaii Nisei Project, copyright 2006–2007, at (www.nisei.hawaii.edu), The Center for Oral History in the Department of Ethnic Studies at the University of Hawaii; based on the account given by Mr. Stanley Masahura Akita (Americans of Japanese Ancestry During World War II), who was imprisoned there.

APPENDIX 3

―――⟫◆⟪―――

Glossary of German Words and Place Names of Note in *The Traitor*

Proper Nouns Are in Roman; Words Are Italicized

Kristallnacht—the Night of Broken Glass—a two-day pogrom on November 9–10, 1938, carried out against Jews in Nazi Germany that resulted in deaths, arrests, the burning of synagogues, and the vandalism/destruction of Jewish businesses.

Putsch—a coup, a revolt, used with masculine definite article *der* (the) in the German language.

Munich—the capital and largest city in the southern German state of Bavaria. Munich, in the early 1920s, became the center of the National Socialist politics and the movement's rise to power.

Juden—Jews (plural); *Jude* (singular).

Rumfordstrasse—a commercial and residential street southeast of the Munich's city center.

Reich—the shortened reference to the Third Reich, Hitler's dream of a thousand-year Germanic rule, sometimes referred to as the Third Empire, the Holy Roman Empire being the first and Imperial Germany the second.

Nazi—the pejorative of National Socialism.

Gestapo—the secret police of Hitler's National Socialist government. It was created in 1933 by Hermann Göring and became a terroristic force against anyone who dared subvert the Reich.

Wehrmacht—the armed forces of the Reich's war machine.

Swastika—the "hooked-cross" adopted by the Nazi Party, displayed on flags, armbands and appropriated for numerous other military and political uses. In recent history, the symbol has come to be identified with fascism and far-right organizations, although the swastika has a long history as a word and character also defined as "good luck."

Reichsmark—the currency in Germany from 1924 until 1948, when it was replaced by the mark in West and East Germany.

Frauenkirche—the Cathedral of Our Dear Lady, serves as the cathedral of the archdiocese of Munich. The current structure dates from the fifteenth century.

Marienplatz—Our Lady's Square, the central square in Munich, with a column devoted to Mary, the mother of Jesus.

SA—a military wing of the early Nazi Party that served various functions, including protecting the party. It eventually was surpassed by the SS.

Nein—no.

Dachau—the first concentration camp opened by the Nazis in 1933 in what has now become suburban Munich. Dachau was the model for all other camps and included a crematorium, along with a gas chamber, which, according to records, was never used on the site.

Neuhauserstrasse—an old and major street in Munich.

Rosental—another street in Munich, in this case the site of a large department store vandalized on Kristallnacht.

Lebensraum—Hitler's ideological principle espousing Germany's need for more territory for expansion of its empire. The lands to the east, including Russia, were prime targets for Nazi invasion under this policy.

Abitur—a qualification conferred upon students in Germany after passing secondary education final exams, a stepping-stone to university admittance.

Verboten—forbidden.

Schwabing—a northern borough of Munich, close to several Munich universities, including Ludwig Maximilians, where Hans and Sophie Scholl were arrested. Now it is a trendy business and residential district.

Leopoldstrasse—a major boulevard and the main street of the Schwabing district.

Haus der Deutschen Kunst—*House of German Art*, it was the first monumental structure commissioned by the Nazi Party. During the war years, it housed what the Reich considered the finest of German art.

Café Luitpold—historic café located near the former Gestapo headquarters in Munich. The headquarters were destroyed in the war, but the café still remains serving coffee, food, and desserts.

Prinzregentenstrasse—one of the four royal avenues, upon which the current House of Art is located. (The former Haus der Deutschen Kunst.)

Odeonsplatz—a large square in central Munich, the site of the fatal shootings during the 1923 Beer Hall Putsch.

Feldherrnhalle—a monumental structure on the Odeonsplatz, modeled after an Italian loggia, the site of the Putsch battle and later a memorial to the Nazi fallen. Pedestrians were expected to give the Nazi salute when they passed by the memorial. Many avoided doing so by walking in a lane behind the monument.

Reichsarbeitsdienst—(RAD) the Reich Labor Service, whose tasks included finding jobs for citizens and promoting Nazi ideology through work programs.

Reichskammer—the head of the Reich Chamber of Visual Art, the state-sponsored arbiter of the visual arts.

Residenz near the Hofgarten—the site of the Degenerate Art exhibit.

Kameradschaft—Comradeship, in this case referring to the large sculpture of two nude men, displaying the Aryan ideal of working together.

Ludwigstrasse—one of Munich's four royal avenues, leading to the university where Hans and Sophie Scholl were arrested.

Siegestor—the Victory Gate originally dedicated to the Bavarian army. It defines the boundary between Maxvorstadt and Schwabing.

SS—the umbrella term for the Schutzstaffel, which included nearly all groups responsible for Reich security. The SS expanded its role through the Nazi years into one of terror as well, and was responsible for much of the genocide perpetrated by the Reich.

Palace of Justice—a large and ornate building in central Munich that served as the site of the trial for Hans and Sophie Scholl. The Palace contains a memorial room to the White Rose.

Stadelheim Prison—one of the largest German prisons and the site of the execution of Hans and Sophie Scholl. Many famous and infamous prisoners have been held in this suburban Munich prison.

Hauptbahnhof—the "main" train station, sometimes referred to as the "central" station.

Frauen-Warte—A Nazi magazine for women, party approved and a source of propaganda that espoused homemaking, childbirth, and other Reich principles, in addition to providing sewing instruction and recipes.

Oberabschnitt Donau—The Austrian SS, a name not officially recognized by the SS.

Englischer Garten—the English Garden, a large park in Munich stretching from the city center to the northeast, bordering the Isar River and holding the Schwabinger Bach, a stream running through the park.

Deutsches Museum—a large museum of science and technology in Munich.

Gauleiter—a leader of the Nazi Party, appointed by Hitler.

Ich hatt' einen Kameraden—(I had a comrade), a lament for fallen German soldiers.

Wittelsbacher Palace—a former royal palace that housed the Gestapo headquarters and a prison during the Nazi years.

Untersturmführer—a mid-level officer's ranking with the SS.

Schattenwald—a fictional asylum not far from Munich. There were many asylums throughout Germany where Nazi atrocities were practiced until banned, which were then carried out clandestinely by administrators and doctors.

Tod—the German word for "death."

Moosburg—a town about forty-five kilometers northeast of Munich.

Lagerstrasse—the central roadway through Stalag VII-A.

THE TRAITOR

V. S. Alexander

ABOUT THIS GUIDE

The suggested questions are included to enhance your
group's reading of V. S. Alexander's *The Traitor*!

DISCUSSION QUESTIONS

1. Those in the White Rose faced danger for even thinking their "treasonous" thoughts. Would you have participated in such a group?

2. There were numerous groups working against the Reich. What would you have done to aid the resistance?

3. In relation to question two, what obstacles would you have faced, knowing that the Gestapo and the SS were always on the lookout for traitors?

4. Do you believe that Garrick had any love in his heart for Natalya?

5. Natalya is forced to make a dramatic choice of life or death. What would you have done at Schattenwald?

6. The character of Gretchen is enigmatic. Would you have found it difficult to maintain such self-control under the circumstances?

7. Natalya and Manfred fall in love in a time of war. Would it have been hard to fall in love during this conflict?

8. What was your reaction to Paul Giesler's speech in front of the students?

9. Was the White Rose doomed to failure from the start? Do you believe they succeeded in their mission?

10. What is your interpretation of the Leaflets of the White Rose, III presented in Appendix 1?

Connect with Us

Visit us online at
KensingtonBooks.com
to read more from your favorite authors, see books
by series, view reading group guides, and more.

Join us on social media
for sneak peeks, chances to win books and prize packs,
and to share your thoughts with other readers.

facebook.com/kensingtonpublishing
twitter.com/kensingtonbooks

Tell us what you think!

To share your thoughts, submit a review,
or sign up for our eNewsletters, please visit:
KensingtonBooks.com/TellUs.